into the pleading eyes of the woman who had landed, uninvited, on his doorstep.

Was this who he had become? So embittered by the death of his wife that he could turn a woman so obviously terrified away from his door?

"Geez. . ." Jefferson muttered under his breath. He was a man who made decisions every day. That was what he did for a living. His decisions often had millions of dollars riding on them, and the livelihoods of thousands of people.

And yet this decision, this split-second decision, about what kind of man he would be, felt bigger than all of those.

Jefferson Stone stepped back marginally from his door. It was all she needed. She catapulted over his threshold and into his house.

Into his life, he told himself grimly. "Thank you," she breathed.

"Nothing has been decided," he told her gruffly, though somehow he knew it had been.

And she knew it, too. She was beaming at him.

"It's not going to be a walk in the park," he told her. He was already ~~annoyed that his decision had~~ been based on a mor⬛⬛⬛⬛⬛⬛⬛⬛⬛⬛⬛⬛le. He had to get thin⬛⬛⬛⬛⬛⬛⬛⬛⬛⬛⬛⬛e she was aware this⬛⬛⬛⬛⬛⬛⬛⬛⬛⬛⬛⬛.

HOUSEKEEPER UNDER THE MISTLETOE

BY
CARA COLTER

MILLS & BOON

Published in Great Britain 2015
by Mills & Boon, an imprint of Harlequin (UK) Limited,
Eton House, 18-24 Paradise Road, Richmond, Surrey, TW9 1SR

© 2015 Cara Colter

ISBN: 978-0-263-25180-7

23-1115

Harlequin (UK) Limited's policy is to use papers that are natural, renewable and recyclable products and made from wood grown in sustainable forests. The logging and manufacturing processes conform to the legal environmental regulations of the country of origin.

Printed and bound in Spain
by CPI, Barcelona

Cara Colter shares her life in beautiful British Columbia, Canada, with her husband, nine horses and one small Pomeranian with a large attitude. She loves to hear from readers, and you can learn more about her and contact her through Facebook.

To all the people who share my love of
the wild and untamed beauty of Kootenay Lake.

CHAPTER ONE

"UNDER DIFFERENT CIRCUMSTANCES," Angelica Wither-spoon muttered to herself, as she drove down a main street where the summer sun was filtered through a thick green canopy of leaves, "this is the kind of place I would adore."

The city of Nelson was nestled in the Selkirk mountain range of British Columbia. It was quaint and charming.

She angle parked her car and noted plenty of activity on the wide sidewalks in front of historical buildings. It made her feel safe enough to vacate her car and get out and stretch. Her muscles were cramped with tension. In the distance, she could catch glimpses of the sparkling waters of the west arm of Kootenay Lake.

Angie sighed with longing. "This is a place I would love to explore." But she reminded herself, sternly, it was her *old* life that would have allowed her to explore the vibrant, artsy and scenic community.

In her *new* life she was extraordinarily tired and on edge. And it took money to explore. Angie had six dollars and twenty-two cents left to her name. She had allowed herself one cash machine withdrawal and was still in shock at how quickly two hundred dollars, the maximum she could take, had evaporated.

Under a colorful awning, just in front of where she had parked her car, there was an outdoor café. The savory smells of rich coffee and of spicy Indian food enveloped her. She felt a pang of hunger. It was the first time in a week on the run that her stomach had unknotted enough for her to feel hungry.

But, she told herself, if she bought a loaf of bread, and some sliced meat she could make her six dollars and change go a bit further than if she gave in to the temptation to sit down to a restaurant meal. She looked around for a corner store.

Tires squealed off in the distance, a jarring sound, and Angelica felt her heart begin to hammer, and a fine bead of sweat broke out on her lip. She fought terror as she scanned the street, making sure she was not being watched.

Inwardly, she talked herself down from the ledge.

"Of course you are not being watched," she chided herself. "How could anyone have followed you when you were not sure yourself where you were going?"

But it was part of this surplus of caution that wouldn't allow her to use the bank machine again. Winston had shown remarkable creativity in invading her life. What if he could track her transactions? No, she would find a loaf of bread. Peanut butter might be a better choice than meat, because it would be easier to keep.

And then what? she asked herself. With her quickly dwindling resources, she was going to have to give this up and go home?

Home. A shudder ran up and down her spine.

He'd been in her home, she reminded herself. Winston had been in her home. In her bedroom. What had he touched?

"Ugh," she said as repulsion shuddered down her

spine, making her uncertain that she was ever going home again. But, realistically, she had to be back at school in September—summer would not last forever. Surely this would be over by then? What if it wasn't?

She thought of faces of her students, the changes she saw in those faces over one school year, the sense they gave her of being *needed*, and she nearly wept at the thought she might not be able to return to them and to the job she loved.

"Never mind that," she told herself firmly. That was all in the distant future. Right now there was a more urgent and immediate question. How was she going to get by for a few weeks until the police apprehended Winston?

"I just need a break," she whispered, heavenward. "One small break."

And that was when she noticed the community bulletin board. She was drawn to it as if it were a magnet and she a dropped pin. All else faded, and she saw only one posting.

In very masculine printing it read:

HOUSEKEEPER NEEDED IMMEDIATELY. MATURE APPLICANTS ONLY. EMPLOYER DESIRES QUIET AND PRIVACY. CHATTERBOXES NEED NOT APPLY. APPLY IN PERSON AT THE STONE HOUSE, ANSLOW, BC.

Angelica snatched the scrap of paper down off the board like a starving pauper who had been tossed a crust. She glanced around surreptitiously, holding the paper close to her chest, as if others might be waiting to pounce on her and wrestle her to the ground for that job opportunity. It occurred to her she might be drawing attention to herself.

But Nelson seemed to be a place that embraced everything from the slightly eclectic to the downright weird, and no one was paying the slightest attention to her. She forced herself to relax and read the notice again, more slowly.

The position was probably long gone. There was no date on it. The paper it was written on seemed frayed around the edges and slightly water damaged. On the other hand, it was downright unfriendly. Only someone desperate—that would be her—would be the slightest bit interested in such a posting.

She wasn't sure how "mature" would be defined, but considered herself a very mature twenty-five. She definitely was not a chatterbox, though she was outgoing and friendly, which was probably what had gotten her into trouble in the first place.

Angelica Witherspoon was being stalked.

Stalked. It was like something out of a movie. Three months ago, she had gone for one cup of coffee with someone she'd felt sorry for. Her life had been unraveling ever since.

Angelica forced herself to focus on the scrap of paper in her hand instead of revisiting what she could have done differently, where she went wrong.

She read it for the third time. In her mind, a picture formed of an elderly gentleman, sweetly crusty and curmudgeonly—maybe like the beautifully animated character in the movie *Up*—who found himself alone and needed some help around his house.

She had asked for one small break. And here it was. She had to grab it. Her resolve firmed within her. With

her background in home economics, she was fully qualified for this job.

"Excuse me," she said. She was startled—and faintly
ashamed—by how timid she sounded. It seemed that a
minor annoyance deepening into something more sin-
ister had changed everything about her in a very short
amount of time.

The man going by her had dreadlocks and a mul-
ticolored striped knit toque despite the mid-July heat.
He also looked as if he was wearing a skirt instead of
pants. But when he stopped and looked at her, she saw
he had friendly eyes.

"Where is Anslow?"

"Take the highway that way, around the lake. It's
only fifty-eight kilometers, but it will take you an hour.
The road is windy."

"Is there any other kind of road in British Columbia?" she asked wearily.

"Ah, an Albertan."

Just like that, without intending to, Angie had revealed things about herself, which Canadian province
she lived in. If somebody was following her and came
asking... Rationally, she knew the chances of this very
same man being stopped and asked about her were slim
to none, but her life was not rational, not right now.

"Saskatchewan, actually," she lied. She was aware
the lie filled her with an odd sense of guilt, which she
shook off. "Have you ever heard of the Stone House
in Anslow?"

"No, but I like the possibilities."

Given his very Bohemian appearance and the faint,
acrid smell of smoke coming from him, Angelica got his
meaning and actually smiled. It was the first time she

had smiled since coming home a week ago to find the campaign to infiltrate her life had escalated. The doors to her new apartment had still been locked, but a brand-new stuffed panda with a red bow around its neck had been residing jauntily against the pillows on her bed. She was sure her dresser drawers had been opened. This had been the final straw in a string of steadily escalating and upsetting incidents that had been going on for the three months since she had said an innocent yes to that cup of coffee.

The shock—finding the bear on her bed, the red ribbon looking horribly like a cut throat—had sent her pell-mell into flight mode. Still, after a week, it felt that no matter where she went, she wasn't far enough away yet.

Now, an hour and a half after leaving Nelson—she'd stopped to wolf down a peanut butter sandwich at a picnic area being enjoyed by several families—following instructions she had received in the town of Anslow, she pulled up to a formidable stone-pillared entrance that would not have looked out of place guarding the entrance to a haunted house. She hesitated but the wrought iron gate hung open, and really...? If she was looking for a place where it would be hard to find her, this was certainly it.

She could not see a house, just a long, deeply shaded drive that wound down to a sharp curve, where it disappeared.

She took the road slowly, around the curve, but still no house, just the drive, weaving its way through magnificent old-growth forest. Angelica opened her window, and birdsong and a wonderful smell, sun on fallen pine needles, wrapped around her.

She felt some of the edginess drain from her. It made the feeling of exhaustion intensify.

The road dropped down and down, drawing ever closer to the water. It wove its lazy way through the forest and occasionally broke out into cleared grasslands that allowed her to see the full and enormous expanse of Kootenay Lake. And then she would be back in the deep, cool shadows of the forest, catching only glimpses of the glinting waters of the lake.

Finally, after a good fifteen minutes of driving, the house came into view.

The name had led her to expect she would see a stone house. Instead, Angie saw it was possible the house was named for its location, anchored as it was into a slab of natural gray stone forty or fifty feet above the placid waters of the lake.

The gate and the picture of the curmudgeonly little old man she had been working on had led her to expect a decrepit mansion.

Instead, the house before her was a masterpiece of modern architecture, blending with the elements around it. The house appeared to be constructed of 90 percent glass, the glass reflecting leaves and trees and sky at the same time as making the interior of the house and its contents seem as if it was an oasis that was magically suspended in the outdoors.

The huge expanse of windows made it possible to see right through the house, past a sectional white leather sofa and a stand-alone fireplace, to the deck on the other side of the dwelling. The deck, though huge, seemed to hold a single hammock, positioned in a way that took best advantage of the breathtaking view of the lake.

The setting and the house were stunningly beautiful.

Angie imagined if you were inside the house it would feel as if nothing separated you from the forest on one side and the lake on the other.

It was not, to be sure, the house she would have expected a curmudgeonly old man to live in!

She suddenly felt ridiculously vulnerable. She was out here in the middle of nowhere, alone. No one, except the person she had asked for instructions in Anslow, knew she was here.

What if she was jumping from the frying pan into the fire?

"What are the chances," she asked herself, "that you could meet another deranged man in such a short span of time? None!"

Realistically, her situation—peanut butter and loaf of bread in the backseat not withstanding—couldn't be more desperate. The past three months had made her steadily more cowardly, but she had to call on what little courage remained in order to do what needed to be done.

She twisted her rearview mirror over and ran a hand through her hair, tried to tidy her blouse and straighten the crumples out of her shorts, which suddenly seemed too short. Despite her efforts, she could not lose the faintly disheveled look of a week of living out of a suitcase.

Then, putting her anxiety about her appearance aside, Angie parked her car under a towering pine. She got out and marched to the door of the house. Okay, she left the keys in the ignition and the door of her car open, just in case she had to make a quick getaway.

As she made the winding walk to the front door, she was aware again of a beautiful aroma, deep and woodsy, and a cacophony of birdsong.

It was a double-entry doorway and it was constructed of stainless steel, etched with a geometric pattern of interlocking squares. The leaves of the trees surrounding the house were casting dancing shadows on the surface. Despite the fact it needed a good scrubbing, it was more like a work of art than a door.

In the center was a ring of steel, and she grasped it firmly and rapped against the door. The sound was loud and pure, like a gong in a Buddhist temple, and it startled her. She was aware of the sound reverberating inside of her when the door swung inward soundlessly.

Angie was pretty sure her mouth had fallen before she snapped it shut.

The man who stood in front of her was about the furthest thing from a curmudgeon that she could imagine.

He was stunningly handsome.

He looked to be in his early thirties. Tall and powerfully built, he had brown hair, the exact color and sheen of a vat of melted dark chocolate. His hair was long enough to touch the collar of an untucked white denim shirt that needed pressing. His hair was faintly mussed, as if he had been out in the wind.

To add to the pirate-straight-off-the-boat look of him, his cheekbones and chin were cast in the dark shadows of a day or two of whisker growth. His legs were long and set apart, braced, which showed the powerful cut of his thigh muscles underneath the faded denim of blue jeans. His feet were bare, which Angie was perturbed to note she found sexy. She hastily lifted her eyes from them to look him in the face.

His eyes were astonishing, the same restless gray blue of the waters of the lake she could see through wall-to-wall windows beyond him. But the water looked welcoming on this sweltering day, and nothing about his expression, and especially not his eyes, welcomed. And still, his eyes were every bit as sexy as his bare feet had been!

He regarded her with a furrowed brow for a moment, the line of his sensuous mouth pulled down in a surprised frown.

"Nope," he said. It was a single word. Despite the fact his voice was a rasp of pure unwelcome, there was something about it that made Angelica even more aware of what an almost criminally attractive man he was, blatantly sexy without even trying.

Apparently, the attraction was not shared. He shut the door. It clicked closed with metallic finality.

CHAPTER TWO

"Nope."

The gravelly rejection rang in Angie's ears for long moments after the door had clicked shut.

Oddly, her first reaction to the door being slammed in her face was relief. She reminded herself she no longer wanted men to find her attractive. It was dangerous. Plus, if he was deranged, he could have taken advantage of the isolation to pull her inside that house. Instead, he was dismissing her.

Though, looking into the strong cast of his face, the intelligence in his eyes, the confidence of his bearing, derangement did not seem like even a remote possibility.

She recognized her relief at the closing of the door, in part, not just because he was obviously not a pervert just waiting for a damsel in distress to land at his door, but because she had reacted to him in a very primal way, and she could not tolerate that in herself.

In the past year her fiancé, Harry, had abandoned her in favor of a beach in Thailand, and a more exciting companion, and now she was being stalked by a maniac. If anyone should be absolutely immune to the charms of the opposite sex, it was her! But apparently she wasn't. So, she should be glad of that door closed with such quiet finality.

But she wasn't. In fact, the relief that she was being dismissed was short-lived, indeed. It gave way to a stirring of indignation at his summary dismissal. And indignation felt so much better than the wound she had carried with her since Harry had shattered her dreams.

And it felt *way* better than the cowering scared-of-her-own-shadow fear she had been living with ever since Winston's escalating invasion of her life.

Angie decided, right that second, that she was not going to be a victim anymore.

Besides, she *needed* this position as a housekeeper. It was an answer to that whispered prayer she had said at the bulletin board in Nelson just a few hours ago.

Angelica took a deep breath. She marshaled her courage. She set her chin and her shoulders. And then she lifted that ring of steel again and rapped it against his door with all the gumption she could muster.

"Damn him," she muttered, when it seemed the master of the Stone House intended to ignore her. She drew in a sharp breath, marshalled her threads of tattered courage, and then she grasped the ring again.

Her hand was clutching the door knocker with the fierce determination of a drowning person clutching a life ring when the door was yanked open.

The unexpected force pulled Angie over the threshold and into the cool, marbled foyer of his house. She stumbled, let go of the knocker—a full second too late—and put out her hands to stop her forward momentum.

Angie's hands ran straight into a solid wall…of man.

She stared at her hands on his chest. Through the fabric of his shirt she could feel the steady, slow beat of his heart and the shocking heat of his skin. She could feel the utter and steely power of him. His scent was masculine, absolutely tantalizing and utterly spellbinding. He smelled of sunshine and lake water and pine trees. Angie dragged her gaze away from the wide expanse of manly and mesmerizing chest in front of her.

Those gorgeous stormy-water eyes were fastened, with some consternation, on the placement of her hands, which for some reason she had not yet removed from his person!

She gulped, came out of her trance, and snapped her hands off his chest and down to her sides. She took a giant step backward.

He raised his eyes from where her hands had been glued to him and tilted his head at her. "You're still here," he said.

His tone was laconic, but his eyes were narrowed with annoyance. There was a little muscle flicking in the uncompromising line of his unshaven jaw. It was fascinating.

"Um," she said intelligently.

"Yes?"

"I just needed to know."

"Know?"

"*Nope* to what?" Angie was trying very hard to regain her sense of equilibrium. She reminded herself to straighten her shoulders and lift her chin.

He seemed surprised that she would have the audacity to even question him. He regarded her piercingly.

"I mean, who answers their door like that? With a single word? Nope? When you don't even know why I'm here." Angie had to remind herself of her vow not to be a victim anymore. Still, she had to fight herself not to fidget, to hold her chin firmly in place and her shoulders square. He regarded her silently, with lowered brows and narrowed eyes. She was certain that he intended to let her stew, to see if he could make her squirm. She held her ground.

Finally, he sighed. The sound was one of pure exasperation, and yet she felt certain his expelled breath had touched her cheek, like a kiss. It was everything she could do to keep her hands at her sides and not touch her cheek.

"Nope to whatever you're selling." His voice was stern and annoyed, not the voice of a man who could kiss cheeks with his very breath.

"But you don't even know what I'm selling!" she protested. Was that a quaver in her voice?

"Yes, I do." His voice was like gravel.

"You don't," she said stubbornly.

"I do."

I do. The words she had expected to be hearing from Harry. Even said out of context, they filled Angie with a longing that made her despise herself. How many kicks in the teeth did a gal have to endure before she got it? There was no knight in shining armor. There was no happily ever after. Those kind of illusions were what got people in trouble.

"Girl Guide cookies," he said, his voice hard, "or your version of enlightenment, or tickets to the high school play. And to all of those, an emphatic nope."

See? This man was the cynical type. He would never fall victim to illusions of any kind.

"As a matter of fact," she said, stripping any trace of quaver—or illusions—from her voice, "you're wrong on all counts. I am not selling anything."

This man was not accustomed to being told he was

wrong. She could see that instantly, when the dark slashes of his brows dropped dangerously.

Angie told herself she needed to be careful not to be off-putting. He was going to be her future boss, after all!

"I've come about your posting on the community board in Nelson," she told him.

The firm line of his lips deepened into a frown. That, coupled with his lowered brows, made it inarguable. Her future boss was scowling at her. He had no idea what she was talking about.

"I'm here about the position you advertised for a housekeeper."

His eyebrows shot up. His gaze swept her. "Oh," he said, "that."

"Yes, that."

He gave her another long look, apparently contemplating her suitability for the position. She tried for her most housekeeperly expression.

"Especially nope to that," he said.

When the door began to whisper shut, again, it was pure desperation that made Angie put one foot in to stop it.

The man—good God, was he Heathcliff from Wuthering Heights—glanced down at her foot with astonished irritation. And then he gave her a look so icily reserved it should have made her withdraw her foot and touch her forelock immediately. But it did not. Angie held her ground.

The master of the mansion glared back down at her foot with deep annoyance, but she refused to retreat. She couldn't!

After a moment, he sighed again, and once more she felt the sensuous heat of his breath whisper across her cheek. 6257845

Then he opened the door wide and leaned the breadth of one of those amazing shoulders against the jamb, the seeming casualness of his stance not fooling her. Every fiber of his being was practically vibrating with displeasure. He folded his arms over the immenseness of his chest and tilted his head at her, waiting for an explanation for her audacity.

Really, all that icy remoteness should not have made him *more* attractive. But the impatient frown tugging at the edges of those too-stern lips made her think renegade thoughts of what was beyond the ice and what it would be like to know that.

These were crazy thoughts. This man was making her think crazy thoughts. She was a woman who had suffered so completely at the hands of love.

First, her Harry had decided all their dreams together were decidedly stodgy and had replaced her with insulting quickness with someone far more exotic and exciting.

And then, a coworker, Winston, had taken total advantage of her brokenhearted vulnerability. She had caved to his constant requests. Angie had said yes instead of no to a single cup of coffee. He had used that yes to force his way into her life.

With that kind of track record, it made her thoroughly annoyed with herself for even noticing what the master of the Stone House looked like. And what his voice sounded like. And what he smelled like. And what his breath had felt like grazing the tenderness of her cheek.

If she had a choice, she would have cut and run. But she was desperate. She had absolutely no choice.

With her foot against the door he was too polite to slam, she said, determined, "I need this job."

He contemplated that, and her, in silence.

"Really," she clarified when it seemed as if he was not going to say anything at all.

"Well, you don't qualify." His determination seemed to match her own. Or exceed it.

"In what way?"

"You're obviously not mature."

"I guess that would depend how you defined mature," she said.

"Old."

"How old?" she pressed. "Fifty? Sixty? Seventy? Eighty?" She hoped she was pointing out how ridiculous he was being. *Old* was not necessarily a great qualification in a housekeeper.

For a moment he said nothing, and then one corner of that sinfully sexy mouth lifted, but not in a nice way. "Older than you."

"I'm sure the human rights commission would have quite a bit to say about not being considered for a job— for which I'm perfectly qualified—because of my age," she said.

The smile deepened, tickling across his lips—cool, unfriendly, dangerous—and then he doused it and lowered the slash of his brows at her. "Are you threatening me?"

It occurred to her that annoying him would be the worst possible way to wiggle her way into this job position.

"No, not at all. I'm just suggesting that you might have attracted a better response to your posting for an available position if you had said you needed someone highly organized and hardworking and honest."

"All of which I'm presuming you are?" he said drily.

She took it as very hopeful that he had not tried

to physically shove her foot out the door and slam it on her.

Not that he looked like a man who ever had to get physical to get what he wanted. That look he was giving her was daunting. Anyone less desperate would have backed down long before now.

"I'm desperate." There she had admitted it to him.

"Your desperation is not my con—"

"I'm willing to guess you haven't had a single response to that ad," she plowed on. "Who would answer an ad like that?"

"Apparently, you would."

"I'm not *just* desperate."

"How very nice for you," he said, his tone so sardonic it had a knife's edge to it.

"I'm also highly organized and hardworking and honest."

"You're too young."

"Humph. I think youth could be a great advantage for this position."

He didn't answer, so she rushed on.

"I will be terrific at this job. You'll love me."

He looked insultingly dubious about that.

How could she have said that? That he would love her? You did not want to even think a word like that in front of a man like this—who could make you feel as if he had kissed you by simply sighing in your direction.

"I'll work for free for one day. If you're not impressed, you haven't lost anything."

He frowned at her. "Look, Miss—"

"Nelson," she filled in, using the name of the town she had just come through. "Brook Nelson." There. A new name. She had used part of the city of Cranbrook that she had passed through on this wild ride, and part of the town of Nelson.

She held her breath, knowing from the tension she felt while she waited that she *needed* the new existence her new name promised her.

CHAPTER THREE

JEFFERSON STONE REGARDED his unwanted visitor. Something shivered along his spine when she said her name. He knew she was lying.

And she wasn't very good at lying, either. In fact, she was terrible at it.

He allowed himself to study her more closely. Brook Nelson—or whoever the hell she really was—was cute as a button. She was dressed in a brightly patterned summer blouse and white shorts. She was a little bit of a thing, slender and not very tall. It looked as if a good wind would pick her up and toss her.

And yet when her hands had been pressed into his chest, he had been aware of something substantial about her. That little bit of a thing had set off a tingle in him— an awareness—that had been as unwelcome as she was.

Hard not to be aware of her, when those shorts ended midthigh and showed off quite a bit of her legs.

Annoyed with himself, Jefferson shook off the thought and continued his study of his housekeeper candidate.

It just underscored what he already knew: she would not do.

She had light hair, a few shades darker than blond, but not brown. Golden, like sand he had seen on Kaiteriteri Beach in New Zealand. That hair was cut short, he suspected in a largely unsuccessful effort to make those plump curls behave themselves. They weren't. They were corkscrewing around her head in a most unruly manner.

Her eyes were hazel, leaning toward the gold side of that autumn-like combination of golds and greens and browns. She had delicate features and it was probably that scattering of freckles across her nose that made her seem so wholesome, even though she was lying about who she was.

There was something earnest about her. Despite her youth, and despite the shortness of those shorts, she seemed faintly prim, as if she would be easily shocked by bad words. Which, of course, was part of the reason she would be a very bad fit for him as a housekeeper.

Because of her size, Jefferson had assumed she was young. But on closer inspection, she looked as if she was in her midtwenties. Still, she was exactly the type you would expect to be peddling cookies for a good cause or wanting to change the world for the better or encouraging attendance at the annual Anslow high school performance of *Grease*, which would be dreadful.

And he should know. Because a long time ago, in a different life, he had been cast as the renegade in that very high school play.

Jefferson shook it off. He did not like reminders of his past life.

Besides, Brook wasn't anything like the ideal person he had in his head for this job, which was gray haired, motherly but not chatty, and someone willing to stay out of his way and keep schtum about his life.

Brook Nelson, in spite of the wholesome exterior and

her claims of honesty, was lying about who she was. He needed her gone.

"Look, Miss, um, Nelson, I've gone through three housekeepers in three weeks—"

"Somebody answered *that* ad?" she asked disbelievingly.

"Not exactly," he had to admit. "*That* ad was a result of the other failures."

The failure was that he had mentioned to Maggie, at the Anslow Emporium, that he was going to need someone.

He hadn't anticipated that telling Maggie—whom he had known since he was six—that he needed some help at his house would be like creating a posting in a lonely hearts club rag.

"Tell me about my three predecessors."

He frowned at that. She was a cheeky little thing, wasn't she? What part of no could she not get? But, since she was immune to slamming doors, why not give her anecdotal evidence of her unsuitability for this position?

"Okay, the first one was *not* mature. Mandy, showed up in flip-flops, and had a most irritating way of popping her gum, except when she was texting on her cell phone, which seemed to require her jaw to stop moving. When she had been here approximately three hours, she knocked on my office door to complain that the internet signal was weak from the deck. And then she acted insulted when I suggested I didn't need her services any longer."

Jefferson did not mention that Mandy had told him that she was prepared to overlook the vast difference in their ages if he wanted to give it a try.

He had escorted her to the door with a sense of urgency almost unparalleled in his life—and before finding out exactly what "it" meant.

"The second one was also not *mature*. She had on too much mascara and her skirt was too short, and she seemed way too interested—"

He stopped.

"In you?" Brook asked quietly.

He didn't want to get into that. He was a small-town boy who had left here, made good of himself and then come home with a wife. He should have figured out, before he took his request to Maggie, that now that Hailey had been dead over three years, he would be perceived, by the good and simple people of his hometown, as a rather tragic figure. Which was nothing new. He'd come to live with his grandparents when he was six, after his parents had died. He sometimes wondered why he had come back here, to this place where he had been and always would be the little orphan.

And now a widower, seen by one and all as much more in need of a new wife than a housekeeper.

"You don't have to worry about that with me," Brook piped up. "I have no romantic inclinations at all. None."

Brook seemed too young to have developed a truly jaundiced attitude toward romance, and Jefferson remembered housekeeper number two's rather frightening avarice.

He focused on her work performance flaws instead of telling Brook the full truth. "She also said *youse* instead of you. *Do youse want the toilet seat left up or down?*"

"You don't have to worry about that with me, either," Brook rushed to assure him. "There are few things I love as much as the English language and its correct usage."

"Hmm. That is not adding up to housekeeper, really. A true housekeeper might have been more concerned about the toilet seat and its correct usage."

A delicate blush crept up her cheeks.

"I'm a student," she said, "desperate for a summer job."

The desperate part was true enough, he could see that. But her eyes had done a slow slide to the right when she had said she was a student.

"My third housekeeper was Clementine." Clementine had been sent after he'd gone back down to the Emporium and read Maggie the riot act.

"She was certainly more suitable in the mature department. She'd actually been a friend of my grandmother's. But Clementine started talking the second she got in the door and did not stop, ever."

Jefferson remembered how even the lock on his office had not stopped her. "She stood outside my office while mopping the floor and polishing the door handle, chattering about her Sam. Husband. Mickey and Dorian. Children. Sylvester and Tweety. Bird and cat."

Suddenly it occurred to Jefferson, he *was* being the chatty one. This stranger standing at his door—whom he had absolutely no intention of hiring—certainly did not need all of this information.

Maybe it was a sign of too much time alone—three failed housekeepers not withstanding—that he just kept talking.

"I barricaded myself inside my office for three days, but Clem showed no sign of moving on to other parts of the house. To avoid discussion, I finally shot a generous check and a nice note about how I really didn't need her anymore under the door. It achieved exactly what I hoped—blessed silence."

He had managed to stop talking before he revealed Clementine's real fatal flaw. She had one divorced stepdaughter and three single nieces, all of whom she thought he should meet.

Brook's lips twitched. That hint of a smile deepened Jefferson's awareness of her as what he wanted least in his house: the distraction of an attractive woman. But that tentative smile also made him aware of the fine lines of tension in her—around her shoulders and neck, around her eyes, around her lips.

"It must have been hard to fire a friend of your grandmother's."

"You have no idea," he said.

But, looking at her, he had the uneasy feeling she *did* have an idea.

"Why the sudden search for a housekeeper? Are you replacing a housekeeper you were quite satisfied with?"

He scowled at her. Who was interviewing whom, here?

"No, I've never felt the need of one before."

"And now?"

He sighed. "In a moment of weakness, I agreed to allow an architectural magazine to photograph the house."

She glanced past him. "A moment of weakness? The house is extraordinary. You must be very honored at their interest."

"I may have been when it was all just an idea. But as soon as a date was set, I realized the house would need attention, which, six weeks later, I am no closer to giving it."

"When is the photo session scheduled?"

"Two weeks." He was aware he was engaging with her, and it didn't seem to be bringing him any closer to getting rid of her.

"I can have your place completely ready for a photo shoot in two weeks. I promise."

Jefferson contemplated that. It was a weakness to contemplate it. But he did need someone to get the place ready, and the date of the photo shoot was creeping up far more rapidly than he could have believed. And he suspected, from the lack of applicants now, that word had spread far and wide through this tight-knit region of the Kootenays that he was impossible to work for.

So, the young woman in front of him could be considered a godsend, if one was inclined to think that way, which Jefferson Stone most definitely was not.

No, Nelson Brook, or Brook Nelson, or whatever her name was, just wasn't going to work out, despite the fact no one else had responded to his blunt posting that had laid out exactly what he needed. He would just have to postpone *Architecture Now* indefinitely. He was aware of feeling relieved at that possibility.

He reached for the door. He was going to gently shove on it until she moved her foot.

But then a crow cawed loudly and raucously in the tree the prospective housekeeper had parked her car under. It dropped a pinecone out of its beak onto the roof of her car, and both sounds, the cawing and the sharp plunk of the cone on her car roof, were loud and unexpected in the drowsy quiet of the afternoon.

She gasped and jumped forward, and she smashed against him. For the second time, in the space of just a few minutes, she was touching him.

Only this time, it wasn't her hands splayed across his chest, which had been disconcerting enough. This time he could feel the press of the entire length of her body against his, and he was acutely aware of the sweet softness of her. He was acutely aware of hesitating a fraction of a second too long before putting her away from him.

"I'm so sorry," she stammered, but he caught the look on her face as she swiveled her head and glanced over her shoulder. It was the frantic look of a deer being startled by wolves. When she turned back to him, despite the fact she was trying hard to school her features, he could see the pulse pounding in the hollow of her throat.

Tension trembled in the air around her, and her muscles had gone taut. It made him notice there were shadows under her eyes and an edginess about her that was far from normal.

Her car door, he noticed, looking beyond her, was open, as if she had planned what to do if she needed to make a quick getaway.

Brook Nelson, or whoever she was, was terrified of something.

What shocked Jefferson was how her fear pierced the armor around his heart. It was as if a little sliver of light found its way to a place that had been in total darkness.

Inside himself was some nearly forgotten sense of decency, some sense of being connected to a human family he'd managed to ignore for three whole years, much to the dismay of the people of Anslow.

Jefferson stood very still. For a moment, he thought of the grandparents who had raised him, in a house not far from here. They had been old-fashioned people, who were decent to the core and kind to a fault. They would have never turned someone in need from their door, and no one had benefited from their generosity of spirit more than him. He could almost imagine the look of disapproval on both their faces if he shut the door now.

Jefferson took a deep breath and looked into the pleading eyes of the woman who had landed, uninvited, on his doorstep.

Was this who he had become? So embittered by the death of his wife, Hailey, that he could turn a woman, so obviously terrified, away from his door?

"Jeez," Jefferson muttered under his breath. He was a man who made decisions every day. That was what he did for a living. The decisions he made altered the courses of entire cities, impacted huge companies and global corporations. His decisions often had millions of dollars and the livelihoods of thousands of people riding on them.

And yet, this decision, this split-second decision, about what kind of man he would be, felt bigger than all of those.

Jefferson Stone stepped back marginally from his door.

It was all Brook Nelson needed. She catapulted over his threshold and into his house.

Into his life, he told himself grimly.

"Thank you," she breathed.

"Nothing has been decided," he told her gruffly, though somehow he knew it had been. And she knew it, too. She was beaming at him.

"It's not going to be a walk in the park," he said. He was already annoyed that his decision had been based on a moment of pure emotion, not rationale. He had to get things back on track and make sure she was aware this was a professional arrangement. "The finer aspects of housekeeping have been neglected for a long time."

He fully intended to tell her that if she didn't put

them right he would not tolerate her presence any longer than he had her predecessors. But she spoke before he could get the grim warning out.

"I could tell that from this door that things have been slightly neglected," she said, tapping the front door. "It needs polishing. You probably use something special for it, do you?"

"I have no idea. That's your job, not mine." He was trying to make up for his moment of weakness in letting her in, but she didn't seem to notice uninviting his tone.

"Do you have an internet connection here?"

"Not one that housekeeper number one, Mandy, approved of, but my career is dependent on being connected."

"I'll just look up online what to use on a door like that one. Is it stainless steel, like kitchen appliances?"

He considered her question. She was focusing on the job at hand and not asking any personal questions about his career. Hopefully, that indicated a lack of nosiness. Hopefully, that indicated his impulsive decision to let her in was not going to lead to complete disaster. "Yes."

"I know I just use a few drops of vegetable oil on mine. At home."

So, there was a home, somewhere, and presumably a fairly nice one if it had stainless steel appliances in it.

Despite his intention to keep everything professional, he smelled man problems in his new housekeeper's personal life. She had already claimed she had no romantic notions, which basically meant *burned by love.* It would be nothing but good for him if she was sour on the whole relationship thing. It could be almost as good protection as *mature* and *silent.* And, despite the fact he had his own history that had turned his heart to the same stone as his name, he sensed a need to keep up his defenses and to demonstrate the same lack of nosiness that she was showing!

Still, she wasn't just having man problems. She was terrified.

CHAPTER FOUR

JEFFERSON CONTEMPLATED HOW Brook's obvious terror stirred an emotion in him that he did not feel ready to identify and, in fact, felt a need to distance himself from.

He'd been living—despite the efforts of the townspeople—without the complication of untidy emotions for some time.

He'd give this woman—Brook Nelson, or whoever she was—a break. That didn't mean he had to involve himself in her drama in any way. The house was ridiculously large. With the slightest effort, during the day he wouldn't even know she was here.

Though that might pose some challenges, because she was in his living room now, and despite the fact the windows let in all kinds of light, it was as if sunshine had poured into the room with her. She flounced into his living room, hands on her hips, eyes narrowed, lips pursed.

"Wow," she said.

He thought she was referring to the architecture, which generally inspired awe, but she turned disapproving eyes to him. "Good grief, I can see neither Mandy nor Clementine got to this room. You mustn't have allergies. How long since this has been dusted?"

"A while," he admitted, instead of *never*.

"And I take it, it would have gone a while longer if it weren't for the photo shoot?"

"That's correct."

"You are a true bachelor, aren't you? Why live in such a beautiful house if you aren't going to take care of it?" she wailed with genuine frustration.

"I'm a widower," he said tersely.

He was not sure why he had imparted that little piece of information. He hoped it wasn't because he thought that would make her more sympathetic to his slovenliness than being a bachelor would.

But, as soon as he saw the sympathy blaze in her eyes, he realized he did not want her sympathy. Arriving in Anslow as an orphan, losing his wife, Jefferson Stone had experienced enough sympathy to last him a lifetime. He did not want any more challenges to his armor. He realized he needed to be much more vigilant in his separation of the professional and personal.

"I'm sorry," she said, her voice a low whisper that could make a man long for a bit of softness in his life.

But he had had softness, Jefferson reminded himself, and had proved himself entirely unworthy of it.

He lifted a shoulder in defense against the sympathy that blazed in her eyes. "My wife was the architect who designed the house."

"Ah, that explains a lot."

He lifted an eyebrow at her.

"You don't really seem like the type of person who would be amenable to having your home photographed. You are honoring her. That's nice."

Jefferson really didn't want her to think he was nice, and he squinted dangerously at her.

She got the message, because she moved over to an enlarged black-and-white photo on the wall.

"Who is this?"

The people responsible for the fact you haven't been sent packing. "It's me, with my grandparents, in front of the old house."

"It's a very powerful photograph."

That's what Hailey had said, too. She wasn't into hanging family portraits, but she had unearthed this photo and had it enlarged to four feet by six feet and transferred to canvas.

"How old are you in it?"

"Six."

She turned and looked at him. "How come you look so sad?" she asked.

He started. Hailey had never asked a single question about the photo. She had considered it an art piece. She had liked the composition, the logs of the old house, the dog on the porch, the hayfork leaning against the railing.

This woman was looking at him as if all his losses were being laid out before her, and he hated it.

"My parents had just died." He kept his tone crisp, not inviting any comment, but he saw the stricken look on her face before she turned away from him and ran her finger along the bottom of the frame.

She looked at her finger but didn't say anything. Her expression said it all. She felt sorry for him. No, it was more than sorry. She was, he could tell, despite the lie about her name, the softhearted type. She didn't just feel sorry for him. Her heart was breaking for him. And he hated that.

"This is a temporary position," he said, his voice cold. "After the photo shoot, I'll return to companionship of my dust bunnies. Maybe you want to consider if two weeks employment is what you are really looking for."

It was a last-ditch effort to let her know this position probably was not going to work for her. Or him.

"Temporary works perfectly for me," she said, as if that made it cosmically ordained. "Two weeks. I have a lot to do."

She had been careful not to express sympathy, and yet Jefferson felt her *I have a lot to do* could somehow mean rescuing him. Just a second. Wasn't he rescuing her? And if she thought she was going to turn the tables on him, she was in for an ugly surprise.

"We haven't come to terms yet. What do you expect for remuneration?"

"I haven't passed the free-day test yet."

He looked at her face. The softness lingered, but he was willing to bet she was one of those overachiever types. He deduced if she set out to impress, he would be impressed.

"Let's assume," he said drily.

She named a figure that seemed criminally low. But then she added, "Plus room and board, of course."

Jefferson stared at her. Why was this coming as a surprise to him? Obviously, some fear had sent her down his driveway, and just as obviously she was not eager to go back to it.

"I'm in the middle of relocating," Brook said vaguely. Then, as if sensing how disconcerted he was, she added, "This looks like a huge place. There must be a spare bedroom? Or two? Or a dozen?"

"I'm not sure—"

"Besides, if I'm going to be a proper housekeeper, I

should probably make you some meals. That would be easier to do in residence, don't you think?"

He saw it again. Behind her I'm-going-to-be-the-best-housekeeper-in-the-world bravado was terror.

She *wanted* to stay here.

Under his roof and his protection. He supposed if you were looking for a place to hide, the Stone House fit the bill quite nicely, as long as the things you were hiding from were outside of yourself.

Jefferson wondered if his new housekeeper would feel quite so eager to seek shelter here if she knew how colossally he had failed the one other woman, his wife, who had expected protection from him.

Meals. He hadn't really even considered a house-keeper providing meals. His search for a housekeeper had been motivated strictly by getting the house ready for the magazine photo shoot. He considered telling her meals would not be part of their agreement but found himself oddly reluctant to do so. He had not had a home-cooked meal in longer than he could remember, and his mouth was watering. His weakness annoyed him.

"Look," he told Brook sternly. "Against my better judgment, I'm giving you a chance, but be warned, if you chatter, you're out of here."

She looked as if she might say something. But then she pursed her lips, brought her fingers up, locked and put the imaginary key in her pocket. But before he could even be properly relieved, she reached into that imaginary pocket, took out the key and unlocked her lips.

"Maybe just before we begin our vow of silence, I should get you to show me around and you can tell me what you'd like to see prioritized. I'll make a list of what each room needs."

It was a reasonable request, and he knew he could not really refuse it.

"Let's begin here," she coaxed, when he was silent.

"This room is the great room," he said. "I noticed the windows are rain spotted."

"The windows would be a priority," she agreed. "But I should probably leave them until right before the photo shoot so they just sparkle that day, right?"

"Right," he said, though of course he had not thought of that.

"Dusting." She looked up at the high vault of the ceiling. "You have a ladder somewhere? I see cobwebs up there."

He frowned up at where she was looking. He did not like spiders. Before he answered, she went and slapped the couch, and a cloud of dust flew up from it. "Vacuuming. If the weather stays nice, I might even put the furniture outside for a bit to air it out."

He couldn't really imagine she was going to get all that furniture outside by herself. The sectional was huge. And apparently she was going to need a ladder. Actually, he was not going to let her up on a ladder, so there was no point in finding one. He needed to make it clear he was not going to be roped into interaction with her. He was going to protest, but then she went on.

"It smells faintly stale in here. I think a good airing of the furniture will change that."

It smelled stale in his house?

"For the photo shoot," she said, a little pensively, "it might be nice to make it look lived in. You don't use this room much, do you?"

"Not really." She was proving to be uncomfortably astute.

"What would you think if we set it up a bit?"

We?

"We could just add a bit of color. Maybe a bright throw over the couch, a few glossy magazines on display, a vase of flowers."

"Don't you think the photographer will do that?"

"Well, if he doesn't think to bring a vase of flowers with him, you'd be out of luck, since the nearest vase of fresh flowers would be quite a distance away. I could make the throw. I'll snoop around and see what you have."

He must have looked unconvinced because she rushed on, "You'd be surprised what you can make things out of. And I'm pretty handy with a needle and thread. I made this blouse."

That made him stare at the blouse for an uncomfortable second.

Thankfully, she had moved on. "It's just that this room—the house—is so beautiful, but it doesn't look very homey. It would make me happy to help it look its very best."

He stared at her. She already appeared much happier than she had when she first arrived, that little furrow of worry easing on her brow.

"I'll leave it up to you to spruce it up however you see fit. If you need to buy a few things, let me know," he said, and was annoyed that he felt he was giving in to her in some subtle but irreversible way. "Stay out of my office. And my bedroom."

The fact that he did not want her in his bedroom, that most intimate of spaces, alerted him to the fact she—this little mite of a woman in her homemade blouse with her wayward curls—was threatening him in some way that he had not allowed himself to be threatened in, in a very long time. If ever.

"But surely they'll want to photograph those rooms, too?"

"I'm quite capable of getting two rooms ready." His tone was curt and did not invite any more discussion, but he was aware that she had to bite her lip to keep herself from discussing it.

"I'll show you the kitchen," he said stiffly, leading her through to that room.

"Whoa," she said, following him, "now *this* is a room you use."

She didn't say it as if it was a good thing.

He looked at the kitchen through her eyes. The sink was full of dishes. She didn't know yet, but so was the oven. His mail was sliding off the kitchen table, and there were several envelopes on the floor. The counter by the coffeemaker was littered with grounds and sticky spoons. He often tromped up from the beach, wet, across the deck and through the kitchen. His bare footprints were outlined against the dark hardwood of a floor he'd allowed to become distinctly grimy.

Instead of looking daunted by the mess, she gave him a smile. "You need me way more than you thought you did."

He looked at her. In this room, as in the living room, it felt as if her presence had made the light come on.

He had the terrible feeling that maybe he did need her more than he had thought he did. His life had become a gray wash of work and isolation.

And damn it, he told himself, *he liked it that way*. What he didn't like was that Brook had been in his domain for only a few minutes, and he already was seeing things about himself that he had managed to avoid for a long, long time.

"Look, I have work to do," he said. "I'm going to let

you poke around the rest of the place by yourself. I'm sure it will become very quickly apparent to you what needs to be done."

He could have left then, but he watched as she wandered over to where the mail had fallen on the floor.

"This one is marked Urgent," she said. She came across the distance that separated them and held out the envelope. He reached for it.

For just a moment, their hands brushed. Something tingled along his spine, an electrical awareness of her. She might have felt something, too, because she spun away from him and went to the kitchen counter. It had a long, sleek window that overlooked the lake. But she did not look out the window. She opened up a cupboard.

"Is this what you're eating?" she asked him, holding up a soup can, and then setting that down and holding up a stew can.

He folded his arms over his chest, uninviting.

She ignored that. "Canned food is very high in sodium," she told him. "At your age, you have to watch things like that."

"My age?" he sputtered.

And then she laughed. It was a tinkling sound, as refreshing as a brook finding its way over pebbles.

"Do you have any fresh food?"

"Not really. There might be a few things in the freezer."

"That's not fresh. What do you eat?"

He thought of the stacks of microwavable meals in the freezer. "Whatever I feel like," he said grouchily.

"Never mind, I'll make a grocery list. How do you get the perishables here? In this heat? I guess ice cream is out of the question."

"I take the boat and a cooler," he said. "Anslow is quicker by water."

"You take a boat for groceries?"

"In the summer, yes."

"That's very romantic."

And then she blushed. And well she should. You did not discuss romance with your employer!

"If you make a list, I'll do a run tomorrow." That hardly sounded like a reprimand for discussing romance with him! It sounded like a concession to her feminine presence in his house!

"Oh, good," she said. "I'll be happy to prepare some meals if I have the right ingredients."

There was that whole meal thing again. A strong man would have just said no, that it was not part of her job, and that he was more than capable of looking after himself. But Jefferson had that typical man's weakness for food.

"What kind of meals?" he heard himself ask. He tried to think of the last time he'd had a truly decent meal. It was definitely when he'd been away on business, a great restaurant in Portland, if he recalled.

Home cooked had not been part of his vocabulary for over a decade, not since his grandmother had died. How she had loved to cook, old-fashioned meals of turkey or roast beef, mashed potatoes and rich gravy. The meal was always followed with in-season fruit pie—rhubarb, apple, cherry. When he had first moved in with his grandparents, his grandma had still made her own ice cream.

Hailey had been as busy with her career as he himself was. She liked what she called "nouveau cuisine," which she did not cook herself. She had made horrified faces at the feasts he fondly remembered his grand-mother providing.

"It is not healthy to eat like that," she had told him.

And yet he could never remember feeling healthier than when his stomach was full of his grandmother's good food.

Jefferson remembered, suddenly and sharply, he and Hailey arguing about this very kitchen.

"Double ovens?" he'd said, when they met the kitchen designer. *"We'll never use those."*

"The caterers will appreciate it when we entertain."

Why had he argued with her about it? Why had he argued with her about anything? As they had built the house, it had seemed as if the arguments had become unending.

If a man only knew how short time could be, and how unexpectedly everything could change… Jefferson felt the sharpness of regret nip at his heels. Some-how, it felt as if Brook, nosing through his fridge, was the reason for this regret. He usually was able to bury himself in work. It prevented being bothered by pesky emotions and, worse, by guilt.

Brook closed the fridge door and opened the freezer side of the huge French-door-styled appliance. She stood with her hands on her hips for a moment, staring at the neatly stacked boxes of single-serving freezer foods.

"I'll make that list," she said, obviously dismissing everything in the freezer as inedible.

"You do that," he said.

Apparently, she meant to make a list right now, while the lack was fresh in her mind. She found a piece of paper on the counter, and a pen. Her brow furrowed with concentration, and as she wrote, she muttered out loud.

"Chicken. Chocolate chips. Flour. Sugar…"

Chocolate chips. And flour. And sugar. Was she going to make cookies? Jefferson felt some despicable weakness inside himself at the very thought of a home-made cookie.

She had obviously been distracted from her request to see the house. "I'm expecting a call in a few minutes, so if you'll excuse me," he said.

Jefferson eased himself out of the room. His mouth had begun watering at the mention of chicken. Again, his thoughts went to his grandmother and platters of golden fried chicken in the middle of the old plank table.

It was a weakness, but he had no power to fight it. Besides, so what? She was signing on as his housekeeper, if she wanted to cook a few things, why shouldn't he be the beneficiary? He'd be signing the paychecks, after all. There were no worries that she would be as good a cook as his grandmother had been. No one was that good a cook.

CHAPTER FIVE

As she watched him go, Angie realized that, in her eagerness not to annoy her new employer with anything that could even remotely be construed as chattiness, she had not asked him his name. Now he was in full retreat and she didn't know where his cleaning supplies were kept or where he would like her to stay.

Instead, she watched mutely as he stalked away, down a wide hallway, turned and disappeared from view. A moment later she had heard the slamming of a door.

Considering how unfriendly he was, Angie contemplated what she was feeling. She felt as if she understood his unfriendliness. Her new employer was a man who had lost everything.

For the first time in a long time—far too long, in fact—Angie was aware that it was not all about her. She had seen in his face that he would not brook any sympathy from her, and though her first impulse had been to offer some, she had listened to her instincts. There were other ways to let him know she had heard him and seen him. There were other ways to offer comfort. After the public humiliation of her broken engagement, she personally knew how hollow words could feel.

Her boss had become an orphan when he was six, and now he was a widower. She remembered the shat-

tered-glass look in his eyes when he had revealed that
about himself, and his quick rejection of what he had
perceived as sympathy even though she had not said
a word.

He didn't want sympathy, and she did not blame him.
He wanted to be left alone, and she did not blame him
for that, either.

But he had let her into his house, and that was a
gift to her. She would give him a gift, too. She vowed
she would be the best housekeeper the world had ever
seen. She vowed for the next two weeks, she would
make her employer's life a little bit easier in any way
that she could.

Angie contemplated the feeling in her. It was nice
that it was not terror. What was it?

She felt *safe*.

Maybe his unfriendliness even made her feel safer.
Look where seemingly friendly male interest had landed
her last time, after all!

But no matter the reasons, for the first time since
she had bolted after finding that stuffed panda on her
bed, she felt something in her relax. Really, the tension
had been increasing for months, as it became more and
more apparent Winston's interest in her was not healthy.

Now, it was as if she had exhaled, after a long, long
period of holding her breath. Looking around the neglected house, it felt extraordinary to have a purpose
beyond her own survival.

With that exhale came a sensation of pure exhaustion, and she let her eyes wander longingly to the hammock that she could see through the kitchen window.
But falling asleep would be no way to make a good first
impression or forward her goal of making her boss's
life a little better!

She made herself focus on the task at hand. From the stack of leaning mail that had taken over the beautiful harvest-style kitchen table, she presumed his name was Jefferson Stone and that he was a business consultant who owned a company called Stone Systems Analysis. She made a mental note to sort the mail for him. Some was obviously junk, but some of those envelopes just as obviously contained checks and business correspondence.

The kitchen cabinets revealed a rather impoverished selection of food. As she went through the cupboards, her grocery list was becoming quite extensive, especially since the thought of cooking for him now was imbued with her sense of altruism.

After she had finished in the kitchen, she went exploring. Off the kitchen was a laundry room. When she opened the washing machine it had wet clothes in it that had been sitting so long they smelled dank. She found the soap and restarted the cycle. The soap was in a cabinet sadly lacking in the cleaning supplies necessary to keep a house. She retrieved her list and added a few more items.

Moving on, feeling like something of a snoop, which was ridiculous, she showed herself around the house. Though from the outside it looked as if it was only one level, she took a stairway off the kitchen that led downward to the next level.

It was not really a basement, but a beautiful above-ground lower level, set up for entertaining. It had a billiards table and a bar, but the cover on the table and the dust on the bottles at the bar suggested no one had entertained down here for a very long time. There was a huge TV on one wall. It looked as if Jefferson did watch that, as there were several smudged drink glasses on the coffee table and a bowl that contained the crumbs of potato chips.

There were two guest suites off the entertainment room with fold-back doors out onto private decks that overlooked the lake.

She could choose one to stay in. Both would probably provide ample separation from the master of the house.

But it looked, she thought with a bit of trepidation, as if it would be very easy to break into this lower level. Besides, maybe the photo shoot crew would need a place to stay.

After making a thorough list of what needed to be done downstairs to make it habitable for the photo crew, should they decide to stay there, she scooped up the dirty dishes and went back upstairs. There was no room in the dishwasher for the dishes, and so she started it, stacking a second load above it. It felt beautifully satisfying to be doing these *normal* things.

Then, she crept down the hall the way Jefferson had gone. The first door was firmly closed, and she went on extra silent feet past it. She could hear him talking, and since he did not seem like the type who would talk to himself, she presumed this was the phone call he had scheduled.

And then she went past his office, farther down the hallway. The next door was open a crack to reveal the master bedroom.

She peeked in. There was a huge window that capitalized on the view. Like all the other windows in the house, it needed a thorough cleaning.

A door led to a private deck, where there was a covered hot tub. Another door, closed, must have led to the master bath.

The bed was king size, with a gorgeous solid head-board of gray weathered wood that looked as if it might have been retrieved from an old barn. Still, the room lost any semblance to boutique hotel chic because the beautiful linens on the unmade bed were rumpled. There were clothes on the floor and overflowing the dresser drawers. There was a heap of magazines sliding off the nightstand, and several empty glasses and plates were scattered about available surfaces.

She moved away from Jefferson's open bedroom door, contemplating how relieved she was he had specifically told her to stay out of his room. She bit back a nervous giggle at the thought of what might be in there. *Good grief, she'd been saved from picking up his underwear off the floor.*

"My heart is overflowing with gratitude," she said softly, out loud, and realized it was completely true. She felt as if she had been plucked from a terrible predicament, but more, she had been given a task to do, and she had a sense of being needed, of having a contribution to make.

She kept going.

There were two more guest bedrooms, and a guest bath. The opulence of these rooms was undisturbed. Except for dusting and freshening—and maybe a vase of flowers—they already looked ready for the cover of a magazine.

At the far end of the hall was a narrow doorway. She thought it was a closet, and opened it to see if this was where extra linens were kept.

Instead she found a narrow staircase, and, intrigued, she followed it.

As soon as she saw what was at the top of that narrow staircase, Angie knew this was where she would stay. Her sense of gratitude deepened. The room was a secret sanctuary, octagon shaped, encased in windows. There was even a tiny bathroom through one door. She peeked in at the claw-foot tub, and at yet more windows overlooking the lake. Then she turned back to the room.

It was a delight in whites: white bed, white linens, white walls. The white draperies, on closer inspection, were silk. She was delighted to see the room also had a small craft alcove with a sewing machine and neat cubicles full of fabrics and craft items.

Angie could not help herself. She went over and inspected the sewing machine. It was a very good model. Growing up as she had, in a single-parent household, there hadn't always been money for the fashionable clothes she wanted. But a sewing lesson in a home economics class had changed all that. By the time she was in high school, she could copy any design she saw and was creating her own designs, too. She had made extra money sewing for her mother's friends and for her own classmates.

At home, tucked away safely in a drawer was a sketch for the wedding dress she had designed herself and hoped to wear down the aisle.

That memory brought her back to reality with an unpleasant snap. She became aware it was also unbelievably hot and stuffy in this room, and she went across the bleached hardwood floor and threw open the windows. Within seconds a gorgeous, cool cross breeze was coming off the lake, fluttering in the curtains and cooling and freshening the room.

Though it was not 100 percent in keeping with her mission of making mental lists of what needed to be done in each room, Angie gave in to the temptation to flounce down on the bed. Her flounce created a cloud of dust, but she lay there, anyway, letting the fresh breeze from the windows carry the dust away. She allowed herself to contemplate the delicious sense of being 100 percent safe.

The windows were low, and even lying down she could see the lake. The view from this room was spectacular. She was looking down at the decks below, the one with the hammock on it, and the other with the hot tub.

She blushed at the thought she could spy on her boss while he sat in that tub. He did not seem like the kind who would wear a bathing suit!

"That's exactly the kind of nosey parker he does not want around," she told herself.

She looked away from the hot tub and could see that, beyond the decks, there were rough stairs carved out of the face of the huge stone the whole house sat upon. The steps led to a crescent moon of a beach and a dock with a sleek motorboat bobbing at its mooring. An afternoon wind was kicking up, and there was a chop on the water, the waves white capped.

She knew she could not go to sleep. She could not. But to find safety after experiencing so much tension? To have a sweet sense of mission after floundering in her own distress for so long?

Her eyelids felt as if they were weighted down by stones. She sighed, snuggled into the somewhat dust scented white of the duvet on the bed, and fell fast asleep.

Darkness fell, and Jefferson was edgily aware as he set down the phone after a long afternoon of conferences that he was not alone in his house.

The envelope she had passed him earlier, marked Urgent, caught his attention and he opened it.

Dear Jefferson,

As I mentioned to you in our recent phone conversation, the town of Anslow hopes to provide a picnic area where the Department of Highways widened the road after your wife's accident. Our intention is to name the area the Hailey Stone Lookout.

Hailey had not been part of our community for very long, but we so want to honor her in this way. Would you please consider attending the fundraiser as our guest? It would mean a great deal to all of us.

The theme is Black Tie Affair and dress is formal. Dinner with dancing to follow.

Will you let me know?

The letter was signed by Maggie, who as well as running the Emporium, was second in command to the mayor, and the town's most goodhearted busybody.

She, like, Clementine, had been a friend of his grandmother's. She had been one of the ones who circled around him after the death of his parents, clucking over him and loving him through all that pain, sewing him seamlessly into life of a small town. She had cheered at his hockey games and been part of the standing ovation for *Grease*. She had been in the front row, beaming at his graduation. She had held his grandmother's hand when they had buried his grandfather, and again when he had gone away to university. It was Maggie who had held his own hand when he came back for his grandmother's funeral.

When he and Hailey had decided to build on this land that had been his grandparents' it had been Maggie who had welcomed them home as if they belonged here.

Had he already known, even at those initial stages, that Hailey would never belong here?

Jefferson glanced at the date. The fund-raiser was two weeks away, the day before the magazine crew was showing up. He cursed under his breath. It was the second time in one day that honoring Hailey had come up. Just like with the photo shoot, how could he refuse? Plus, he didn't want to let Maggie down. But he had a horrible feeling the whole thing was just a ruse—not to honor Hailey but to parade the whole town's eligible women before him.

The people of Anslow meant so well, but none of them could believe a life worth living could be had without family. They thought it was "time" for him to get over it and get on with it, as if these things could be done on a schedule. But couldn't they see? For him family was forever connected to loss. And it was loss he could not bear any more of.

"I'll think of a way," he decided. He wished his new housekeeper had never handed him the envelope.

His new housekeeper. He listened. He thought he would hear sounds of her rummaging around, but there was nothing. In fact, he was pretty sure, now that he thought about it, that he had not heard a sound for hours.

He slipped out of his office and into the hallway. Night was falling and his house was in deep shadow. He sniffed the air. He knew there was hardly anything to cook with, so why was he disappointed that she had not made him dinner, and then sharply annoyed at his disappointment.

He had done fine without her for all these years.

He noticed the doorway at the end of the hall was open, and he went toward it, and then quietly up the dark staircase.

He paused as he came into the room. There was very little light left in it. It had been Hailey's favorite room in the whole house design.

"Like a secret room," she had said.

It had seemed to him it was the kind of room their kids might have adored, back then, when he had still held the hope he would one day create a family of his own.

But Hailey had designed the room not for kids but for crafts.

Crafts? He remembered the astonishment in his voice. Because his wife, the consummate professional, did not do crafts any more than she did double ovens.

The knife ache of pain throbbed along his temples. Because he had had a dream of settling here, and having kids here, and the night that Hailey had run off into the storm, it had been apparent their dreams were entirely different.

He had failed her so colossally.

Then, as his eyes adjusted to the dimness in the room, Jefferson saw Brook on the bed. She was curled up on her side, facing him, and she was fast asleep, her golden sand curls scattered over the white pillow cases.

It occurred to him he should feel annoyed. This was hardly the way for her to make the stellar impression she had promised. And yet seeing her sleeping, the anxiety completely relaxed from her face, Jefferson did not feel annoyed.

He felt as if he had done the right thing, and maybe the only thing. A thing that would have made his grandparents proud of him. This was his grandparents' land.

They would have never turned away someone in need. That was the unspoken creed they had lived their lives by, and no one had benefited more than he from their strict adherence to the golden rule.

He stood there for a moment too long, because Brook's eyes opened, sleepy and disoriented at first, and then they widened.

She sat up on the bed. A scream of pure terror erupted from her. She scrambled backward, knees to her chin, pulling the covers along with her and putting her back into the corner.

"Hey," he said. "Hey, Brook, it's okay. It's me."

That apparently was not reassuring, as she screamed again, a scream of fear so primal it made the hair on the back of his neck stand up.

"Jefferson Stone," he said, but then it occurred to him he had not volunteered his name as of yet, so it might not reassure her at all. It also occurred to him, the light in the room was very dim. All she could see was a hulk standing in her doorway.

He stood there for a moment trying to get his eyes to adjust more fully. She scooted out of the corner bed, and he lost sight of her in the darkness. And then something crashed down on his head. By instinct, he reached out, connected with the arm of his attacker and pulled her in close to him.

"Let me go," she screamed, fighting like a wildcat.

Instead of letting her go, Jefferson pulled the panicky woman into his chest and held her hard and tight. She pummeled him with her fists. She reared back and hit his chest with her head. He was afraid she might bite him. But he would not let go.

"Brook, stop it," he said quietly. "Stop it. It's just me. Jefferson."

Finally, his voice seemed to penetrate all that panic. The wriggling strength of her went suddenly still, though he could feel the rabbit-fast beat of her heart against his chest.

"Jefferson?" She tilted her face up at him, and he could see the glitter of gold in her eyes as she stared up at him, frightened and baffled.

"Jefferson Stone, your new boss?"

Silence. And then, recognition pierced the glaze in her eyes, and for the first time he thought she might actually be wide-awake.

"Oh, my God! My new boss. I just hit my new boss with a lamp."

"Yes, you did."

"I'm so sorry. No. I'm beyond sorry. I'm mortified. Devastated. Appall—"

"I get it," he said drily.

She seemed to realize she had made no effort to pull away from him. He realized how delicate she felt pressed into the length of him. He realized what he wanted to realize the least: that his life had become too vacant, lacking almost completely in this most basic of human needs. To be touched.

Jefferson Stone was far too aware that Brook felt good. And smelled good, and that a man could live to see eyes like that searching his face for goodness.

And finding it.

She seemed to realize now that rather than fighting to get out of his arms, she was clinging to him. Embarrassment painted her cheeks a delicate shade of pink. She dropped her arms to her sides and took a wobbly step back from him. After a moment, she lifted her arm and pushed her hand through her rumpled curls.

"I think you should sit down," he said.

No argument. She retreated to the bed. She sat on the edge of it, peering through the darkness.

He reached over and flicked on the overhead light.

Jefferson had never seen terror as naked as what remained in her freshly illuminated face. He held up his hands, like a cowboy who had dropped his weapon, and he backed toward the door. "I'm not going to hurt you."

But now comprehension was dawning in her own features.

"Of course, you're not," she said. "I know who you are now. I thought you were…" She dropped her head into her hands. Her whole body shuddered.

"Are you crying?" he asked. It was the first time since this whole thing had started that he felt panic.

"N-n-no."

Clearly she was lying. Sheesh. She was the world's worst liar.

Jefferson hesitated in the doorway. What he wanted to do was run from the sheer need in her. She was about to hit emotional meltdown.

"I'm practically a hermit," he told her. "I don't know how to help you."

"I—I—I don't need any h-h-help from you."

But she did. She needed, obviously, to be comforted.

He was in no way qualified to do that. His every inclination was to keep backing up until he was all the way down the stairs.

But what he wanted to do, and what he did, were two separate things.

"Has anyone ever told you that you are the world's worst liar?" he asked.

CHAPTER SIX

"THAT WOULD BE a good thing, wouldn't it?" Brook sniveled. "Being a bad liar?"

In any other circumstances, Jefferson would have agreed with her. But at the moment? He would have liked to believe her. That she did not need any help from him.

Jefferson told himself that rap on the head with her bedside lamp was preventing him from thinking rationally. He was shocked at himself when he did not retreat from Brook's naked need but, instead, dropped his arms to his sides and moved with measured steps into the room, around the shattered lamp and across to the bed.

She looked very vulnerable, still in the blouse and shorts she had arrived in, though now her outfit was quite crumpled. He was ready to stop the second she indicated he should, but she never did. He arrived at the bed, and felt large and oafish, towering over her. She peeked through the fingers that covered her face. She drew in a long, shuddering breath.

She was trembling. It reminded him of aspen leaves in a breeze. Given how frightened she had been, he was sure his very size intimidated.

"I'm sorry," he said softly. "I feel like an ogre in a fairy tale."

She hiccuped, glanced at him through her fingers again and tried for a wobbly smile. "Then I hope it's Wreck."

"I don't have a clue who that is," he admitted.

"*Wreck and Me*? It's a kid's movie about an ogre."

"I'm not up on my kids' movies."

"Wreck turns out to be the good guy, despite appearances." She wasn't sobbing uncontrollably anymore, so he was making progress. Maybe. Did he want her to think he was a good guy? Not really.

Women like her pinned their hopes and dreams on men they perceived to be good guys. Like most, he would eventually let her down.

But not tonight. Tonight he could be a good guy. He hesitated, looking for a way to not be quite so big against her tininess. And then, seeing nothing else to do, so he was not hovering over her from a great height, he sat down on the edge of the bed. The mattress gave under his weight, and she slid toward him. Their thighs touched. Hers were bare.

A truly good guy would not be so suddenly and painfully aware of her.

She did not try to scoot right through the wall, but regarded him with wide eyes studded with tears.

"So, Brook, who did you think I was?" he asked.

For a moment, she didn't comprehend the name, confirming that she was just about the world's worst liar and that she had lied about who she was. But that lie was somehow connected to this terror and to the tears trickling down her cheeks. Now was not the time to press her for the truth.

"I—I—I thought you were someone else," she managed to stammer.

"That's reassuring." He deliberately kept his voice

flat and calm. "I can be grumpy, yes. But I don't think terrifying enough to deserve a lamp over the head."

"I'm so sorry."

"I've certainly never had a woman react to me like that before."

He saw the faintest glimmer of a smile and was encouraged by it. It was like trying to win the trust of a wary deer in a meadow.

"No, I don't suppose you have," she said.

This was going from bad to worse. She was blushing delicately. She probably would have liked to lie about the fact she thought he was attractive. There was no need for him to preen. He needed to recognize the danger. His housekeeper thought he was attractive. *And* a good guy.

She was obviously going to survive. He ordered himself to get up and leave.

The stupid good guy vetoed him.

"Who?" he asked. "Who the hell is scaring you like this?"

His tone was all wrong, he realized, the fury at whoever it was having crept, entirely unbidden, into his voice. She seemed to shrink in on herself, as if being terrified was an indictment of her, as if somehow her being terrified was her own fault, an unforgivable weakness.

"It was just a bad dream," she said, her voice muffled.

She was lying again. It had not been just a bad dream. But he let it go. He shouldn't have pursued it in the first place. It fell strongly into the *none of his business* category. It was time to extricate himself from this situation.

The good guy was not ready to go. The good guy was struggling to find words to bring her comfort. Of course the colossally self-centered guy had been in charge so long, he could find none. The analyst had long ago banished sensitivity as a weakness that could not be tolerated.

The good guy could not fail to notice she was still trembling, that tears were still slithering out between the fingers that covered her face.

The bad guy in him sighed with resignation and went, somewhat unwillingly, where the good guy told him to go. It was not a place of numbers. Or words. Or equations. Or analysis.

The good guy in Jefferson Stone went to the place where his grandmother had gone when a frightened and heartbroken waif had been delivered to her.

"Are you okay?" he asked.

"Yes."

But she wasn't. Her voice was wobbling as if she was running a jackhammer. She scrubbed furiously at her tears with the palm of one hand.

Some instinct or memory of the little boy he had once been, some primal recognition of what goodness was and what was required of him made Jefferson slide his arms under her and tug her over onto his lap. Her hesitation—a sudden stiffening, a small resistance—did not even last a breath. And then she was snuggled into his chest, her curls tickling his chin, her tears washing through his shirt, her warm weight a puddle against him.

"It's okay," he said. His voice was rusty, unaccustomed to reaching for that gentle note. "It's okay, sweetheart. You're safe."

Sweetheart? Desperation to make her feel better was obviously making him crazy. What was he doing calling her *sweetheart*? But somehow he didn't want to call her Brook, to invest in the obvious lie she had told him about her name.

It added to his sense of craziness that making physical contact with his new housekeeper seemed to be becoming a regular event!

But, at that moment, the good did shine through. Because despite the sweetness of her curves, despite her warmth pooling against him, despite her designated role in his life, despite the lie of her name between them, she felt not like the beautiful woman that she was. She felt only like a frightened child, as he had once been. And he felt only like a person reaching deeply and desperately within himself for the decency to comfort her, as his grandmother had once done.

And so he stroked her hair and told her over and over again, in a crooning voice that he did not recognize as his own, that she was safe. He could feel the tension draining out of her, her muscles relaxing, her breathing becoming more regular, the hard pulsing of her heart slowing.

And she must have felt safe, because she finally said, her voice low and tentative, "You know how you said I'm not a very good liar?"

"Hmm?"

"My name isn't Brook."

He waited.

She sighed as if she were weighing the wisdom of what she was about to do. "It's Angelica. Angie."

He waited, again, to see if she would go on, if she would explain the necessity of the subterfuge to him, but she didn't. In fact, he felt her relax totally, and then her breath came in even little puffs against his chest. Her hair had fallen forward, shielding her face, and when he tucked it back, he saw she was asleep.

He sat there for a long time, afraid to waken her. Finally his arm felt as if it was going numb. He wondered, as he worked his way out from under the slight weight of her, if she had ever truly been awake.

He settled her back in the bed, drew the covers over her and gazed down at her for a moment.

Her face looked relaxed, angelic even, the perfect face for someone named *Angelica*. He bent and kissed her cheek, as if she was a child he had tucked in.

And then he turned swiftly from her, embarrassed by his tenderness. "I hope," he muttered, "neither of us remembers a thing about this by morning."

She had a chance of that. He did not.

He glanced once more at the sleeping woman, then went quietly down the steps and closed the door to the turret room behind him.

Jefferson was aware of steeling himself against whatever he had felt in that room. It was one thing to be a good man. But it was another to care about others. To care about others was to invite unspeakable pain into your life. He would use this incident to shore up rather than lessen his resolve for their relationship to be professional only. He would withdraw himself, as completely as it was possible to do while they were under one roof. Withdrawing was something he was an absolute expert at. After the blow of Hailey's death, he'd withdrawn quite successfully from the world for the past three years.

Though it was now late at night, he was aware he would not sleep. He went into his office and shut the door. He was in the middle of a contract to revamp the computer systems for the City of Portland. This was what he loved and this is what he could lose himself in: researching, planning and coordinating the selection and installation of the software systems that gigantic enterprises, towns and cities, corporations and businesses counted on for smooth and efficient operation.

He sat down at his computer and sighed with satisfaction at the reassuring world devoid of emotional complexity. This was his world: analysis. Numbers and graphs and statistics appeared on the screen before him.

"Two weeks?" he told himself. "That's nothing."

CHAPTER SEVEN

ANGIE AWOKE IN the morning, bright light embracing her. For a moment, she had no idea where she was. But the ceiling had a display of dancing light on it, the windows reflecting patterns off the nearby water. She remembered the lake. She remembered arriving at the Stone House. And finding this bedroom and surrendering to the exhaustion that had been building in her.

And then, she remembered last night.

She remembered the panic that had clawed at her throat as she woke up to see a man's figure silhouetted in the doorway.

Disoriented, her fears and stresses must have been playing out in her dreams, because Angie had thought, *Winston found me.* She had reached for that lamp and attacked with full force.

But it had not been Winston. She hoped it had all been a bad dream.

But, no, it was all true. There was the lamp, with a large chunk missing from its glass base and the shade completely crumpled, lying on her floor.

It hadn't been Winston. It had been a man she barely knew. It had been her new employer, Jefferson Stone.

Heat raced up her cheeks as she remembered him comforting her even after she had smashed a lamp over his head. When he had climbed onto the bed? That's when she should have protested more convincingly that she did not need him! When he had pulled her onto his lap? That's when she should have put the wall up and resisted with all her might.

But, no, instead, weakling that she was, she had surrendered into it, allowed herself to feel something she had not felt in months, not even with the police.

It was a sensation beyond feeling safe. Angie had felt protected.

Even if Jefferson hadn't said to her, over and over, that she was safe, she would have felt protected by him. It was not his words that had comforted. Unlike her, he was incapable of lying about who he was. She had felt the truth that was at the core of Jefferson Stone. She had felt the great strength and calm in his physical presence.

She had felt he was that man—that one-in-a-million man—who would lay down his life to protect someone he perceived as weaker than himself, or vulnerable.

Fresh from terrifying dreams—not to mention months of uncertainty—she had not been strong enough to resist what he had offered. It was what she had wanted most since her terrifying ordeal with Winston had begun. To feel safe again in the world.

And after she had felt safe? After she had realized she was in a lovely bedroom at a house on a lake that most people would not be able to find, even with a map? Then she should have told him to go, released him from that primal duty he felt to protect someone not as strong as him.

But, oh, no, she had given herself completely over to the temptation of being weak. She had relished his presence. The solidness of his chest, that delicious scent

that was all his, the tenderness of his hand in her hair.
She had lapped up his attention like a greedy child lap-
ping up ice cream, and in the light of morning, that was
exceedingly embarrassing.

Had he really kissed her cheek before he left the
room? Her hand flew there as if she would be able to
feel the evidence of it lingering. She had let down her
guard. She had told him her name was not Brook. It was
a moment of terrible weakness that had allowed these
indiscretions. She vowed there would not be another.

Though maybe that would not be her choice. She had
admitted she had lied to him. She had hit him with a
lamp! He would be within his rights, in the cold light
of day, to ask her to leave. Or at least to demand an explanation.

A half hour later, showered and dressed and ready
for her first day of official duties—if she still had a
job—she realized her new boss must also have a plan
of avoidance. Obviously, she had managed to embarrass him, too.

His office door was shut when she went by it. There
was coffee ready in the kitchen, but investigation did
not show much else for breakfast. The man did not
even have a loaf of bread! There was an empty box on
the counter.

She picked it up and read the label. Apparently Jefferson had indulged in a microwavable bean burrito for
breakfast. It was quite pathetic, actually.

She remembered her resolve, even before last night's
kindness, to make his life better while she was here.
Now, standing there holding the burrito box, she committed more fully to that. She would see that he had
proper meals and clean clothes, and that every surface
of his house shone, reminding him of what a beautiful

place he lived in. Maybe reminding him that it was a beautiful world.

That awareness, that it was a beautiful world, had evaporated from her in the past while, too. Maybe, in helping him discover it, she could recover some of her own faith in the world.

A little frightened, Angie realized she was allowing the most dangerous thing of all into her world.

She was allowing herself to hope.

That hope infused her as she did normal things. She made a grocery list, put dishes in the dishwasher, cleaned crumbs off the counter. It was a testament to how crazy her life had become that doing these small things filled her with such pleasure. She had never really appreciated how wonderful it was to just be normal.

Still, she could not use these simple pleasures as an excuse to delay seeing Jefferson this morning. With her list in hand, she approached his office door. It was true her boss had made it plain he didn't like interruptions, but she couldn't very well ignore the events of last night. And she needed to know if he planned to oust her over her deception about her name.

Standing in the hallway, she was aware her heart was beating too hard. She rehearsed what she would say. If he did keep her on, she needed him to know that his tender concern, while appreciated, was not in any way expected by her. The exact opposite, in fact. She would prefer they stay on less familiar terms. The list was a pretext to get into his office and make her speech.

She knocked.

"Yes?"

She opened the door a crack and peeked in. Jefferson looked exhausted. Here, she had vowed to make his life better, and it was apparent it was already worse!

"You haven't been up all night, have you?" she asked, appalled, her rehearsed speech forgotten.

He glowered at her. "You're my housekeeper, not my mother." His tone was unnecessarily curt.

But all she heard was *you're my housekeeper*. He wasn't firing her!

She was relieved that the tenderness she thought she had experienced last night had been largely imagined. At the same time, she was aware that she was ever so faintly annoyed that he had reached the conclusion, all by himself, that his tender concern would not be necessary in the light of day.

"I just wanted to apologize for last night," Angie said, the opening line of her speech. It would be a shame to let the whole thing go to waste. She opened the door a little more, though he clearly had not invited her to.

"No need." He waved a dismissive hand at her. The message was clear—*Leave me alone.*

"I was very tired…" She felt driven to explain, stepping over the threshold into his office. "I'm sure it won't happen again."

"Great," he said. He glanced up from his computer, acknowledged the fact she was actually in his office with a slight frown and looked back at the computer. "I only have so many lamps."

This was very good. He was going to make it about the lamp instead of about her. And him. And embarrassingly tender moments.

"I'll pay for the lamp," she insisted, following his lead. Let's make it about the lamp. Only that was harder than it should have been. Even with that scowl on his face, he was a very attractive man. It was not so easy to dismiss the fact she had been on his lap last night.

"I don't care about it, actually." Apparently, it was easy for him to dismiss it.

"Well, I do. I'll pay for it. I insist."

"Whatever." This was a discharge.

In case she didn't get that, he waved a hand at her, as if she was a bothersome fly. She noticed a lump on his head and stepped in to his office even farther. She didn't stop until she was standing right in front of him.

He looked up from his computer and folded his arms over his chest, clearly annoyed. "You've apologized. We've established you are paying for the lamp. Was there anything else?"

"Are you having any symptoms of concussion?" she asked. "Because you have quite a large lump right—"

She reached for him; he reared back. She snatched her hand away and touched her own forehead above her eyebrow. "Here," she finished weakly.

"I am not having the symptoms of a concussion," he said.

"How's your head?" He had a lump rising above one of his slashing eyebrows.

She thought he would at least express some curiosity about her real identity, but he did not.

"Aren't you going to ask me why I gave you a false name?" she said.

He studied her for a moment. "No."

"Oh." She realized she was disappointed in his lack of interest—not that she wanted to get into the whole tawdry tale of her failure to discern a bad person from a good one. Still, she felt driven to say something else.

"I just want you to know, I'm not a person you can't trust."

He looked at his watch, a hint that she didn't have to say anything else.

For some reason, she babbled on. "I don't have a list of aliases. There is no dead person in an attic somewhere that can be attributed to me. I'm not on the run from the law."

Something like a smile tickled at the edges of his lips. "You think you had to tell me that you're not a murderer or a fugitive?" he asked.

She nodded vigorously.

"It's imminently apparent that you are not."

"That's good," she said, though she wasn't so sure. He had managed to say that as if she had *boring* written all over her, as if she was exactly the kind of woman whose fiancé would leave in search of excitement elsewhere.

"It's also imminently apparent that something, or someone, has thrown a very bad scare into you. If it's a man—" the smile had disappeared completely and something dangerous darkened his eyes "—you need to get rid of him and never look back."

She opened her mouth to say something and then closed it again. Jefferson was already looking back to his computer. It was a man, but it was too complicated to explain, and he clearly did not want an explanation. Despite the advice, he was letting her know that theirs was a temporary arrangement and that she had to handle her life herself. He had absolutely no interest in her personal dramas. He did not want a repeat of last night any more than she did.

Except that looking at him, she did feel a strange longing to see the tender side of him again, to feel his hand in her hair and his lips on her cheek.

After a moment, he glanced at her, and she realized

she was still standing there, trying to reconcile this cold indifference with the man who had comforted her last night.

Yes, that lump on your head, right over your scowling brow, needs some attention. And I would love to finish what I started, to lean over and put my fingers on it, as if somehow I could soothe the pain away. The way you soothed mine away last night.

But he was looking at her like the man least likely to want his pain soothed away. She thought of the little lost boy in that photograph in the living room. And she suspected the lump on Jefferson Stone's head was the least of his pain.

She was glad she had the grocery list and didn't have to make up an excuse for the fact she was standing there staring at him. "You asked me if there was anything else and yes, there is. There's this."

Trying not to feel as if she was scurrying under his impatient eye, she crossed the room and thrust the list in front of him.

He picked it up and studied it. The annoyed scowl creased his brow again. "Good grief, are we supplying a barracks?" he said, lifting his eyes to hers.

"It's really just basics."

He glared again at the list, then lifted those cool gray eyes to hers. "Cumin is a basic?"

His pronunciation of cumin was way off. He made it sound like something quite erotic.

"It's a spice! You don't have any spices," she sputtered. She willed herself not to blush over something so silly as the pronunciation of *cumin*.

"Well, I doubt if they have anything quite so exotic in Anslow. There's no big-box supermarket there. It's a little family general store."

"It's not exotic," she said. Good grief. She sounded defensive over a spice. She was pretty sure she was blushing.

"Well, I'm still not going to go ask for it. People would get the wrong idea entirely." He took a pen off his desk and put a line through cumin.

"They might indeed get the wrong idea if you said it like that." She could not resist commenting. "It's not *coming*." Now her cheeks felt as if they were on fire. "It's pronounced *coo-men*."

"Huh." Unsaid: *I don't give a damn*, though he was watching her face with interest now.

"I use it in homemade guacamole. I make really good burritos. You'll never want a frozen one again." She was hoping to get him to put cumin back on the list and to distract him from her schoolgirl reaction to what was simply a wrong pronunciation.

"That's the problem with improvements," he said. "They make you dissatisfied with the way things were before."

"Well, in terms of frozen burritos for breakfast, that can only be a good thing."

He appeared about to remind her, again, she was not his mother. Instead, he looked back at the list.

"I don't know where any of this stuff is," he said. "Cornstarch. Where do you find that? In the vegetables or in the laundry supplies?"

She pressed her lips together to keep from laughing.

"How essential can something called cornstarch be, anyway? I don't even like my shirts starched. That was my grandfather's generation." He took his pen and struck another item from her list.

"It's for thickening sauces, not for doing laundry," she said, but he did not appear to hear her.

"Dark chocolate ice cream? Not just ordinary chocolate?"

She had been planning on making iced mocha for the heat of the afternoon. In truth, it was all part of her plot to make him *happy*.

It was more than obvious happiness did not come naturally to him. Rather than seeing that as a challenge, she should just admit to herself that she had set an impossible task.

If only bringing someone happiness could be as simple as giving them an iced mocha on a hot afternoon.

CHAPTER EIGHT

"The ice cream may not be essential," Angie admitted, though she was reluctant to give ground.

"Good." Jefferson crossed it off the list with a little too much enthusiasm, and then muttered, "If I was going to get ice cream, it wouldn't be chocolate, anyway."

"What kind would it be?" she asked, curious despite herself. You could probably tell a lot about a man by the kind of ice cream he liked.

But he only spared her a glance that made her feel as if the question had been highly personal, like asking if he preferred boxers or briefs.

"You know," he said, displeasure deepening his voice even more, "I offered to pick up a few things in town because I have another errand to do there, but a list like this? I'll be wandering in the market for hours. They'll have to send in a Saint Bernard to find me, hopefully with a keg of brandy around his neck. Brandy." He squinted at her list and crossed something off. She was fairly certain it was the cooking sherry.

"I hate going to the market, anyway," he admitted.

"That explains the frozen bean burrito for breakfast."

"Yes, it does," he said unapologetically. "One-stop shopping. I stop at the freezer, fill my basket, and leave. I can be done in forty-three seconds."

"Well, you should at least be familiar with where the ice cream is if you're such a fan of the freezer section," she said. She should leave it at that. Really, she should. But she didn't. "Why do you hate going to the market?"

"These people have known me since I was six years old. They have an annoying tendency to fuss over me," he snapped. "You're not the first person to think my food selections are not that great. All those busybodies peering in my basket."

Not everyone, she guessed. Women. It was a small town. He was probably its most eligible bachelor. And damned unhappy about it, too. She could just imagine them clucking over him at the supermarket.

She made a note to herself. *No clucking. No fussing.* He was right. She was not his mother.

"There's only one solution," he said.

She held her breath. Either he was going to throw out the list or reconsider her employment.

But as it turned out, there was a third option, which she had not even considered.

"You'll have to come and do the shopping yourself." He held out the list, and she snatched it from him, trying not to show her delight at this unexpected turn of events. "I'll send you off to the market while I run my other errands."

"It won't put you out in the least to have me along," she said. It sounded like a promise.

"Yeah, whatever." He didn't have the grace to appear even slightly grateful she was going to get some decent supplies for him. He glanced at his watch. "I can't go until later this afternoon. Can you be ready around four-thirty?"

She sighed. "That means frozen bean burritos for lunch, I'm afraid."

"You say that as if it's a bad thing," he said drily.

It was when she left his office that she remembered he said he went to Anslow by boat. And she had said she thought that was romantic, even though she shouldn't have done. Anyway, she scolded herself, if that was her idea of romance, it was no wonder that her fiancé had left her for someone who wanted to live on a beach in Thailand!

Well, if she was not Jefferson's mother, she was even less likely a romantic prospect. Luckily for her—and for tired-of-women-fussing-over-him Jefferson—she was completely disillusioned in that department. Harry, and then Winston, had seen to that.

What a relief. Because feeling romantic about her boss in any context, including a boat ride, could lead to dreadful complications, even in two short weeks.

But for some horrible reason, even as she vowed off romance, Angie thought of his lips brushing her cheek the night before. And she blushed even more deeply than she had over the mispronunciation of a word.

She squeezed as much activity as she could into the day. By the time four-thirty rolled around, the dishes and laundry were completely caught up and the kitchen was gleaming. It was hot, though. A thermometer on the outside of the kitchen window told her it was a hundred and two degrees outside when she slipped up to her room and showered the day's grime off.

Angie had hauled her meager suitcase up the stairs to her room. She had not, in her panicked flight from Calgary, packed one thing that might impress Jefferson Stone. It was too hot to impress, anyway. She slipped on a clean white T-shirt and a very simple wraparound skirt she had designed and made herself. Then she ran a brush through hair that was springing up all over the place.

"Ready?" he asked as she came down the stairs.

"Is it always so hot here?" She regarded Jefferson. He didn't look hot at all in a summer sports shirt and light khaki shorts. He looked cool and confident and composed—a man who did not invite fussing at the supermarket.

"This is a pretty average summer day. You could have turned on the air-conditioning."

"I was hoping to freshen up the house by leaving all the windows open. I think I've succeeded only at letting the heat in. How are we going to keep the groceries from wilting?"

We. As if they were a partnership. She contemplated how easily the "we" had slipped from her lips.

He grabbed a large cooler from the storage cabinet by the back door and then led her out the back door and across the deck. She noticed he did not bother locking the door they came out. He paused before taking the stairs down, scanning the nearby mountains.

"What?"

"Just looking at the clouds," he said.

She followed his gaze. The clouds were huge, pure white and fluffy as cotton balls, obliterating the tops of the mountains. "They're beautiful," she said. "Can you see anything in them?"

He cast her a glance, shook his head and snorted.

"Well, I can," she said stubbornly. "It looks like a horse kicking up clouds of snow behind it."

He looked back at the clouds, squinted, then shook it off.

"It's not unusual to get a thunderstorm late in the day when it's hot like this," he said. "Hopefully, it will hold off."

"I don't know. I feel as if I'd love to stand out in the rain right now." The heat was absolutely withering.

He looked as if he was going to say something but, with one more glance at the clouds and at her, changed his mind.

They went down a steep staircase, carved into stone, that led to a crescent of private white-sand beach and to a boat dock. It seemed with every step closer to the water, the air cooled.

"Oh," Angie said, looking at the sleek boat bobbing at its moorings. "It looks like something out of James Bond." Come to think of it, *he* looked like something out of James Bond!

He stepped from the dock to the boat with absolute ease despite the cooler in his hands and the bobbing of the boat.

"Wait," he snapped when she tried to follow. He stored the cooler and came back. He reached out his hand to her, and she took it and leaned forward for the long and rather scary step down. He sensed her hesitation and let go of her hand. Then he put his hands around her waist, lifted her easily into the boat and set her back on her feet.

For a moment they stood there, looking at each other, his hands still cupping her waist. She glimpsed the man he had been last night. Angie had a sense of time stopping, of being highly aware of the way the hot afternoon sunshine felt on her skin and of how it looked in the crisp darkness of his hair. She was aware of the shape of his lips and the moody gray of his eyes, the strength in those hands that practically encircled her waist. She was aware of the birds calling all around them, the annoyed chatter of a squirrel, the gentle lap of water against the hull of the boat.

She was aware of feeling exquisitely alive.

Then Jefferson abruptly released her. He tossed a cover over a seat beside the wheel, and she took it, aware of the scorching heat coming up through the cover. It was the kind of gorgeous white leather she thought was reserved for higher end cars.

He was back out on the dock releasing the boat from its moorings. He tossed the lines in the boat then gave it a shove with his foot before leaping with mountain goat agility over the swiftly widening gap of water between the dock and the boat.

He took the seat beside her, put a key in the ignition and powerful engines thrummed to life.

He motioned to a sliding panel located between their seats, slid it open briefly to show her a staircase leading into the hull of the boat. "Life jackets are in here, if we should need them. And facilities."

There was a bathroom on board? "I've never been on a powerboat," she murmured. "It seems very *Lifestyles of the Rich and Famous*."

He snorted at that. "It's the reality of living on a lake. I'm afraid the realities of living in a place like this are easy to overlook on a beautiful summer day like this."

She cast him a glance, but his lips were pressed together as if he thought he had said too much.

He snapped the slider shut, then expertly backed the vessel out of its mooring, guided it to the mouth of the bay and opened the throttle.

"But you like it, don't you?"

"Absolutely. But I grew up with it. I understand there are certain hardships and inconveniences associated with living in a remote place."

There was something about the way he said *I* that alerted Angie of something deeper going on.

"Your wife didn't like it," she guessed softly.

"She thought she would, but—" He shrugged. His

voice drifted away, and he squinted intently at the water ahead of them.

"But?" she prodded carefully.

He shot her a look. "But she didn't," he said tersely. "Look, there's an eagle."

The fact that he had pointed out the bird to distract her did not make it any less magnificent. She watched, awed, as the bald eagle floated on the wind current.

Then, clear of his bay, Jefferson opened it up. The nose of the boat lifted, and they rocketed across the smooth surface of the water, cutting it cleanly, leaving sprays of white foam in their wake.

"Oh," she called gratefully over the sounds of the engines, "it's as if the air-conditioning has been turned on." She could feel a fine spray of water misting her skin. The wind tangled in her hair. It was glorious on such a hot day. It was so sensual it made her feel almost delirious. Angie laughed out loud.

Jefferson glanced at her, and his gaze held before he looked away. The stern line that had appeared around his mouth at the mention of his wife softened.

"I've never done anything like this before," she called to him over the powerful purr of the engines. "It's fun. Oh, my gosh, this is so much fun."

Jefferson glanced at her. Angie's face was alight, and she laughed out loud again as he opened up the throttle even more. The boat lifted from the water and then went back down with a bone-jarring whack that sent spray right over the windshield. The wind was wreaking havoc on her curls.

It was so completely different from last night when she had awoken in terror that he gave himself over to it a tiny bit. He was trying his best to hold himself away from her, but her laughter and her genuine enjoyment were an enchantment.

He reminded himself, sternly, what he had said to her this morning.

That's the problem with improvements. They make you dissatisfied with the way things were before.

Jefferson was well aware that Angie could be that kind of problem. She could storm his world and it wasn't just because she was so cute with the wind tangling in her hair, and her T-shirt molded to the front of her, her slender legs shown off to advantage by a red-and-white flowered skirt. It went deeper: her vulnerability and her laughter, her recipes and ideas. She could pry secrets best left untold—like the secret of Hailey's growing discontent with the lake life—from him. She could make him dissatisfied with the life he'd had before she had arrived.

Despite her diminutive size, he was well aware she was a powerful presence. And right now, with the wind catching in her hair and the laughter bubbling out of her? She was beautiful.

In fact, it was dangerous how attractive he found her. He reminded himself of what he had told himself last night. It was an equation, not unlike the equations he put together for companies and corporations. One plus one equals.

And this equation went like this: caring about somebody equaled pain. It left you wide-open to a world of hurt.

And yet, if he contemplated the past few years of his life, where he thought he had evaded more hurt at all costs, he saw a great stretch of emptiness that he was suddenly and acutely aware had caused pain of its own.

He *hated* that. Angie had been in his life one day. It

was just a little over twenty-four hours since she had arrived on his doorstep and cajoled her way into his house and his life. And something was shifting. That something was his own perception, which he was aware could be the most powerful thing of all.

Even knowing that, even knowing that he was playing with fire, he could not resist her smile.

"So, you have seriously never been on a powerboat before?" he called over the powerful thrum of the engines.

"Grew up in a place that was landlocked," she said. "It was just my mom and me. We would have never had the resources to go on a boat."

"Where was your dad?"

The carefree look disappeared from her face. "He left when I was ten. It was a shock. Nothing had seemed really wrong between him and my mother. Someone else caught his fancy. He didn't really factor into our lives, much, after that."

"It may be the way of the world," Jefferson said, and he could hear the tightness in his own voice, "but I always feel put out when I hear people have thrown away a family—for something as ridiculous as something or someone else catching their fancy—when mine was taken from me. Do they not understand the value of what they have?"

Angie reached across the space that separated them and laid her hand on his wrist. It was just for a second, a small gesture, but in that moment he felt as if she got it. She got exactly what he was saying.

"My grandparents' generation had many things right," he said. He had inherited strong traditional values from them. He still remembered his shock when Hailey had told him *after* they married that she didn't want children. It was the kind of thing they should have discussed first, but they had been so caught up in the passion they hadn't. And he would have never left her because of it. Never.

"They did have many things right," she agreed.

The mood had become somber, and Jefferson realized he wanted to make her laugh again. He was ridiculously pleased by the total lack of worry and tension in her as she embraced the mild adventure of a boat racing across a lake.

He gave in to a small temptation to show her how much fun it could be, and began to cut powerful S patterns through the water. The boat was so responsive. It leaned deep into the twists.

Instead of hanging on tight, she threw wide her arms. She held out her hand to catch the spray. She chortled with uninhibited delight.

And a trip that should have taken him ten minutes took double that, as he traveled the long way, cutting big looping S's across the mirror surface of a lake that they had all to themselves.

He finally pulled into the mouth of Anslow Bay.

"It is so beautiful," she whispered.

He followed her gaze to the shoreline. It was beautiful. He felt as if he was looking at it with fresh eyes: the cluster of pastel-colored houses, visible through the thick greenery of trees, climbing up the hills around the bay. A church spire shone brilliant white in the afternoon sun.

But he had seen Anslow from the water a thousand times before. He was aware, again, of the sway Angie was holding on his perception. He dared to glance at her.

She was what was beautiful. He made himself look

away, cut back the engines and focus on docking at the
public pier that was at the heart of downtown Anslow.

He was almost afraid to look at her, again, and he
was annoyed with his fear. Still, he leaped out of the
boat and onto the dock to moor his boat. When he
looked back at her after fastening the lines, he understood his fear completely. Angie's skirt had ridden up
her legs. Her hair was crazy. Her cheeks were bright
from wind and sunshine. Freckles were darkening over
that little snub of a nose. Her lips were curved up in a
delighted smile. And her eyes were shining with a light
that a man could live to see.

It was with reluctance that he leaned from the dock
and held out his hand to her. As he suspected, when she
took it, it was as if an electrical circuit had been completed. His awareness of her was jolting. Her hand was
soft in his, and yet strong. He gave a little tug and she
flew up onto the dock beside him. He didn't release her.
They stood staring at each other.

"There are no words for the way you just made me
feel," she whispered.

Because of the boat ride? Or the confidences they
had shared? Or the way it had felt, just now, when their
hands touched and the circuit was completed?

And then, he supposed because there were no words,
she stood on her tiptoes and kissed his cheek, in almost
exactly the same way he had kissed hers the night before.

Her lips were as soft as a hummingbird's wings on
his skin. He felt that electrical awareness of her tingle
right into his belly.

"Thank you," she whispered, and stepped away from
him, embarrassed. As well she should be!

You didn't kiss your boss! But, somehow, the words

evaporated within him. Instead, he said, "The store is right across the street. Just walk to the end of the pier, go through that gate, turn right and cross the street. Have them put everything on my account."

She wasn't fooled that he hadn't been affected. It bothered him that she wasn't fooled. Then she ducked her head and scurried away.

He touched his cheek. That moment of weakness—of *wanting* to make her happy—had cost him. He knew that. He knew something so small as that kiss could change everything. It could make a man dissatisfied with what he'd had before.

If he let it.

"Hellooo, Jefferson."

He had just left the dock area and was making his way through the summer-crowded streets to the post office. He whirled around.

Maggie. He hoped she had not seen him receiving kisses on the dock.

"I've been hoping to run into you. Are you going to come, Jefferson? To our fund-raising event? A Black Tie Affair?"

Jefferson was annoyed with himself. He'd been so distracted by that damned grocery list, and by Angie, that he hadn't really prepared himself for an encounter with Maggie. For him, going into Anslow was often like running the gauntlet.

He looked at Maggie's face. In its wrinkled lines he saw wisdom and compassion and caring...for him. She was trying so desperately to try to make something good come from something bad. She was trying so desperately to bring him back from the abyss.

A few days ago, he would have made an excuse. He would not have been able to see the naked caring in her face. No. Maybe he would have seen it. But he would not have allowed himself to feel it.

But now, after he had just lectured about people throwing away the things that mattered? But now, after he had made an effort to be better man? After he had comforted the crying, terrified woman instead of walking away? After he had committed to giving her that moment's enjoyment she had not experienced as a child? After he had committed to making her laugh? It was hard to put that particular horse back in the barn.

He reached out and touched Maggie's shoulder. "Of course, I'm coming," he heard himself say.

"Oh, Jefferson, that means so much to me."

Her eyes had tears in them. He was not sure he could handle any more tears this week. He was at his quota. So, he gave Maggie's shoulder one more squeeze and went on his way.

He wanted to believe nothing about him was changed.

But the fact that he was considering *feelings*—those pesky unpredictable things—meant something major had changed already, not needing any kind of permission from him.

CHAPTER NINE

ONCE JEFFERSON HAD turned back to the boat, Angie touched a finger to her lips. She had just kissed her boss.

Oh, it had been a casual thing, an impulse when words had evaded her. She had just wanted to let him know how much she had loved the boat ride, and she wanted to acknowledge she knew he had made an extra effort to make it pleasurable for her. Maybe, she had even wanted him to know, in that brief touch of her lips to his cheek, that she saw, despite how much he did not want her to see it, that he was a good man.

She could tell he felt guilty about his wife not liking the lake, that it was a burden that had become heavier because Hailey had died. Maybe she had hoped that kiss could tell him what she could not: that his guilt was uncalled-for.

It was a lot to expect of a kiss.

And it had rocked her world more than she had expected it to. She had intended a light peck on his cheek, and really, that was all it had been.

And yet she had been so aware of the rough scrape of his whiskers, the sun and water scent of him, the color of his eyes, the easy strength and confidence of him.

"No more kisses on the cheek or otherwise," she ordered herself internally. *Otherwise?* How had that crept in there? But you did not kiss a man like Jefferson Stone on the cheek without wanting more, without contemplating the sweetness of his lips.

Distracted as she was by the pure and unexpected pleasure of the boat trip—and her lips on the roughness of his cheek—Angie made herself focus on Anslow. She had passed through here briefly just yesterday. It was a measure of how fraught with anxiety she had been that she had barely noticed the town.

Now, she saw the sleepy lakeside village was like something you would see on a postcard of a perfect place to be in the summer. The pier jutted out from the main street. That street had a row of single-story false-fronted stores on one side of it, facing the lake. The buildings were authentically old, mostly whitewashed, though some were weathered gray. Oak whiskey casks, cut in half, served as planters, and spilled abundant displays of colorful flowers. All in all, downtown Anslow looked like a set for a Western movie!

Along the wooden boardwalk the Emporium was front and center, but there was also a post office and a museum, an ice-cream parlor and a law office. There was a bookstore and a place to rent canoes and bicycles and, farther along, a barn-like structure that was the community hall.

Apparently, many people shared her view of Anslow's summer perfection, because the main street was currently clogged with tourists. The general store, which billed itself as the Anslow Emporium, was packed with holiday goers. Just a short while ago, the crush of people might have made Angie panic. Today, all that summer happiness cemented her sense of well-being.

Or maybe it was knowing that Jefferson was just a

few steps away, going about his errands, somewhere on that boardwalk. Though it might be silly, she felt as if his mere presence in such close proximity was protecting her. It felt to Angie as if he would never let anything happen to her. That made Angie feel as at ease as she had felt in months.

Exploring the shop, which stocked everything from clothing to lawn mower parts to groceries, Angie was taken, again, with how delightful it felt to be normal and to be shopping for normal things. She snooped contentedly through the crammed aisles of the general store with a sense of discovery instead of with the ever-present fear shadowing her.

She came to a rack, a slender portion of which had been dedicated to bathing suits. Angie hesitated. In her rush to leave her apartment, swimming had been the furthest thing from her mind.

But now the water of the lake beckoned on these sultry, hot days. The selection was tiny. The one-piece model was a leopard print with no back that was available in four sizes, small to extra-large. The two-piece selection was not much better: the scanty bikinis were available in two different prints, leopard or red polka dots, in the same four sizes.

She snatched a small red polka-dot one before she changed her mind. He never had to see it, but it would allow her to enjoy the lake. She could pay Jefferson back for it out of her first check.

She almost sighed out loud. Enjoyment had not been part of her vocabulary—or her experience—for quite some time!

After that one impulse buy, Angie focused on her list. While Jefferson had been right that it did not stock anything exotic, it did have all the basics and a nice selection of spices, too. Since getting to the store was not an easy matter, even if it was delightful, she planned several meals in advance. Was it delightful to be normal? Or was it delightful to be planning meals for Jefferson? She ignored the heavy black lines he had drawn through many of the items on the list.

When she got to the checkout counter, there was a stand of movies for rent. The rental period was a surprising two weeks. When Angie saw the movie *Wreck and Me*, she could not resist adding it to the purchases. As instructed, she put them on the Stone House account. The clerk looked at her with interest but asked no questions, for which she was thankful.

Her things were loaded into her cart, which she took out into the bright sunshine. The thunderclouds were building over the mountain and there was an ominous pressure in the air. The heat had become absolutely stifling. There was not a breath of wind.

She began to push the buggy toward the dock, but Jefferson materialized at her side and began to lift bags from it. Between the two of them they got everything down to the boat in just one trip. She stowed it under the deck, absently putting her frozen items in the cooler he had brought while contemplating him. Was he avoiding looking at her? Was it because of that kiss? Should she apologize?

When she came back above deck, he was eyeing the clouds and she could sense a certain urgency about him.

"Ready?" he asked tersely. He didn't wait for her reply. She took her seat, and he ignored her completely, scanning the water and the clouds with intensity of focus. Was she a little disappointed that his terseness might be more related to the building clouds than the building tension between them?

When they came out of the protected bay in front of Anslow, she was taken aback at the change to the water. The wind was quite ferocious out in the open and the water had gone from silky smooth to choppy.

"That was sudden," she said.

"This lake can turn in a hair," he said. Under the gathering wind, the chop deepened. The boat began to feel as if it was climbing in and out of swells.

Angie watched Jefferson's face. He looked grimly determined, but not in the least afraid. And then the rain began to pelt down. Lightning hit the water, seemingly right in front of them, and the thunder was so close that the boat shuddered.

The brightness of the day was swallowed in the darkness of the storm. The heavens opened up and the rain began to pelt down.

"This falls into the be-careful-what-you-wish-for department," he told her.

She remembered saying, when they had set out this afternoon, that she had wanted to stand in the rain. "I'm not at all sorry I wished for it," she said. "It's exhilarating."

He cast her a surprised glance, and she grinned at him. He returned to focusing on what he was doing.

Angie was aware she could allow herself to feel the exhilaration because of him: unruffled by the storm, radiating confidence in his ability to handle it. She experienced, again, the exquisite sense of being protected.

She could feel the electricity in the air; she could feel the pitch and power of the water beneath the boat. After the heat of the day, having the water pour down, soaking her hair and then her clothes, felt lovely and sensual in a way she was not sure she had felt before. She felt no danger at all, only the exhilaration of being on such intimate terms with the storm, of sharing this experience with him.

The boat rolled, and she rolled toward him and then away. She realized there was no one she would rather be with in these circumstances than him. Despite the powerful twin engines at the back of boat, the boat was bobbing like a cork on the stormy waters.

"Summer storms like this don't usually last long," he called over the noise. "I'm going to pull into one of those coves and drop the anchor. We'll wait it out."

The water calmed as soon as he made it past the mouth of the cove and into its shelter. He dropped the anchor, and they stood side by side watching the fury of the storm out on the main lake. The lightning show was amazing. The echo of the thunder was caught in the steep mountain sides of the forested land around the lake.

Angie was so aware of everything: her clothes plastered to her, and his to him. The rain plastering her hair to her head, and his hair to his head, the water running down her face, and his. The blessed coolness in the air after the heat of the day. The feel of the boat moving beneath them, as if it were a living thing—a dragon—that they were riding.

Finally, the thunderstorm moved by them, though they could still hear it as it pressed down the lake.

"That," she finally said, "was amazing."

"Yeah," he said, "it was. We still won't be going anywhere for a while." Despite the storm passing, the wind remained, and the waves in the main lake were huge.

Was it wrong to *love* that, to love it that she could hang on to the intensity they were sharing for just a little bit longer?

"Jefferson?" Yesterday she had not even known this

man. But after she had accepted his comfort, and offered him some of her own? After she had seen how the man handled a storm on a lake? Her sense of knowing him deeply was complete.

"Hmm?"

"We have a problem."

He turned and looked at her. His eyes went dark as he took in her soaked shirt. She could see the outline of his chest through his own wet shirt.

"Please, don't tell me the boat is leaking." His tone suggested he knew that was not the problem.

"No."

The problem was that the storm had passed and the electricity still leaped in the air between them.

"What's the problem?"

She looked at the slick wetness of his hair. The problem was she wanted to run her hands through it. The problem was that she wanted to press her wet body against his. She gulped and looked away from him.

The problem, she reminded herself. Her mind was blank for a moment, and then she remembered.

"Ice cream!"

"Huh?" He ran a hand through that wet hair where her own hand wanted so badly to go. It freed droplets that ran down the line of his temple, and then his cheek and his jaw.

"You know you took the ice cream off the list?" she said in a rush. "I bought it anyway."

"Why am I unsurprised?" he said, his voice full of irony.

"And the cooler is not going to prevent it from melting."

"No, it won't."

"That's our problem. We have to eat it now. All of it."

"Sounds like kind of a fun problem to have," he said.

"And since you didn't want dark chocolate, I bought two kinds. The dark chocolate for me, and one for you. I tried to guess what you might like."

"And?"

"Salted caramel."

"I have to know," he said drily, "what would make you look at me and think salted caramel?"

"The contradictions," she blurted out. "Sweet and salty."

"Don't kid yourself. There is nothing sweet about me."

But that, she knew, was a lie. She remembered his tenderness from the night before. She thought of how he had deliberately made the boat ride to Anslow exhilarating. Still, she played along with him. "It was Salted Caramel or Nutty Road."

His lips twitched. And then he laughed. It was no less delightful because it was so reluctant.

"I hope you like Salted Caramel. A lot. Because you have to eat a whole bucket of it."

"We don't exactly *have* to," he pointed out pragmatically.

"I should have got the Nutty Road because only a nut would even consider letting ice cream melt,. Even with the cooler it won't last long in this heat."

Aware that something was easing between them, Angie went below and retrieved the two containers of ice cream. She came back topside and he turned from where he had been digging through a side compartment. In his hand he had one of those Swiss Army combination knife sets. He unfolded it to reveal a spoon.

"We're going to have to share," he said. "Only one spoon."

The danger of the storm had nothing on this: sharing a spoon with him. The new ease between them became laced with something else, something as sensuous and unpredictable as that storm.

Jefferson gestured to a bench seat at the back of the boat, sat down and patted the seat beside him. She took the seat, not quite touching him but close enough to be aware of the heat radiating from under his damp shirt. She set down one bucket of ice cream, put the other on her lap and popped the lid off it. She looked into a vat of chocolate the same color as his hair.

"It's already started to melt," she said.

"That lends a sense of urgency to the whole situation," he said.

She glanced at him and realized he was teasing her. The ease and the electricity braided themselves together even more completely.

He dug the spoon in and then held it, heaping with dripping ice cream, out to her. She moved into the circle of his electricity and closed her lips over the spoon, her eyes locked on his.

Without breaking the hold, he took the empty spoon and dug it back into the chocolate. Seeing his tongue dart out to free the ice cream from the spoon was way too sexy. But then he was holding the spoon, filled again, out to her. She closed her lips around the spoon, aware that his lips had just touched that same place. Ever so slowly, she tugged the ice cream off.

And then she watched him take that same spoon and dip it back into the ice cream and put his lips exactly where hers had just been. His eyes met hers. He did something exquisite to that spoon with his tongue.

When it was her turn, she did something just as exquisite with her tongue. She heard him give a little gasp of surprise.

And longing.

Sharing that spoon became an exploration of sensuality almost as powerful as a kiss. She was so aware of him: the wet transparency of his shirt, the shape of his lips, the light in his eyes, the solidness of his wrists, the strong columns of his fingers as they held the spoon to her lips.

"So, would you say this ice-cream flavor—dark chocolate—is a reflection of you?" he asked.

She gulped. "In what way?"

"Sweet, but with surprising depth and a hint of mystery."

Was he flirting with her?

"You need to be writing ice-cream labels," she said.

"You write the next one."

He reached over her, and took the second bucket of ice cream. He pried the lid off the salted caramel one and dipped the spoon in. He held it out to her and she took it.

"What do you think?" he said. "What would you put on the label?"

"Subtle, but sensuous with hints of salt." Was she flirting back?

He ducked his head and dipped the spoon back into the ice cream and tasted it slowly, rolling the ice cream on his tongue as if he was at a wine tasting.

"I like it, but—" he dipped the spoon back into the chocolate and then into the salted caramel "—who knows what could happen if you combined two such different flavors?"

Was he talking about ice cream? Or was he flirting? Whatever he was doing, she liked it. She never wanted it to end.

With her eyes still locked on his, she slid the ice cream off the spoon. The whole experience was so exquisite it was almost painful. She had to shut her eyes against it.

When she opened them, he was sliding a spoonful of the mixed version between the sultry mounds of his lips.

"The ice cream tastes like ambrosia," he said gruffly.

"What does that mean, exactly, ambrosia?"

"Food of the gods."

"That's what we will call this new flavor then, Ambrosia."

And this experience, in her mind, also had a name. Ambrosia. Surely, this was the kind of experience the gods fed on? Not food but the quality of air, and the static from the storm, and the hint of danger between her and him right now.

They ate ice cream until they could not eat another bite. They put the lids on the now melted containers and put them aside. While they had been eating the ice cream, darkness had been sliding over the lake. They sat there, side by side, rocking gently on the waters of the cove, while just beyond them the lake rolled, white tipped and violent.

The waves appeared as big and violent as they had during the storm. The wind outside the cove howled a warning.

She shivered, whether from cold or from eating too much ice cream or from awareness she was not sure. Jefferson went below and came back with a blanket.

Again, he had just one. He tossed it over both their shoulders and pulled it tight around them. The warmth from him and from the blanket crept into her. They were sailors, marooned, and she loved it. Night fell and the stars winked on, one by one, studding the pure inky blackness of the sky.

It was crazy, and beautiful.

Going for groceries by boat was definitely the most romantic thing that Angie had ever done.

She was so amazingly aware of everything: the wind, and his warmth and solidness of his shoulder underneath the blanket and the flavor of ice cream in her mouth. She was so aware of how he was not watching the restless waters of the lake, but her.

"What?" she whispered.

"I'm just trying to figure you out."

"Really?"

"Because it is apparent to me that there's nothing about you that is a shrinking violet. It is apparent to me you are very courageous. So, I want to know what has you so frightened."

"This morning you weren't interested," she reminded him.

"I was interested," he admitted. "I just didn't want you to know I was interested."

"And what has changed?" *Besides everything*, she thought to herself.

"This morning we hadn't eaten ice cream off the same spoon."

She sighed deeply. And surrendered.

CHAPTER TEN

JEFFERSON WAS AWARE of the surrender, not just in her but in himself. Had he actually been flirting with his housekeeper?

No, he told himself sternly, he had not. Being with her had coaxed his more playful side to the surface. Okay, he was more than surprised that he had a playful side, but he blamed the storm for cutting down his defenses, placing them in this predicament where they had to share a spoon.

And sharing that spoon had led to this. The complete collapse of defenses. They were going to share even deeper confidences.

"I'm not a housekeeper," Angie confessed solemnly.

"Yeah, I kind of figured that part out."

"I'm close, though, and qualified. I'm a high school home economics teacher in Calgary."

Jefferson contemplated that. He could feel the truth of it—he thought of her making her lists and organizing his kitchen. He thought of her home breaking up, and her longing. He was not surprised that she had chosen a career where she would teach people how to make a home. And superimposed over this knowledge of her, he thought of the taste of ice cream, mingled with her taste, still sweet in his mouth.

"Or I *was* a teacher," she said pensively. "I don't know when I can go back there." She shuddered.

Jefferson pulled the shared blanket more tightly over their shoulders, pulling her more tightly into him. "What happened?"

"First, I need you to understand *why* it happened."

"Okay."

"I met my fiancé in university."

"Your fiancé?" Jefferson felt the shock of it. And the relief. All the electricity between them didn't matter. She was taken! But his relief was short-lived.

"Not anymore," she said sadly. "We broke off. That's what made me so vulnerable when…well, I'll get to that. Harry and I had been engaged since the second year of our studies. We graduated at the same time, and both got wonderful jobs. I secured my dream job teaching home economics in high school, he got on with one of the banks. I assumed it was time to take the next step, but every time I tried to set a date for the wedding, Harry would become evasive."

He heard inside himself *oh-oh* but did not say it out loud.

"In fact," she said, her lips pursed with remembered annoyance, "had I been paying more attention, I would have seen the whites of his eyes rolling in pure terror at the mere mention of spending a lifetime with me."

"A lifetime with you doesn't seem as if it should make eyes roll in terror."

Her mouth popped open in surprise. She studied his face, as if she was looking for the lie. She smiled. He realized he was treading very dangerous ground, indeed.

"Finally, he worked up his nerve to tell me the truth. He had discovered his career in finance was a terrible mistake. He was bored."

"God forbid we should ever be bored," Jefferson said. He tried to keep his tone dry, but in fact, he felt angry.

"And unfulfilled. He had just discovered he didn't want what other people wanted. He did not want a boring life in the suburbs with two-point-five children and a bus trip into work every day. And guess what? He'd already found someone who didn't want the very same things he didn't want and it wasn't me."

"Aw, Angie."

She held up her palm. "Please don't feel sorry for me. I should have picked up on the signs long before I did. And, besides, this is just the story before the story."

"Go on."

"So, in the space of a week, he quit his job and asked me for his ring back."

"He asked for the ring back? That's scummy."

She wrinkled her nose. "Thank you. I thought so, too, especially after he told me he intended to sell it to finance his tickets. Make that two tickets."

Jefferson was forming a very low opinion of a man who would not only ask for the ring back, but tell his ex-betrothed the reason he had to have it. "Loser," he muttered.

"Thank you," she said, as if she had desperately needed someone else to see it. Angie looked adorable all wrapped in the blanket, her hair curling wildly as it started to dry. But when she wrinkled her nose like that? How could anyone have ever pried themselves away from her?

"Thailand," Angie went on, tilting her chin bravely. "That's where he and Loxi—can that possibly be a real name?"

She glared at him as if she expected an answer.

"No, I don't think it can be a real name."

"Not that it stopped her from traveling! How can you even get a passport with a name like that?" Her question was full of indignation.

"I'd like to know," he agreed.

She sighed at his agreement. "Anyway, that's where he and Loxi had a plan to live on the beach and teach yoga or some such thing."

"I'm sorry."

Her eyes searched his, and her chin quivered. In denial of that emotion, she said quickly, "You don't have to be sorry. I'm just setting up why I was vulnerable. I'm over it now."

He doubted that. He could see she carried the pain of the betrayal as if it were somehow her fault, as if she had accepted her fiancé's abandonment as a judgment of her. That she somehow was not worthy.

"But I wasn't over it then. Right after it happened, I was in a shocked daze. Naturally, in the staff room, my missing engagement ring was noticed eventually. I had to tell people Harry and I were no longer an item. I didn't tell anyone the Loxi or Thailand part. It was too humiliating."

Jefferson thought of her carrying that on her own, trying to keep her head up high, and ached for her.

"Anyway, I went from discussing wedding plans and poring over bridal magazines with two other teachers who were engaged to being the subject of gossip and pity."

She sat very still. She pulled the blanket a little tighter around her and gazed out at the dark waters of the pitching lake beyond the cove.

"There was another teacher there," she said, her voice strained. "Winston."

He saw a flinch crawl along her skin.

"I can't say I'd ever paid the least attention to him besides a casual good-morning. He was quite an unassuming little fellow, given to wearing bow ties."

"Never trust a man who wears a bow tie," he told her.

"Now you tell me."

She gave him a little smack on his chest and continued. "He confided in me that the very same thing had happened to him. I could actually see the tears in his eyes when he said it. He asked me if I wanted to go for a coffee with him.

"It seemed safe enough. My God, he was a fellow teacher. I felt sorry for him. I thought maybe he just needed to talk about it. I actually thought *Oh, look, other people beyond you have problems.* I thought it would be good for me to get out of myself for a bit. So, I agreed. One coffee.

"But I could tell, once we were out of the school environment, that there was something a touch off about him. I'm not sure I could put my finger on it, but it made me uncomfortable, and I gulped down my coffee and left with murmured sympathies about the pathetic state of his personal life.

"The next day in the coffee room, he was entirely inappropriate, sitting too close to me, putting his hand on my knee, touching my hair. It was creepy. I took to avoiding him, even taking breaks in my classroom. But he tracked me down, and I did not want to be in my classroom alone with him."

She stopped, troubled. Her hands were wound together and she stared down at them.

Jefferson could see they were trembling. He covered her hands with his own and felt how shockingly cold they were.

"The more I rejected him," Angie whispered, "the

more strongly he pursued me. He bugged me at school. He called me at home. He gave me unwanted gifts. He sent flowers.

"I finally had to talk to my principal about it. Winston was warned to stay away from me. He didn't. It actually got worse after the principal talked to him. Within a few weeks, he'd been fired.

"The phone calls really started to come in then. I changed my number three times. He always managed to get it. Sometimes he'd be raging that it was all my fault. Other times he'd tell me he had forgiven me for ruining his life. Other times he would be crying. Pleading with me to come back to him. Come back to him? We'd had a single cup of coffee.

"I had to involve the police. I had to get a restraining order. He started hanging out across the street from my place, just out of range of the order. I moved to a new apartment with what I thought was better security. Despite all that, he just kept coming at me. I was a wreck. I was as jittery as if I drank a hundred cups of coffee a day. I startled if one of the children came up behind me suddenly. I barely slept, and when I did I had terrible dreams.

"I started to question my sanity. I wondered if I was overreacting. I wondered if I was making things worse than they were. I wondered what I had done to lead him on. I pondered, constantly, what I should be doing differently.

"On the last day of school before summer break, I went home to my new apartment. The door was locked. Nothing seemed amiss or out of place. I went into my bedroom. The first thing I noticed was that my dresser drawers had been opened.

"And the second thing I noticed was that there was a

stuffed bear on my bed. A huge stuffed bear, a panda, almost as big as I was. It had a red ribbon around its neck that made it look as though its neck had been slashed."

She shuddered at the memory, and Jefferson tried to contain the pure fury that was coursing through his veins.

"I called the police, and they said they would arrest him…if they could find him. I have never felt such terror or felt so unprotected. I tossed a few things in a bag, and got in my car. I let a few friends know I was going away, and why I was going away, but that I couldn't tell them where.

"Because I didn't even know where I was going. It seemed it didn't matter how far I drove, it wasn't far enough. I was so paranoid I would not use my phone or my bank card. I checked in with the police on pay phones—do you know how hard it is to find a pay phone these days—but there was no sign of him. I began to feel as if he was hot on my heels. I was running out of money and hope. And then I saw your ad."

She was silent for a long time. "And that's why," she finished softly, "in a boat in the middle of a lake, right now, I feel exhilarated. Because finally, I am in a place where he can't get at me."

Jefferson knew he should be relieved that it was not their togetherness filling her with exhilaration. He told himself he wasn't relieved—or disappointed—because the emotion he was feeling drowned out every other one.

He had never felt such a killing fury as he felt now at the two men who had brought Angie to this point. But he controlled himself. He could see she had had enough of men who could not put her first, whose self-centeredness was so complete they could not control their own impulses in the interest of someone else.

"You can stay," he said gruffly.

"What?"

"You can stay at the Stone House. As long as you need to."

"Oh, Jefferson." Her eyes clouded with tears. "I don't know what to say."

And just like before, when she had not known what to say, she leaned into him. He knew what was coming. He had plenty of chance to back away from it.

"You knew," she whispered. "You knew I wasn't really a housekeeper. You knew I was a damsel in distress."

That was plenty of warning. What was a damsel in distress looking for, after all? She was looking for a knight in shining armor.

And he knew he was not that, even as he could feel the storm quieting all around them. The roar of the wind dropped, and the waters of the lake quieted. He knew it was time to break away from this, but he could not.

He was caught in a moment: the intensity of the storm, the sweetness of the ice cream, the warmth of her trust, his need to protect her, his sudden aching awareness of his own loneliness. All of those things were swirling around in him, making it impossible not to take what she offered.

Her lips.

She offered him her lips.

And he leaned in close and took them.

They tasted as he had known they would. Of chocolate and salted caramel, and of something sweetly feminine and trusting.

Her lips tasted of ambrosia, food of the gods. And he, a mere mortal, could not resist it. And so he tasted her, and he put his hands in her wet curls and drew her more deeply to him and tasted her more completely.

And remembered that another woman had trusted him to protect her and keep her safe and he had failed completely.

It took all the strength he had to draw away from Angie. He staggered to his feet. He knew it was not the motion of the boat making him feel so unstable. He'd offered her the sanctuary of his house for as long as she needed it.

It was up to him to make sure she was not *more* damaged when she left. And that meant he had to be better at controlling his needs than the other men in her life had been. He had to be better at putting what she needed ahead of what he wanted.

Because what he wanted was to explore every road that kiss could take them down, to climb every mountain it promised, to discover every valley, to let it open the possibility of new worlds.

His voice was too harsh.

"I am not your knight in shining armor. I am not anyone's knight in shining armor. Do you get that?"

She nodded, but she looked as if she was going to cry again. He left her sitting there, wrapped in the blanket, and he pulled the anchor and turned on his nighttime running lights. He prepared to go.

The water had calmed, and the stars were like jewels shining in a black velvet sky. The light could not even hope to pierce the darkness of his own self-awareness.

When they got to the dock, he moored the boat. In stilted silence she went below and brought up all the groceries she had bought. She passed him up bag after bag of groceries and, finally, two ruined buckets of ice cream. When he offered her his hand to get out of the boat, she refused it and scrambled up on the dock by herself.

Loaded with groceries, he went up the steep steps to the house. She followed him. In the kitchen he set them down.

"I'll look after them," she said tightly.

"I think you should check in with the police again," he said. "Maybe your stalker has been apprehended."

"I'll do that," she said, that same tight note in her voice. But then her forehead wrinkled. "Do you suppose it's safe to call them from your line?"

Jefferson could not even imagine being this afraid. For a moment, his every defense was undermined. He just wanted to take her into his arms and soothe her, kiss away that furrow from her brow.

Instead, he managed to strip all the emotion from his voice. "I have no doubt your stalker is insanely clever, but I somehow doubt he has managed to tap a police line."

She nodded. "Yes, of course you are right. I will call them in the morning. If they've apprehended him I can go right away."

He barely knew her! How could he possibly be aching at the emptiness she would leave behind?

"And, regardless, I won't stay beyond our original agreement, despite your kind offer," she said, reading between the lines. He would shelter her as long as he *had* to. "I will get the house ready for the magazine, and then I'll go. I can't let this thing go on indefinitely."

He wanted, again, to sweep her up in his arms, to not let her feel she had to deal with *this thing* by herself. But what thing couldn't she let go on indefinitely? Her thing with the stalker or her thing with him? He wanted to finish what they had started.

But wouldn't that be all about what was good for him? Filling some gaping hole inside him? It wouldn't be about what was good for her. He was thankful she was putting a time limit on her stay, even though he had foolishly told her she could stay forever.

Forever.

He could imagine forever with a woman like her. He could imagine starlit boat rides and facing storms. He could, all too easily, imagine campfires on the beach. And decorating a nursery.

But again, that was about some need in him that he had managed to outrun for a long time. He did not deserve that life. He had had his chance at forever. He had even vowed it. And he had not lived up to those vows. He had blown it completely.

But for two weeks? What was that in a lifetime? For two weeks, he could be the better man. Even if that meant staying the hell out of her way.

CHAPTER ELEVEN

ANGIE WATCHED JEFFERSON stalk away and heard the far-off slam of his office door. She sank into a kitchen chair, stunned by all that had transpired since she had climbed on that boat with him in the pre-storm heat of the afternoon.

She touched her lips, and it was as if she could still feel the electricity of his kiss there. The intensity that had leaped up between them had been just like that storm—just as powerful and just as unpredictable.

She could not believe she was capable of being swept away so completely in such a short time. She had known this man just a little over a full day. It wasn't rational to feel so strongly about him.

But that was what storms did. They came unexpectedly. They swept in, sucked everything into their vortex and swept back out, leaving a trail of destruction.

Or maybe not always destruction. The storm that had just passed over Kootenay Lake had probably also left life-giving water on the surrounding forests and land.

Still, Jefferson had been right to pull away. Hadn't he? Despite the sense of intimacy nurtured by being stranded together in the boat, by facing into the teeth of that storm, by sharing buckets of ice cream and the same spoon, they barely knew one another.

On the other hand? So what? What did knowing each other have to do with anything? Angie had been rational her whole life. She had been mapping out carefully the life she wanted since the divorce of her parents when she was a child.

She wanted the sense of safety and security that being part of a family had given her, before the split of her parents. She had determined that solid, unexciting Harry was exactly the kind of man to pin those kinds of hopes and dreams on.

She had *known* him. She had known he woke up at precisely seven-ten every morning. She had known he would always order grilled cheese at the university cafeteria. She had known he preferred the news over *The Big Bang Theory*. Angie had thought that what she had shared with Harry was intimacy and that it would lead her directly to the safety she craved. She had thought their entire lives were predictable enough to make her comfortable.

But in that boat, sharing a spoonful of ice cream with a near stranger, she had felt as if she was digging into the tip of the iceberg that was intimacy. She had felt exhilarated by the potential for danger, not afraid of it. In fact, the exhilaration was in part because, for the first time in far too long, she had not been afraid. She had been the opposite of afraid.

She had been fearless.

And she knew that feeling of being fearless was not going to go willingly back into its box.

She glanced at a clock. It was really too late to do anything and yet she felt too energized by her encounter with Jefferson to go to sleep. She unpacked the groceries and put them away, smiled at the video of *Wreck and Me*. If she left it out for him to find, would he watch it?

Still filled with a restless kind of energy once the groceries were stowed, Angie decided to make some blueberry muffins.

"If he gets nothing else from my stay here, he will be able to see there is life beyond bean burritos," she muttered to herself.

Three days later, Jefferson felt like a prisoner in his own house, marking x's on his wall. He was well aware that in the course of human history, three days was a very short time.

But in the context of having Angie aka Brook Nelson under the same roof as him, it was a torturous eternity. In his efforts to avoid her, she had driven him underground. He'd always enjoyed working at night; now it felt compulsory.

But despite seeing her only occasionally—her crazy hair hidden under a babushka obviously of her own invention, her legs looking long and coltish in shorts and skirts, T-shirts clinging to her, the sweat beading on her neck, the cobwebs sticking to the rubber gloves she always wore—there was no pretending she was not here. Even though she seemed to be avoiding him just as scrupulously as he was avoiding her, the house smelled different since she had arrived.

If it was just the smell of cleaning supplies and fresh air, it would not have been so disturbing. But no... Her scent—faintly spicy, clean, feminine—clung like a faint vapor in every room she had been in. Which, as far as he could tell, was all of them, except this room and his bedroom.

Also disturbing was the noise. If it was just the noise of the vacuum cleaner and the dishwasher and the washing machine and dryer, it probably would not have been so disturbing. But, though she was probably not aware of it, the more involved she got in some task, the louder she hummed.

Christmas tunes, of all things. "Jingle Bells" and "Here Comes Santa Claus" and "Silent Night." On more than one occasion she had burst into bloody song and it had stuck in his head—*Here comes Santa Claus, here comes Santa Claus, right down Santa Claus lane*—long after she had moved out of hearing.

The problem was she sounded so happy that he could not bring himself to tell her to stop. Even though he was avoiding her with all his might, on those occasions when he could not avoid bumping into her, Jefferson could see the tension she had arrived with had eased from her.

She was still easily startled—he'd come up behind her one day while she was vacuuming, and his eardrums were still ringing from the scream—but was losing that terrified, hunted look he'd first glimpsed on her first day when the pinecone had dropped on her car.

It was not just that the house was undergoing a transformation, which it surely was. Dust was disappearing. Cobwebs were being banished. Floors were emerging from under a layer of grime. Windows were, one by one, beginning to shine.

The biggest transformation was in his kitchen. The day's mail was neatly sorted. Every surface was gleaming. Every dish he left there in the dark of night was swept away. The fridge had real cream in it for his coffee, and milk for the selection of cereals that had appeared. There were single-serving containers of yogurt, and lettuce and tomatoes. There was a selection of drinks. There was fresh fruit in a bowl on the counter.

Best of all—or perhaps worst of all, depending how you looked at it—were the meals that she left for him.

Though the heat was climbing into the nineties and was over one hundred again, once, every day she had the oven on for something.

The rich smells tantalized him even before he took his nocturnal journey down to the kitchen to see what she had done. Muffins. Fresh bread. Cookies. Last night, she had left him a roast chicken dinner.

Tonight she had left a steak, and a tinfoil-wrapped potato with careful instructions how to grill it.

He set down her note, aware he felt like a wild animal being lured in by the promise of food. His anticipation for what she would make for him grew every day.

If she wanted to discuss things with him she left him a note. He was uncomfortably aware that he was looking forward to the notes as much as the food. He looked around for today's and found it next to the stack of other ones.

He went through the old ones, aware he was smiling. Hers...

Have you got a ladder I could use outside?

His...

DO NOT UNDER ANY CIRCUMSTANCES GET ON A LADDER.

Would tomorrow be a good day to put the furniture out on the deck for an airing?

DO NOT UNDER ANY CIRCUMSTANCES TRY TO MOVE THAT FURNITURE BY YOURSELF.

I have a system figured out.

NO.

Tonight, he read her response to that, aware he was looking forward to it.

I'm going to put the couches on dishcloths, like coasters, and slide them across the floor. Must you write in all caps like that? It's disconcerting.

NO, YOU AREN'T, he scrawled with great enjoyment. AND YES, I MUST WRITE IN ALL CAPS. I FAILED PENMANSHIP IN SCHOOL.

He hesitated. Too much information? Stop analyzing everything. Admitting he'd failed penmanship in school was not the same as admitting he'd had a terrible row with his wife, and she had gone out into a storm…

He shook that thought off. A gentleman would offer to help Angie move the furniture.

But no, the two weeks minus the time elapsed would be so much easier to get through if he stayed on his path of avoidance. It was good, anyway. He was way ahead of schedule on the Portland project.

He went out to the deck and lit the barbecue as per her instructions. He stood there for a moment, taking in the dark surface of the lake, the lights across the way, the night sounds. It occurred to him it had been a long time since he had felt something like this: just simple enjoyment.

It occurred to him, even though she wasn't beside him, that she was here. In his house. And somehow, it was changing everything. He wished she was down here with him.

He forced himself to suck it up. To repeat his mantra. *Two weeks. Two weeks. Two weeks.*

Angelica surveyed the kitchen with satisfaction. The early-morning light poured through the windows. Jefferson had eaten his steak dinner and gobbled up the cookies she had made yesterday.

She looked for his note, read it and smiled. He'd failed penmanship? Really, it was hard to imagine him failing anything. She put that note with the others, aware she was collecting them.

She went over to the grinder, and put in coffee beans. In a few minutes fresh coffee was dripping into the pot. She savored the smell of it and the light and the birdsong—and Jefferson's note. She felt so supremely rested. She felt alive and happy.

The phone rang, as she poured herself that first cup of coffee, and she felt herself tensing. Jefferson's house phone rarely rang. For too long, the phone ringing in her life had meant the sound of breathing on the other end. Or a hang-up. Or a sobbing explanation. Or a begging plea.

She reminded herself she was fearless now and, coffee in one hand, she picked up the phone without checking the call display.

"Stone House," she said cheerfully.

A moment later the cup, filled with coffee fell from her hand and shattered on the floor. She stared at the mess, put the phone receiver back in its cradle. She wondered, dazedly, if proclaiming herself fearless had been like a challenge to the gods.

Jefferson appeared at the kitchen door. "I heard a crash." He took in the smashed coffee cup. "Thank God," he said. "I thought you'd finally managed to fall off a ladder."

She shook her head mutely.

He crossed the room in a single stride and gazed down at her.

"What is it?"

"The police just called," she managed to croak. "The Calgary police. I took your advice and called them after…"

That magical night shimmered, momentarily, between them, like a mirage.

And that's what it was, she told herself. A mirage. Real life was different. "Angie?" He took her shoulders and gave her a gentle shake. She looked up into his eyes, and tried to feel the sense of safety she had felt that night, and really ever since. But maybe that had been part of the mirage, feeling safe in an unsafe world.

"Tell me what's happened," he ordered her.

"You know that girl Winston told me he had been dating? The one who supposedly dumped him at the same time Harry dumped me?"

He cocked his head at her, frowning, still holding her shoulders, thank God, anchoring her to his kitchen and him and not allowing her to fly toward her fear.

"She's missing. The police suspect foul play. And they suspect Winston is connected to it, and no, they have not located him yet."

He said a word under his breath that should have appalled her. Instead, for a reason she couldn't decipher immediately, it made her feel reassured, but still she trembled. She could feel panic quaking within her, just below the surface.

"I feel I need to do something," she said. "But I don't know what it is. Scream? Cry? Lock myself in the bathroom? Run away?"

"You aren't doing any of that." He pulled her in close to him and held her tight.

In the circle of Jefferson's arms, she could feel the trembling begin to subside. "I'm not?" she whispered.

"You aren't going to scream, or cry. You aren't going to lock yourself in the bathroom, and you most certainly are not going to run away."

She sighed against him. She wasn't so sure she wasn't going to cry. "I—I—I guess you're stuck with me for a little while longer, then."

He put her away from him, at arm's length.

"Well," he said, all business, "let's make the most of it, shall we? Did you want to move furniture today?"

She stared at him, stunned by his sudden change in demeanor. "What?"

"Look, I'm not letting you move it by yourself. The last thing I need is a Workers' Compensation claim. And I happen to have a clear day as far as my schedule goes."

Her mouth worked soundlessly. Suddenly, she knew exactly what he was doing. Somehow he knew if he left her alone or even let her make her own decisions, they would all be bad ones. He could probably tell she was a hair away from dissolving into hysterics. Somehow he knew he had to get her focused on something else.

"You should have something to eat. I can recommend the chocolate chip cookies," he said it as if it was an ordinary day.

"Chocolate chip cookies are not breakfast!"

A tiny smile played along his lips, satisfied. He had managed to distract her, and he was pleased about it.

"I had them. I seem to be okay," he said. He held one out to her, wafted it underneath her nose.

She grabbed it from him and took a bite. Surprisingly, it felt as if it might not be such a bad breakfast, after all. She gobbled down three of them. Surprisingly, it felt as if the knots of anxiety in her stomach were eased. By the cookies, or by him, she couldn't quite be certain.

While she ate cookies, he went and surveyed the living room.

"I have a plan," Jefferson announced. "I have a furniture dolly out in the shed. I think it might work better than the dishrag system you outlined."

She was ashamed of it, but she could not even let him out of her sight when he went to get the dolly.

"You might as well come with me," he said, as if it was his idea, as if she was not already stuck to his heels like glue. "There are other things we might need from the shed."

She followed him outside into the morning. She stopped for a minute, gulping in the freshness, the call of the birds, the chatter of an indignant chipmunk.

At the shed door, he stopped and looked back at her.

"Something else?" he said quietly. "He's not coming for you here. And if he did, he'd have to get past me. And you know what?"

She shook her head.

"He's no match for me."

And she knew, looking up at him, that that was absolutely true. She knew why she had been reassured instead of appalled by that dreadful word he had said.

Because in that single syllable had been this message.

Jefferson Stone would lay down his life for her. And though Angie had lost the lovely sensation of fearless that she had felt over the past few days, something in her relaxed as she watched him fling open the shed door.

"There it is."

She saw the red handles of a dolly poking out from behind a weed whacker, a sack of lawn seed and several boxes. It seemed to her that her idea of sliding the furniture out of the living room was better than his, but she said nothing.

She reached to take the first dusty box from him. Their hands touched. His closed around hers and squeezed. She realized Jefferson was offering her his strength until her own returned.

CHAPTER TWELVE

ANGIE WAS FEELING STRONGER, already, as she set down the first box, and Jefferson passed her another. Finally, he unearthed the dolly and managed to wrestle it out of the shed.

He brushed himself off while she looked at the dolly. "It's covered in spiderwebs. We just need to—"

She caught Jefferson taking a giant step back out of the corner of her eye.

"What?"

"I don't like spiders," he said.

"You're kidding, right?"

He made a face. She was aware he was not kidding, not entirely.

"For someone who does not want to be mistaken as a knight in shining armor, it was a very brave thing to go inside that shed if you're afraid of spiders."

"I don't recall using the word *afraid*."

"Maybe we're all afraid of something," she said gently.

He rejected her gentleness. "I'm not afraid of them. I just don't like them."

"Look! There's one crawling up the handle. It's huge."

"Don't touch that!"

She ignored him and let the spider crawl onto her hand.

"Put that down."

"He's cute. Look." She held out her hand.

Jefferson stepped back. She stepped forward. He scowled. She giggled. She took another step forward. He retreated, then turned on his heel and darted through the trees.

She shrieked with laughter and went in hot pursuit of him. He plunged through the trees and leaped over fallen logs, shouting his protests.

She followed on his heels, shouting with laughter.

Finally, when they were both gasping for breath from running and laughing and leaping logs and dodging trees, Jefferson put the huge trunk of a live tree between them. He looked out from behind it. She lunged one way. He went the other.

Then his hand snaked out from behind the tree and grabbed her wrist.

"You made me drop him," she protested. In actual fact, she was pretty sure she had dropped the spider a long time ago.

"Thank God," he said. He threw himself down on the forest floor and lay on his back, his hands folded over his chest as if he was monitoring the hard beating of his heart. "It's already hot," he said.

It felt like the most natural thing in the world to lie down on the forest floor beside him. It smelled of new things and ancient things, blended together perfectly. She looked up through the tangle of branches at a bright blue sky. And then she turned her head to look at him, drinking in his strong and now so familiar profile.

New things. The way she felt about him.

Ancient things. The way men and women had come together for all time and against all odds.

"Are you really afraid of spiders?" She suspected he

wasn't. He wouldn't be lying here in all this forest duff if he was afraid of creepy-crawly things, would he? "Or were you just distracting me from my own fear?"

"Maybe you were right. Everybody's afraid of something."

"What are you afraid of? Really?"

He was silent for a long time. "Isn't it obvious?" he asked quietly.

She thought of that. She thought of him being an orphan and first losing his grandparents and then his wife. She thought of his extreme isolation. Of the fact that he didn't even want a housekeeper who was chatty.

He was afraid to let anyone in. He was afraid to lose anything else.

"Yes," she said, "it's obvious."

"It's too hot to move furniture today," Jefferson announced, obviously not prepared to probe his fears any further, obviously fearing he had already said way too much. And so there it was. Full retreat.

Except it wasn't. She recognized a miracle when it was presented.

"You want to go out on the boat?" he asked softly.

Angie thought of the boat and how safe she had felt there through the storm, and how much it must have taken for him to offer her this. She thought of the boat as the place where pure magic had unfolded between them.

"Yes," she said. "I want to go out on the boat. And suddenly, I'm starving. I knew cookies were not a good breakfast! Should I pack a lunch?"

"Sure. And don't forget your bathing suit."

"How do you know I have one?"

"It was on the bill."

She thought of that bathing suit. She was pretty sure she did not have the guts to wear it in front of him. On the other hand, he was testing his courage. Maybe all of it, all of life, was a call to courage.

He got up and held out his hand to her. She took it and he never let it go as they walked to the house together.

"What is that?" Jefferson asked, when Angie met him at the boat a half hour later.

"What?"

"What you are wearing."

"It's a bathing suit cover."

"It looks like a cross between a monk's frock and Mexican serape. Where did you unearth it?"

"I made it," she said, as if she was quite pleased with herself. "I mean I didn't sew it. I didn't have time. I just found some fabric and cut it. I've always been good at making things."

"Hmm, *good* might be a bit of a stretch," he said, and realized he felt comfortable teasing her. It was a terrible thing, but he felt glad about that phone call this morning. It had broken the impasse he had created between them.

He wanted to give her—a woman who had suffered just a little too much—carefree days of summer. He wanted to do that, even if it cost him.

He took the boat out onto the lake, and they did a tour of some of its hundreds of miles of coves and inlets and arms. And then he brought them back to a place that was not that far—and yet a world away—from where his house was located.

"Let's go ashore here for lunch," Jefferson suggested.

"What is this place?" Angie asked, handing him the picnic basket and then taking his hand and letting him help her out of the boat.

"Watch the pier. It's a bit rotten. This is where my grandparents' house used to be. You can still see the foundation."

She wandered over and looked at the crumbling stone foundation. "What happened to the house?"

He went and stood beside her, nudged a stone with his foot. "It burned down a few years ago. It had been abandoned for some time."

"What a beautiful spot." She reached for the basket and pulled a blanket from it. She set it out and they both settled on it. "I'm surprised you didn't build your new house here."

"It wasn't practical. This spot is nearly inaccessible by land. My great-grandfather ran a trading post here for lake traffic. When I came here, my grandparents were still almost exclusively using a boat for transport."

"How did you go to school?"

"Until high school, by correspondence. Then, my grandparents bought a place for us in Anslow. They said it was because they were getting older, but I know it was so I could have a normal high school experience, make some friends." He grinned at the memory. "Meet a girl. My grandfather was always concerned about me meeting a girl."

It occurred to him his grandfather would be very pleased, indeed, to see this girl eating a picnic lunch by the old homestead.

"What kind of normal did you have here?" she asked.

He thought he should probably stop talking, but on the other hand, it was good to distract her and to see her growing more relaxed by the minute.

"The best kind," he said. "I grew up using a boat, and chopping wood and hunting and fishing. I knew every inch of these woods. It helped me. It healed me."

He was shocked to hear himself say that. He was not sure he had ever said it before. If he had been able to say it to Hailey, would she have understood?

"I could never sell it," Jefferson heard himself say.

"Sell it?" Angie looked at him, astonished. "I think it would be criminal to sell it."

As they ate lunch, she seemed to know all the right questions. And so he found himself talking of things he had not spoken of for years. He told her of the basset hound named Sam who had followed him through the days of his boyhood, and of a baby squirrel he had bottle-fed. He told her of the winter the snow had piled up past the roof, and of being on the lake in twenty-foot swells. He told her of bear encounters and afternoons in the hills picking gallons of huckleberries that his grandmother turned into pies and preserves.

"People see this place as magical in the summer, but my favorite time of year here was Christmas," Jefferson said.

"Really? Why?"

"My grandmother used to have a Christmas gathering every year, right on Christmas Day. She sent out a blanket invitation. Everyone was invited, and everyone came. My grandfather and I were put to work a month in advance. We had to find the perfect Christmas tree, and make sure there was enough wood to have a bonfire down by the lake. The main body of this lake never freezes, but sometimes the arms do, and I can remember my grandfather going out there with a saw, every day in December, to check the depth of the ice. We were allowed to skate if the ice was over four inches thick. The day he pronounced it safe was better than Christmas for me. I can remember skating on it when the ice was so clear it was like skating on a sheet of glass over the water.

"It could be hard to get here in the winter, but they came for the Stone Christmas, anyway. There were no gifts allowed at her gathering—my grandmother said the gift was each other. And so people came from miles around, and the women got around her gift rule by bringing pies and homemade bread and buns and jars of preserves.

"Families prepared skits, and we sang songs, and we ate food until we could barely move. We kept a bonfire going, and there was sledding and snow fights and snowman building competitions. Lots of times people came prepared to stay, and there were sleeping bags on the floors, and the gathering lasted for days."

It seemed, as he spoke, he was being restored to some part of himself that he had forgotten.

"It sounds wonderful," she said wistfully. "What happened to it?"

"We had a smaller version of it once we moved into town. My grandparents got older, families grew up and people moved. It just kind of faded away."

They sat there in silence for a long time.

"Are you up for a bit of a hike?" he asked. "There's something I'd like to show you."

He contemplated that invitation, even as he took her hand. He'd never taken anyone to his secret place before. Hailey would not have wanted to go. She would have complained incessantly about bugs and branches snagging her clothes. She would have worried about bears and cougars and wolves.

He guided Angie to a trail that was sadly overgrown, though the animals still used it, so it was passable. Even though her footwear was entirely inappropriate—a flimsy pair of flip-flops, she was un-complaining as they wound their way steadily upward through the forest growth and the steadily increasing afternoon heat.

The trail ended an hour later at a waterfall. It cas-caded out of a rock outcropping fifty feet above them and ended in a gorgeous green pool.

He watched, not the waterfall, which he had seen a thousand times, but her.

Her face was a study in wonder.

"This," she declared softly, "is the most beautiful place in the world."

They were both hot and sticky after the hike, so he stripped off his shirt.

"Ready to swim?" he asked her.

She hesitated and then tugged the hem of that serape/frock invention over her head.

He was aware his mouth fell open. He snapped it shut. He ordered himself to look away. He didn't.

"Sorry," she said. "It's all they had at the Emporium."

Sorry? She was a goddess. She was a vision. He had to turn from her and dive into the water to break away from the spell she was casting on him in that tiny polka-dot bikini.

He surfaced. She was standing at the edge of the pool. Her arms were wrapped around herself. She was a self-conscious goddess.

"Come in," he called.

She stuck her toe in and emitted a very un-goddess-like shriek. He swam over to her, took the flat of his hand and splashed her.

"Hey! I'm getting in my way. It's very cold."

"It's mountain fed. Of course it's cold. Get in."

"Quit being bossy."

"I'll be bossy if I want. I'm the boss."

She giggled at that. "I'll have to look at my contract," she said, putting a finger to her chin and tapping. "I'm not sure if you're the boss here, or just in the house."

He exploded from the water, wrapped his arms around her, and fell backward into the pond, taking her with him.

She broke from his embrace and the water, sputtering wildly and shaking water droplets from her curls. She glared at him. She stomped toward him. He moved away. She moved after him.

"Come back here," she demanded.

"That seems as if it would be foolish," he said, moving a bit farther from her.

What he knew, and she didn't was that the floor of the pond dropped away suddenly. He took one more step and was treading water.

She took one more step and was in over her head. When she came up for air, paddling to keep her head above water, the laughter rumbled up from someplace deep inside of him. It felt so pure and so good.

"I'm going to get you," she said.

"If you can catch me. You couldn't this morning. I don't see what has changed."

"You are infuriating."

"Yes, I know." He splashed her.

"Oh!" She plunged after him.

Now that the bathing suit—or lack thereof—was hidden by the cool, pure water, the same playfulness that had been between them with the spider erupted again.

He wanted to keep her from thinking of that phone call. And he wanted to make her laugh again.

Soon they were chasing each other around, splashing and shrieking. Their laughter rang off the walls of the mountains surrounding them and echoed in the rocky cavern behind the waterfall.

Finally, he allowed himself to be caught, and good-naturedly suffered a decent splashing. He guided her under the water of the falls. They could stand up here, and he helped her find her feet. He put his arms around her naked midriff to steady her against the pummeling of the water. She lifted her face to it. And he lifted his.

He stood there, in awe of it, of being baptized by mother earth, cleansed, purified, as if he was being prepared for a new beginning.

Finally, cooled, drenched, pleasantly exhausted, they dragged themselves out onto a huge sun-warmed rock beside the pond. They lay there side by side, until their breathing had returned to normal.

She reached out and laid her hand on his naked back as if it was the most natural thing in the world.

"I never want to leave here," she said.

And he heard himself saying, "I don't, either."

He closed his eyes. He let the energy ooze from her hand like heated oil, thick and healing, onto his back. And then through the skin of his back and inside of him, bringing light to a place that had been in darkness.

And days later, he knew the place had not been about the waterfall, because they had left the waterfall and yet that feeling of a warm energy, of something deeply comfortable and playful, remained between them.

Jefferson told himself he was allowing this to happen only because he was being a better man. He was distracting Angie from the pure terror of discovering her predecessor in Winston's affections had gone missing.

But somehow it wasn't a job he was doing. There was a kind of joyous discovery of the world they were sharing. His world was boats and water and woods and

waterfalls. They took the boat out; they swam, they pic-
nicked, and one memorable afternoon he taught her how
to catch a fish. In the perfect marriage of their worlds,
she taught him how to cook it.

After the success of that, she invited him into her
world even further. He could see what an amazing
teacher she must be as she taught him how to make
cookies and the correct way to do his laundry and how
to sew on a button.

"When I have young guys in my class?" she said. "I
consider it my obligation to their future wives to make
sure they have a few rudimentary skills."

Who would have guessed gaining a few rudimentary
skills would be so much fun? And so intense?

The awareness between them was like a storm circling. The electricity crackled around them. It was in
their eyes meeting and in the accidental brushing of
their hands. It was in *everything*.

And yet, he would not allow himself to follow it. He
was always the one who pulled back, reminding himself, sternly, that she was here under his protection and
that she was as vulnerable as she had been after her fiancé had left her.

He could not take advantage of that.

It was Angie who reminded him they had a house to
get ready for a photo shoot.

And somehow, doing that, was also a journey in discovery.

A few days later, Jefferson watched as Angie settled
back into the deepness of the couch and sighed with
contentment. The house was nearly ready. They were
sitting outside on his deck in the comfort of his living
room furniture. It was the last big job they needed to
do, get the furniture out. She had insisted on spending

a very hot afternoon scrubbing the floors and waxing them.

Now, as they waited for them to dry, the sun was going down. Jefferson, without asking, had placed a glass of wine in her hand.

"I should have thought of this before," Jefferson said, looking out over the lake. "This furniture is great out here. Very comfortable. I think I'll leave it out here."

They were sprawled out on the sofa. He was covered in sweat, and so was she.

As far as romantic moments went, moving furniture was probably way down the scale. But honestly? If you wanted a woman to see your muscles? Woo-hoo.

"You will not leave it out here," she said. "You'd wreck it."

"Who cares? I barely use it anyway."

"Don't you like it?"

He was silent.

"You don't like it."

"Hailey picked everything for this house."

"Ah, so it has sentimental value."

"The funny thing? I don't think she much liked it, either."

"But why, then?"

"It's a long story." He did not feel ready to tell it. For when he told her the truth about his marriage, all this magic between them would dissipate. She would see who he really was, that there was nothing remotely heroic about him. But for now, he was not strong enough to break the enchantment between them.

"I think I can hook up the TV to work out here," he said. "You want to watch *Wreck and Me*?"

"Yes!"

And so, as the stars winked on in a glorious night

sky, they sat on his couch outside and watched the movie about a solitary ogre who reluctantly falls in love.

Jefferson found himself frowning. That ogre, living alone in his cave, enjoying his life of solitude, reminded him of someone. The beautiful princess, who so desperately needed the reluctant ogre's help, reminded him of someone, too.

He had refilled her wineglass several times, and when the final song, "A Night for Us," came on, it made her bold.

"Dance with me," she whispered. "There's nothing in the living room. The wax is dry. It makes for a perfect dance floor."

"I'm not much of a dancer." He had to stop this nonsense before he created a problem worse than the one she was running from.

"I love to dance," she said.

"Did you dance with him? With your fiancé?"

She smiled, a touch wryly. "No. He *hated* dancing. I don't think we ever danced together. Once, I bought tickets to a ball. They were very expensive. He said he would go, but then he was conveniently ill that night."

Jefferson contemplated that. If you loved a woman and you knew she liked something, was it not part of what you had signed up for—to put yourself out a bit?

"What did you love about him?" he asked. He wished he could take the words back. Why did he want to know?

She sighed and took the last sip of her wine. "Looking back on it now? It's more like I selected a candidate than fell in love."

"Selected a candidate?"

"I wanted the things I lost when my father abandoned

our family. I wanted to feel secure and safe. Now, I'm not so sure what that has to do with love."

Jefferson felt a shiver along his spine. Why would she know more about love now than she had then?

"It seems to me," she said softly, "maybe love is a leap into the unknown rather than retreat into the known."

This was not going well, Jefferson thought. He was sitting out on his deck on a star-studded night, discussing love with a beautiful, beautiful woman.

The well-known female vocalist's voice soared out over the lake. It seemed to mingle with the stars and the warmth of the summer breeze.

"'We have come through every valley, we have come through every plight,

"'Let me take your hand and show you the magic of the night...'"

Jefferson did the worst possible thing. He needed to avoid this discussion. At the same time he felt a deep, masculine desire to show her he was a better man than Harry.

In his haste to do both, he held out his hand to her. He said to her, his voice a hoarse whisper, "Let's dance."

He realized, too late, he had just taken that great leap into the unknown.

CHAPTER THIRTEEN

ANGIE DID THE worst possible thing. Even though she had instigated this, even though she knew Jefferson had asked her to dance because he felt sorry for her that Harry had been such a boob on the subject, even though she knew it was moving them toward uncharted territory, she put her hand in Jefferson's.

She let him lead her into the house. With the doors of the living room folded open to the night, they swayed together to the hopelessly romantic music. She gazed upon the face she had become so fond of and contemplated what she had revealed, not just to Jefferson, but to herself, about the nature of her and Harry's relationship.

She hadn't loved Harry. She had picked him as the most likely to give her the life she had wanted ever since her father had walked out the door with hardly a glance back.

She knew that now. She had not known it then.

She thought about why she knew it now when she had not known it then. Because now she had eaten ice cream during a storm. Now she had chased a man with a spider, the air ringing with their laughter. Now, she had stood under a waterfall. And squealed as a slippery fish had landed in their boat. Now she had watched *Wreck and Me* under the stars.

Now, she was dancing in an empty room with no one watching.

She stared up at Jefferson and drank in the face that had become so familiar to her. She felt the heat of his body and the strength of it where it was pressed into her.

It occurred to Angie exactly why she knew now that she had not fallen in love with Harry when she had not known it before, even when he left her.

She stopped dancing.

Jefferson stopped dancing.

"Would you like to come to a real dance with me?" he asked. "The town is having a fund-raiser in Hailey's memory."

She knew it would be craziness to say yes.

"It's going to be very hard for me to go alone."

Which made it impossible to say no.

"It's called A Black Tie Affair."

There was her excuse. She did not have a single thing to wear to a function called A Black Tie Affair.

She started to say it and then snapped her mouth shut.

That was the Angie she had been, before. Before she had driven down that long and winding road and knocked on the door that had led her to this man. To Jefferson.

That was the Angie who had been afraid of everything. Even before she had been stalked she had played it safe, tried to arrange a life that would make her feel comfortable and secure.

Playing it safe, she realized, had not gotten her one single thing that she wanted. The exact opposite was probably true.

"I'd love to go to the dance with you," she said.

"It's on Saturday."

"What day is it today?"

"I have to think about it," he said wryly. "I've lost track of time. Tuesday. Today's Tuesday."

She broke away from him. "That's only four days away. And the photographer from the magazine is coming on Monday. I have a great deal to do."

Not being swayed by the bemusement in his eyes, she fled from Jefferson and went up the stairs to her room.

She knew she should say no to going to the dance, but she could not. She sat down and did a sketch, and stared at it.

It was even more beautiful than the wedding dress she had designed. It had a strap over one shoulder, the other shoulder bare. The upper portion of the dress, bodice to waist, was fitted. And then it flared out in a cloud of whimsy. She had only a few days.

It occurred to her she really did only have a few days. It had been their agreement that she would leave after the photographer came. Her job here would be done. Her time here.

But she felt as she had lying on the sun-warmed stone by the waterfall.

I want to stay here forever.

She reminded herself that Jefferson had broken that spell. That Jefferson broke all the spells. She wanted things to deepen between them. He did not.

And that was good. It was a good thing that one of them could be pragmatic when the storm was building all around them, threatening to pull them right into its vortex of power.

She looked at the dress again. If ever a dress could challenge a man's best intentions, it would be this one. Is that what she wanted to do?

It was what she wanted to do. She did not want to be safe anymore. She wanted to fling herself into the storm, to put herself at the mercy of love.

Love.

She looked at her drawing again and let that word wash over her, felt the power of the feeling that accompanied it. Could she really pull this off?

She thought with longing of the woman she had been, ever so briefly, when that storm was over.

Fearless.

She wanted that again. She wanted to be fearless.

What about getting his house ready for the photographers? She was going to have to do both. She was going to have to be fearless and pragmatic.

Well, anyone who could coax cookies and a sewing project out of thirty reluctant teenagers could most certainly handle the pragmatic aspects of the assignment she had given herself.

She got up from her desk. She went over to those cubbies filled with fabric and sorted through them. They were swatches. It was almost as if they had been put here for show—to add splashes of bright color to the room—rather than to be of use. Angie had managed to scavenge her bathing suit cover from these, but the dress in the sketch was another matter.

She went to the window and stared out at the darkened lake. The breeze lifted a curtain and it caught her eye.

Angie laughed out loud. It was pure white silk. She caressed it with her fingers. She couldn't use his curtains for a dress, could she?

The old Angie might not have been able to. The new Angie got on a chair and tugged the draperies down off their hooks.

* * *

Jefferson would not admit how much he missed Angie. Since that night they had danced in the living room, and in a moment of weakness when he had wanted to give her everything she wanted, and had invited her to a real dance, he had barely seen her.

She was a flurry of motion—racing through the house, cleaning crazily, organizing for the photo shoot and then disappearing up the stairs to her room.

She was making meals—in the middle of the night?—and leaving him notes on how to cook them, but he missed her. He was glad they were going to have a whole evening together to just enjoy each other.

On Saturday evening, he came out of his room. He and Hailey had often gone to events that required this kind of garb—the opera, plays, fund-raising balls. He had not dressed like this for a long time. He had never felt like this about it, either. Strangely awkward, almost shy. Standing in the hall, he put a finger between his collar and his neck, trying for a bit of breathing space.

He heard a sound on the stairs that led to Angie's room.

He turned slowly. He dropped his finger from his collar. It was hopeless. He was never going to be able to breathe. Every thought of the impression he was going to make on her fled him as the sight of her—the impression she was making on him—filled his every sense and stole his breath away.

Could this woman be Angie?

Even in that ultra-sexy bathing suit, he had never seen her look like this.

She floated down the staircase toward him on a cloud of white. The dress hugged her upper body, showed the sensuous curve of her recently sun kissed shoulders, then flared out, sweeping around her. She looked like a princess in a fairy tale.

"What?" she asked, pausing on the stairs.

Could she not know what a vision she was?

"Where on earth did that dress come from?" he managed to choke out when that was not what he wanted to say at all. "I'm pretty sure the Emporium does not stock anything like that."

"Have you ever seen *The Sound of Music*?"

"Uh, yeah."

"Curtains," she said. "I'm afraid I owe you a set of curtains."

He vaguely recalled a scene in that movie where curtains had been transformed into play clothes. It was a movie. They would have had a team of tailors and seamstresses working on that.

"How did you do this?" he asked. Another movie came to mind. Cinderella, where the cleaning girl was transformed.

As if drawn to her by an invisible cord, he went and stood before her, looking up the stairs at her, at the sweep of the dress, the delicacy of her naked shoulder, the formfitting bodice.

"This is what I always wanted to do," she said. "I wanted to design clothes."

"And you didn't, why?" He could hear the astonishment in his own voice.

"Because I was told to pick a practical career, and that's what I did. Instead of following my own heart."

She was looking at him with an unnerving intensity, as if that was all changed now. As if she fully intended to follow her own heart from now on.

He realized it was not the dress, alone, that made her beautiful. He realized it was her radiance. He had invited her to go to the dance as a gift to her, to give her something she had always wanted.

Jefferson contemplated the nature of gifts.

For this one had come back to him. It felt as if what he had given her since she arrived, the gift of sanctuary, had unveiled her bit by bit.

Now she stood before him, confident and radiant, the woman she really was, the woman she had always been meant to be.

And so the gift was returned to him. In leading her back to herself, it was he who had come fully alive. This gift of awareness did not fall gently against him. No, it smashed into him with all the force that was needed to take what was left of the severely compromised armor he had put around his heart and leave it in shards.

It felt as though he was stepping over that shattered armor as he reached for her, as her hand came into his, as he placed his kiss of recognition and welcome first on the top of her hand and then on her cheek.

He could fight no more.

They went by boat to Anslow. That journey, through inky waters, the spray from the boat white against blackness of the sky and the lake was the beginning of the magic. When they arrived he had to squeeze in to find a place to tie up, there were so many boats at the dock. A horse and carriage were at the end of it, waiting to take guests who had arrived by water to the community hall.

The interior of the hall had been transformed with thousands of bright fairy lights. They illuminated the line of the roof, climbing the walls like vines, tracing the outlines of linen-covered tables.

The place was packed. The people of Anslow loved an occasion—weddings, graduations, fund-raisers—

they kept finery that would not have been out of place in New York City for these community events.

There were no speeches, just a dinner followed by a clearing of the tables, a bar being set up, a band taking their places on the raised stage at one end of the room.

He introduced Angie to people who had been his family and his friends and his neighbors since he was six years old.

They welcomed him into the fold of their lives as if he was a soldier who had been away from home for too long. They extended their acceptance of him to Angie. But almost too much so! He could not get near the woman he had escorted to the dance.

She quickly became the belle of the ball. For the first set, every old geezer in Anslow had to claim a dance with her. By the second set, the young men who had been fortifying their courage at the bar were jostling to have a turn around the hall with her.

Angie, amazing in that dress, was an astonishing dancer. Her movements were fluid and natural and unconsciously sensual. Her laughter carried through the hall. Her face was flushed. Her eyes were radiant. She was a princess, casting an enchantment.

Watching her, dance, watching her shine, Jefferson had a sense of having done the right thing. This is what she had led him to again and again since she had arrived at his door.

She required him to do the right thing. She forced him to be a better man.

And then, for the third set, he wearied of all the attention being paid to her and went and claimed her for his own. When Gerry Mack tried to cut in, he told him no. By the time the fourth and final set of the evening arrived, no one was trying to cut in anymore.

They danced until their feet ached. They danced until they could hardly breathe. They danced until the last dance, when he held her tight, rested his chin on the top of her head and realized something had happened that he thought would never happen again.

He was happy.

The evening broke up, and the poor old horse and carriage could not keep up with people flocking down to the dock, so he and Angie walked along the boardwalk, hand in hand. The night was filled with the laughter and chatter of the crowds. They were not the only ones walking.

As they turned at the entrance of the dock, a flurry of farewells filled the air.

"So good to see you, Jefferson. Angie, nice to meet you."

"Safe journey over the water, Jeff. Angie, thank you for coming."

Finally, he helped her into the boat and settled her in her seat. He went and got the blanket from below and tucked it over her shoulders.

"They love you," Angie said, tugging the blanket around herself. She was glowing.

He contemplated her words. How right it seemed for the word *love* to have floated into the enchantment that was tonight.

He started the engine, put on the running lights, backed away from the dock and pointed the nose of his boat toward the dark main body of water of Kootenay Lake. Driving at night was extraordinarily beautiful, but it held some extra challenges.

"Jefferson?"

He turned his focus from the water, looked at her.

"They love you. And so do I."

For the second time that night, it felt as if his breath had quit and his heart had stopped. What was he doing? Hadn't he known all along this is where it was going?

"They only think they love me," he told her. "And so do you."

"No," she said stubbornly.

Rather than respond, he checked for other boats leaving the harbor and, seeing none, opened up the throttle. Everybody only thought they loved him. If only they knew how unworthy he was.

He realized he could give the boat all the gas he wanted, but he could not go fast enough to outrun what had to be done.

He had to tell her. He had to put this to a stop right now, before he undid every bit of good the past two weeks had done for her.

He didn't respond to her at first. He drove them over the quiet lake—so much of it now held memories of their times together—and pulled into the cove where they had taken refuge from the storm. He stopped the boat and put out the anchor.

The boat rocked gently. The night air was as warm as an embrace. He could still hear voices and laughter drifting over the lake. Angie sat looking at him, the dress a dream around her, so beautiful it made him ache.

"It is a perfect night," she said. "Or would be if I had ice cream."

It had been. It had been a perfect night. But it wasn't going to be anymore. Because every good memory he had of this night would be overridden by what was going to happen next. This was the night it was all going to end.

"I have to tell you something," Jefferson said quietly.

CHAPTER FOURTEEN

I HAVE TO tell you something.

It seemed to Angie as if every horrible event of her whole life had begun with those words.

Her mother looking at her with red, swollen eyes, her voice broken. "I have to tell you something. Your father and I are getting divorced. He moved out this morning."

Harry, biting his lip and then looking away, before clearing his throat and saying in a firm voice, "I have to tell you something. It's not good news, I'm afraid. I'm not happy. I can't be happy here. I've met someone."

Her father had met someone, too, not that she had known it at the time. If she had known, maybe she could have been more prepared for how her life was about to change.

And then Harry turned out to be exactly like her father, as if she could spot a philanderer across a crowded room, when what she was looking for was the exact opposite.

So, what did Jefferson have to tell her? Selfishly, she wished he would wait until morning. She did not want to end what had been one of the nicest nights of her life on a sour note! How cruel of him to park the boat in the middle of a lake where she had no option to run and hide once he had told her.

But that's what she got for declaring her love. That's what she got for being fearless when she was the person least inclined that way. Why hadn't she just accepted who she was instead of pushing her boundaries?

"I had no right to enjoy tonight as much as I did," Jefferson announced quietly.

She felt suddenly panicky. "You can spare me the details," she said. "I think I can guess. You have a girl-friend tucked away somewhere, don't you? I should have known, really. A man like you—so gorgeous and so much fun and so successful—could not possibly be alone for so long. I—"

"Angie. Stop it! Of course I don't have a girlfriend."

Her relief was short-lived. "A horrible ailment," she decided. "Are you dying?"

"No. Angie, just let me speak. Please."

"I'm trapped on a boat. What choice do I have?" How could she have been so dumb? How could she have de-clared her love for him? Now, he had to make excuses. She braced herself for it. She could imagine what was coming. He didn't love her. He was going to try and let her down gently. *I like you very much. I hope we can remain friends.*

"Are you listening?" he asked.

"No, I'm contemplating jumping off the boat. Un-fortunately, the weight of the dress, wet, would prob-ably drown me."

"As if I would ever let you drown," he said, annoyed.

That made her look at him. There was a protective fury in his voice. And there was something tortured in the way he was looking at her.

"Okay," she said, taking a deep breath, "I'm listening."

"Those people, who you so correctly pointed out love me, are trying to help me. They were so insistent I come tonight, because they are trying to bring me back to their world. But I feel their love is with an illusion, because they have no idea who I really am."

She stared at him. He was standing at the back of the boat, his weight rocking easily from foot to foot with the boat's motion. How could he believe people had no idea who he was when he radiated who he was?

All that quiet confidence and strength.

"Everybody is trying to make me feel better about what happened that night with Hailey. They're trying to make me feel better, they want me to get on with my life. But I would have to absolve myself, and I can't."

"Absolve yourself?" she whispered.

"Here's the truth no one knows," he said harshly. "Here's the truth you need to know before you make your declaration of love.

"We fought that night. That's what sent her out onto those terrible roads. We had had a terrible fight. And I was so mad, I didn't go after her. I knew she didn't know those roads. I failed her. I failed to protect her. Isn't that what I swore I would do, when I said those vows to her?"

"Jefferson, what happened?"

He looked out over the lake, pensive. When he spoke again, his voice was quiet. Angie had to strain to hear it.

"I could not believe my ears when Hailey said she wanted to build a house on the land I'd inherited from my grandparents. My grandparents' house had already burned down by the time I met her, so our trips to the property were not exactly successes. We tried camping once. That was a disaster. We stayed at the hotel in Anslow twice, and that didn't meet her standards.

"That's nothing against her—she was a big-city girl, with a high-powered career that was just reaching its pinnacle. I knew that when I married her.

"I was fine with our life. I loved my wife. We had a swanky apartment in downtown Vancouver. Both of us traveled a lot with our careers. When we were together it was fancy dinners and theater and entertaining friends. I was content with all of that.

"Until she said she wanted to build a house here, on my land, on Kootenay Lake. And then I knew how much I had missed it and how much I wanted to come home. Then, I knew I harbored other dreams beyond the amazing success I was enjoying. Of having a family, and of campfires on summer nights and long days on the boat.

"We started building in the spring. It was a huge undertaking. Summer was the best part of the whole project. We lived in a holiday trailer, but everything seemed exciting—things were happening, the house was taking shape. We'd work all day, then swim and sit around a little campfire roasting hot dogs.

"But, right from the start, there were disagreements. She picked an impractical location for the house because it would "showcase" her skills. The whole project very quickly seemed to become about showcasing her skills. Budget went out the window with the building of the road to the house site, and it went downhill from there.

"Double ovens in the kitchen? She didn't even cook. A craft room? You could not meet a person less interested in being crafty than Hailey.

"Then the build went into the fall. It was wet and

grim. By the time we finished and moved in, Hailey hated it here. It's cold that close to the water. It's foggy. Because of where she chose to put the house, it was incredibly difficult to get in and out of it.

"But, finally, we were nearing completion. That's when she started picking furniture. Every single thing seemed to be about how it looked instead of how it felt.

"And that night when we fought, she was placing furniture and it slipped out that she was staging the house. Staging. That's what you do to manipulate people's impressions of a space—it's like you're creating a fantasy they can walk into. It's not what you do if you're planning on living there.

"So, I pressed her on that, what she meant by staging, and she admitted all of it had really been with an eye to a future sale. The property, by itself, is probably worth millions. With the house on it?

"She figured with the proceeds of this sale we could buy a piece of property in any big city in the world that we wanted, and she could build our *real* house there. Our real house, the house for the busy professional couple, with no children. She actually laughed when I asked her where our kids fit into the picture.

"I'm not proud of what happened next. I lost my mind. I started smashing all her little staging items— her expensive vases and her pictures that didn't mean anything to anybody. I'm not sure I have ever been so angry.

"And she left. She left in the middle of a snowstorm and drove away. And I didn't go after her.

"No, I sat and brooded over the mistake I'd made, and asked myself how I couldn't have seen sooner what was coming. I didn't think—not once—about all the things I loved about her. The way she laughed, and how smart she was, and how she liked to play jokes on me. I didn't think about all the good years we'd had before we started to build that house, or all the things we had in common. No, I got rip-roaring drunk, and I passed out on the couch.

"I woke up to a knock at the door. It was the police. She'd made it up our road to the highway. But she had tried to take a corner too fast. It was slippery. She'd gone off the road. She died on impact, when the car hit the water."

Angie could feel the tears streaming down her face. She got up from where she had been sitting and stood behind him. She wrapped her arms around him and leaned her head into his back.

He jerked away from her. He spun and looked at her. His eyes were dark with a fury that made her take a step back from him, even though it was obvious the fury was directed at himself.

"That's the me that nobody knows," he said grimly. "I killed her. She had nowhere to go when I got mad like that. I might as well have put a gun to her head and pulled the trigger."

Angie gasped at that, but he wasn't done.

"You were right. Those people love me. They've loved me since I was a six-year-old boy. But they don't know me. And I don't think they'd be trying so damned hard to make something good come out of something bad if they knew the full truth."

"Jefferson," Angie said, her voice a croak of pure pain, "it was an accident. You did not kill your wife. That is a terrible burden you've been carrying. You are a good man."

He looked at her long and hard. And then he pushed past her and took his seat at the controls of the boat. He flicked it on and gave it full throttle. The nose lifted so quickly, she was thrust into one of the back seats. They shot over the still water like a rocket that had been launched.

When they arrived at his dock and he helped her out of the boat, his face remained grim.

"Don't love me," he said. And then he turned and walked away.

Angie watched him go. It was already too late for that. She already did love him, beyond reason. The fact that he carried this terrible burden of guilt, along with his grief, did not make her love him less.

But it did make her see the truth. Perhaps it was the truth he had already seen.

She was hiding here. Cowering, really, from what life had handed her. To love him, to lead him through everything that love meant she could not cower.

She had to face her life head-on.

She had to show him she did not need his protection. He had set himself up in that role, a role he already thought he had failed at.

And she had allowed it. She had taken great comfort in it.

But it had done what it needed to do. It had helped to heal her. Now, to love him, she had to come to him whole, not in fragments of fear and not a hostage to her own history. She had to dig deep within herself and be the person he had shown her she could be. She had to give him back what he had given her. She had to lend him her strength, just as he had lent her his.

And she could see only one way she could do that.

Angie had to be fearless.

* * *

Jefferson went to his room without waiting to see how Angie would react to all he had told her. In the morning, he expected she would look at him with the disdain of someone who had been shown a truth that was different from what they had believed.

He expected he might see signs she had been crying.

Instead, when he ventured out of his room in the morning, he saw Angie was already busy. The muffins were fresh baked, as always. He heard her in the living room.

"The photographer is coming tomorrow," she called to him.

He resisted an impulse to yell he didn't give a damn about the photographer. Was she going to pretend he hadn't said anything last night? He grabbed a muffin and went and stood in the door of the living room.

The princess was gone, and Cinderella was back, her hair hidden under one of her babushka creations, her shorts showing off the slenderness of her legs, her T-shirt clinging. She had a small mountain of pillows on the floor.

"Where did those come from?" he asked gruffly.

"I made them."

How was it possible to like this as much as the goddess she had been last night? How was it possible to *love* this as much.

Love.

There was that word again. And the truth smashed into him. He loved her. Enough to let her go on to the life she deserved.

"When?" he asked.

"Last night. I couldn't sleep."

So, she was more distressed by what he had told her than she was letting on. He could see that now. She was avoiding looking at him.

He stuffed the entire blueberry muffin in his mouth, as if somehow, that could help him stuff back the terrible sensation of loss that was sweeping through him, even though she was standing right here.

"You need to go see if you can find some flowers," she said, placing a pillow on the couch. She scowled at it, then karate chopped the top of it. "I should have asked to have the ones from the dinner tables last night."

He scowled. He had just laid an earth-shattering truth about himself at her feet, and she was going to talk about flowers?

Well, fine, he'd go along with that. He'd go find some flowers. He didn't want to be around her anyway. It caused an ache in him that felt as if it would never go away.

Grabbing another muffin, he went out the door.

He made sure he was gone a good long time. He emptied Anslow of flowers and then, as an afterthought, he pulled off the lake and picked a bouquet of wildflowers from the hills. The wildflowers, he somehow knew, would delight her more than the ones he had gotten from the tiny flower shop in Anslow.

Why, he asked himself, was he picking wildflowers for her.

Because, at the very core of every man, was a little light that flickered, that would not be put out, not even if you threw pails of water on it.

That light was hope.

But that light died in him when, laden with flowers as she had requested, he went back into his house.

Maybe, subliminally, he had registered that her car

was not parked under the tree where it had been since the day she arrived.

Maybe, subliminally, he had registered there was no movement in the windows, no lights on, as he had come up the staircase from the lake.

Whatever it was, he knew the instant he walked in the door. He knew before he called her name and walked room to room looking for her. He knew before he took the stairs, two at a time, up to her room and found the closets empty and her suitcase gone.

The wildflowers fell from his hand and scattered across the bleached hardwood floor.

He had known before having evidence, because it was as if her essence was gone from the house.

He walked back through, more slowly. It was strange, because the house was as perfect as it had ever been. As he went from room to room, he saw it looked exactly as Hailey had dreamed it would look. Staged, to give the illusion it was someone's home.

There was a throw over the couch, and a wooden apple crate beside it filled with magazines. There was a hardcover book, turned over, open, making it look as if someone had sat here reading and they had just gotten up for a second. The fireplace, that had never been used, was laid for a fire as if it was just waiting for a match.

The kitchen had a platter of cookies on the island and a basket of the small green apples that grew wild on the road down to the house. He knew them to be inedible, but they were a delight to the eye and created that illusion of homeyness. On the counter, there was a cookbook open on a reading rack, and a bottle of wine with two glasses.

She had disobeyed him and gone into his bedroom. There were candles on the bedside tables, and the scent of freshly laundered sheets filled his nostrils. And right underneath that scent was one that reminded him of her. She didn't know that he had saved Hailey's pillow, and he went to it and pressed it to his face.

Hailey's scent was gone from it. And after what he had revealed last night, that seemed fitting.

There was not a nook or corner of his house that had not been cleaned to sparkling. The little details were everywhere, but she was not.

Angie was gone.

And he did not blame her for going. She had fulfilled the letter of her agreement with him. She had refused his further protection, which given his failure to Hailey, was understandable.

Jefferson fought down the feeling of panic rising in him. There was a nut job out there who wanted Angie and who was most likely responsible for the disappearance of another woman.

He scoured his house for a note from her that would leave him a clue to where she was, but he found nothing.

Even though he had brought this on himself, he felt furious with Angie for the impotence he felt. He had known last night's revelations would force her to leave if she was smart, which he knew she was.

But, somehow, he had thought he would engineer the exit plan, so that he could know she was safe. How dare she wake him up—to the point he could feel again—and then leave him with this sense of abject helplessness? Leave him to face his demons: he had failed to protect Hailey, and now he could not protect Angie either.

No doubt, she would go into deeper hiding than ever. She was clever. If she didn't want to be found, he was pretty sure Winston would not find her.

But he wouldn't, either. For his own sanity, he had to

know she was all right. How was he going to do that? He was a man with resources. And plenty of them.

Within an hour, he had the most elite private detective agency in the world looking for Angie. Vibrating with tension, needing something to occupy him, he turned his attention to the final stages of getting the house ready for the magazine.

CHAPTER FIFTEEN

ANGIE SAT AT the window of the coffee shop, sipping a cup of tea, waiting. She should have felt nervous. But she didn't. She felt strangely and wonderfully elated.

She had experienced an epiphany that night of A Black Tie Affair, coming home on the boat with Jefferson. He had told her everything about himself, exposed what he perceived as his weaknesses to her. She knew he had been trying to chase her away.

What he had done was the exact opposite. Angie realized she had pursued love for all the wrong reasons for her whole life. She had wanted to feel safe and secure. It had always been all about her.

But what she felt for Jefferson—what had grown over their two weeks together and culminated on his boat that final night—was so much bigger than that.

It made her realize who she had to be to love that man. And that realization made her feel bold and fully alive for the first time in her life. The realization that she loved the man beyond reason required her to fearlessly embrace the unknown, not retreat into safety. It required her to be whole and strong, not to go to Jefferson weak and afraid and filled with neediness.

A voice crackled in her ear. It startled her, but she

resisted the urge to reach up to her ear and adjust the tiny bud that had been planted there.

"We have the subject parking his car. He's out. He's coming to the door."

"Okay," she whispered.

Hidden in a brooch she had attached to the lapel of the suit jacket she was wearing was a microphone. She was "wired" just like in the movies.

Angie watched as the door to the restaurant slid open. She felt her heart begin to beat hard. Up until this point, they had not even been sure the message she had left on Winston's Facebook page had reached him or if he would respond to it if it had.

Winston stood there, scanning the room. Angie's sense of confidence evaporated. He was innocent enough looking: an ordinary bespectacled man in a sports jacket and jeans. The bow tie, and blue-checkered shirt, added to the air of benign befuddlement, as if he was a professor trying to figure out which class he was supposed to be in.

But underneath that, when he narrowed his eyes and caught sight of her, Angie saw the truth of him. His gaze was that of a predator who had spotted prey. There was the glint of pure malice before it was masked with a smile. She fought a desire to shudder and, more, to get up and bolt.

She took a deep breath. She reminded herself she was in a crowded room. She reminded herself that the police were right outside, and that they would listen to every word. She reminded herself that this wasn't just about her. Or even about Jefferson. It was about putting away a dangerous man; it was about protecting another unsuspecting woman, or maybe even more than one.

She had, with police help, rehearsed a script. She

needed to put Winston at ease enough to talk about the woman who was missing.

Winston sat down across from her. A little smile flickered across his face as he looked at her. What was it? Suspicion? Hope? Slyness?

"Hello, Angie," he said.

She took another deep, steadying breath. She reminded herself of the fearless woman she had been on the deck of that pitching boat. Her lips stretched into what she hoped was a smile of amiable greeting.

"Hello, Winston."

It was a game of cat and mouse, luring him into her confidence. After a few pleasantries, she began to talk about Harry and his new girlfriend. She claimed she had gone away because she needed to think, to recover from Harry's betrayal. She had to manufacture indignation, because these days, she saw Harry as a necessary step to being put on the most important road of all. The road to herself.

Once she had talked about Harry, it was an easy enough thing to turn the talk to Winston's ex, to follow a carefully crafted script that led him deeper and deeper down a road he could not retreat from.

As his barriers dropped, Angie had the chilling feeling Winston *wanted* her to know what had happened to his ex. That he was pleased with himself. That he wanted her to know what he was capable of, so that he could use it to control her.

He told her everything. He trusted her. He incriminated himself. He, no doubt, thought that even if she wasn't so frightened she would never speak of this again, no one would ever believe her if she repeated this chilling tale.

"Good job. We've got him," the voice said in her ear. "Tell him you have to leave now."

She looked at her watch. "Oh! Look at the time. I have to go, Winston. It's been nice catching up."

He looked stunned at this easy dismissal. And then he looked angry. He was seething as he followed her to the cashier.

"I'll get it," he snapped, when she reached for her purse.

But the thought of his money paying for one thing she had ingested nauseated her. She shook her head. She was pretty sure he noticed her hand trembling as she passed the bills to the cashier.

"When am I going to see you again?" he demanded.

"I'm just not sure."

He stared at her. "There's someone else," he said. "Isn't there?"

She was not safe yet. She edged toward the door.

"I can see it in your face," he said. And then he sighed with what might have seemed like defeat if she was not so wary of him. "I'd like to give you something. To remember me by."

She was sure that was true.

"Just walk out to my car with me."

She had no doubt he would love her to accompany him to his car, that he would look for an opportunity to overwhelm her.

"Sure," she said, and went out the door. He was gloating over her acceptance. She had rehearsed this part with the police, too. Get out the door. Go instantly right. A policeman grabbed her and pulled her out of the way.

Winston, still gloating over the fact she had agreed to accompany her to his car, did not even see it coming. He was on the ground in a sea of blue in the blink of an eye. Then he was yanked to his feet.

Panting, he pulled against the arms that held him, glaring at her, radiating pure malevolence. "I'll get you, you bitch," he promised.

Angie stared at him. And then she actually threw back her head and laughed. "Don't you get it? I got you. Your game is over."

And then, feeling as free and as fearless as she had ever felt in her life, she turned and walked away.

Now, she was worthy to love Jefferson.

Jefferson's phone rang. He snatched it out of his pocket and felt a whoosh of pure relief at the number on the screen. He had been waiting for this call for three days.

He had not been able to work. Or sleep. Or eat. The photographers had come and gone with him hardly noticing their presence. He was not sure if he had ever experienced the sense of helplessness that had gripped him over the past few days.

"Have you found her?" he demanded.

"Yes, we've located her."

"Is she safe?"

"Oh, yeah."

Jefferson felt as if he had been holding his breath and was finally allowed to breathe. He was not sure what to make of the cavalier tone in the PI's voice.

"What do you mean by that?" he asked.

"She's more than fine. Angelica Witherspoon is quite the woman."

"Excuse me?"

"I tracked her down through a source at the Calgary Police Service. She was at the center of a sting. They got that bastard. Because of her."

"Huh?"

"My source says he's been doing police work for twenty-two years and has never seen anyone perform like that. She was so calm and cool, and confident. She walked him right into a trap. He'll never breathe another free breath."

"She did what?" Jefferson sputtered. "We're talking about Angie? Angelica Witherspoon?"

His detective repeated the whole story with great relish and more detail.

Jefferson tried to make this line up with the woman who had arrived at his door four weeks ago.

He couldn't make it happen.

But as he thought of who she had become over their two weeks together, he knew what he was hearing was true.

She was braver than he had ever believed. And she was stronger than she had ever believed.

Still, when he hung up the phone, what he felt was an abject sense of loss. He felt the desolation of a man who had somehow touched heaven and was being sent back to earth.

Her foolhardiness only reminded him of what he already knew. Life was capricious. Things had turned out well, but they could have just as easily gone the other way. He could have gotten a phone call that reminded him, again, of his impotency. Of his failure to protect.

His phone rang again.

He saw Angelica Witherspoon flash across the screen. He wanted to talk to her more than he had ever wanted anything in his life. He wanted to scream at her for her foolishness and tell her to come home.

Home.

The place that both held hope and dashed hope. The

place that tantalized with a vision of love, and then could take it all away.

He didn't answer her call. And when he listened to her message and heard her words, he was so glad he had not.

I love you.

He clicked it off without listening to the rest of the message. She loved the one who could not protect her. Had he heard her speak those words, his every strength would have fled him. He would have begged her to come and fill this empty void his life had become.

Instead, he turned off his phone and tucked it away. He would get about the very serious business of proving to himself and to her he could go on without her.

It felt like a mission as he made his way to the kitchen, opened the freezer, remembered some particularly wonderful thing she had done with chicken breast. He had seen in her eyes, that first day, when she had looked at his tinned collection of food, that she had felt pity for him.

And one thing about Jefferson Stone? He despised pity. He had been on the receiving end of too much for his entire life. His parents. His grandparents. Hailey. He was not going to be the object of anyone's pity, ever again.

He probably had some kind of curse on him. The curse of loss.

His resolve to stand on his own, to not ever invite anyone else into his wretched life, firmed. If he truly wanted chicken dinner and muffins, he was quite capable of doing that for himself. He did not *need* Angie Witherspoon aka Brook Nelson. He did not *need* anyone. It was safest that way.

He returned to his office, but only to pick up his electronic tablet. He put what he needed into the search engine, and snorted to himself at how ridiculously easy it was to cook a rosemary chicken breast. Buoyed by that success, he also looked up muffins.

It occurred to him that he didn't know where the mixing bowls were or even if he had any. Wasn't it high time he found out?

Whistling with grim determination—and not Jingle Bells, either—Jefferson renewed his vow of complete independence. He found the bowls and some rudimentary ingredients. He began to slap things together.

Angie set down the phone. Jefferson had not answered. She felt the first real fear she had felt since she had returned to snare Winston. She looked at her watch. She could be back at the Stone House in a matter of hours.

But what if he didn't want to see her? What if it was over between them? What if she could not restore his faith in himself?

This, she told herself, was not the time to allow her courage to fail her.

She made the trip in what she imagined was record time. She was surprised she had not gotten a speeding ticket.

Now, she stood outside that door where she had stood just a few weeks ago, when she was a totally different person. She took a deep breath, and she gripped the knocker firmly in her hand.

She could hear him coming.

The door swung open.

She stared at Jefferson.

Oh, beloved, she thought to herself. He had regressed. His shirt was rumpled, and his hair was uncombed. He didn't look as though his face has seen a razor since she had left. He looked utterly exhausted.

She loved him more than she had ever loved him, more even, than that night of enchantment when he had been dressed so beautifully in a formal suit, and she in a gown suited to a princess.

"Nope," he said.

It was hardly the declaration of undying love she had hoped for after her absence!

He started to close the door, but not as firmly as he would have if he really did not want to see her. Come to that, if he really didn't want to see her, he wouldn't have even come to the door.

She stuck her foot in it before he managed to get it closed all the way.

He reopened it and glared at her foot, before lifting his eyes to hers. There were walls up that a less determined person—a less courageous person—might not be able to scale.

"Are you burning the house down?" she asked. "Because it smells as if you are."

"What's it to you? You didn't even leave a note."

She saw the hurt in him before he quickly masked it with a scowl. "Yes, I did. I left it right on the kitchen counter where you would be sure to see it."

"There was no note. What did you say in it? That you were going to single-handedly apprehend a very dangerous person?"

"How did you know that?" she asked.

He glared at her.

"It wasn't single-handed," she said. "I had an entire police team working with me. Jefferson, something is burning. Could we—"

He turned from her, and she followed him through the living room to the kitchen.

It was a shambles.

"No wonder you couldn't find the note," she said.

"It didn't look like this, then."

Black smoke was pouring out of his oven.

"Hell's bells," he snapped.

She was not sure how it was possible the room could be in worse shape than the day she had first seen it, The overhead lights were on, shining an unforgiving light on the disaster and illuminating the thin wisps of smoke that layered the air despite windows opened wide.

Gooey bowls were over on their sides. The countertops dripped mysterious substances onto the floors. A muffin tin—which looked suspiciously as if it was filled with partially cooked muffins—was upside down on the island.

And Jefferson Stone stood, with his back to her, cursing. His hair was silky and just a little too long, and it touched the collar of that same rumpled denim shirt. The shirt showed off the incredible breadth of his shoulders and how the wideness of his back tapered to narrowness at his waist. The untucked shirttails, thankfully, covered most of the enticing curve of his bottom but clung to strength of his legs, set wide. His feet were still sexily bare.

Angie felt an almost animal awareness of how beautifully he was made, how mouthwateringly masculine he was. It made the mess all around him fade.

He turned from the oven to her. She hoped it wasn't the little gasp of pure weakness that rose in her throat and escaped past her lips, like a sigh of longing, that turned him.

He swung around to her, and her sense of being too aware of how beautifully he was made, intensified. The shadow of whiskers on his cheeks and chin had darkened even more. His features were honed and masculine and perfect.

She knew she had been traveling, and her appearance was probably disheveled. She had been so eager to see him she had not even stopped to run a comb through her hair or dab a bit of lipstick on her lips. She put a hand to her tangled hair. His eyes followed her hand, his gaze so dark and direct it sent a delighted shiver up and down her spine.

Stop it, she ordered herself. They had things to say to each other. Or at least, she had things to say to him. But the awareness that hissed in the air between them, like static, like the coming of a storm, was distracting.

A blackened, smoldering chunk of something was dangling from a fork in his hand.

"Is that on fire?" she asked, dragging her eyes away from the piercing gray-blue of his eyes to the welcome distraction of what he held in his hand.

He looked down at the chicken breast, turned quickly and tossed it into the sink before swiveling back to her. "Of course not."

She sniffed the air and raised an eyebrow at him.

He frowned. "Smoldering."

"Ah."

"Prefire, at best."

"Of course."

"The smoke detectors didn't even go off."

"Maybe they aren't working properly," she said, and that earned her a scowl. "Have you tested them recently?"

He was silent.

"I'll add it to my list of things to do," she decided out loud.

"Your things to do?" he sputtered.

"How did the photo shoot go?"

"Swimmingly," he bit out.

She hazarded a few steps in, stopped at the kitchen island and lifted the upside-down muffin tin with cautious fingers. Gluey strings tried to hold it to the counter top, but she succeeded at flipping it over. She stared down. The openings were filled with half-cooked batter that had evidently risen over the confines of the wells provided for them.

"What on earth were you trying to accomplish?" she finally managed to ask him, lifting her eyes to his.

"I had a sudden inexplicable need to lower my sodium intake," he said, crossing his arms defensively over his chest and glaring at her as if this was all her fault.

"I'm sorry. I'm sorry I went away."

He lifted a shoulder as if he didn't care. "You can go away again," he said, his voice hoarse, his posture so stiff it looked as though the tiniest nudge would break him in two. "Clearly, I don't need you."

"Clearly," she agreed softly.

He glared at her with suspicion. He nodded at his mess as if it were a success. "Your presence is unnecessary," he said, lifting his chin in defiance of the wreckage all around him. "I am quite capable of looking after myself."

"Yes," she said soothingly. "Yes. I can clearly see—"

A terrible little giggle escaped her. She tried to stifle it by putting her fist to her lips. It didn't work.

"I wanted the chicken like that. Blackened."

She swallowed hard and spoke over her fist. "Of…course…you…did." Between the words were the strangled remnants of suppressed laughter. She really had said quite enough, but she felt compelled to add, "And the desire to cook…muffins came from?"

"Men," he informed her proudly, "are extremely suggestible animals, particularly when it comes to food. I wanted a muffin, I saw no reason I should not make one for myself."

"A statement of independence," she said.

He looked annoyed at her deduction.

Laughter. It had become, until a few weeks ago, as foreign to her as a forgotten language. Her life had been so strained. She had lived with the extreme tension of feeling hunted and not safe. All that had changed. Her laughter died when she realized that Jefferson was not in any way, shape or form sharing her enjoyment. In fact, Jefferson Stone looked downright grim.

"I wasn't laughing at you," she said, contrite. "It's just that it feels so good to be here. And so right."

Jefferson frowned at that. In case she mistook his silence as an invitation to exchange confidences, he looked long and hard at her, and then gave his head a shake. "I can't see how this is possibly going to work," he muttered.

"We could give it a free trial," she suggested softly.

"I already told you. I don't need you."

"If you decide it's not what you want, I'll refund your misery."

"I told you," he said, "I don't need you."

"What if it's not about need, Jefferson? What if it's not about what either of us needs?"

He didn't say anything.

"What if it's about want? About wanting a different kind of life, not needing it?"

He looked unimpressed. How he reminded her of the

man who had first stood in his doorway, arms folded over his chest, his one word—*nope*—hanging between them.

She hadn't let his attitude stop her then, and she wasn't going to let it stop her now. Just like then, it felt as if her life depended on changing that nope to something else. "Can I tell you what I see?"

"Please don't," he said, his voice hard and cold.

She smiled, because she had already seen beyond that mask. She had already seen the strength and the decency that were at his very core.

"I see a man," she said quietly and firmly, "who despite his dizzying career and financial success, lives with an abject sense of failure. I see a man who viewed himself as helpless when it counted the most, when he most wanted to be powerful.

"I see a man who has suffered way too much loss, and all that loss has left him feeling guarded about love, unwilling to risk such terrifying powerlessness and loss again.

"I see a man who doesn't *need* love but who wants it desperately. And yet he'll say no to that—to rediscovering the richness of his emotional life, to learning to laugh again—because the risk of pain seems like too great a risk."

"It is. Too. Great. A. Risk. And I don't want to talk to you about risks. How could you have done that? Put yourself in the path of that psychopath?"

"I had to."

"But why?"

"Because I was like the Cowardly Lion, I had to find my courage."

He snorted.

"Because there is no love without courage. To choose

love? Even though it has wounded you? That is the greatest courage of all."

Angie heard the firmness in her voice, the new strength of a woman who had found the courage to face down her own fears—all of them. "It's the only risk worth taking. The tremendous payoff is worth the risk. The payoff is love."

When Angie had laughed he had known the gig was up. The minute he had let her in that door, all those weeks ago, he had opened up a whole world of danger to himself.

Her laughter had shown him, all too clearly, who she really was.

And who she really was? Vivacious and fun, alight with life. Smart. Capable. And now this added element: pure, unadulterated courage. What could be more dangerous to his shut-down world than someone like her who was willing to grow and change, to let life teach her all its lessons, both easy and hard? What could be more threatening to the comforting darkness he had come to live in, than her promise of light?

Still, he tried. He cleared his throat.

"Let's look at the facts," he said.

She wrinkled her nose at him. He *hated* it that she did that. It made her look so adorably cute.

He cleared his throat. She had been back in his house less than three minutes and he was already *reacting* to her.

"That moment of madness when I decided I was capable of making muffins?"

"You totally miss me," she said.

He scowled at her. "It is the result of your intrusion on my world, influencing me, filling me with a desire to prove things that did not need proving a mere month ago!"

He had thought, when she had first arrived, that it was only for two weeks. That was all. He'd been clear about that. A man could handle anything for two short weeks.

She moved toward him. He had plenty of opportunity to move away. Plenty. But he did not.

She came and stood before him. Everything she was, was before him. It was in her eyes, sparkling with unshed tears, and in her posture and in her exquisitely beautiful but tentative smile. She was courage and she was delicacy. She was strength and she was tenderness. She was tears and she was laughter.

She was offering him a world that would go from black-and-white to full color; she was offering him a world that would go from bleak to glorious. All of that was in her as she reached out her hand and cupped his jawline, her fingers stretching out to touch his cheekbones.

He froze. He could feel the utter tenderness of her touch. In her shining eyes was love and acceptance. He understood every man dreams of such a thing, without knowing that it was his greatest longing.

Jefferson Stone's strength completely failed him, crumbled like rock from an ancient wall.

Or maybe that was not it. Maybe that was not it at all. Maybe it was that his strength was replaced with the courage she had talked about. And that courage unfurled within him like a flag that had felt the wind.

The wind was her love, showing him all that he could be and all that they could be and all that their world could be.

Because, instead of moving away from the promise

of her touch, he moved toward it. He covered her hand with his, and then he guided her hand to his mouth and kissed her fingertips with the reverence of recognition.

Of who this amazing woman was and what she was offering him.

She felt his moment of surrender. Her eyes widened, and the tears were finally freed. Her mouth formed the most delectable little O. And then she was crying, and laughing at the same time.

He gathered her in his arms and felt the pure homecoming of his heart finding its way back. He whispered his thanks to her and to the universe and to whatever forces had guided them toward this moment.

This exquisite moment, when all the world stopped, when every other single thing fell away in insignificance, when all the world bowed before the glory of it.

When all the world acknowledged that there really was only one truth.

And that one truth was love.

EPILOGUE

JEFFERSON STONE WENT and stood at the window for a moment. The moody waters of the main body of the lake were swathed in the chill gray cloud of winter, but the water at the edges of the sheltered bays was freezing up nicely.

The wind howled under the eaves of the house and tossed pebbles of slanting snow against the window. Here, inside, the contrast was sharp and delicious. The house was warm and cozy. He could smell pumpkin pie cooking. December would not be everyone's favorite time to be on the lake, but it was his.

Had December always been his favorite month, with its mercurial weather changes, and with skating on the lake and Christmas right around the corner? Probably it had not been. Once, he had wandered away, like a man lost, from the magic of all those things.

He and Angie had married on Christmas Day. He had offered her the big spring wedding, knowing that dream had been yanked from her once without warning.

But Angie had said no, that wasn't her dream anymore. She said a big wedding was about a day, but loving each other was about a lifetime. And she had been so impatient! She was not about to wait until spring.

So, instead of a church and a dinner, instead of all

those traditions she had once longed for, they had done as his grandmother had once done, and sent out a blanket invitation to spend Christmas with them. It had been like the days of old, the house filled to overflowing with joy and love. The wedding had been a surprise for most of their guests. A few, like Maggie, had been in on the secret.

So, after dinner, with only a few in the know, they had gone outside and lit a bonfire against the gathering darkness. Jefferson stood at the bonfire, down by the shores of the freshly frozen edges of the lake.

He still smiled with remembered delight as he thought of the surprised faces of their friends and neighbors when Maggie's granddaughter had begun to play the wedding march on her flute. The notes had been so clear and beautiful on the crisp air that it had stunned their guests into silence. And then Pastor Michael had appeared, on cue, in his full vestments.

And then, the music had fallen away, and a pregnant sense of waiting had filled the gathering with a delightful sense of anticipation. Snow had fallen from the limb of a tree and landed with a poof of magic that had drawn all eyes there.

And there Angie had stood, at the edge of the old-growth forest, looking like an enchantment, looking every inch the angel he had always known she was, splendid in a white dress and a beautiful fur cape. Those curls had been sewn with tiny snowdrops, and she had come to him, through a path in the snow, her eyes never leaving his face, holding promises he could not have ever anticipated for himself.

They had spoken their vows on the shores of the lake, and now that spot was, forever, the most sacred of places. He could see it from where he stood at the window, now.

They had lit torches around the lake and strapped on skates, and that was where he had had the first dance with her. That year, the lake had frozen like glass, and they had been able to see the dark water far beneath them as they glided along. They had fire-roasted marsh-mallows instead of cake, and one of their friends had brought a guitar. They had sat by the fire singing and listening to the guitar and the flute dance with each other as the stars came out. He could not think of that day without his throat closing with pure emotion at how real every single moment of it had been.

Could it really have been three years this month? Sometimes he longed to stop the race of time, to hold each moment in his hand so that he could feel it more deeply, savor what he had been given.

He heard a shriek of laughter and grimaced good-naturedly. He turned back to what he was doing: painting this room a delicate shade of white that had the faintest blush of pink in it.

"It's the very same color," he had groused to Angie when she had shown it to him.

"No," she had said, "it's not," and so that had become the color of the nursery. He slid a little glance at the crib he had assembled yesterday and he gulped.

Were they ready for this? Could you ever be ready?

Angie had said to him once, on the most important day of his life, that there was no love without courage. She had said that to choose love, even though it wounded, was the greatest courage of all.

But in a month, they were going to have a baby in this room, in that crib with its bumpers and blankets with vivid pink monkeys cavorting across the fabric as if it was all fun, somehow. Fun? A real, live, breathing, cooing, little girl. He was not at all sure he had the courage for this.

Not just for bringing the baby home, but for the first day of kindergarten, and for wiping away tears because some boy had been mean to her, and for deciding whether she should be in hockey or ballet.

Was he ready to be a daddy? So much potential for love. And so much potential for loss. And so much potential for the place where those two things met.

Because even now, with his baby girl still safe in the womb of her mother, Jefferson ached with awareness.

That there would come a day, when she might want a long, dress of white or she might not, but there would come a day when she would stand in a place of sanctuary, looking at a man who was not her daddy, with an aching love in her eyes.

The laughter came again, floating up the staircases as if the house was overflowing with it.

Jefferson contemplated that. His house, once a lonely fortress on a rock, was filled with the sounds of his friends and neighbors, gathering from far and wide to celebrate Christmas here at the Stone House. It was remarkably easy to breathe new life into an old tradition. But then, really, Angie made so much look remarkably easy.

Angie had never returned to teaching home economics in high school. Instead, after they had married, she had started an organization called Prom-n-Aid.

She remembered, so clearly, being the child of a single parent, unable to afford what other girls could have. Trust Angie to turn this into her gift to the world. She proudly headed an organization that did not give girls dresses, but showed them how to create them.

"I don't just want to give them a dress," Angie had told him in that earnest way of hers. "I want them to discover the power of their own creativity—their ability to use the force of creativity to make the world match their dreams."

But really, for all those words, it was just a variation on love.

It had grown unbelievably. Angie taught seminars to teachers and clubs all over North America, showing them how to get sponsors to donate everything from thread to tiaras, how to reach out to the girls who needed this the most.

"There you are!"

Jefferson turned slightly. His wife—would he ever get accustomed to those words in relation to Angie—was glowing. For some reason, pregnancy had made her hair even curlier. How he loved the wild chaos of her hair. The maternity dress was of her own design, proudly hugging the huge roundness of her belly. She had been talking lately about starting a maternity division of Prom-n-Aid.

"It's beautiful," she whispered of the color.

"It's the same as it was before," he said, just for the sake of argument, even though he could clearly see it wasn't. The new shade had a delicacy and warmth that the old one had not had.

"Are you hiding?" she demanded, ignoring his invitation to argue with him, her eyes twinkling with the knowledge that she had his number.

"No. I just wanted to finish it, in case."

She did not accept his answer, watching him.

"Maybe," he admitted. "Maybe I'm hiding."

"Why?" she whispered.

He put his hand to his face and pinched his nose at

the bridge, as if he could stop the emotion he was feeling. "I don't want everyone to see how scared I am to have this baby."

Angie came and tugged his hand away and looked at him in that way of hers that made him feel as if he was the strongest man in the universe.

And just like that, something flared between them, the something that never cooled or grew old. That allowed his wife to wrap him around her finger!

He carefully balanced the paintbrush on the open tin and left his hand in hers.

He heard the noises from downstairs again, and Maggie's laughter rose, joyous, above the others. She was so happy for him. They all were. It was as if he and Angie's love had become a part of the house, and it drew people here, into its circle. This is what love did.

It expanded. It gave back. It served.

It made the world better in ways that were too numerous to count, in ways that were as infinite as the stars in the sky.

Suddenly, he didn't feel afraid of having his own little girl at all.

Suddenly, he knew the biggest truth. His wife, his beautiful, wise, funny wife, could be wrong sometimes.

She had said, on the day she had come back for him, on the day she had refused to sacrifice him to the abyss of loneliness he would have chosen, that there was no love without courage. She had said to choose love, even when it wounded you, was the greatest courage of all.

But now, Jefferson saw a deeper truth.

It wasn't the *greatest* kind of courage, after all.

Choosing love was the *only* kind of courage.

"Are you ready?" Angie said.

She could have meant anything. Was he ready to join

the others? Was he ready for Christmas dinner? Was he ready to welcome a baby into their lives?

"Yes," Jefferson said. He said it to the bigger question, the one that required the only kind of courage.

He said yes, again, just as he had three years ago, to the force that humbled a man completely, that was so much larger than anything he could ever be, that had plans for him that were so much bigger than anything he could have ever planned for himself. Jefferson Stone said yes to love.

* * * * *

Dear Diary,

The Matchmaking Mamas have found our latest project! There are lots of lonely hearts to heal this Christmas, but we've discovered a special two-some that we hope will meet under the mistletoe on December 25.

Keith O'Connell is a handsome lawyer who's headed home for the holidays. . .but not to celebrate with his family. Sadly, he was estranged from his mother, who's since passed away. Now he's back in town to sell his childhood home.

So far, we have seen a few signs of Keith opening up to someone, a woman he's known for years. She's beautiful and smart, and she seems to be luring him out of his shell, bit by bit, this holiday season.

I know Kenzie Bradshaw had a crush on Keith back in junior high, but they're both all grown up now. And she's still got a thing for the guy in a buttoned-up suit with a closed-off heart. Keith is one puzzle that Kenzie is determined to unravel, but will they realize how perfect they are together in time for Christmas? I can't wait to watch and find out.

Love,

Maizie

Matchmaking Mama Extraordinaire.

COMING HOME
FOR CHRISTMAS

BY
MARIE FERRARELLA

Published in Great Britain 2015
by Mills & Boon, an imprint of Harlequin (UK) Limited,
Eton House, 18-24 Paradise Road, Richmond, Surrey, TW9 1SR

© 2015 Marie Rydzynski-Ferrarella

ISBN: 978-0-263-25180-7

23-1115

Harlequin (UK) Limited's policy is to use papers that are natural, renewable and recyclable products and made from wood grown in sustainable forests. The logging and manufacturing processes conform to the legal environmental regulations of the country of origin.

Printed and bound in Spain
by CPI, Barcelona

USA TODAY bestselling and RITA® Award-winning author **Marie Ferrarella** has written more than two hundred and fifty books for Mills & Boon, some under the name Marie Nicole. Her romances are beloved by fans worldwide. Visit her website, www.marieferrarella.com.

To
Elliana Melgar,
Welcome
To
The
World.

Prologue

It felt very odd to be back.

In all honesty, he never thought he'd be back here again. Not back in this city. Certainly not back in this house.

But then, he never thought his mother would become someone he'd be forced to think of in the past tense, either.

Granted, he and his mother hadn't spoken in almost ten years. But despite his criticism the last time words— angry, hot words—had been exchanged between them, she had always struck him as being a force of nature. Forces of nature didn't just cease to exist. They continued. Whether or not someone was there to witness the force, it continued.

Somewhere in his unconscious, he had thought his mother would be the same way. She would just continue.

But Dorothy O'Connell didn't continue. Quite abruptly, without any warning, without any lingering diseases, her heart just suddenly gave out and she died. If it hadn't been for the phone call he'd received from her neighbor, he wouldn't even have known this had transpired.

Well, now he knew. Knew when there was nothing further he could do about it. Knew that there would never be an opportunity to mend the rift that had existed between them.

Not that there would have been much chance of that, even if she were still alive and they had another twenty years. The wounds had gone too deep.

And he had lost his mother long before he'd walked out of the house that day.

Keith sighed as he looked around the first-floor family room. You would think, after ten years—and knowing that she was gone—he wouldn't expect to see her come walking into the room. Wouldn't, on some level, strain to hear the sound of her voice as she called out to him, or to Amy.

Or both.

The house had always been filled with her voice and her presence. At least, he amended, for most of the years he'd lived in it. It was only after—after the car accident—after Amy wasn't around anymore—that everything changed.

And somehow, in an odd sort of way, it had stayed the same. Except tenser. So much tenser. He supposed that part of it had been his fault, too.

Keith shrugged even though there was no one there to see him do so. No one there to call him on it.

It didn't matter. All the tension, the things that were said, the things that *weren't* said, none of it mattered anymore. It was all in the past now.

Just like his mother was in the past.

He was here. Here to tie up all the loose ends, to tend

to the arrangements. To shut down that chapter of his life and put it all away in a box.

After all, life went on. Except, of course, when it didn't.

Keith resisted the fleeting temptation to go upstairs and look into rooms he hadn't looked into in ten years. There was no point to that. He wasn't here to thumb a ride down memory lane. He was here for one purpose only: to sell the house and everything in it. The items in the house were of no use to him and hadn't been for a very long time.

Squaring his shoulders, Keith got down to business. The sooner he was finished, the sooner he could get back to the firm up north in San Francisco and to his life.

And forget all about the house on Normandie in Bedford and the woman who had lived in it.

Chapter One

With her trim figure and attractively styled light blond hair, Maizie Sommers looked far younger than the actual years noted on her birth certificate. She liked to tell people that her family and her real estate company kept her vital and young, which was true.

And then there was her other hobby, the one she was involved in with Theresa and Cecilia, her two best friends since the third grade. The hobby that, she firmly believed, aided her in finally getting the son-in-law and grandchildren she'd always hoped for. She, Theresa and Cecilia were very skilled at, quite unashamedly, matchmaking.

Specifically, covert matchmaking. The unassuming objects of their selfless efforts were never aware of what hit them when love came barreling into their lives.

The matchmaking tasks were usually undertaken at the behest of either one unwitting participant's relative or the other, most often a parent. And the ladies happily took it from there.

As it turned out, they were enabled in their altruistic endeavors because of the companies they had formed during the second half of their lives. After each woman had raised her child—or, in Theresa's case, children—and found herself squarely faced with widowhood, all three friends had met the resulting emptiness in their lives the same way. They turned their attention to whatever skills they had and transformed those into what eventually amounted to lucrative livelihoods. Maizie went into real estate, Theresa undertook catering and Cecilia, always the very last word in organization and neatness, began her own housecleaning service.

Each of these three businesses, now quite nicely successful, brought into their collective lives an ever-changing and growing pool of people.

It was within this pool that the three friends found their likely candidates: unattached people who were in need of soul mates in order to reach their own full potential and thrive.

Maizie, Theresa and Cecilia thought of their matchmaking as a calling.

Even as they conducted business as usual, all three women were on the lookout for their next matchmaking success stories.

And none was as proactive as Maizie, whose cache of candidates was always changing.

Maizie had an eye not just for excellent property buys, which in turn were responsible for bringing money into her company, but also for loneliness, no matter how well disguised that loneliness might be within the person who crossed her path.

Such was the case, she felt, with her latest client. The tall, good-looking young man walked into her office on a Wednesday morning, wearing a somber expression and an expensive gray suit. He had green eyes and very precisely cut thick, dark brown hair, and his incredible straight-arrow posture made his broad shoulders appear even broader than they were.

"Maizie Sommers?" Keith asked as he approached her desk.

He'd gotten her name from the same neighbor who had notified him of his mother's sudden passing. He felt one real estate firm was as good as another, but perhaps a smaller one was a little hungrier than a corporation so the agent could be persuaded to sell the house faster. At least, that was his reasoning when he'd found her on the internet and then came here immediately after that.

Maizie looked up into his eyes and gave the young man her best maternal smile. It usually went a long way in disarming her prospective clients and getting them to trust her.

She didn't do it for any devious or self-serving purpose. What she was trying to convey to her clients was that it wasn't a matter of her versus them but a matter of them *and* her. She thought of herself and her clients as a team, and she intended to be on her clients' side.

Sales were not final until the clients were happy with the home they were buying. She took any misgivings they might entertain very seriously. Their ultimate satisfaction was *always* her bottom line.

And if, along the way, said client also turned out to be an unattached person who would be decidedly happier as part of a twosome—Maizie was a very firm believer in love—well, so much the better.

That part of what she and her friends did—the matchmaking—was undertaken without any thought—or collection—of financial rewards. Maizie, Theresa and Cecilia all unequivocally believed that the soul needed nurturing as well as the body. And in the case of their matchmaking efforts, with each success—and thus far, they had *only* successes—they felt even more fulfilled than they did when the actual jobs they did collect fees for were successfully executed.

Thus, until she knew otherwise, Maizie viewed the young man who walked into her office this morning as quite possibly a candidate on two fronts.

The smile on her lips came from deep within.

"Yes, I am, young man," she told him warmly. "What can I do for you?" she asked, rising ever so slightly from the seat behind her desk to shake his hand.

The woman reminded him of his mother.

It wasn't so much that this Maizie Sommers he had come to see actually resembled his mother visually, but there was an enthusiasm—as well as a kindness—that seemed somehow to *radiate* from this woman. Such was often the case with his mother.

At least, his mother the way she had been those years when he was growing up. The years before Amy had died. The three of them had been a happy unit then, bolstering one another. And no matter what, he and Amy had always been secure in the knowledge that although there was no father in the picture for a good deal of the time, all was well in their lives because their mother was with them. They were convinced Dorothy O'Connell could handle anything. Nothing would ever hurt them as long as she was around.

It turned out to be a lie.

Keith realized that he had lapsed into silence when he should be saying *something*. Attempting to recover ground, Keith cleared his throat and took a stab at apologizing, something he hardly ever did.

"Sorry, I didn't mean to stare," he said, deliberately

averting his eyes from her. "For a minute, you reminded me of someone."

Maizie's bright blue eyes crinkled at the corners as she smiled at him. "A pleasant memory, I hope."

"Yes, well, it was. Once," he allowed, stumbling ever so slightly over the words coming out as he continued looking away.

"I see," she responded, hoping he'd continue. Her prospective client appeared to be somewhat uncomfortable, though. One of the things she prided herself on the most, an ability she had honed both as a mother and as a successful independent businesswoman, was putting someone at ease.

Glossing over the young man's last words, Maizie purposely went on to the reason she assumed that he had come to her in the first place. In her judgment, he appeared to be the type who was more comfortable sticking to the business at hand than touching upon anything even remotely personal.

Still, she couldn't help wondering if he was married or, at the very least, spoken for. The young man was clearly the kind who fell into the "drop-dead gorgeous" category, as Cecilia's daughter liked to say. If he wasn't married, well then, she just might have met her newest challenge.

"Are you here looking to buy a house, Mr...." She let her voice trail off, giving him the opportunity to state exactly why he was here as well as introduce himself.

"Oh, sorry." Keith upbraided himself. He really wasn't on his game today. Going straight from the airport to the house and then staying there overnight had done that to him. He would have been better off booking a hotel room.

He was going to have to see to that as soon as he finished up with this woman.

"Keith O'Connell," he told her, shaking her hand be-

latedly. Given their proximity and difference in height—
Maizie was petite while he was six-foot-two—he didn't
have to lean over her desk because she was standing up.
"And I'm looking to sell, not buy, actually."

"Sell," she repeated slowly, as if she was pausing to
taste the word. "You own a home here in Bedford?" she
asked.

"In a manner of speaking."

He couldn't think of himself as being the actual owner.
That had been his mother, who had worked long and hard,
stitching together disjointed hours so she could be home
for Amy and him when they were younger and needed
her, but still provide for them. It was his mother's sweat
and dedication that had managed to pay for the house.
He had just lived there—until he didn't. And now it was
his by default.

Because there was no one left.

"It is—*was*," Keith corrected himself, "my mother's
house."

Maizie sensed another wave of discomfort sweeping
over her client-to-be and interpreted it the only way she
could. He was having second thoughts about the fate of
the house.

"Are you sure you want to sell it?" she questioned
gently.

"Yes." The single word was emphatic, exploding from
his lips almost like a gunshot. And then Keith backped-
aled just a shade. "I live and work in San Francisco, and
there's no reason for me to maintain a house down here.
I'd like to sell the house as quickly as possible," he added.

Maizie had remained on her feet. "Well, then, let's go
take a look at it, shall we?" she suggested brightly.

Keith nodded. "My car's parked in front of the restaurant," he told her. Striding ahead of the agent, he opened the office's front door and held it for her.

Maizie glanced over her shoulder at the young woman seated at a desk in the corner. "I should only be gone for a little while, Rhonda. Hold down the fort," she instructed her assistant cheerfully.

The woman she addressed looked as if she was eager to be the only occupant of the "fort."

"Yes, ma'am!"

"She's in training," Maizie confided to her client-to-be once they were outside the office and the door had closed behind them. "More willing than able at the moment, I'm afraid. But with luck that should change soon." At least, she hoped so. "We'll take my car," she announced as she stopped in front of a cream-colored Mercedes.

Keith glanced over toward his own dark blue sedan parked several yards away. He was accustomed to taking charge, no matter what the situation. He was also accustomed to being the one behind the wheel. "I thought that—"

Maizie neatly cut him off, her maternal smile widening considerably.

"No reason for you to use up your gas," she informed him cheerfully. Aiming her key fob at her vehicle, she pressed it, and a melodious signal announced that the door locks had been released.

Without hesitation, Maizie got in, buckled up, then looked to her right and waited. After a beat, her would-be client got in on the passenger's side. She hadn't quite comprehended how tall the man was until he more than filled that section of her vehicle.

Hands resting on the steering wheel, she paused until Keith buckled up before saying, "Now, if you just give me the address, we'll be on our way."

.

Keith gave her the house number, adding, "That's in the—"

"West Park development," Maizie acknowledged. She flashed a smile at Keith as she pulled away from the curb. "I've been at this for a while now," she told him.

Good for you, Keith thought as he stared, sphinxlike, straight ahead through the front windshield. With luck, this would wind up being one of his last drives to his mother's house.

"It's a lovely home," Maizie concluded after her tour of both floors, the three-car garage and the backyard.

She preferred to build up her own rapport with the house she was to sell, but many of her clients insisted on leading the tour. She'd noticed Keith had hung back a little after he'd unlocked the front door.

It was very evident he had no desire to be here.

Either that or Keith was reluctant about selling the house in the first place but found himself in a financial situation forcing him to take this path.

"How fast can you sell it?" he asked her abruptly the moment he saw that she had finished her initial inspection.

Maizie watched her newest client for a long moment, studying him before she finally replied.

"I'm afraid that all depends on the market, the price of the house, what you—"

"You do it," he said abruptly.

"Do what, exactly?" Maizie asked. He looked to be on edge. Why? she wondered. Did it have to do with the house or something else? There were a lot of gaps she would have to fill. It didn't necessarily help with the sale of the house, but the information would be useful in other ways.

"You determine the going price for the house and sell it for just under that," he explained.

"Under the going rate?" Maizie questioned. Why would he want to sell it short? This was one of the more popular models in the development, and its orientation was ideal. The morning sun hit the kitchen and family room first. By the time the afternoon arrived with its heat, the sun was hitting the driveway, leaving the house enveloped in comfort.

Maizie looked at her new client more closely. "What's wrong with the house, Mr. O'Connell?"

"Nothing." He had to hold himself in check to keep from snapping. That wasn't going to help. Besides, it wasn't Mrs. Sommers's fault that closure felt as if it was eluding him. "There's nothing wrong with the house. I just want to get rid of it. I told you, I don't live in this area anymore, and I just want to sell the house and get back to my work."

"What is it that you do, Mr. O'Connell?"

"I'm a lawyer." Usually he experienced a tinge of pride accompanying that sentence. But this time there was nothing, just this odd, hollow feeling, as if being a lawyer didn't matter anymore.

That was ridiculous. Of course it mattered. He was just fatigued, Keith insisted, silently scolding himself for the irrational thought.

"A lawyer," Maizie repeated with an approving nod of her head, surprising him. "The son and daughter of one of my best friends are both lawyers," she told him conversationally. And then she sobered slightly and she asked in as kind a tone as she could, "Did your mother die at home, by any chance?"

Because if the woman had, that put an impedance on the idea of a quick sale. Legally, at-home deaths had to be stated as such, and there were a great many people who wouldn't dream of buying a home that supposedly came with its very own ghost to haunt its hallways.

Keith blinked. "What? No. Why?" The single-word sentences were fired out at her like bullets, shot one at a time.

Maizie's tone continued to be kind as she answered him. "I thought that might explain why you seem so... tense," she finally said for lack of a better word.

She didn't want to offend the young man, but she did want to get to the heart of what might be troubling him, because he *was* troubled. Anyone could see that.

"Jet lag," Keith told her dismissively, as if that explained everything.

"San Francisco is in the same time zone," she pointed out gently. There was no reason for him to be experiencing any sort of jet lag.

"Of course it's in the same time zone. I'm not an idiot," Keith protested. "Sorry," he murmured, doing his best to bank down his temper. Over the years, he'd schooled himself to be emotionally reserved. But what he'd learned was escaping him right now. "I was in New York on business when I got the call that—" Abruptly he changed the course of his response, correcting his last words. "My firm took a call from my mother's neighbor saying that my mother had passed away. My assistant called me. So I caught the next plane back," he told her.

And then he stopped cold.

Keith wasn't accustomed to explaining himself. He hadn't done that in a very long time. This had all caught him completely by surprise, and he was revealing more than he'd intended.

"That doesn't have anything to do with anything," he informed her stiffly.

"No," she agreed, "it doesn't. But I was just trying to get a feeling for the situation—and you. It helps me do a better job." Maizie knew she had to sell this to the young man, who needed far more than the sale of this house to tie up loose ends.

He needed peace, she thought.

"I don't care what you get for it. Just sell it," Keith was saying. "I don't want it hanging around my neck like the proverbial albatross."

"You might not care about the sale price now, but you will someday soon. Perhaps even very soon." Maizie paused, her sharp eyes sweeping over everything in the living room. "If you don't mind my asking, what are you planning on doing with the furnishings?"

"Furnishings?" Keith repeated uncomprehendingly.

"The furniture, the clothing in the closets, the books—"

He hadn't even thought about that. He supposed he was still coming to grips with the idea that as far as his mother was concerned, there would be no more tomorrows and all that entailed.

Replaying the agent's words in his head, Keith waved his hand, dismissing the problem. "Get rid of it. All of it." The things she'd enumerated represented a place in his life he had no intention of revisiting. "Throw it all away."

That would be a terrible waste, and Maizie wasn't about to be wasteful if she could possibly help it. "I think if you do that, if you just throw all this away, you'll live to regret it."

He was already regretting this conversation. However, he told himself that it cost him nothing to hear her out. "All right. What do you suggest?"

Maizie thought of the conversation she'd just had yesterday with Theresa over a late lunch. It involved the daughter of a mutual friend.

The *single* daughter of a mutual friend.

A wide smile blossomed on Maizie's lips. "I think I have an idea you just might like."

Chapter Two

"You do realize you work too hard, right?"

Marcy Crawford aimed the question at her younger sister, MacKenzie Bradshaw, as she followed her sister around a showroom that was nothing short of an obstacle course for anyone who wasn't a size three. And in her current state of pregnancy, Marcy admittedly hadn't been a petite size three for a little longer than eight months now.

Her question was a rhetorical one, and it was meant to get Kenzie, the youngest of five and the one everyone in the family doted on, to reassess her present life. However, her supposedly impromptu visit to Kenzie's place of work wound up getting the latter to fall back on her usual evasive maneuvers. Whether or not she actually meant to, Kenzie was weaving her way in and out of small pockets of space. Pockets that Marcy was frustratingly finding close to impossible to get into. Thus she was completely unable to follow.

Kenzie glanced over her shoulder, pausing only long

enough to blow her light blond bangs out of her eyes—she *had* to find time to get a haircut, she silently noted. With Christmas almost here, business had been good lately, really good. The turnaround at her shop, Hidden Treasures, both with items coming in and going out, had been more than a little gratifying.

"Said the woman who's more than eight months pregnant and carrying a fourteenth-month-old around in her arms," Kenzie pointed out.

She dearly loved her sister—loved all four of her siblings and her mother—but she instantly went into withdrawal mode the moment Marcy or the others felt compelled to change around the structure of her life. She liked it just the way it was—busy and profitable.

"Exactly my point," Marcy said, shuffling so that she was finally able to move in front of her sister by coming in from the other side. The less than fluid movement managed to trap Kenzie with an ornate carved turn-of-the-century credenza at her back while she, with her sheer girth, barred her sister's escape from the front. "All this effort you keep putting out, it should be going toward your own family, not toward pawing through dead people's junk."

"Hidden treasures," Kenzie corrected her with just a touch of indignation, taking offense for both her clients and the one-of-a-kind items in her shop. "One woman's junk is another woman's prized possession."

"Call it whatever you like," Marcy told her with a sigh. Alex, her sleeping fourteen-month-old son, was growing increasingly heavy and she shifted him from one side to the other in an effort to balance his weight. "Just say you'll come to dinner tonight."

"I'd say it," Kenzie replied willingly, "but you know I don't believe in lying." She fixed her sister with a penetrating look. "Look, Marce, I'd come over in a heartbeat if you weren't setting me up."

"Setting you up?" Marcy echoed, torn between sounding utterly innocent and completely indignant at the suggestion that she would do something so underhanded—even though that's exactly what she was doing. Her free hand was pressed against her offended breast. "Who's setting you up?" she asked, her voice cracking as it went up just a little too high at the end of her question.

"You are," Kenzie replied without blinking. Turning, she found an opening next to a vintage Singer sewing machine console and wiggled through it, leaving Marcy to lumber over to a wider aisle.

Marcy valiantly attempted to keep up the ruse. "I am not. Why would you say that?" she demanded. When Alex began to whimper in response to her elevated voice, Marcy was forced to lower it to a whisper. "Why would you say that?" she repeated in almost a hiss.

Kenzie gave her a knowing look. "You told me not to wear my jeans and to remember to fix my hair."

Because of her hectic schedule and the fact that she had to dress well for work, in her off hours Kenzie enjoyed kicking back and being comfortable during her get-togethers with her family. Apparently, in her sister's estimation, there was such a thing as being *too* comfortable.

Marcy sniffed. "I just happen to think you look nice with your hair up."

Kenzie felt compelled to point out the flaw in that excuse. "Marcy, you spend your days running after a kid whose energy levels rival the Energizer Bunny and you're about to give birth in a month or less. Why would you even *care* if I shaved my head before I came over for dinner?" she challenged. "Unless, of course," she went on, "you're inviting an extra guest to attend that dinner."

Marcy sighed, giving up the pretense. "Okay, you got me. I had Bob invite his friend George to dinner. But George is very nice—"

Kenzie immediately cut her off. This line of conversation had no future. There was no point in letting Marcy just go on and on.

"I'm sure he is," she said, patronizing Marcy just the slightest bit, "but I'm never going to find out because I'm not coming over to dinner."

Marcy looked at her pleadingly. "C'mon, Kenzie, don't be stubborn."

"You call it being stubborn. I call it surviving. Stop pulling a Mom on me," Kenzie requested, then added a little more kindly, "I have no desire to be set up. My life is full enough as it is." With that, she went on adjusting a new display of furnishings.

Marcy cast a disparaging look around at her sister's most recent acquisitions. "Yeah, full of dust and allergens," she grumbled.

Kenzie paused for a moment to pat her sister's cheek. "C'mon, Marcy. Don't pout. Your face might set that way," she teased. It was something their grandmother used to threaten them with when they were little and scowled at being reprimanded.

"What am I going to tell George?" Marcy asked. "I've already built you up to him as the greatest thing since sliced bread."

"Tell him I ran off to feed the masses," Kenzie joked. And then she sighed, shaking her head. She would have thought Marcy would know better by now. "This can't be coming as a surprise to you. You know how I feel about setups."

Marcy shifted Alex over to her other hip again, clearly physically uncomfortable. "But that's when Mom does them."

"That has nothing to do with it," Kenzie pointed out. "A setup by any other family member would be just as rotten."

Marcy played her ace card. Her eyes narrowed as she looked at her youngest sister. "You're not getting any younger, you know."

"Nobody's getting any younger, except for Brad Pitt when he played that weird guy in that movie a few years ago." Kenzie congratulated herself on delivering the comeback with a straight face.

Marcy's hands were full as she held onto her son. Otherwise she would have used one to anchor her sister and get her to agree to dinner tonight. "I'm serious, Kenzie."

"And so am I, Marce. I've got a rocking chair with my name on it at the retirement home. The second I turn thirty, I'll be sure to get my butt over there and start rocking in it."

"This isn't a joke, Kenzie," Marcy complained. She clearly wanted her sister to enjoy the sort of happiness she herself had a handle on: home, husband and an expanding family.

"Neither is being set up." Maybe if Kenzie issued a blanket warning, her siblings would cease and desist once and for all in attempting to manage her life. "Pass the word along to Marilyn. And while you're at it, you can also tell Tom and Trevor in case they're entertaining any ideas to jump in and pick up where you dropped off. *I don't want to be set up.* Got that?"

"I got it," Marcy grumbled with a sigh. "But someday, you'll regret this when you find yourself alone."

Kenzie suppressed a laugh. "Marcy, I have four married siblings with seven kids among them. I will *never* find myself alone. Besides, this way I get to be Fun Aunt Kenzie to the short tribe.

"Now please, I've got work to do and I'm going to be here all night if you don't let me finish it." She paused for a second to kiss her sleeping nephew and brush her lips against her sister's cheek. "I appreciate what you think you were doing for me, but trust me, setting me up will only lead to disaster. Now go before Pablo comes in with his duster. If you wind up staying here, you'll be sneezing for a week," she promised. "Go, Marcy."

Scowling her disapproval at the way things had turned out, Marcy murmured a few disenchanted-sounding words and then backed out of the space she was in. She was still scowling when she slowly made her way out the front door.

Kenzie breathed a sigh of relief. *Finally!*

She had exactly sixty seconds all to herself before the phone rang.

She made it to the counter, where the store phone was located, by the second ring. Managing to collect herself to convey cheerfulness, Kenzie lifted the receiver from its cradle and declared, "This is Hidden Treasures. How may I assist you today?"

The moment she heard the voice on the other end of the line, the smile she had deliberately forced to her lips widened of its own accord, generously spreading to the rest of her.

"Hello, Theresa," she said warmly to her mother's close friend and the woman who had handled several catered affairs for her. "What's up?"

It was a nice house.

Kenzie recognized it instantly. It was nothing out of the ordinary, but still very nice. And well kept.

The company her mother had founded and then passed on to her six years ago had her traveling up and down the California coast, visiting estates, regular homes and houses that fell somewhere in between. It was the middle group that tended to present her with the most surprises, yielding the occasional hidden treasure—which was why she had decided to change the shop's name to that.

Her work had taught her never to judge a book by its cover. She'd discovered that the most incredible things could be found in old cigar boxes—or their equivalent— left forgotten in the recesses of an attic, under a bed or in a seldom opened closest. Anything—from a vintage pack of playing cards once held in the hands of a famous gun- man, to a great-grandmother's precious missing cameo, to a deed to forgotten property—could turn up if some effort was given to the hunt.

What she liked most about her work was entering a different world while she assessed the belongings and, in some cases, prepared to undertake the sale of them. She always gave 110 percent of herself so her clients wound up receiving the maximum amount for their things while the items found homes with people who appreciated their worth.

Kenzie liked to call her undertaking a win-win situ- ation.

Every place, be it a simple home or an estate, had its own kind of hidden treasure, no matter how unimpres- sive that item might appear to an outsider. With that in mind, Kenzie couldn't help wondering what she would find in this pleasant residential home that Theresa Ma- netti had sent her to.

She knew it was just serendipity that brought her here because she doubted Theresa had any idea she'd once known Amy, the girl who had lived here—or that she'd had a wild crush on Amy's older brother.

Parking her car next to the curb, Kenzie got out and slowly made her way up the front walk. She did a cursory evaluation of what she saw as she went.

The property had been well maintained, although there was one hearty weed making its way up against the fence as if waiting to let loose with a growth spurt the moment no one was looking. The rest of the front yard, though, had been well tended.

The house was at the end of a cul-de-sac in an upper-class residential neighborhood. All the houses in West Park appeared to be cared for. Holding a successful estate sale here with just a little bit of advertising would require next to no effort on her part, Kenzie decided just as she reached the front door.

For a second, snatches of memories came scurrying her way, stirring questions.

One thing at a time, Kenzie, she told herself.

It seemed to her that the exact instant she touched the doorbell and pressed it, the front door flew open. She hoped she managed to hide her surprise from the tall, dark-haired man who answered the door.

Oh, God, is that...?

Yes, it is him. Keith. This is still his house, then.

Kenzie struggled to subdue her erratic pulse. She forced herself to breathe normally.

Had he been standing by the front window, waiting for her? Or was this just a coincidence? Mrs. Manetti had told her that according to her real estate agent friend, Maizie Sommers, the owner of this house was extremely eager to sell it and everything inside.

But somehow, until this moment, she hadn't made the

connection. She knew Keith had moved away but assumed that his mother had, too.

Because of what Mrs. Manetti had said, she should have realized this was still the O'Connell house. She supposed it was the story that threw her. Mrs. Sommers had said the seller had grown up here, which meant it was his childhood home. If anyone had told her that her parents' house was being sold, she would have been upset, not indifferent. And if she were forced to pack up whatever belongings she wanted to take with her, she would have had to hire a large moving van, not carelessly ask to have it all sold off to strangers.

But then, not everyone was as sentimental or attached to things as she was. And, she supposed, in a way there was a cloud over this house. Maybe that was what Keith had been thinking when he said he wanted everything sold.

The moment she looked up at Keith, that old queasy-stomach feeling came over her. She had to fight to keep it in check. This was business, Kenzie reminded herself. Her smile increased its wattage. Partially it was the saleswoman in her, and partially it was just the woman in her responding to the man.

He had only gotten better looking.

It figured. Was he married?

It had been ten years since she'd seen him. *Of course* he'd gotten married.

Hadn't he?

Kenzie dealt with a great many people in her line of work, and she was accustomed to all types crossing her path. As far as looks went, Keith, with his chiseled features, somber expression and sad green eyes, was definitely in the top 3 percent. She allowed her well-organized mind to wander just a little bit.

She had to admit that if Marcy or Marilyn had wanted to set her up with someone who resembled Keith, she probably wouldn't have turned the offer down, principles or no principles.

The next moment, Kenzie sternly upbraided herself for allowing her mind to wander this far off course, even for a split second. Even if it *was* Keith.

Grow up, Kenzie.

This was definitely *not* how she conducted business. It didn't matter if this was Keith, just as it didn't matter if she was dealing with a man who looked like Prince Charming or resembled a diseased frog. The only thing that mattered was whether or not she could help him sell the possessions inside his house. She could if those items were in decent condition or, barring that, if they were unique and interesting.

And even if that *wasn't* the case, she could offer suggestions on the measures he needed to take to make some money on the items.

All these thoughts went racing through her head in far less time than it took for an outsider to actually review what had happened.

Showtime, Kenzie thought. She was ready. She liked to think of herself as *always* ready.

She handed him her card. "Mr. O'Connell?" she asked, her throat feeling remarkably dry as she formally said his name. She waited for him to recognize her.

Green eyes went up and down the length of her, taking measure of her. Her breath backed up in her lungs.

"Yes?" Keith answered. There was absolutely no recognition in his eyes.

Banking down her disappointment—reminding herself that she had done a lot of transforming since she'd been in high school—Kenzie forced a smile to her lips and extended her hand to him. "Mrs. Sommers called to tell me that you were looking for someone to help you find a new home for your things."

The woman standing in front of him with the thousand-watt smile seemed far too youthful to be handling anything with the word *estate* in it. He felt as if he had just accidentally wandered into a children's story time. The underage woman made it sound as if his mother's things were animated with lives of their own.

Which was beyond ridiculous.

A distant, formless memory hovered about his brain, teasing it, but when he tried to capture it, to nail it down, it eluded him.

The woman on his doorstep reminded him of someone. Who?

He pushed the thought aside.

"Technically, they're not my things," he informed her. "I don't care if they find a home or not. I just need to get them out of the house. Mrs. Sommers seems to think the house will show much better—and sell better—if there are no distracting pieces of furniture scattered through-out the house, cluttering it up."

Kenzie nodded, hurt that there was no recognition in his eyes when he spoke to her. Reminding herself that she looked quite a bit different now didn't help.

Give it time, Kenzie.

"Okay," she said gamely to him once she was inside the front door. "Why don't you show me around so I can see what I've got to work with?"

He hadn't been into all the rooms since he'd returned home himself. More specifically, he hadn't seen most of the rooms since he'd left home ten years ago.

Even when he'd returned yesterday, he'd deliberately remained downstairs, sleeping on the living room sofa.

When he'd woken up after a less than restful night, he'd ventured only as far as the kitchen to make himself some breakfast.

As for the rest of the house—his room, Amy's, his mother's bedroom, the bonus room they used for a TV room—he hadn't gone into any of it. And he wanted to keep it that way until he felt up to viewing the other rooms—if that time came.

But saying anything of the kind to this woman felt far too personal.

Keith supposed he could just beg off, or murmur some noncommittal excuse that accomplished the same thing. But he had a feeling this woman wasn't the type to accept no for an answer, at least not without a really good reason.

To be fair, he decided to make one attempt at accommodating her while maintaining the balance he was searching for.

"You can just find your own way through the house. I don't mind if you poke around," he added, thinking she probably wanted a chance to review what might sell and what just needed to be carted away.

The smile was lightning fast as she attempted to coax him into accompanying her. "I'm bound to have questions," she told him. When he made no response, thinking she'd take the hint, she just continued. "If you come along as my guide, it'll go faster that way. I promise." Turning on her heel, she led the way to the staircase.

He was really beginning to regret this.

Chapter Three

Walking ahead of him, Kenzie had just managed to climb up one step on the staircase when melodic chimes announced that there was someone on the other side of the front door.

Keith looked from the door back to the woman standing just ahead of him. He was hard-pressed to say which bothered him more—going upstairs with the woman he was still trying to place, or dealing with what had to be a prospective buyer. He wanted the house emptied almost as much as he wanted it sold. He just didn't want to be the one dealing with either firsthand.

Looking at his expression, Kenzie could almost read his mind. It occurred to her that for a relatively uncommunicative man, Keith didn't keep his thoughts all that well hidden.

"It's too soon for a prospective buyer to be turning up on your doorstep, and even if there was one this fast, he or she would be coming in with Mrs. Sommers. They wouldn't be here on their own, ringing your doorbell—I'm assuming you gave her a set of keys."

How had he forgotten that? Though he hated to admit it, even to himself, all of this had shaken him up more than he thought it would.

"Yes, I did," he answered.

As if on cue, the doorbell rang again, sounding a little more demanding this time around, if that was actually possible.

Kenzie withdrew from the first step, facing him squarely, toe-to-toe. "I can get that for you if you'd like," she offered.

"No, thanks. I can answer it myself," he retorted stiffly, then glanced at her expectantly.

It took her a second, but again, she seemed to sense what he was thinking. "Why don't I just start the tour without you?" she offered.

His grunt told her that she'd guessed right again. "That sounds good."

Having no other recourse, Kenzie turned back around and went up the stairs. It was only after she had reached the landing and the doorbell had rung for a third time that she heard any sort of movement on the floor below. Keith was finally opening his front door.

Kenzie shook her head. She remembered a far different Keith. While not exactly gregarious, he'd been popular and friendly. What had happened to him in the past ten years to change him into this stoic, distant man she'd met today?

Putting Keith out of her mind, she scanned the small bedroom she'd entered. Amy's room. Judging by the soft decor, the pastel accent colors and the white eyelet comforter on the four-poster double bed, the bedroom had not been touched since the girl had died.

Amy had been a very pretty, popular teenage girl, Kenzie recalled, looking at the photographs tacked onto the cork bulletin board above the small desk. The montage included some shots from her childhood, but for the most part, it depicted her high school years. There was even, Kenzie realized as she drew closer, a picture of Amy and her. Her heart ached a little as she looked at it. It had been taken at one of the baseball games they'd attended at school. She could remember standing next to Amy when someone had snapped it.

The next moment, another photograph caught her eye, and Kenzie paused to examine it. Amy had her arms around Keith, who appeared to be teasing her.

That was the Keith she remembered. A wave of nostalgia hit her. The man she'd left downstairs seemed to be light-years away from the teenager in the photograph she was looking at.

He was decidedly happier in the picture, Kenzie thought. He had laughter in his eyes. The man answering the door downstairs didn't appear as if he actually knew *how* to smile.

Kenzie swiftly took account of the closet and the other items in the room. Although the bedroom had apparently been cleaned on a regular basis, nothing had been touched or moved. It had been preserved like a shrine to Amy's memory. She guessed that had been Amy's mother's doing, because unless she'd read him incorrectly, Keith was definitely reluctant to come up here.

Had he been here since Amy's death? The thought saddened her that maybe he hadn't. Taking it a step further, she began to think that quite possibly he hadn't even been back to the house in all this time, which meant that he and his mother had been estranged at the time of her death.

Her first impulse was to run downstairs and throw her arms around him, saying how sorry she was. Of course, since he didn't seem to remember her, that would only spook him. She'd approach this more subtly, she decided—but she did intend to get to the bottom of this and find the answers to her questions. If nothing else, she owed it to Amy to see to it that Keith made peace with whatever demons were haunting him.

Kenzie went through the other two upstairs bedrooms as quickly as she could. After doing this job for a number of years, she'd developed an eye for what could sell and what would be passed over. Since Keith had told her he wanted to get rid of everything, she inventoried the clothes and furnishings, placing everything into two categories: what would sell and what would ultimately have to be disposed of in some other fashion.

When she was finished, Kenzie made her way downstairs quietly. She was just in time to hear the person—an older woman—who had rung the doorbell tell Keith, "I could drive you over to the funeral home if you'd like."

Keith guided the woman in his mother's foyer toward the door. He'd been polite, letting her elaborate on how she felt when she'd let herself into the house and found his mother unconscious on the floor, but he didn't know how much longer he could maintain his facade. He didn't want details. Details would only reel him in, and he wanted to remain distant.

It was time to send the woman on her way.

"No, I know where it is. Thanks, anyway, Mrs. Anderson."

Peggy Anderson lingered in the doorway. "It's just not going to be the same without your mother living next door to me," she told him sadly. "Your mother had a way of lighting up everyone's life the second she came in contact with them."

"So I've heard," Keith replied, an extremely tight, polite smile underscoring the words.

Observing him, Kenzie could see that he was holding himself in check. Keith was probably afraid that if he allowed his guard to go down, he'd fall apart.

Sympathy flooded through her.

It intensified as she drew closer.

Ushering Mrs. Anderson out of the house, Keith closed the door firmly behind the talkative woman. He stood there for a moment, looking at the closed door, his entire body a testimony to rigidly controlled grief.

Or so it seemed to Kenzie.

There were men who wanted only to be left alone when they were dealing with their darkest hour. However, she had never learned how to accommodate them, because everything within her cried out to offer a grieving person as much comfort as she could render.

And besides, this was Keith. There was no way she could stand on ceremony.

Coming up behind him, she placed her hand on his rigid shoulder, trying to convey her availability to comfort him in his grief. She said with a great deal of sincerity, "I'm so sorry."

Keith almost jumped when he felt her hand on his shoulder. He'd forgotten all about her. How long had she been standing there? She was supposed to be upstairs, taking inventory, not down here, eavesdropping.

He swung around to look at her. "You can't sell any of it?" Keith asked, assuming that her apology referred to the things she'd found in the upstairs bedrooms.

"What?" It took Kenzie a minute to untangle his reaction. And then she understood. They were talking about two entirely different things.

"Oh, no, I'm not apologizing about anything that has

to do with your estate. I just wanted to tell you how very sorry I am about your loss." And then Kenzie frowned, shaking her head. "The words are trite," she was quick to admit, "but that doesn't make the sentiment any less genuine."

"I'm sure it is," he said crisply, cutting the young woman off in case she had more to say on the subject.

This whole thing was much too private, and he didn't want to talk about it. However, he could see that she felt she had to say something. He shrugged away any obligation she might have thought she had in this case.

"Everyone's got to die sometime, right?" He needed to get out—and he actually did have somewhere else to be. "I have to leave for a while. Go on with your tour. Let me know if you think you can sell these things and what they might go for."

"Absolutely," she promised, then asked, "Where are you going?"

He wasn't prepared to be questioned, so he didn't have a lie on tap. Which was how the simple truth wound up coming out. "I've got to go see about making funeral arrangements."

Now there was something she'd find oppressive if she had to face it on her own. "Are you going alone?"

Again, she'd caught him off guard. And there was that weird feeling again, as if he knew her from somewhere. But that wasn't possible, was it?

Either way, Keith thought that was an odd question for her to be asking him. "Yes. Why do you ask?"

"I just thought you might want some company. You know, someone to talk to. This isn't exactly a run-of-the-mill errand you're about to undertake," she pointed out.

He turned the tables on her by saying, "If you need to talk to me, we can meet later."

With that, and a mumbled "See you later," he walked out before Kenzie had a chance to say that she thought he was the one who needed to talk, not her.

Instead of going back to her work—she had yet to inventory the first floor—Kenzie went to the front window, moved aside the curtain and stood in silence as Keith walked down the driveway to his car.

Here was someone who was either oblivious to, or more likely in denial about, the extent of his own grief.

Watching him, Kenzie made up her mind.

There were too many damn questions to answer, Keith thought wearily half an hour later.

Mrs. Anderson had told him that, per his mother's wishes, upon her death, Dorothy O'Connell wanted to be laid out at Morrison & Sons Funeral Home. He'd assumed from this information that all the paperwork had been taken care of.

He'd assumed wrong.

He supposed he could have just taken the easy way out, called the funeral director to ask about the costs and then assured the man that the check would be in the next day's mail. To be honest, Keith still wasn't entirely sure what he was doing here. It all seemed rather perverse and against what he'd always felt his role would be after his mother's final breath had been taken.

This process wasn't supposed to matter to him, but it did.

He supposed that somewhere—very deep inside—was still a sliver of the kid he had once been. The kid who had gotten along with his mother and had wanted nothing more than to take care of her and his sister. He'd wanted to be the man of the family.

He must have been all of ten or eleven years old at the time.

Before the age of reason, Keith silently added.

"I can write up a full accounting," Abe Morrison Sr. was telling him.

The funeral director looked exactly the way Keith would have expected the man to look. Tall, thin, somber, with a touch of gray at his temples and a soft voice, as if he knew that speaking above a certain decibel level would be intruding on the next-of-kin's grief.

But Keith was hardly listening to the man. He just wanted this part of it to be over with.

Hell, he wanted *all* of it to be over with.

More than anything, he wanted to be on a plane flying back to San Francisco and his life, his future, not sitting here with a stately old man, stuck in the past as he listened to him talk about a woman who was in essence a stranger to Keith and had been so for close to ten years.

Abe Morrison, however, seemed to know her very well. Why the thought irritated him so much, Keith wasn't sure, but it did and that contributed to his feelings of intense restlessness.

The man's whisper-soft voice was beginning to annoy him, as well.

"She was very explicit, your mother," Abe was saying. "She didn't want to burden you with a lot of details." A mass of wrinkles around his eyes became prominent as the funeral director offered him what appeared to be a fond smile. "Not all our clients are as thoughtful as your mother was."

Keith nodded dismissively. He didn't want to be here in this place where the dead were made to look lifelike. He took out his checkbook, hoping that would signal an end to Morrison's narrative.

Placing his checkbook on the edge of the man's mahogany desk, his pen poised, Keith asked, "So, what do I owe you?"

"Nothing," Abe replied serenely.

Keith looked up at the man. Was this some sort of a game? If it was, the point of it was lost on him. "Nothing?" he questioned.

"Nothing," Abe repeated, then went on to explain. "Your mother wrote out a check once she'd decided what she wanted. Always knew her own mind, that lady," Abe commented with just a hint of an appreciative laugh. "She prepaid her funeral expenses. She just wanted you to fill in the paperwork."

He should have known. She'd become almost flighty in that year after Amy's death, but at bottom, she was an exceedingly proud, responsible person who always insisted on paying her own way. He supposed funeral expenses were no different for her. Making him fill out the paperwork was just her way of reminding him that she was still in charge, even though she was no longer around.

Closing the checkbook again, he slipped it into his jacket's inside breast pocket. "So I guess if there's nothing further you require from me, I can be on my way."

Abe's finely curved eyebrows drew together as his brow furrowed. He gazed at Keith as if he couldn't comprehend what had just been said.

"Don't you want to view the body?" he asked, seemingly convinced that Keith hadn't really meant he wanted to leave without seeing his mother. "Our in-house cosmetic artist did an excellent job," he added quickly. "In case you think seeing her this way might be too difficult for you, I assure you that your mother just looks like she's sleeping." The lanky funeral director was already on his feet, ready to lead the way into Dorothy O'Connell's viewing room. "Come, I'll take you to the room myself. You'll be the first one to see her—other than my staff, of course."

Keith wanted to tell the man there was no need to bring him to his mother's viewing room. He wanted simply to beg off and leave. After all, he hadn't spent any time with his mother in the last ten years of her life. Why would he want to spend any time with her now that she was dead?

But he had a very strong feeling that if he left, the funeral director would only keep after him until the man got him to change his mind—or lose his temper. He might as well spare himself the aggravation. And this way, after he got this viewing over with, he'd be done with it once and for all.

So, against his better judgment, Keith allowed himself to be led into the viewing room.

He was prepared to mumble a few token words of grief for Abe Morrison's benefit and then leave the funeral home and this part of his past once and for all.

What Keith *wasn't* prepared for was that the funeral director would leave him alone in the viewing room.

And he definitely wasn't prepared for the impact that being alone with his mother's body would have on him. Logically, he knew it wasn't her. It was just the empty shell of what had once *been* his mother.

And yet…

She still seemed to be right there, a part of everything. A part of him.

Keith felt as if someone had stolen the breath out of his lungs, then sat on his chest, daring him to suck air back in.

He couldn't.

For just a second, before he regained control over himself, Keith thought he was going to black out.

"Guess you got in the last word, after all, didn't you?" he asked his mother, the question barely above a whisper.

Keith felt tears gathering in the corners of his eyes, and he damned himself for it and her for making him have to go through this.

"This doesn't change anything, you know," he told her gruffly. "This death thing isn't going to soften me and make me decide you were right and I was wrong. I wasn't wrong. *You* were. Wrong to act like life was one great big party, wrong to act like you were a teenager, living life to the fullest—and more.

"I know what you were trying to do," he told the still form lying in the blue silk–lined casket. "You were trying to live Amy's life for her after she couldn't live it herself. But you couldn't do that," he pointed out, the very words he uttered scraping against the inside of his throat. "Nobody gets to live someone else's life. Everybody's got one chance to live, and if that's taken away, well, then it's gone."

He leaned over the casket just a tad, bringing his face in closer to hers. Damn it, the funeral director was right. She *did* look as if she were sleeping.

He felt as if Death—and his mother—were rubbing his nose in the fact that she was gone.

"There are no do-overs, even if you thought there should be. *You* don't get to decide things like that," he informed her. And then his voice grew louder as his anger came to the fore. "Don't you think it tore me apart, seeing you do that? Acting like Amy when Amy wasn't there anymore? You were her mother—*my* mother. You were supposed to act like one, not like some teenage girl with a mission.

"And where did all that get you in the end?" he demanded heatedly. "Nowhere, dead on a slab, that's where it got you." Because now that he thought about it, his mother's erratic, age-denying lifestyle must have contributed to her demise. "Now your life's gone, too, just like Amy's."

The disgust abated from his voice, and it softened again just a hint. "Maybe you could have lived longer if you hadn't lived so crazy. I don't know, and it's too late to find out." He turned to leave, then stopped, another wave of recrimination hovering on his lips. "But you shouldn't have done it. You shouldn't have," he repeated, stopping short of raising his voice to the level of shouting.

He didn't want to attract anyone to the room. Having a meltdown here in the middle of the funeral home was bad enough without it being witnessed by a bunch of strangers.

Still, Keith stood there in the room for a few more moments, doing his best to pull himself together. Searching for a way to reconcile the fact that he was never going to see his mother's face again. This was to be the last time he'd see her, and he told himself that he shouldn't care.

But he did.

Calling himself a fool, Keith squared his shoulders and turned to walk out of the small viewing room. He didn't have time for this, didn't have time to let something as useless as grief eat away at him. He had loose ends to tie up and a busy life to get back to. He wouldn't stand around and mope over a woman who had had no regard for him whatsoever, who had shut him out when he'd tried to reach her and make her accept reality.

This, he thought, taking one last look at Dorothy O'Connell, was the final reality.

Turning, he took a long stride out of the room—and walked straight into the young woman he couldn't quite place, who was standing just outside the room.

And who was apparently, if the expression on her face and the tears glistening in her eyes were any indication, listening to every word he'd just said to his late mother.

Chapter Four

It was a toss up whether he was more surprised or angry to find her there.

"Please tell me you've found a buyer for all those things in the house. Either that, or you suddenly need a funeral home, because otherwise, you have absolutely no reason to be here right now, hovering outside my mother's viewing room," he informed her.

He wasn't all that sure he could tolerate the truth, but he wasn't about to put up with any kind of lie.

"You're my reason," she told him, her voice as quiet as his was sharp.

Stalker.

The word flashed through his head in big, bold letters. Was that what he'd done, hired a stalker? The possibility made him angrier.

The scowl on his face was meant to be intimidating. "You're going to have to explain that. Carefully," he warned.

His eyes held her prisoner, as if to say that he could see right through her and would immediately know if she was lying to him.

Because he seemed so angry, Kenzie deliberately curbed her habit of speaking quickly. Instead, she enunciated every word that she uttered so he could absorb it.

"You were coming here alone, and this isn't the sort of thing a person should have to face alone," she told Keith with feeling. "I thought you might need a friend, so I came."

Keith stared at her. "You're not my friend. We have a working relationship," he reminded her tersely, then added, "I don't make friends that easily."

That she could readily believe, despite how popular he'd once been. Still, even though he had apparently changed, that didn't alter the way she felt about what he was going through or what had initially compelled her to come to the funeral home, looking for him.

Given what she'd heard him say when he thought no one was listening, she knew better than most what he was going through.

Kenzie approached the subject slowly. "I had an argument with my father."

Keith's scowl deepened. "I'm not your priest, either, which means I don't do confessions." And then his curiosity about what she was thinking got the better of him. "What does your argument with your father have to do with me?" he demanded.

Kenzie pretended that he hadn't asked any impatient questions. Instead, she went on as if the man she addressed was quietly waiting to be enlightened.

"My father definitely had opinions about my lifestyle, my choice of friends. You know, all the usual reasons fathers and daughters butt heads. I put up with it for a while, then decided that if that was how he felt, it was his loss, not mine, and I stopped talking to him. I refused to return his calls and, to make a long story short—"

"Too late," Keith informed her tersely.

He was making it difficult for her to get her point across, but she pushed on. "I smugly put him in his place— or so I thought." Her voice became more serious as she continued. "I also thought there was all the time in the world to resolve these differences between us when I was good and ready to."

Kenzie took a breath. She and her father had had more than their share of differences, but she'd loved him, and it still hurt to think about him no longer being part of her life.

"My father died before that happened. To this day, I really regret not mending those fences. And I regret not getting off my high horse and just declaring those differences we had to be meaningless water under the bridge." She looked up into Keith's eyes. "So I know firsthand what it's like to have someone die on you before you have a chance to make up."

"I had no intentions of making up," he informed Kenzie.

Kenzie shook her head. "You say that now, but you don't really mean it."

"Look—"

Kenzie wasn't about to back down from her position. She was certain that she was right and he was in a state of stubborn denial.

"No one but the Tasmanian Devil wants to live in a state of perpetual warfare." She looked past Keith's shoulder toward the casket. "I'd like to pay my last respects to your mother."

That *really* didn't make any sense to him. "Why would

you possibly want to look at the earthly remains of Dorothy O'Connell?"

Moving into the room, Kenzie gazed down at the woman and then at Keith before turning back to the deceased again. "I'm looking at more than that."

"An estate sale with a side order of philosophy," Keith said sarcastically. "Does that come as a package deal, or am I required to pay extra for it?"

"You know," she said in a tone that was devoid of judgment and composed solely of concern, "you might do a lot better getting along with yourself if you just dropped the attitude—and the 'philosophy,' as you call it, is free. As for our business arrangement, I only get a percentage of the total sales once they're final," she pointed out. "That's written in the contract I brought with me," she told him before he had a chance to ask about it.

Circumventing him, Kenzie went straight to the casket for a closer look at his mother. "She was always a pretty lady," she observed softly. Her mouth curved a little as she added, "She looks so young."

He shrugged, telling himself he didn't care about his mother, about any of it. "That was her goal."

His retort was cynical. Kenzie raised her eyes to his. When had his soul become so tortured? she couldn't help thinking.

"Everyone deals with grief in their own way." Her comment had him eyeing her quizzically. "I heard you talking to her," she told him, thinking it was best not to elaborate any further right now.

"Of course you did," he responded. She could tell he struggled to curb his annoyance.

She watched his expression as she said, "I was just trying to help."

"You want to help?" he retorted. "Don't eavesdrop.

Don't follow me. Just sell the damn things in the house. That's all I need or want from you."

He needed more than that, Kenzie couldn't help thinking, even if he didn't consciously realize it. But for now, she pretended to go along with his instructions and nodded her head.

"I still have to go over some of the inventory with you."

He'd hired her at the agent's suggestion so he *wouldn't* have to deal with any of that. Now she seemed determined to pull him in to do exactly what he didn't want to do.

"Why?"

"So I can put a proper price on the items," she replied innocently. She had more of a motive than that—she wanted to help him deal with his feelings and the past—but saying so would only accomplish the exact opposite.

"Isn't that up to you?" he asked. "You're supposed to be the one with the expertise in vintage clutter."

He was hiding behind insults, but she had an idea that wasn't how he felt about it, not really, not deep down.

"I'd need you to point out the items that have more sentimental value for you—"

Keith immediately cut her short. "Well, that's easy enough. There aren't any."

The house was filled with clothes, photographs and other things. It seemed impossible to her that he didn't have at least a few favorite items amid the rest.

"None?" she asked.

His answer was firm. "None."

Kenzie studied him for a long moment. "I don't believe you."

"Believe me or not. I really don't care *what* you believe. All I want from you is to deal with the facts as they exist."

When it came to battles, Kenzie had learned that picking the time and place gave her some advantage. For now she acquiesced. "If you say so."

His eyes narrowed. "I say so."

His voice was firm, but Keith didn't believe what she'd just said for an instant. This woman didn't strike him as the type to withdraw suddenly like that. Even after only a couple of hours, she seemed a bit more of a fighter than that. If he were to put a bet on it, he'd say the woman was a great example of sneak attacks and most likely was the human personification of guerrilla warfare.

Kenzie pressed on in her own fashion. "I'd still take it as a favor if you would give me some sort of a bottom-line price on some of the things I found in your mother's closet."

Keith grunted something unintelligible in response as they left the funeral home. He had no desire to go through the things in his mother's closet.

Kenzie turned toward him once they were outside in the parking lot and asked, completely out of the blue, "When's the funeral?"

There was nothing boring about this woman, Keith thought. "In three days. My mother, according to Mrs. Anderson and confirmed by the funeral director, left very specific instructions as to what she wanted. She thought three days would give all her friends enough time to say goodbye." He was reiterating what the director had told him.

It was obvious to Kenzie that he did not appreciate the time frame. Stepping over to the side, she tried to put what he seemed to view as an ordeal in a more flattering light.

"That was very thoughtful of her."

He, apparently, didn't see it that way.

"Or vain," Keith countered. "Think what it says for her to believe she has enough friends that they would fill up three days of a calendar. I don't know of anyone short of a Hollywood celebrity who could have that sort of a following."

What had made him so bitter? Kenzie wondered. There had to be something else at work here, not just an estrangement between a mother and her son. Had Amy's death been the trigger?

"Oh, I don't know," she told him. "I'd like to think that people who touch other people's lives on a regular basis might get that kind of a send-off when their time comes. Your mother obviously meant a lot to many people."

Keith studied her for a moment before turning away and going to his car.

This woman his agent had recommended was definitely a Pollyanna type, he thought disparagingly. Just his luck. The last person he wanted in his life right now was Pollyanna.

He made an attempt to set her straight, admittedly more for his sake than hers. There was just so much cheerfulness and optimism he could put up with listening to, and he was past his limit.

"People aren't nearly as nice as you seem to think they are," he told her.

"And," Kenzie interjected, "they're not nearly as evil, self-centered and hot-tempered as you seem to think they are." The look she gave him said they were at a stalemate and for now, she was willing to let it go at that.

"Better safe than sorry," he pointed out.

She pressed her lips together, aware that since he was the client and she was in essence working for him, she should just drop this.

And she did.

For about five seconds.

"Being safe is highly overrated," she told him.

Kenzie paused for a moment, back to debating whether or not to reveal who she was. Initially, she'd decided not to mention it, but as things began to progress, she'd gotten more and more tempted to let him in on the truth.

She decided to begin slowly and see where this went. "You know, it's okay for you to grieve. People will understand."

"What they won't understand is *not* grieving," he pointed out, then shrugged as he added, "But, well, you can't show what you don't feel, right?"

"I don't believe that," she told him quietly. His comment didn't jibe with what she knew about him, or had once known, at any rate.

Keith was about to tell her that he didn't care what she believed or didn't believe. But he never got the chance, because she went on to say with more conviction than he felt she should exhibit, "Your mother was a very special lady."

Keith sorely disliked people preaching on things they couldn't possibly have any idea about. "And you came to this conclusion how?" he demanded. "By standing and looking at her for a total of, oh, about sixty seconds?"

"No, it was a lot longer than that."

There was contempt in his eyes. "Maybe you'd better learn how to tell time."

Okay, now she had to tell him the rest of it, Kenzie decided. The moment she'd recognized him and realized who he was, she'd wavered on whether or not to tell him right off the bat. But he'd been so removed, so distant, she'd decided there was no point in saying anything. He might even be suspicious why she'd bring this into their dealings. But now she didn't see how she could avoid it.

"I don't have any trouble telling time," she informed him.

Keith ushered her impatiently over to the far edge of

the sidewalk, away from the funeral home's entrance. "What are you talking about?" he asked.

She took a breath before beginning, then plunged in. She began with the most obvious line. "You don't remember me, do you?"

"Remember you?" Keith repeated, confused. Okay, something familiar about her had been nagging at him, but she had no way of knowing that. "You came to my door this afternoon, saying that my agent sent you. I admit I'm out of my depth here, but my memory's not exactly Swiss cheese. I remember you from this afternoon."

She made no comment on his response. Instead, she went straight to the part he needed to hear. "We went to school together."

His eyes narrowed as he focused on her face. "'We' as in you and I?" he questioned suspiciously.

She nodded, then added, "And Amy."

Kenzie watched as her client's face darkened. She could tell that he thought she was making this up. That for some perverse reason, she was using his sister to get him to trust her or open up to her.

Nothing could have been further from the truth.

"I don't remember you," he told her in a low, somber and dismissive voice. He meant for it to terminate the conversation before it went any further.

But it didn't.

"I was in Amy's homeroom and a few of her classes. We were friendly." She could see that he still didn't believe her—most likely because he still didn't recognize her. In an odd way, she took that as a compliment. It had taken her a long while to learn how to play up her assets, how to style her hair and perform all the other small tricks that it took to make a silk purse out of what had been, in her opinion, a sow's ear.

Taking out her phone, Kenzie began to flip through something on the bottom of her screen.

"Are you planning on calling someone to back you up?" Keith asked.

"No, I thought this might jar your memory a little—not that we exchanged more than about five or six words in high school." It had been the classic scenario. "You were the sophisticated senior at the time, and I was the klutzy sophomore."

What she was flipping through were the photographs on her phone. Most of that space was devoted to the merchandise she had acquired and was attempting to sell in her store.

But in addition to those photographs, she also had a good many photographs of her family. And she had made it a point to have one photograph of herself in that collection. The photograph captured the way she looked back in high school. She kept it to remind her never to allow herself just to coast along. Appearance, success and everything in between required constant work.

Settling for a status quo eventually led to failure.

"This was me in high school." Turning her phone around, she held it up for his perusal. "Now do you remember me?"

He'd only meant to glance at it and dismiss what she was saying. But the second he looked down at the screen on her phone, a memory began to stir within the recesses of his mind.

The distant memory that been elusively playing hide-and-seek with his brain was back again. He stared at the photo for a handful of minutes—and then the light bulb went off in his head. Stunned, he looked at her in disbelief.

"You're Clumsy Mac."

The wince was automatic. She hadn't heard that name in years and would have thought she had risen above reacting to it.

Obviously not.

"Not the most flattering nickname, but yes," Kenzie admitted, "I was called that."

Taking the phone from her, Keith stared at the screen, then looked back at her before looking down at the photograph again.

There was only one word that was applicable here. "Wow."

Kenzie's generous mouth curved. "I'll take that as a compliment."

He hardly heard what she said. He was having a great deal of trouble believing that Clumsy Mac and the woman standing before him were one and the same person. He asked the obvious.

"Did you have surgery done?"

She tried not to pay attention to the fact that his question could be taken as an insult. She sensed he hadn't meant it that way, which was all that counted.

"Actually, no. This is the result of a good hair stylist and learning how to use makeup."

"Learning?" he echoed. "I think you graduated," he murmured, looking back at the person captured on her mobile phone.

The difference between that teenager and the woman standing in front of him was like night and day—and, in his opinion, nothing short of a miracle.

Chapter Five

Keith wasn't sure how he felt about the idea that he knew the person handling the so-called "estate" sale of the furnishings and other items within his mother's house.

In recent years he'd come to feel that there was something to be said for anonymity. Since he and Kenzie had, in a manner of speaking, a vague sort of history together, he had an uneasy feeling that he was leaving himself open to an invasion of privacy somewhere down the road. He had little doubt that Kenzie would believe their having attended the same high school entitled her to ask questions and be on a familiar footing with him, whereas if they were actually strangers, he would be able to keep her at a distance more easily.

He was overthinking this, he told himself. After all, MacKenzie Bradshaw was a professional, and he sincerely doubted that his agent would have suggested her for the job if Kenzie wasn't up to getting the job done—and more than just adequately.

Besides, he wouldn't have to put up with any of this for long. He was flying back to San Francisco the second the funeral was over. His presence here certainly wasn't necessary for the sale of either the house or the things that were in it. That was why he'd come to Maizie Sommers to begin with.

Sanctuary would be his very shortly, Keith promised himself—provided, of course, that he survived the next few days. There were times that he wasn't sure of the inevitability of that outcome.

In a bid for simplicity and moving things along at an acceptable pace, Keith had reconsidered checking into a hotel as he'd planned after the first night. He'd grown up in this house, he reasoned, so he could endure staying here for a few more days rather than commuting back and forth from the hotel, braving traffic and steep hotel rates.

Ever practical, he saw no reason to complicate matters and have to pay premium prices just for a place to sleep, which was all that his stay at a hotel would have amounted to. The rest of his time while he was in Bedford would be spent either fielding Kenzie's free-flowing questions or being involved in myriad details connected to his mother's funeral.

He discovered that he didn't have to tackle them alone if he didn't want to. Kenzie proved to be good at not just her job but also a whole host of other things. Like deciphering what amounted to illegible handwriting in his opinion.

When she found him in the living room less than an hour after they returned to the house, he was frowning over the unreadable entries in his mother's worn little red address book. Kenzie was *not* shy about asking him what was wrong.

Kenzie was not shy about *anything*.

He didn't bother hiding that he was less than happy about whatever needed doing next. "I'm going to have to call my mother's friends to let them know where and when the funeral service will be held."

Kenzie apparently picked up on his reluctance. "Would you like me to call them for you?"

For just a moment, he allowed himself to savor the wave of relief that washed over him. He was more than willing to have her take over this tedious, not to mention uncomfortable, chore.

But the next moment, reality set in, as it always did. "And say what?" he asked. "That you're my administrative assistant and you're making these calls about Dorothy O'Connell's passing on the behalf of the only family she has left?"

Kenzie inclined her head, indicating her basic agreement with his assessment. "That would be the gist of it, although not exactly in those words." In her opinion, he'd sounded not just detached but also a tad sarcastic, neither of which would work in this situation once he started calling and talking to his mother's friends. "I thought all lawyers knew how to charm juries."

Keith frowned again as he looked down at the page he'd opened the book to. "The people in this book aren't a jury," he pointed out.

Okay, so her choice of words left something to be desired. "Maybe not, but the charm thing can still work. Besides, juries are comprised of people, and these *are* people you'll be calling," Kenzie said, indicating the address book.

Keith sighed, frustrated. "Illegible people." He shook his head. "My mother had the world's worst handwriting. A chicken with its beak dipped in ink could write more legibly than my mother did." And that was being charitable. "For all I know, this could be an annotated list of a herd of ponies," he grumbled, waving the address book.

"May I?" Kenzie held out her hand toward him, her indication clear. She wanted him to surrender the book to her so she could see firsthand what she would be up against.

Keith gladly surrendered the cause of his eyestrain and blossoming headache. "Be my guest. And if you can read any of those names and numbers, I'll buy you a filet mignon dinner."

The grin Kenzie gave him told Keith how game she was even before she said, "You're on."

Kenzie skimmed down the first couple of pages quickly before she raised her eyes to his again. She fixed Keith with a mesmerizing look he found almost too hypnotic. Drawing his eyes away proved to be a real problem—which in turn annoyed him. He didn't need extraneous thoughts right now.

"What restaurant?" she asked him, the grin still playing along her lips.

He looked at her sharply. She had to be bluffing. "You're kidding."

"Frequently," Kenzie allowed. "Going along with the popular belief, laughter really *is* the best medicine. However," she went on, "I'm not kidding this time. Would you like me to type these names and numbers up for you?" she offered.

"You can read them?" he asked in disbelief.

"Absolutely," she told him without hesitation.

For a moment, he was going to accuse her of lying, but why would she lie? She had to know he'd call her on it, and she obviously was ready to back up her claim by recreating the entries.

Getting up, he circled around her until he was looking over her shoulder at the same page she was.

Incredible, he thought.

"Do you want me to write them down?" she offered again, prodding him for an answer.

He wouldn't have use for any of those names once the people listed in it were notified.

"No need," he told her. "As long as they know the date, time and location of the funeral—"

"And the reception," she added. Didn't he realize that there was always some sort of a reception held after a funeral?

Obviously not, she thought, judging by the blank expression on Keith's face when he looked at her. "What reception?"

Kenzie gave him the benefit of the doubt. Maybe the man had never been to a funeral before. "The one you're going to be holding for everyone after your mother's funeral."

"No, I'm not. I'm not holding anything. I'm flying back to San Francisco right after the funeral," he told her firmly.

"Are you expecting some sort of an emergency?" Kenzie questioned innocently.

He saw right through her and it irritated him, but there was no point in letting her see that. After all, she was just trying to help here. But he could be honest with her.

"The emergency is that I can't take being here for any length of time."

Kenzie very politely shot down his plans for an early escape. "Hold a reception," she told him. "Trust me, you'll regret it if you don't. It doesn't take all that much to throw a reception together if you know the right people to ask." That she knew such people went without saying. "Your mother's friends will expect it."

"I'm never going to see any of these people again. Why should it matter to me what they think?"

She refrained from pointing out the obvious—he would be doing it to honor his mother, and that sort of thing was expected. Instead, she tried to appeal to his practical side.

"Call it tying up loose ends. You'll feel better about it when you look back."

For a relative stranger—despite their common background—Kenzie Bradshaw seemed awfully confident that she knew how he'd react to something when he would have occasion to look back on it someday in the future. He almost called her on it, then decided there was no point.

Besides, he needed all the help he could get, and for whatever reason, this woman seemed perfectly content to handle all this for him.

"Okay, we'll have the reception." Then he tapped the edge of the tattered address book. "Now see what you can do with this."

She flipped over to a few more pages in the same worn condition. "Do you want everyone in the address book notified about your mother's funeral and reception?"

He shrugged. On his own, he wouldn't have known who to call and who to leave out. "Might as well." And then he thought of one restriction. "Just the people who are located in the States."

He was not about to postpone the entire funeral service just because someone couldn't make immediate travel arrangements. This was already getting too drawn out.

Kenzie nodded. "Understood."

Holding on to the tattered address book, Kenzie sat down and made herself comfortable on the sofa. She took out her cell phone.

"You can use the house phone," Keith told her. He had no idea who her carrier was or what data plan she had.

She was essentially doing him a favor, and he didn't want it costing her anything on top of that.

"This is fine," Kenzie assured him. "Besides, the house phone won't reach over here." She pointed to the landline, which was located on the kitchen wall, and smiled as she said, "Your mother didn't appear to be a supporter of cordless phones."

He hadn't taken any notice of that. Now that he did, Keith laughed shortly. "I guess some things never change," he commented. The phone in the kitchen looked as if it was the same one that had been there when he still lived at home.

Just for a glimmer of a moment, she thought she saw nostalgia flash in Keith's eyes. She wanted to ask him about it, but she instinctively knew where that would lead. Keith wasn't ready to talk. She could see that. Whether this involved unresolved issues between Keith and his mother or something else, he'd have to approach it slowly, in stages, not all at once like a firestorm. And right now, he had trusted her enough to ask for help.

That was step one.

"I'd better get started," Kenzie told him as she opened the address book and turned to the first page, her cell phone ready in her other hand.

Taking his cue, Keith left her to it.

Or thought he did.

The problem was that the house was so quiet, it was almost eerie. There was no competing noise to draw his attention away from the sound of Kenzie's voice as she made call after call, saying, essentially, the same thing over and over again.

Even with a room between them—he was in the tiny room that had been used as a study—he could still hear her clearly.

Kenzie's voice, he thought, sounded almost melodic despite the fact that it was infused with the proper sub-dued decorum as she called the first of many people to announce solemnly his mother's passing.

He caught himself being drawn to the sound of her voice even though he tried not to listen.

He fully expected Kenzie to keep her end of the con-versation identical from call to call. But after listening to her phone what he assumed were the first two people in the book, he realized she was tailoring what she said.

Kenzie Bradshaw was nothing if not personable. He found himself admiring her.

He had spent the first night here on the sofa rather than going upstairs to his old bedroom. But with the sound of Kenzie's voice filling up the living room and perforce the surrounding area, he decided he needed to escape. So he reluctantly went upstairs to his room, thinking he'd give what he'd left there ten years ago a cursory look on the off chance that there actually *was* something he might want to keep from that period of his life.

As he climbed up the stairs, Keith couldn't help think-ing that he'd lucked out hiring Kenzie. What she was doing right now was definitely over and above the call of duty. He appreciated that she had taken on what would have been to him nothing short of an ordeal. Notifying people that someone they knew and presumably liked was dead was an onerous task. That went double since the deceased was his mother.

Yet Kenzie had taken the job on more than willingly.

He wondered why she'd done that.

Was she playing some sort of an angle? And if so, what?

He'd been a lawyer much too long. Otherwise, he wouldn't be on his guard like this. Not everyone had an underhanded motive in mind, he reminded himself. Sometimes a kindness was just a kindness.

The embroidery-worthy slogan caught him up short as it popped into his head.

That was something his mother used to say. Now that he thought about it, she had always been a champion of good deeds for their own sake, not for any sort of financial gain or reward other than a feeling of satisfaction.

And then he frowned, remembering that their last argument had been about just that.

A strong feeling of déjà vu swept over Keith the moment he crossed the threshold into his old bedroom. Until this point, he had been convinced he was in no danger of feeling even remotely nostalgic. After all, he'd left in the heat of anger, and anger had continued to be his shield all these years.

When he thought of the house on Normandie, there was no overwhelming fondness vying for his attention. There was just that feeling of anger, anger that effectively managed to cocoon him.

So where was that shield, that cocoon now? he silently demanded.

Keith felt naked and exposed, and he definitely felt vulnerable.

He almost turned on his heel and walked out again, but that would have been cowardly and he refused to be a coward, even if only in his own eyes.

So he forced himself to remain in the room, opening bureau drawers and looking into his closet.

Much to his frustration, the feeling of nostalgia refused to abate. It grew. Grew until he could feel it emanating from every corner, from every nook in his room.

Even looking at his high school jacket, the one with the

letter he'd been so proud of, wound up being another occasion for nostalgia to ambush him. It happened not just when he put it on but also when he slipped his hands into the pockets. He expected them to be empty.

They weren't.

His fingers in his right pocket came in contact with something soft. When he pulled it out, he found it was a ribbon. For a moment, he stared at it, unable to remember whom it belonged to.

And then he remembered all too well. His stomach tightened.

The ribbon had belonged to Amy. It had come undone from her hair and she'd lost it. He'd found the ribbon, and out of habit, he picked it up. Amy was always losing things. Ribbons, schoolbooks, those funny little dangling earrings she loved so much. He'd teased her, saying that with her penchant for losing things, she was lucky to have kept her clothes on.

Trying to shake off the feeling, he shoved the ribbon back into his pocket and stripped the jacket off. He threw it into the bottom of his closet and quickly closed the sliding closet door, as if hiding it from view could somehow erase the feeling he was experiencing.

It didn't.

Kenzie chose that moment to come walking in. "It's done," she announced.

His mind still elsewhere, Keith looked at her uncomprehendingly.

"I called all the people in your mother's book." To say that it had been a grueling ordeal would have been an understatement. But no one had forced her to do it. She'd volunteered, she reminded herself, so she had no right to complain. "Everyone is profoundly sorry to hear about your mother's passing. They had some really nice things to say about her. It might have been good for you to hear," she couldn't help telling him. "I jotted some of the things down if you want to see for yourself."

She held the pad she'd used out to him.

Keith deliberately ignored the pad. Rather than accept it, he just shrugged. "I'll take your word for it." He got back to the only thing that mattered here as far as he was concerned. "So it's done?"

"The notification part, yes. It's done."

"What other part is there?" he asked, then realized what she was probably referring to. "Oh, you mean attending the funeral."

"Actually, I was referring to the arrangements for the reception."

The reception. He was hoping she'd forgotten about that. He should have known better.

"Yeah, about that. There're too many details to see to at this late date. I don't think that I can—"

"But I can," she interjected, reminding him of what she'd said earlier. "I'll handle it for you," she volunteered.

She was turning into his own personal valet, and he had to admit, he really did appreciate the help. But he had to draw the line at this. There was such a thing as abusing an offer of help, no matter how willing she seemed to be.

"It's too much," he maintained stubbornly.

She glossed right over his protest.

"We can hold it here—after all, this is where all of your mother's friends were probably accustomed to coming. The house has that kind of warmth to it," she added when he looked at her quizzically. "And the reception doesn't have to be anything fancy. All it has to do is *be*," she stressed.

And then she tackled the biggest obstacle that he could raise before he had a chance to do it. "I happen to know someone who could cater this for you at a more than reasonable price," she promised, thinking of Mrs. Manetti.

Okay, this was getting into the realm of being too good to be true—which meant that it ultimately wasn't. Somewhere down the line, there had to be a catch.

"So, aside from selling vintage furnishings, you moonlight as what—a magician, is that it?" Keith asked almost accusingly.

"No," she told him, doing her best not to pay attention to his skeptical tone. "I just happen to have a lot of connections."

I just bet you do, Keith couldn't help thinking. Anyone who looked the way this woman did undoubtedly had *lots* of connections.

[illegible faint text from facing page bleed-through]

Chapter Six

In the end, though it was against his better judgment, Keith gave in and told this woman who had popped up out of his past to go ahead with the arrangements for the reception.

It was proving to be easier to say yes than to argue with Kenzie. To the casual observer, she might appear to be incredibly easygoing, but obviously in this case looks not only could be deceiving but also actually were.

The enterprising young woman was tenacious. *Extremely* tenacious. Keith quickly discovered that when she thought she was right about something, Kenzie just dug in. He had a feeling that if he didn't tell her to go ahead with the reception, she would keep chipping away at him until he finally gave in.

This way spared him a lot of useless grief.

What actual business this was of hers he had yet to figure out, but since his mother's friends did seem to expect there would be a reception held after the funeral and

Kenzie was willing to make all the arrangements for him, he figured there was no point in fighting it.

He supposed it was, in essence, a win-win situation—except that he didn't actually want a reception after the funeral in the first place…

But then, he really didn't want to have to go through with the funeral service, either. However, there was just no way around it.

The situation he found himself facing made him think of one of the senior partners at his law firm, Nathan Greeley. Greeley had a large family, and one or more of them were always giving the man grief. He'd once asked Greeley how he put up with it. The senior partner had told him he just threw money at the problem until it finally went away.

At the time, he'd thought the response seemed like a rather cold—not to mention wasteful—philosophy. But he could fully appreciate the man's thinking right now. He could also readily embrace it now that he was dealing with Kenzie and his mother's funeral.

Keith supposed that, in all honesty, he couldn't really complain. Kenzie was actually doing the work. He just had to pay the bills.

For the second time, he couldn't help thinking that he had certainly gotten more than he'd bargained for by hiring Kenzie.

In more ways than one.

She was definitely a far cry from the awkward, unsure teenager he only vaguely remembered from high school.

But then, to be fair, he supposed that *he* was a far cry from the person he had been back then, as well.

Shrugging, Keith pushed any further examination of those years aside. It served no purpose. He was who he was.

A man without a family.

The thought just seemed to pop up in his head out of nowhere. Jagged and painful in its brutal simplicity, it proved to be hard to push aside.

The funeral, and everything that was associated with it, was supposed to have been just a sidebar. The sale of the house and its furnishings were supposed have taken center stage for him until they were effectively history for him, as well.

But things weren't progressing nearly as swiftly as he would have liked. It felt as if the sale was on temporary hold until after the funeral and reception were over.

He wasn't quite sure how that had happened. Kenzie had mentioned something to him in passing that postponing putting the house up for sale was just showing the proper respect for his mother. He'd been tempted to say that his mother never bothered showing him any proper respect, but he bit his tongue and refrained.

The funeral would be held in three days, and he supposed he could wait until then.

Besides, mercifully, Kenzie seemed to be really invested in making all the arrangements. To her credit—if he could call it that—she did try to pull him into every decision, but he kept abdicating his position and telling her to do what she felt was best—as long as it remained simple.

Even so, Kenzie kept trying.

She even came to him with a choice of three different menus for the reception.

He was on the sofa at the time, trying to distract himself by finding something vaguely entertaining on television. Never an avid viewer, he was striking out rather badly.

Armed with printed material, Kenzie bent over the coffee table and spread out the menus for him to review.

"What looks good to you?" she asked.

Keith glanced away from the set and looked in her direction. The first thing he noticed wasn't any of the menus she'd laid out for him. It was the way her light blue blouse dipped down, allowing him to glimpse just the slightest hint of cleavage—only enough to distract him—as she fussed over the menus.

As if his brain was on some delayed timer, when he realized what he was doing—and that she was looking at him—Keith said the first thing that came to mind that didn't include her.

Or food, for that matter.

Clearing his throat, he muttered, "A shot of vodka comes to mind."

Kenzie effortlessly took his response in stride, incorporating it in her answer. "There'll be a bar for those who feel the need for something a little more bracing than soda." Straightening up as unobtrusively as possible when she realized that her neckline had dipped down, Kenzie tapped an index finger once on each of the menus. "I meant, which of these menus do you want at the reception?"

None stood out from the other two. They looked equally acceptable. Keith waved a dismissive hand at the array. "It doesn't matter."

The look he caught her giving him in response said that it did matter.

"Okay, you pick," he told Kenzie, adding for her benefit, "I defer to your judgment. You seem to be in tune to what these women want."

She couldn't help wondering if Keith knew how aloof he sounded. She refused to believe he really felt that way. There was a human being underneath all that. She was sure of it. He couldn't have changed all that much from the person she remembered when she'd had that massive crush on him in high school.

"What they want is the opportunity to get together and trade favorite stories about your mother. And what I want," she added quietly, catching him by surprise, "is for you not to patronize me."

Keith frowned. He hadn't realized that he'd allowed his facade to slip down. He was usually a lot better at keeping his mask in place when dealing with a distasteful situation.

"I wasn't patronizing you," he protested.

Kenzie laughed dryly and rolled her eyes.

"Oh, please. I'm an optimist, not an idiot. You're angry. I get it. But eventually, the anger's going to pass. If you don't do this, if you just turn your back on your mother, her friends and everything else, you're going to regret it. And regret has amazing staying power. It has a tendency to haunt us for a very long time."

He doubted that Kenzie had ever regretted anything in her whole life. He, on the other hand, did. And that was what he was attempting to deal with right now.

"More philosophy?" he asked flippantly.

"Call it whatever you like. And no, it's not part of a package deal. It's on the house," she added with a tolerant, lopsided smile.

With that, she scooped the menus up off the coffee table and began to walk out of the room.

The woman was trying, and he shouldn't be making it this hard for her. With an inward sigh, he called out to her. "Kenzie?"

Kenzie paused, then glanced at him over her shoulder. "Yes?"

"Which one did you decide on?"

"The one with chicken. There are people who have issues with beef or pork, but almost everyone likes chicken," she told him.

It made sense, and Keith nodded. Just as she did cross the threshold, he added what he'd left unsaid. "Thanks for doing this."

Again, she looked at Keith over her shoulder and smiled. "No problem," she assured him.

And she sounded like she actually meant it.

It was the smell of coffee that woke him the next morning.

At first, as the aroma wafted into the misty domain comprising his dormant, unconscious state, Keith was sure he was just dreaming.

But he could still smell the strong aroma when he opened his eyes.

What the…?

He was certain that he hadn't set the coffee machine on a timer. Last night came back to him, and he remembered watching *Executive Decision*, a favorite movie he must have seen at least twenty times, if not more. Flipping channels, he'd encountered it—a few scenes into the story—on one of the cable stations, and it was like running into an old friend.

Watching it was somehow comforting. He couldn't recall falling asleep, but he must have.

When had he turned off the set?

Or had he?

As Keith struggled to clear his head and piece together the tail end of his evening, the scent of coffee became stronger.

And then he realized why.

"Hi, you're up," Kenzie said as if it was an event she'd

been waiting for. She placed a large cup of coffee—
black—in front of him.

His brain still hadn't fully clicked in, but he distinctly
remembered Kenzie going home last night. "What are
you doing here?"

"Putting coffee in front of you," she responded brightly.
Kenzie knew that he wasn't really asking that, so she answered what she assumed was his actual question. "I let
myself in this morning. I hope you don't mind."

The fog was still hovering around his brain, clouding
it. "I gave you a key?" Keith couldn't remember doing
that.

And, it turned out, with good reason.

"No," Kenzie answered. "But there was an extra front
door key hanging on the key rack in the kitchen, so I took
it last night. I need to get an early start this morning, and
I didn't want to wake you up."

The information was going in, but it still wasn't finding
a proper home. "Early start?" he echoed. "Doing what?"

"Inventory," she answered. And then she prodded his
memory a little more. "You hired me to organize an estate sale, remember?"

"I know," he bit out impatiently, "but what I remember
is you taking over my mother's funeral arrangements—
not that I'm not glad you did," he quickly interjected,
afraid that she might just back off and subsequently out
of everything if she thought he was complaining. Now
that apparently everyone was coming to the house after
the funeral, he definitely wanted Kenzie to remain and
act as his buffer.

Looking to move on, Keith picked up the mug from
the coffee table. The coffee immediately drew the focus
of his attention. In this day and age of designer coffee, his
own taste in coffee had remained unchanged.

After taking an appreciative first sip, he raised his eyes to hers and asked, "How did you know that I take it black?"

"I guessed," Kenzie confessed. "No cream, no sugar, just black. It seemed to me that would be your style," she added.

"And strong." Which he discovered after taking his second sip of the hot brew. His first reaction hadn't been a fluke. The coffee tasted as if it could double as a paint remover.

"Another guess," she admitted. "There's also breakfast in the kitchen if you like," she added. Keith must have looked puzzled, because she elaborated. "Eggs, bacon, toast. Nothing fancy, just hot."

"I didn't see any eggs or bacon in the refrigerator."

"That's because there weren't any. I stopped at the store on my way here."

That seemed to him unnecessarily complicated. "Would've been easier stopping at a drive-through," was his assessment.

"Maybe," Kenzie conceded. "But I like to cook, and most breakfasts are simple enough to make. This certainly was," she added. "So, if you're interested, the plate's on the stove, still warm."

With that, she turned away and headed toward the stairs.

"Where are you going?" Keith asked. He got up, holding the coffee mug in both hands.

"Upstairs. Inventory," she answered again. Then she asked with a patient smile, "Remember?"

Keith frowned. He figured that he had to in order to maintain the ruse that he was effectively keeping Kenzie at arm's length, even though that length was definitely shrinking—by the moment, it seemed.

He wasn't happy about it. At the same time, he didn't seem to be able to do anything about it.

In self-defense, he allowed his temper to surface.

"Yes, I remember," he answered curtly. "I'm not senile yet."

"Yet," Kenzie echoed with a grin, clearly amused.

It was slowly working out, she thought as she hurried up the stairs. He sounded reasonably awake and somewhat cheerful—until he realized he was thawing and made a stab at grumpiness. She figured it was best to quit while she was ahead.

Besides, she had a lot of work cut out for her that had nothing to do with the state of his disposition—even though it interested her a great deal.

Later, she promised herself.

He'd finished eating and the dishes were in the sink, obviously waiting to be washed at some future date, whenever he felt like getting around to it.

Since Kenzie hadn't been gone all that long, he was surprised to see her.

The expression on her face was difficult for him to decipher. As a lawyer, he'd learned how to read jurists, but she was a challenge. Though she was deceptively laid-back with amusement in her eyes, he knew there was a great deal more to her than was visible at first.

"Something wrong?" Keith asked.

She wouldn't have called it "wrong" but just something that needed to be addressed. "I found a box," she began slowly, wondering how he was going to react.

"So?" he asked, waiting for some sort of further explanation.

"It's a box of letters," Kenzie told him, sounding slightly

breathless as she placed the box on the coffee table in front of him.

Keith shrugged. He refrained from touching it, as if not touching the box allowed him to negate the validity of whatever might have been inside. He regarded it uneasily without knowing why.

"Put it in the trash," he told her. "Nobody's going to want to read someone else's letters."

"The letters are ones your mother wrote to you," she told him quietly.

Keith looked at her sharply. There was an angry accusation in his eyes.

What sort of game was she playing? "I never got any letters from her," he informed Kenzie coldly.

"They weren't mailed." She glanced down at the box. "They were addressed, stamped, signed, but she never mailed them."

He felt a ripple of curiosity forming—and smashed it. "I told you, put them in the trash."

She stared at him as if he'd just instructed her to set the house on fire. "Don't you want to read what she wanted to tell you?"

"If my mother *wanted* to tell me anything, she would have mailed the letters," he said coldly. "Consequently, what she wrote there was for her own conscience. It had nothing to do with me."

She didn't believe that—and neither did Keith, she thought. "But—"

Keith cut her short. "Look, I know you think you're helping, but you're not," he said forcefully. "You've already done more than you're supposed to, and no matter what misguided notion you might have, it's not your job to be my conscience. Either stop, or I'll pay you for the time you've put in so far, and I'll get someone else to handle this so-called estate sale."

She suppressed a sigh, picking up the box again. "You're going to regret not reading these."

"My letters, my regret."

Kenzie looked down at the box she'd picked up, then moved it against the crook of her arm. "Have it your way."

Finally!

"Thank you," Keith said. The words were polite and perfunctory. He'd honestly expected more of an argument out of her than that.

Kenzie merely nodded her acknowledgment as she walked out of the kitchen, carrying the offending box of letters out with her. She cradled the box against her as if she were carrying a baby.

She disappeared from view, and Keith turned back around again, fairly certain that the incident was closed. Nonetheless, he strained to hear the familiar sounds of Kenzie going out of the house so that she could throw the letters away.

And then he did.

He heard the front door open and then close again. He sat, waiting to hear it open again. When it didn't, he began to wonder if Kenzie had opted to take him up on the alternative that he offered and decided to leave.

He remained at the table, straining to hear some movement from the front of the house.

When he finally heard the door opening again, he released the breath he'd unconsciously been holding.

She hadn't left.

The relief he felt surprised him.

And worried him, as well.

Chapter Seven

Keith had no time to examine his rather strong—and positive—reaction to the fact that Kenzie hadn't left. The moment she walked back into the room, she hit him with a question.

"Are you planning on going to the funeral home today?"

He thought it was rather an odd question, coming from her. After all, her actual function here was to organize what was in the house, put a price on it and, hopefully, sell it. Granted, she was being helpful in other ways, but she *had* volunteered her services. He hadn't recruited her. In no way was that even remotely associated with his attendance—or nonattendance—at the funeral home.

"No," he responded. "Why would you want to know that?"

She shrugged carelessly and said, "No reason. I just thought you might want to be there to talk to some of her friends in case they had any questions or just wanted to talk to you."

"I'll be at the funeral," he reminded her somewhat stiffly. "If they have anything to ask, they can do it then." Although the very thought of being subjected to any sort of questions regarding his mother's final days—or even her final years—left him feeling exceedingly uncomfortable. He wouldn't be able to answer any of them because, quite frankly, he didn't know anything about the last ten years. His mother's supposed letters to him notwithstanding, there had been no contact between them during that time.

"Or they can ask you at the reception," she reminded him.

For a second, he'd forgotten about the reception. More to endure, he thought wearily. He didn't even bother attempting to contain the less than happy sigh that escaped. "Yeah, there's that, too."

She squashed the desire to offer him any comfort. The Keith standing before her wasn't the type to accept any overt gestures. That was why she had to go the indirect route she was taking.

"Well, if you're not going to the funeral home, why don't you come with me?"

"Come with you where?" he asked suspiciously.

Instead of answering his question, Kenzie hit him with a question of her own. "You don't like surprises, do you?"

"Surprises don't usually turn out to be a good thing."

She thought of the family gathering she was trying to bring him to. A fondness slipped over her, the way it always did whenever she thought of her family en masse. "Well, in this case I can guarantee you good food, good spirits and maybe even some singing." He still appeared rather skeptical about the whole idea—and she could tell that the singing part was definitely *not* a selling feature.

Still, she tried to make him come around by promising, "It'll be good for you."

The frown on Keith's face deepened. "The last time I heard that line, I was facing a plate of steamed vegetables."

Kenzie suppressed a laugh. "I promise this experience will be way better than a plate of vegetables. And it'll help you unwind."

That only managed to put him on his guard. "What makes you think I need to unwind?"

Kenzie rolled her eyes in response to his question. She couldn't help it. "Oh, please. I've seen balls of yarn that were less wound up than you."

Passing by him at the table, she crossed over to the sink. Kenzie turned on the water and began washing the dishes.

Still nursing the last of his coffee, Keith half rose in his seat. "You don't have to do that," he protested.

Maybe not, but someone had to, and she'd learned that molehills were a lot easier to tackle than mountains.

"Mrs. Sommers'll be showing the house soon. You don't want to let things like dirty dishes start accumulating."

She was doing it again, acting as if she knew him better than he knew himself. "What makes you think I wasn't going to wash those?" he asked.

Kenzie stopped washing for a minute and looked at him over her shoulder. Her answer to that was simplicity itself. "You're a man."

Keith scowled. "What's that supposed to mean?"

The smile on her lips softened the sting. "There are certain edicts out there in the cosmos. One of them states that men don't do dishes. They buy dishes, break dishes, sometimes borrow dishes, but they don't wash them if they can avoid it at all."

"Doesn't that smack of sexism?" he asked, prodding her.

"Maybe," Kenzie allowed generously. "That still doesn't change the fact that it's true," she concluded with a smile, then got back to her initial topic. "So, since you're not going to the funeral home, two o'clock okay with you?"

He was still distrustful of where this was going. Being a lawyer had changed the way he looked at everything. "For what?"

"For me to pick you up so you can come with me," she told him innocently, then asked, "Are you always this inattentive?"

"Only when I'm not interested," Keith replied truthfully.

"This'll do you good," she promised.

"You keep saying that. Just what sort of good would going off with you do me?" he asked.

Was she coming on to him? he suddenly wondered. He wouldn't have thought so. He had to admit that the idea was definitely not without its appeal. The woman was extremely compelling and, under other circumstances, he could see himself being really attracted to her—and acting on it. But he wasn't going to stay here long enough to even entertain that possibility, much less explore it. And he had never been into one-night stands.

"That's where the surprise part of this comes in," she told him glibly, coming full circle.

He fixed her with a look. "I think we've had this dance before."

Kenzie merely smiled, unfazed by the fact that he was leveling an accusation at her. "We have," she acknowledged, then proposed, "This time, just for fun, why don't you let me lead?"

What did he have to lose? Keith asked himself gamely. After all, in just three days, four at the most, he wasn't even going to be in the same longitude and latitude as this woman or as anyone else around here, for that matter.

Besides, he had to admit he did like her company—for the most part.

"Okay, why not?" he said with a shrug, surrendering—for now.

"Great," she answered. This had actually turned out to be easier than she thought.

Enthused—and because she did know him and they did go back all the way to high school—Kenzie allowed herself to go with her impulse. It was her way, but not usually with someone as standoffish as Keith had become.

Turning from the sink, her hands still wet from the dishes she'd just finished washing, Kenzie threw her arms around his neck and kissed him.

Her aim—and intention—had been to kiss his cheek. But, surprised by her sudden movement, he'd turned his head at the last second to look at her, puzzled.

He was about to ask her what she was doing, which was how his mouth happened to be open when her lips missed their intended target and instead locked onto his.

To say that he was surprised would have been a huge understatement.

In actuality, they were *both* surprised.

And even more surprising than that was the realization that something was going on here that went beyond the simple contact of lips. Way beyond.

This was the fantasy that she had nurtured the two years they had both been in high school at the same time.

Night after night, she'd dreamed about what it might actually feel like, kissing Keith. *Being* kissed by Keith.

Dreams, she now realized, didn't begin to do the actual sensation justice, even though this kiss had been unintentional.

Kenzie felt as if she had swallowed a match. A *lit* match, and it was setting her on fire. But it was a very pleasant, enjoyable fire, and with very little effort—

No, hold it, the voice of common sense all but screamed in her head in an attempt to redirect her attention. This just couldn't happen. At least, not by accident. If it did, that almost made her a predator. Whether he would admit it or not—whether he even *knew* it or not—Keith was very vulnerable right now, and she was taking advantage of that as surely as if she was a stalker, jumping at the first glimmer of an opportunity.

It didn't matter that she was as caught by surprise as he was. That she hadn't meant to do anything more than kiss his cheek. Circumstances had abruptly changed, and she needed to take that into account and backpedal as quickly as she could before something happened that couldn't be undone.

In a second, something inside her promised breathlessly, stalling for time.

He'd told Kenzie the truth. He didn't like surprises. But this—this was different. While it still fell under the general heading of being a surprise, it was so much more. He had no idea where to begin to categorize it or file it away. He clearly hadn't meant for this to happen, but now that it had, he was forced to look at Kenzie in a whole different light.

This was the girl he had gone to school with? The one everyone had laughingly referred to as Clumsy Mac?

Talk about still waters running deep. There was an entire sea here.

When contact between them was abruptly severed—and she had been the one to sever it, just as she had been the one to initiate it—Keith saw her flush and then mumble something that sounded like "Oops."

The word echoed back in his head, as if he'd somehow hit instant replay. The whole scenario struck him as ludicrous.

Before he could stop himself, he started to laugh.

Laugh so hard that his sides actually shook. And then tears came to his eyes. Whether they'd initially been stored there against anticipated further sorrow, he didn't know.

The laughter and the accompanying tears didn't abate immediately, not until he was almost exhausted.

Kenzie joined in and couldn't seem to stop, either, not until they both collapsed onto the floor in a crumbled heap, both too exhausted to move.

Finally, drawing in deep breaths, Keith found that his sanity was slowly restored.

"What just happened here?" he was finally able to ask, still bemused.

"I'm not sure," Kenzie told him honestly as she gathered herself together. "But I think we both needed it."

Though he wanted to protest, he knew she was right. He didn't exactly feel rejuvenated, but the oppressiveness that had been weighing him down the last few days seemed to have taken a few steps back, allowing him to regain his sense of self.

"So now what?" Keith asked, curious as to what she would say.

"Now we each take care of a few minor things that we need to see to, and I'll be back by two to pick you up."

Keith took in a deep breath. He was already having second thoughts that he'd said yes too soon and that he was going to regret this.

"About that—" he began.

Kenzie immediately began to shake her head, as if his words wouldn't be able to gain access to a moving target. "Sorry," she said, cutting Keith off before he could get any further. "My hearing seems to be clogged. Must have happened during that laugh-fest we just shared. Gotta run," she announced quickly, deliberately talking too fast for him to be able to get in a word edgewise.

Keith opened and then closed his mouth one last time as he heard the front door close with finality. He felt a little as if he'd been blitzkrieged.

The odd thing was, he discovered he wasn't angry or even mildly annoyed about it.

Instead, his mouth was curving in just the vaguest hint of a smile.

Kenzie wasn't true to her word. She wasn't back by two.

She was back *before* two.

MacKenzie Bradshaw was the only woman he'd ever encountered who was early, Keith thought with grudging admiration.

Though he had a feeling it was futile, he attempted to beg off one last time. "Look, I know I kind of agreed before, but—"

Kenzie flashed the same innocent look in response. "Still have that hearing problem," she told him. "Maybe it'll clear up by the time we get there."

It was a game and she knew it. A game because if Keith really didn't want to go, there was no way she could actually *make* him go. So these were just motions he was going through, possibly to satisfy some inner need to tell himself that he'd tried to resist but had gone along with what she proposed for reasons of maintaining the peace.

"Exactly where is 'there'?" she heard Keith asking her even as he followed her out of the house.

"The place we're supposed to be," she answered evasively, waiting for him to lock the front door.

Keith pocketed his key. For some odd reason, this effervescent woman had stirred his curiosity. He pretended to resist for form's sake, and he knew that she was aware of it. There was no question that if he really didn't want to do something or go somewhere, he didn't. It was that simple. He wasn't exactly a ninety-eight-pound weakling who could be flung over an adversary's shoulder and carried off, fireman style. At six-two, Keith couldn't be carried off anywhere.

But he wanted to see exactly where Kenzie felt he needed to go, so he went along with this, telling himself at he could bail at any time, calling a halt to it and just going home.

He noted that Kenzie, who was always dressed attractively, hadn't done anything out of the ordinary to her appearance, so they weren't going anywhere that required formal wear.

Apparently that was the only clue she was dispensing, because when he asked for more information, Kenzie very deftly sidestepped and avoided his attempts to extract it from her.

"And if I just refuse to go?" he asked as he watched her slide behind the steering wheel of her car.

"You promised me a filet mignon dinner if I deciphered your mother's handwriting in her address book, remember?"

He remembered. When he'd made the bet, he'd done

it knowing that if she won, it would allow him to take her out without the formality of actually *asking* her out. "We're going to dinner?" he questioned.

"No, but this can be in place of that." Kenzie put it in simpler terms. "You come with me, I absolve you of that bet. Fair enough?"

"Fair?" he echoed. In all honesty, he couldn't really answer that without getting further information to work with. Information he already knew he wasn't about to get ahead of time. She'd made that abundantly clear. "Ask me again after I get back," he told her.

A smile that could be described as nothing short of sexy, even by the most oblivious of people, curved the corners of her mouth.

At first glance, Keith found his reaction to the sight of her smile rather unsettling. And yet at the same time, the sight of her smile directed at him was oddly appealing.

At the root of it all, he had to surmise, was the accidental kiss they'd shared this morning. It had placed an entirely different spin on just about everything going on between them.

It certainly affected how he looked at her.

Maybe it had something to do with where he found himself right now—at loose ends, maybe even cast adrift. In two days he would have to go through the motions of a pantomime he had no desire to endure.

At this funeral, the attendees would be expecting him to play the part of a grieving son, but he'd been that already. Ten years ago he'd been that grieving son, as well as a grieving brother.

To lose Amy had been extremely rough on his soul. To lose his mother in the bargain had been all but crushing for him. He hadn't lost his mother literally—she was, after all, still breathing—but for all intents and purposes, he had lost the mother he had known all his life up to that tragic point.

After Amy died in the accident, his kind, loving, levelheaded mother had suddenly transformed into what amounted to a reckless teenager. As far as he was concerned, there was nothing more pitiable than a fifty-year-old teenager, but she had refused to listen to anything he said. He tried to reason with her, even asked her to seek help, but she'd turned him down. Desperate, hurting, he had continued to cajole and plead until finally he'd lost all patience with her.

And then one day, the collision he knew was coming came. Heated, angry words were exchanged. Words that, once they were out, couldn't be taken back.

Words that destroyed all the bridges that connected them to each other.

And even if those words could be taken back, they certainly couldn't be erased from memory. That was where they remained forever, and because they were there, nothing else was allowed to thrive.

"Are you all right?" Kenzie asked him gently.

Snapping out of it, Keith looked at her. "Yeah, sure. Why?"

"You got really quiet there, and you've got this strange look on your face," she told him.

Keith forced himself to smile for a second, pretending he hadn't been preoccupied with any sort of serious thoughts. "Just contemplating what kind of torture you have in mind for me."

Kenzie wasn't sure she believed him, but she played along, anyway. There was no point in pressing him. "Not torture," she promised. "And you'll see soon enough."

"I suppose I will," he replied quietly.

He didn't fool her for a minute, but the game continued, anyway. She was counting on her family to help her bring him around to the person she knew he used to be.

Chapter Eight

"It's a house," he said in surprise as Kenzie began to slow down at the curb before the well-kept two-story structure.

They'd turned in to a residential development, so he shouldn't have been surprised, but for some reason he'd thought she might be taking him to a more public place.

There was amusement in Kenzie's eyes as she smiled at him. "Nothing wrong with your powers of observation, I see."

He had no idea if she was being sarcastic or not. Had the words come from anyone else, he would have gone with the former. But from what he remembered of her from high school and what he'd been exposed to currently, Kenzie was far too positive a person to waste her time with sarcasm.

"It's my mom's house," she told Keith as she brought her vehicle to a complete stop and turned off the engine. Kenzie could see that he was less than thrilled about being

exposed to family, even if that family belonged to someone else. "Ginny's having a birthday party."

He left his seat belt buckled even though she was undo-
ing hers. He had no idea who Kenzie was talking about.
"Ginny?" he questioned.

Kenzie nodded, wondering if he was going to give
her a hard time, after all. "One of my nieces. She's three
today."

"You brought me to a kid's birthday party?" he asked
in disbelief. This was what he got for letting his guard
down and going along.

"I brought you to a *family* birthday party," Kenzie corrected him. "It just happens to be Ginny's birthday. If this
had been two weeks ago, it would have been my mother's
birthday. Most of the family live pretty busy lives," she
went on, opening the door on her side. "Birthdays are the
excuse we use to get together for a few hours."

He wasn't moving. Pausing, she bent down and looked
into the car at him. "The car's too big to fit in the living
room," she said matter-of-factly.

His eyebrows drew together. "What?"

"You're still buckled up," Kenzie said, nodding at the
fastened seat belt. "And I just thought you'd want to know
that the car is too big to take in with you, so you're going
to have to unbuckle the seat belt."

He was clearly having his doubts about attending.
"Maybe I should just stay here until you're done."

"Maybe you shouldn't," Kenzie countered cheerfully.
"The whole point is to get you out of the house and clear
your head," she told him.

He had his own way of unwinding that didn't involve
pretending to be interested in what strangers were talking about. "A glass of wine will clear my head."

"Not hardly," she told him. "Wine just makes things

fuzzy. C'mon," she coaxed him. "I've got a very friendly family and they don't bite—I promise. Besides, if you come in with me, you'll be doing me a favor."

"What kind of a favor?" Keith asked suspiciously. His hand hovered over the seat belt, which remained buckled.

She thought back to the other day and her sister's attempts to set her up with a blind date for dinner at her house. "If my siblings see me coming in with a breathing male under the age of fifty, they might leave me alone for a while."

He was no more enlightened now than he had been a moment ago. "I don't get it."

Sighing, Kenzie spelled it out for him. "They're all married. I'm not. I'm the youngest and somehow, through no fault of my own, I became everyone's favorite match-making project. If they see you, they'll cease and desist— at least for a little while—and I can breathe and focus on doing my job well instead of having to fend off their efforts."

Now he understood. "That sounds reasonable enough, I guess."

"Great." She closed the door on her side. "Now take a deep breath," she advised. "And let's go."

The second Keith got out of her car, Kenzie aimed her key fob at the vehicle and pressed it. Four locks all closed simultaneously.

The sounds of people talking, laughing, calling out to one another were all around him long before the front door of the house was opened.

Echoes from long ago rose up to meet Keith, and he stopped short of the front step.

He didn't know if he was up to this, willingly walking into a situation that was already resurrecting memories he had absolutely no desire to revisit.

Memories that had been, until now, too painful for him.

The next moment, just before he started to turn away, he felt Kenzie weaving her arm through his as if it were a long practiced maneuver. Before he could say a word in protest—or tell her that he had definitely changed his mind—the front door opened, and he found himself drawn inside by a woman with warm eyes and a warmer smile. A woman, he realized, who looked exactly like an older version of Kenzie.

"Come in. You're just in time," she told them.

"Just in time?" he repeated more quietly, glancing at Kenzie as they followed the woman into the living room—a room filled with people, large and small.

"She means that they haven't sung 'Happy Birthday' yet. Mom," Kenzie said, raising her voice as she called out to the older woman. When Mrs. Bradshaw turned around, Kenzie said, "You remember Keith O'Connell. Keith, this is my mom, Andrea."

"Yes, of course," Andrea replied, taking his hand and shaking it.

He didn't see how that was possible—he had no memory of ever encountering the woman—but he played along and returned the smile.

Keith still didn't want to be here, but he couldn't leave without causing a scene. That seemed like rather a ludicrous thing to do, given that the people here were participating in a child's birthday party, so he refrained.

Making the best of it, Keith told himself that for the duration of an hour or ninety minutes, he could put up with this charade. For some reason, Kenzie wanted him here, and in a way, he did owe her. After all, she had handled all the extraneous details surrounding the funeral and reception for him. And that, in turn, had taken some of the weight of this whole experience off his shoulders.

"Kenzie, you made it. And you brought a man." The woman who swooped down on them from the left looked as if she were another older version of Kenzie. Younger than her mother, so this had to be a sister, he guessed. An older, *pregnant* sister, he amended as he got a better view of the woman who was currently giving him a very thorough once-over.

"Yes, I did, but he's not for Ginny," Kenzie responded, smiling at her sister. "This," she continued, placing the gaily wrapped package she had brought with her into her sister's hands, "is for our birthday girl."

"And this is?" Marcy asked, clearly not easily diverted. She also didn't bother to hide the fact that she was still giving her sister's companion a very close inspection.

After another moment, Kenzie gathered from the expression on Marcy's face that Keith had met with her sister's guarded approval.

"Is Keith," Kenzie answered, deliberately being mysterious and leaving out his last name. "That's all you need to know. Keith, meet Marcy Bradshaw Crawford. She's just one of my meddlesome siblings," she warned him. "All four of them smile and look harmless, but trust me, they're not. This, however," Kenzie declared, never missing a beat as she scooped up her niece, who had launched herself at her from across the room, "is a regular little charmer. However, she's prone to sneak attacks."

Laughing, she swung the little girl around in a circle before putting Ginny down again. "Don't turn your back on her for a second," she told Keith.

She said it so seriously that Ginny looked up at her, an impatient expression on her small, thin face. "Don't worry. I won't hurt him, Aunt Kenzie."

"I know, Pumpkin. But you're quick, and I'm afraid that my friend here isn't used to that." She'd said that strictly for Ginny's benefit, so the little girl would feel more confident about herself. An anticipated new arrival in the family was a time for shifting dynamics and self-doubts, and she just wanted to be sure that her niece was equipped to weather it well.

Kenzie tousled the little girl's hair, knowing the day wasn't far away that Ginny would be looking to disentangle herself from her parents and the rest of the family and go off with her friends.

Way of the world, she thought with resignation.

Keith had assumed that he could just remain on the sidelines, hidden in plain sight, so to speak. That way, he didn't have to get involved in any of the conversations that were going on all around him.

Or so he thought, only to discover he was sadly mistaken.

There was no such thing as standing on the sidelines when it came to Kenzie's family. He found himself engulfed in warm voices, had questions directed at him that rang with genuine interest and was on the receiving end of amusing stories to the extent that he quickly discovered he didn't even know which way to turn or whose question to answer first.

He also discovered that there was no place to hide. Even more surprising, he didn't really want to, at least not all that much.

To his relief, Kenzie came to his rescue when he found himself facing questions about the cases he took on as a lawyer.

"No shop talk, Tom," she told her brother, wedging herself in between her oldest sibling and Keith. "I promised Keith that this afternoon was all about unwinding, not grilling."

Slipping her arm through his, she gently led Keith away from the small cluster of guests.

"I take it we're not leaving yet," Keith said. To his own surprise, he wasn't having that bad a time. This experience, forced though it was, was not without its merits.

"Soon," she murmured, drawing him over to another gathering.

She repeatedly came to his rescue several more times that afternoon and early evening.

Contrary to what he thought was happening—that he would stay for a total of sixty minutes, maybe ninety— by the end of his self-imposed time limit, Keith discovered that he was more than amenable to remaining for a little while longer.

That officially ended as dusk was creeping up out of the Pacific waters, looking to embrace whatever it could in order to remain around.

At first, Keith had really tried not to take part in the conversations. He thought, after remaining deliberately closed-mouthed once or twice, that would be the end of it.

However, he had no idea just how unobtrusively persistent Kenzie's family members—from the oldest member to the youngest—could be when it came to doing something they believed, in their heart of hearts, was the right thing. Apparently, getting him to talk fell under that heading.

Drawing him out in conversation had been tricky to say the least, but to Keith's amazement, he was no match for even the youngest of Kenzie's clan.

And just like that, he was pulled in.

Pulled into the conversation and consequently, by and by, pulled into the family dynamic, as well.

That was how one hour turned into two and two into

four. Before he knew it, most of the day had gone by. Moreover, he wasn't the least bit annoyed by this.

He liked these unassuming, down-to-earth people even though he initially felt that he had nothing in common with them. But he—and they—had all initially come from a working class mother and father who took on any kind of work to keep their children dressed and fed. That, he discovered, was the American dream to Kenzie's parents, and they had captured it in the palms of their hands, passing it down to their children.

And although it was very much against his will at first, when Kenzie's mother came up to him to exchange a few words later that evening, Keith couldn't help thinking of his own mother—the way she had once been, not the woman whose burial service he was going to be attending the day after tomorrow.

With a great deal of effort, Keith shook off the memory. Nothing good would come of going there. He had to remember that—and resist the temptation to do otherwise.

"I think our birthday girl is ready to be taken home, don't you?" Andrea asked him.

The little girl was sitting beside him on the sofa, her head lolling to one side. She was obviously asleep and had been for the last twenty minutes or so, after valiantly struggling to keep her eyes open. She'd finally lost the battle. Her even, measured breathing attested to that.

"It is getting late," Keith agreed. His mother had been very strict about bedtime when he was Ginny's age. Apparently, Kenzie's family didn't feel the same way.

Kenzie picked up his cue. Looking at Keith, she inclined her head so that only he could hear her and said, "You've more than paid off your debt. Would you like to go back to your house?"

The candles had been blown out and the cake had long

since been eaten. Ginny had gone on to daintily remove the wrapping paper from her gifts. Some of the paper, evading cleanup, still littered parts of the floor. Ginny might have fallen asleep, but her older cousins were awake, and some of them were playing with her gifts, all under their mothers' watchful eyes.

All in all, it was a scene out of a Norman Rockwell painting, only done one better. Keith felt a very odd sensation of longing stirring inside before he managed to block it and lock it away.

"Are you serious?" Keith asked, surprised that Kenzie would come around so easily—and on her own, too. He had become fairly convinced that in order to leave the premises before midnight, he would be forced to come up with some sort of an elaborate escape plan.

Not that he really wanted to all that much.

Maybe there was something in the punch, Keith thought.

Obviously amused by his response, Kenzie grinned at him. That grin was getting to him, working its way under his skin. He was finding her harder and harder to ignore or even keep at bay.

"It would be too cruel to tease you like that," she told him, whispering the words into his ear and creating, unbeknownst to her, waves of warmth that undulated through him. "Yes, I'm serious," she assured him.

To prove it, Kenzie rose to her feet.

The birthday girl chose that moment to wake up. Rubbing her eyes, Ginny looked up at her aunt. The expression on her face silently asked if the fact that Kenzie was on her feet meant that another present was possibly coming her way.

"We've got to get going, sweetie," she told Ginny— and thereby also informed all those who needed to be informed that they were leaving. "We've got a lot of things to do tomorrow."

Rather than say anything to her, Ginny turned to look at Keith. With all the guile of a four-year-old, she asked, "Are you gonna come back?"

The little girl had caught him completely off guard. When Keith opened his mouth, it was to offer what he felt was a valid excuse. "I don't live around here."

"But you can always come back," Ginny pointed out.

"Maybe some time," Keith conceded evasively, not about to get into involved explanations. It occurred to him that he couldn't remember the last time someone had actually *wanted* his presence enough to question the excuse he offered.

"He's going to be very busy, Ginny," Kenzie said, once again coming to his rescue.

"But sometime?" she questioned hopefully, looking at Keith with large, soulful blue eyes.

"Sometime," Kenzie echoed, making the nebulous word sound more like a promise.

Ginny flashed Kenzie a big smile, then surprised Keith by jumping to her feet and awarding him a quick, fierce hug before turning her attention back to her newly acquired loot.

"You look stunned," Kenzie observed as they made their way to the door amid a chorus of goodbyes from the people who remained. "Never been hugged by a little girl before?" she guessed.

He thought of making some sort of flippant remark or excuse, then reconsidered and went with the plain truth. "Not to my recollection."

"Makes you feel good, doesn't it?"

He grunted something unintelligible. It was enough to make her smile to herself.

"I think you made a big impression on my niece," Kenzie said as they were walking back to her car. "As well as on my family," she added.

To her surprise, Keith had actually remembered most of her family's names during the course of the day. That nice guy she'd been trying to reach was beginning to surface.

The moon lit their way, allowing her to see Keith's expression. It had been a long day, and part of her had expected him to be annoyed or, at the very least, beleaguered. But he appeared to be neither. That was another nice surprise.

"Yeah, well, that worked both ways," Keith told her after a couple of beats.

Kenzie got the impression that he had first debated the pros and cons of voicing his reaction to the little girl before saying anything.

"You have a nice family."

He couldn't have said anything better or more meaningful to her.

"Thanks. I think so," she said without any hesitation or embarrassment. "There are times I'd like to strangle one or more of my siblings, but for the most part, I have to agree with you. They really *are* nice." Then she added, "I'll bet you're really tired. I'd better take you home so you get enough rest to help me tackle the pricing tomorrow."

"Pricing?" he echoed, confused.

"Of the things going into the first wave of the estate sale. I decided that it should start tomorrow." That had changed from her original plan, but she thought it best to keep Keith busy rather than dwelling on the situation— and his loss, even if he didn't want to admit it. "Remember? I asked if you had any objections to doing it before the funeral, and you were all for getting started."

He grunted in agreement, but the truth of it was, he'd actually forgotten that conversation. Attending the birthday party, being transported down memory lane by a family-friendly scenario that was so similar to what he'd grown up with, had temporarily driven thoughts of everything else out of his head.

But it all came back to him now as reality returned to wrap him in its cold embrace.

He pushed the emotion aside and dwelled only on what needed to be done.

Chapter Nine

He'd meant to be gone before the whole thing got underway.

When he had fallen asleep last night, Keith had had every intention of being gone before the estate sale, or even the preparations for displaying the items, had begun. Although if he were being honest with himself, he hadn't really a clue as to where "gone" was physically located. He hadn't gotten that far along in figuring out his escape plan when sleep had suddenly—and silently—overtaken him.

Sleep had brought dreams, something that he hadn't experienced in a very long time. Years, as a matter of fact. Nocturnal episodes in his life these past few years were defined by being awake, then finding himself waking up. Sleep, obviously, occurred in between those two end posts, but it brought no dreams with it that he was aware of, certainly none that he could summon once his eyes were open and his brain shook off its fuzzy, unfocused state.

But last night had been different. Last night, when he'd fallen asleep, he'd had dreams, tiny snatches of dreams. Dreams that couldn't have lasted for more than a few moments. Dreams that he was in this house, the house where he'd grown up, but rather than Amy and his mother, the people inhabiting his childhood home had been Kenzie's family.

A couple of times during these disjointed, rambling segments that seemed to fill his head, he thought he'd caught sight of Amy. When that happened, he immediately attempted to follow her. But whenever he entered the room he was positive she was in, he found he was wrong. She wasn't there. In her place were a whole bunch of nieces and nephews and various assorted other relatives, all of whom belonged to Kenzie.

And yet, somehow, there was this unspoken feeling that these relatives infiltrating his dreams also belonged to him.

Part of him was convinced, during these recurring sequences, that he was in fact dreaming, and all he needed to do to end this was to wake up.

Easier thought than executed.

No matter how hard he tried, his eyes just would not open, and as long as they stayed closed, he remained within the confines of this endless dreamlike state.

After numerous attempts, when Keith finally *did* manage to pry open his eyes—his lids felt as if they weighed a ton—daylight wasn't tiptoeing into the bedroom.

It had come *stomping* into the room.

The moment his brain registered that fact—as well as the fact that it was the morning of the sale—he sat bolt upright.

The sudden movement brought a severe penalty with it. His head began to pound, producing one of those inexplicable morning headaches that insisted on haunting him every so often. He'd suffered through them on occasion ever since he'd been a child. They made thinking clearly nothing short of a challenge.

Keith sat perfectly still for approximately thirty seconds, taking in a deep breath and vainly trying to center himself. When that failed, he threw off his bedclothes and went directly into his bathroom. After shedding his clothing, Keith got into the shower stall. With quick, efficient movements, he did his best to wash the imagery out of his brain as he showered.

Seven minutes later, he'd dried off, dressed and was walking out of his bedroom. In his conservative estimation, he had about fifteen minutes to vacate the premises before Kenzie arrived and descended on him.

He estimated wrong.

The second he was in the hallway, walking toward the stairs, Keith instantly knew he had sorely miscalculated. The warm, inviting aroma of coffee was wafting up the stairs and tantalized him.

It also mocked him.

He knew he hadn't had the presence of mind to program his coffeemaker last night. That meant either he had a warm, hospitable burglar who had broken into his house and decided to make coffee for him while he was at it—or Kenzie was here early, champing at the bit to get the sale underway.

Making coffee was more her style.

Keith caught part of himself rooting for the burglar. At least then he could quickly leave the premises without having to offer any excuses or to beg off.

Reminding himself that he was the one in charge here

and that Kenzie, in point of fact, actually worked for him did absolutely no good.

It wasn't that he felt he couldn't stand up to her and make his point known. It was just that for some reason, while he was standing up and making his point, Kenzie seemed able to steamroller right over logic—and him.

He ran into her on the stairs.

Kenzie was going up holding a steaming cup of hot coffee in her hands—her bribe of choice—and he was on his way down, still vainly hoping to execute some sort of an eleventh-hour great escape before she saw him. That boat, of course, had instantly sailed off the moment that their eyes met.

Kenzie grinned as she stopped walking. "You're up," she noted cheerfully.

"Looks that way," he responded, silently berating himself for not setting an alarm to wake him up earlier.

Keith glanced over her shoulder at the front door. He was just several yards short of an escape, he couldn't help thinking almost wistfully.

So near and yet so far.

"I brought you coffee," Kenzie told him.

His attention was drawn back to the woman directly in front of him. "I figured that part out on my own," he responded flippantly.

Kenzie wasn't about to comment on his less than sunny disposition. Kenzie thought his surliness might have something to do with the fact that people would be going through, paying for and carting off bits and pieces of his former life.

That had to be rough. But that was exactly why she *had* given him the option of holding some things back, of vetoing any item from going on sale.

However, he had declined to even entertain the idea,

much less executing it, saying, "As far as I'm concerned, you can sell the whole household as one big lot if it means getting rid of everything."

In her heart, she refused to believe he actually meant that. At least, she was sure he didn't mean it about *everything* in the house. The man whom she'd gotten to interact with her family was definitely not devoid of all feelings and emotions.

Those emotions and feelings were most likely buried rather deeply because of his sister's death.

People reacted differently to tragedies of that magnitude. Some rallied, and it became their finest hour. Others fell to pieces and were never quite the same again.

Most people, however, fell somewhere in between, with an entire spectrum of emotions. And she wanted to help him navigate the spectrum if she possibly could.

Surrendering the coffee cup to him, Kenzie made a U-turn on the stairs and headed back down. "There's breakfast in the kitchen if you're interested," she added.

"Good place for it,"

Hand on the banister, Kenzie paused and looked over her shoulder at him. "*Your* breakfast."

He did his best to seem disinterested, fully aware now that if he gave Kenzie an inch, she would create a little village on it.

"I didn't ask for any."

The coffee felt like liquid heaven going down, though. He was forced to admit secretly that the woman really knew how to make one hell of a cup of coffee.

"No, you didn't," Kenzie agreed. "But you do need to eat and keep up your strength."

He stared at the back of the blond head as he walked behind her. That was an odd thing to say, he thought. Why would she think he needed strength? "Are you entering me in a weight lifting contest?"

Coming to the bottom of the stairs, she turned around to look at him. "No, but I would like you to carry some things out to the driveway for me. Pablo pulled a muscle, so I told him to stay home and take care of himself."

"Pablo?" he echoed. Who was that? He was fairly certain he hadn't met anyone by that name at her niece's birthday party last night.

"Pablo's my assistant and general, all-around handy person," she explained.

"I take it he's not very handy with a pulled muscle." Finishing off the coffee, Keith left the cup on the first flat surface nearest the staircase.

"None of us is." Deftly she scooped up the cup, quickly carrying it to the kitchen, where his breakfast was waiting for him beneath a covered dish on the kitchen counter. "And, like I said, he's home, resting. I arranged everything that's going on sale today in boxes, but now the boxes need to find their way outside to the tables."

"Tables?"

Nothing was making immediate sense to him. Keith was beginning to feel like Alice in Wonderland after she slid down the rabbit hole. Quite an identity crisis for a thirty-two-year-old male, he couldn't help thinking.

Kenzie nodded, patiently explaining, "The ones I set up under the canopy in your driveway."

"My driveway—the driveway," he amended, still doing his best to distance himself from the house and the woman who had lived alone here for the past ten years, "doesn't have a canopy."

"It does for today," she contradicted him. "And for later this week when the sales resume."

Because she wanted to be respectful of his mother, she

was putting the sale on hold the day of the funeral. But since Keith was in a hurry to have it all over with, the sale would resume the day after that.

"The canopy catches the neighbors' eye—and it also protects some of the more delicate items from being damaged by the sun," she added. "Don't forget, some of the things are old and very delicate."

Keith just shook his head. She had gone too far in her efforts to protect things he had no use for or desire to preserve.

"You're the expert," he commented in a tone that said what he thought was the exact opposite.

Kenzie took pride in the fact that she was good at her job and even better at not getting drawn into any sort of a confrontation about minor matters. Long ago, she had learned to pick her fights, and this was definitely not meant to be one of them. She sensed that despite Keith's bravado, he *was* having a hard time with what was happening.

For all she knew, he hadn't even made his peace with his mother's death. If that was the case, it would hit him really hard down the line.

"Thank you for that," she said quietly. "Now eat your breakfast while it's still warm and then come out and help me show off the first wave of items to their best advantage."

Keith picked up the dish from the counter, removing the cover and leaving it behind. He sat down at the table. He noticed she'd set utensils out for him. She didn't miss a thing.

"It's a glorified garage sale," he pointed out. "There *is* no showing things off to their best advantage, no matter what you try."

Kenzie was not easily dissuaded. Flashing one of her

dazzling smiles, she told him as she left the kitchen, "You'd be surprised."

And, he discovered shortly thereafter, he was.

Half an hour after he had carried out close to ten boxes of memorabilia and then retreated into the house, Keith moved the curtain aside from the living room window and saw that there were people lining up on his driveway, waiting their turn to approach the very end of a long table.

They were holding items they had discovered at the sale in one hand and money in the other. They were all queuing up to reach Kenzie. She was on the other side of the long rectangular table, ringing up these found treasures on what looked to be an old-fashioned cash register.

Keith decided that it was time for him to make himself scarce.

He had no attachment to these items, he silently insisted for the tenth or so time. But watching them being snatched up and then paraded out to waiting vehicles still felt somewhat disconcerting to him.

Rather than attempt to explore the reason he'd feel this way, Keith decided not to witness any of it.

Grabbing a jacket—December in Southern California didn't exactly bring visions of icicles to mind, but for this area, it did feel rather cold this year—he made his way out of the house.

His car was parked a little down the block. He was aware that if he got back too soon, his space and just about every other space, would be taken, but right now, all Keith could focus on was making a successful escape.

He thought he could slip out unnoticed, but he should have known better.

Apparently Clumsy Mac had developed eyes in the back of her head as well as what amounted to a sixth sense.

As he tried to leave, she called out to him, asking him a question that made absolutely no sense to him. "So, are you going to go out to look for a tree?"

Completely baffled by her question, he turned around to look at Kenzie. Several people in the immediate area, he noticed, appeared to be invested in this possible exchange between them. But given that she was ringing up sales and surrounded by people, he couldn't very well take her aside to ask her what she was talking about.

He did his best to ignore the others, mostly women, listening in as he crossed over to her and asked, "Come again?"

"A tree," she repeated, enunciating the words slowly. "Are you going out to look for a tree?"

"Why would I want to look for a tree? There are trees all over the place here."

Kenzie smiled at him, and he caught himself wondering how a smile could be both sensually appealing and damn annoying at the same time.

"A Christmas tree," Kenzie specified.

Okay, now she was either kidding or she'd lost her mind, Keith concluded.

"I can't think of a single reason why I'd want to go out to buy a Christmas tree, of all things." His tone was dismissive as he turned to walk to his car.

Kenzie quickly made her way around the long table to reach him. "I'll be right back," she promised the person who was about to be rung up. Catching up to Keith, she took hold of his arm so that she could slow his pace. "Mrs. Sommers said that it would help with the sale of the house."

Keith frowned as he tried to remember the real estate agent telling him that. This was news to him. "When did she say that?" he questioned, giving Kenzie the benefit of the doubt.

"She mentioned it to me when she gave me the details about this job. She said that houses were hard to sell this time of year because kids are in school and the holidays are coming up. But according to her, the one thing that helps sell a house even around Christmas is highlighting the season, emphasizing that warm, fuzzy, greeting card commercial kind of thing. Ergo, getting a really terrific Christmas tree and displaying it in a prominent place in the house."

He couldn't believe he was hearing her correctly. A house was a house. It was either a good buy or it wasn't. How was adding what amounted to disposable ginger-bread supposed to change that?

"You're serious?" he asked in disbelief, giving her the opportunity to recant.

"Are you serious about selling the house?"

To his credit, he managed to contain his impatience. "Yes."

"Then I'm serious. It's not my suggestion," she pointed out. "It was hers."

A wave of frustration washed over him. "I don't even know where to find an artificial tree," Keith began.

It had been ages since he'd even had a Christmas tree. The last time was roughly ten years ago, in his dorm room. He didn't bother celebrating the season these days. Once Amy was gone, Christmas had ceased to mean anything to him.

Kenzie shook her head. "No, not an artificial tree. A *real* Christmas tree," she insisted.

He blew out a breath. "Even more of a mystery," he told her.

She held up her index finger as if that would somehow hold him in his place. "Give me a few minutes."

"And you'll do what? Conjure up a Christmas tree?" he asked, only half kidding. At this point, he wasn't sure just what MacKenzie Bradshaw was capable of, but he put nothing past the woman.

"No," Kenzie told him. "I'm going to 'conjure up' re-inforcements."

If he were thinking clearly, he would have just waved a dismissive hand in her direction and gotten into his car, going in search of not a Christmas tree—that was just absurd—but some peace and quiet. Most of all, in search of some much-needed rest from all of Kenzie's seemingly never-ending, relentless cheerfulness.

He always liked to believe he was a clear thinker.

And yet, for some reason, against all logic, he stayed where he was—just as she'd asked him to.

Chapter Ten

"Exactly who are you waiting for?" Keith asked her impatiently ten minutes later.

As he spoke, he circumvented the long display table to get on the other side, where she was standing. He knew she'd placed a call when she'd asked him to wait—and then she'd gone back to business as usual.

He turned his back to the eager-looking older woman who had just, in her words, "scored a really fantastic deal." The woman had one arm wrapped around each of the two tall, sturdy antique lamps, lamps that had stood on the nightstands that flanked his mother's bed for as far back as he could remember.

Though he had told Kenzie to get rid of everything, seeing the lamps being carried off by someone else felt decidedly strange.

With effort, he focused on the question he'd put to Kenzie and not the oddly bittersweet memory.

"Them," Kenzie answered with a touch of relief in her voice, happily pointing to someone directly behind him.

Turning around, Keith saw that Kenzie's mother and one of her sisters—the one who wasn't pregnant—were coming toward them from the curb where they'd parked a car.

Kenzie's mother smiled at him first before addressing her daughter. "Keith, how nice to see you again so soon."

If he closed his eyes, he could have sworn he'd just heard a deeper version of Kenzie's voice. "The feeling is mutual," he replied. The lawyer in him produced automatic responses.

Andrea Bradshaw turned her attention to her daughter. "You're lucky you caught us."

"Talk about giving short notice," Marilyn commented, shaking her head. "This has to be your all-time best—or worst, given your point of view."

"Desperate times, desperate measures," Kenzie said to her sister, then turned toward her mother. She paused to kiss the woman's cheek first. "Hi, Mom. Thanks for coming."

"What's so desperate?" Andrea asked. She was directing the question to her daughter but looking at Keith, making it rather obvious that she thought the source of the emergency might very well lie with him.

Without a second's hesitation, Kenzie said, "We need to go Christmas tree shopping."

Keith was about to deny her statement, saying that not only there was no need but also he wasn't about to go shopping for anything, much less a Christmas tree. He noticed that Kenzie's mother appeared to take the whole thing in stride, as did some of the women who were browsing through his mother's possessions.

Only her sister, Marilyn, appeared confused. "Come again?" she asked, giving him a very curious look.

He began to issue his denial, but Kenzie cut him off. "Long story. I'll explain later," she promised, getting her purse from a box she had tucked beneath the long table. "Besides, I knew you two miss the thrill of selling unique things." Kenzie paused to brush a quick, affectionate kiss against her mother's cheek. "We won't be gone long."

"Take as much time as you need," Andrea told her youngest, waving Kenzie on her way. "Make sure you pick a good one," she added, addressing her words to Keith before turning her attention to the next woman in line.

"The thrill of selling?" Keith echoed. With her arm through his, Kenzie was hustling him away from the driveway with its teeming buyers and eager customers and toward the light blue SUV she had driven today.

"My mother ran the business before she opted to retire and sell it to me. Marilyn worked at the store part-time when she was in college, same as me." Kenzie smiled at him over the hood of her car just before getting in. "See, I didn't leave your goods in the hands of amateurs."

He shrugged, doing his best to cling to his aloof stance. "Wouldn't matter if you did. Whatever's left, you can have some charity pick up." Getting in, he pulled the door shut and then buckled up. "Just so we're clear, I'm not looking to fund my 401-K with the net proceeds from this sale."

"We're clear," she assured him, turning on the ignition. "And just for the record, you don't have to justify anything to me. Whatever you want is fine with me."

Whatever he wanted.

Funny how that choice of words seemed to nudge thoughts into his head that hadn't been there a moment ago. Thoughts that had far more to do with this whirlwind behind the steering wheel next to him than with the business of wrapping up loose ends.

Whatever he wanted…

What if what he wanted wasn't some formless thing or a concept but something a great deal more real than that? What if he wanted to step out of the moment and into a scenario that had far more to do with the needs and desires between a man and a woman?

Between himself and Kenzie?

What was going on with him? The woman was talking about his mother's possessions, not about anything personal.

Maybe this concept of not having any ties to anyone was getting to him, and subconsciously he was trying to make a connection, *any* connection.

Could that be why he suddenly found himself having feelings *for* and feelings *about* Kenzie?

Ridiculous. He didn't have feelings for Kenzie, he silently insisted. He needed to get a grip.

What he really needed was to be away from her, not confined with her in a space that was smaller than the average closet.

He had to get out.

"Look, why don't you just drop me off somewhere and go on ahead by yourself?" he suggested, scanning the area they were passing to see if it looked familiar to him.

Kenzie spared him a glance as she quickly squeezed through a yellow light. "And why would I want to do something like that?"

"Because you have more experience at this tree-buying thing than I do, and you obviously like the idea of shopping for a Christmas tree." Shifting so that he could reach the wallet in his pocket, he wrapped his fingers around the smooth leather and extracted it. "You can get two of them. One for yourself—my treat," he emphasized, producing two hundred-dollar bills.

"You're too late," she told him, amused.

"You've already got a tree?" he guessed, surprised.

Kenzie looked at him as if she couldn't believe he was actually asking the question. "Christmas is in a few days. Of course I have a tree."

"Of course," he echoed.

The words were no sooner out of his mouth than he had to brace his hands against the dashboard to keep from leaning into her. Kenzie had taken a sharp turn into a parking lot. It was located before a cluster of stores. A supermarket filled up more than half of that area.

"Why are we—? Oh." Keith had started to ask why they were stopping here, but then he saw the answer.

There, in a roped-off section before the entrance to the grocery store, was a collection of Christmas trees of varying sizes. They were clustered over to one side, each apparently in need of a good home. At least, that's what he assumed she'd say to him if he happened to ask.

Kenzie turned off the engine, unbuckled her seat belt and slid out of her seat. She was about to close her door when she saw that he still hadn't budged.

"Well, c'mon," she urged. "The tree isn't about to select itself and jump onto our roof. We have to single it out and pay for it first."

This whole trip was silly. It only made him acutely aware of the fact that being in an enclosed space with Kenzie aroused him, which was just about the very last thing in the world he wanted.

"You know, having a tree in the living room or wherever isn't going to sell the house any faster," he told her cynically.

"Maybe not, but not having one might just send a bad

message to the prospective buyer about the so-called 'vibrations' that came with the house," she told him. "Trust me, you need to do just about everything you can to tip the scales in your favor. And it never hurts to take your agent's advice. Real estate can be a rather a cutthroat competition at times."

Maybe she had a point, after all. In any event, they were here. Shrugging, he said, "Sure, why not? I'll get a tree. Anything else? Warm kittens? A fuzzy puppy?"

"If you had a fuzzy puppy, that wouldn't hurt, but it's too late to get one and try to train it to respond to you on cue for the buyers' benefit. That sort of thing always backfires. But having a pretty Christmas tree should do the trick," she assured him. "Not to mention that putting the tree up and decorating it might just cheer you up, as well."

His back went up automatically. "Who says I need cheering up?" he asked. When she started to laugh, he decided to drop that line of questioning. But she'd also said something else he couldn't just ignore. "What do you mean, 'decorating'?" he asked.

"Decorations. You know, balls, garland, some tinsel." She paused, looking at him, waiting for the light to dawn or, barring that, the frown to fade. When it didn't, she asked, "What part of that don't you understand?"

"The part where I'm the one doing it," Keith answered bluntly. "I don't decorate Christmas trees," he informed her flatly.

"Ever?" she questioned incredulously. She remembered Amy talking about the ritual that had been involved in decorating her family Christmas tree. One day just for setting the tree up, two days for the lights and then one day for all the rest of the decorations. Her friend had never indicated that Keith wasn't part of this tradition.

"Not in the last ten years."

It seemed to her that everything of any true meaning in Keith's life had come to an abrupt stop with his sister's death. Her heart ached for him.

"Then maybe it's about time you got back in the game," she told him gently.

Though he got out of the vehicle, he felt wounds opening up. Old, painful wounds. "Why? Because you say so?"

"No, because it's the right thing to do," she answered quietly.

He looked at Kenzie pointedly. She was trying to manipulate his life. What gave her the right? "According to?"

"Everybody," she answered without hesitation. "Don't resist so hard," Kenzie gently cajoled, treating him with kid gloves. "Why not put that energy toward getting the job done?"

He knew exactly what he wanted to do with that energy, and putting up a Christmas tree was not it.

Even so, he fell into step beside her as they went to look at potential Christmas trees. But he didn't want her to think that it wasn't under protest. "I'll help you get a tree, but I'm not decorating it."

"Uh-huh." Kenzie smiled.

"About time you got back," were the first words out of Marilyn's mouth when she saw her sister and Keith getting out of Kenzie's vehicle. "I was beginning to give up hope."

"Don't let her snow you," Andrea spoke up, handing a young boy who had just bought his mother a Christmas present his change. "She's been having the time of her life."

Marilyn tossed her head, her hair bouncing against her shoulders. "That's because I'm such a good actress."

Andrea ignored her older daughter's play for sympathy. She smiled warmly as she scrutinized the fruits of Kenzie and Keith's hunt.

"I see you got the tree. Very nice," she approved. "Marilyn and I can stay on out here while you decorate it."

Marilyn groaned, then murmured, "Sorry," to the woman in front of her who was examining an intricately carved vase.

Kenzie laughed. "That's okay, Mom. You and Marilyn have done more than enough. The tree'll keep. Keith and I can decorate it after we close up for the day."

Her comment surprised Keith. He thought that this argument had been settled earlier when they had gone looking for this damn Christmas tree she'd been so set on finding. He really should have known better. "Wait, what?"

"The tree can keep for a few hours," she said to him before turning back to her mother. "I can take over now, Mom. And thanks for all your help," she added with sincerity. Turning toward her sister, she said, "You, too, Marilyn."

Her sister muttered something unintelligible in response. Kenzie knew better than to ask Marilyn to repeat it.

The first day of the estate sale lasted until the appointed time on the flyers she'd posted around the development: five o'clock. At exactly one minute after five, Kenzie tendered her regrets to the handful of stragglers left, promising to reopen the estate sale in two days, at which time the remaining items would be available.

"Why not tomorrow?" one woman asked.

Aware that Keith might be within earshot, Kenzie worded her answer carefully. "The lady who owned this house is being buried tomorrow. It wouldn't seem right to hold the sale during her funeral."

"Oh." The single word was laced with contrition and unspoken apologies.

"Thank you for your business, ladies," Kenzie announced, officially closing down the sale.

She waited for the women to leave the driveway and make their way to their vehicles. Satisfied that the last of the potential customers had left the premises, Kenzie began to pack up the items that still hadn't sold.

As she tucked them into boxes she'd kept under the tables, she was surprised, not to mention pleased, to have Keith pitch in. He began putting the remaining items away without saying a single word.

"You don't have to do this," she told him. This was really her job, not his. That had been part of the initial arrangement.

"It'll go faster this way," he responded.

Finished packing, he realized that she was planning on closing up the tables and putting them into the garage for the time being. He was about to tell her to leave them out when it occurred to him that she wanted them cleared away because of the funeral reception tomorrow. She seemed more concerned about decorum than he was.

Blowing out a breath, he got on one side of the table and pushed after she'd removed the extension, closing the section so that the table was one half its original size. Done, he dragged the table into the garage, then closed it.

"Thanks," she told him, flashing the smile that he caught himself looking forward to seeing.

"No problem. Does that get me out of decorating that thing?" he asked, nodding at the house. They'd carried in the Christmas tree earlier.

"If you really don't want to decorate the tree, you don't have to. I can do it by myself." It was a simple statement of fact and not punctuated with a pout.

He eyed her suspiciously and shook his head.

"What's the matter?" she asked him.

"I'm beginning to know you. You don't give up that easily."

"I'm not giving up, but I certainly can't strong-arm you into doing it," she pointed out. "That would be physically impossible." She paused before adding, "But I do think you should decorate the tree."

"Why?" he challenged her. He sensed that he was doomed and that he'd wind up decorating this tree, but he wanted her to work for it.

"Think of it as a tribute to your mother," she urged him. "The women coming back from the funeral will find it very touching that you went out of your way like this to keep the magic of Christmas alive for her even though she's not here to enjoy it anymore."

His face darkened. "Why would I want to pay tribute to a woman who dropped out of life? Who was so fixated on her pain, she didn't notice that anyone else was in pain, as well?"

So that was it, Kenzie thought. He hadn't forgiven his mother for not being there for him after Amy had died. He'd been hurting and his mother didn't reach out to him. Instead, she was trying to find a way to deal with her own pain. Both of them had been isolated without realizing that the key to everything lay within each other.

"Because she's your mother," Kenzie insisted, trying to break through the wall he'd constructed around himself once and for all.

"Maybe that's not enough of a reason," Keith fired back.

"Well, it's going to have to be," she told him matter-of-factly.

With that, Kenzie left the driveway. After a beat, Keith followed her inside, albeit exceedingly reluctantly.

He would ignore her. If she wanted to spout nonsense and pretend that decorating a tree was going to change anything, that was her problem. Nowhere did it say that he had to decorate the Christmas tree he had been forced to buy.

He certainly didn't have to stay in the same room and watch her do it, either.

Just because he still didn't feel like going into any of the other rooms after all these years didn't mean he had to hang around the living room, watching Kenzie struggle with Christmas lights that always seemed to be knotted up no matter how carefully they had been put away the previous year.

He could go anywhere he wanted to.

Somehow, like a moth to a flame, he still managed to wind up staying in the living room.

Standing beside the tree that was still bundled up and lying on the floor, Kenzie could *sense* that he was behind her. She glanced over her shoulder to see that he was just inside the room's threshold. But that didn't mean he was going to help her.

Kenzie worked with what she had. "Have you decided to supervise?" she asked.

The sound of her voice broke through the jumble of thoughts that were circling around his brain, as tangled as the Christmas lights always were, year after year.

"What? No, I haven't decided anything," he answered. At this point he was just trying to resist offering to help her decorate the tree for as long as he could.

"Because you could, you know," she went on, slowly drawing him in. "That way you could be part of it without having to compromise any of whatever principles you feel you're trying to maintain in this battle of dueling philosophies."

Coming closer to her, Keith shook his head as if to clear it. "You know, sometimes I don't understand a word you're saying."

Kenzie laughed, the warm sound wrapping itself around him. "That's okay. Sometimes I don't, either. But what I'm trying to tell you right now is that you can still maintain your distance—if that's what you want—but be part of this by telling me where you want me to put the various ornaments. This way, the tree'll get decorated with your help, but without you having to touch any of the decorations."

"I have nothing against the actual touching of decorations," he protested.

"Okay, if that's how you feel, wonderful. Touch away," she encouraged him.

He looked at her, then started to laugh. "Do you have any idea how crazy that sounds?"

"Maybe," she conceded. "But it got you to laugh, didn't it?"

That was when he realized his laughter had been her goal all along. "Okay, you win. I'll decorate the tree with you."

The exceedingly pleased expression on her face more than took the sting out of his surrender.

Chapter Eleven

"You do realize that I don't know where anything is?" Keith asked her the next moment.

He glanced at the tree lying on the floor, still tightly bound up like the hostage of Christmas Past. He'd made his peace with decorating it—he was here, Kenzie was here, the tree was here, and he had some time to kill, so what would it ultimately hurt? But the practical problem that now confronted him and this relentless Christmas elf beside him was the unknown location of these decorations.

"And by 'anything' you mean…?" Kenzie let her voice trail off, waiting for him to elaborate.

"I mean the tree stand, the ornaments and whatever else that thing—" he waved a hand at the tree on the floor behind him "—requires."

He had to admit that he expected Kenzie to throw in the towel when faced with this news. He didn't expect her to flash that dazzling grin of hers and then shoot down his eleventh-hour glimmer of hope. "That's okay. I do."

Of course you do, he commented silently. Out loud he voiced his natural skepticism. If he didn't know where the decorations were kept, why would she? "How would you know?"

Her mesmerizing grin turned into a patient smile. "I took inventory, remember?" Then, before he could question anything further, she volunteered the ornaments' location. "The decorations are in your pull-down attic. As for the tree stand, that's in the corner in the garage behind the black plastic box of wires and extension cords," she informed him cheerfully.

He knew he'd agreed to do this with her, but he wouldn't have forgiven himself if he hadn't given this one last try. "Look, if the decorations are all tucked away, why don't we just leave them there?"

Kenzie didn't even blink—or accuse him of reneging. "Because then the tree'll stay naked. Since we bought the tree—"

"And whose idea was that?" Keith reminded her pointedly.

Kenzie blissfully continued making her argument, pretending to take no notice that he had interjected anything. "It might as well be decorated," she stubbornly concluded.

The last time he'd been in that attic, Amy had been filling out applications to different colleges. The memory brought a bitter pang to his heart.

"And you expect me to climb up into the attic and get the decorations," Keith assumed.

"Expect?" she echoed and then shook her head. "No. I don't put demands on people," Kenzie told him just before she left the room.

Now what? Was this a show of temper? "Where are you going?" he called after Kenzie.

Rather than returning, Kenzie just raised her voice so he could hear her answer. "Well, since I haven't figured out how to make decorations come when I call them, I guess I'm going into the attic to get them."

The next second, he heard the door leading into the garage open and then close again. Kenzie had left the house.

"Darned woman," Keith muttered under his breath, hurrying after her.

He walked into the garage just in time to see Kenzie lowering the folded ladder that led up into the attic. Balancing it, she pulled at the rung to extend the ladder.

"Move out of the way," he told her gruffly just as she snapped the locks on either side of the ladder into place, strengthening it.

She wasn't sure what Keith intended to do, and she wanted to get on with decorating the tree. "But—"

"Don't argue with me," he ordered. Taking hold of both her shoulders, Keith literally moved her to the side, giving him clear access to the attic's entrance above.

"I wouldn't dream of it," she responded. She punctuated the innocent statement with an equally innocent smile.

He wasn't taken in for a second. Kenzie had orchestrated this, he thought.

"Ha!" The single word echoed behind him as he climbed up the ladder.

"Don't forget to flip on the light," she called up after Keith. She positioned herself at the base of the ladder so she could take the various boxes from him as he handed them down one at a time.

"Whose attic is this, anyway?" he retorted.

"Yours," she answered as if he was actually asking her

a serious question. "I just thought that after all these years, you might have forgotten about the light in the attic."

Maybe he had forgotten, Keith thought as he stood on the top rung of the ladder, looking around the dimly lit enclosure. Forgotten about the light—it still worked. Most of all, forgotten there were vivid memories attached to the things tucked away up here. Memories that in turn stirred bittersweet feelings within him, slicing through him like the whirling blades of a helicopter.

Kenzie shifted from foot to foot as she looked up the ladder. "Do you see them?" she asked, raising her voice so that he could hear her. He was being too quiet.

"Yes, I see them," he answered, more to himself than to her.

This was a bad idea, Keith thought again. But he couldn't very well say anything because he didn't want Kenzie to think he was affected. He wanted her to believe that he could remain detached from all this. Her sympathy would be too much for him to take right now.

He especially didn't want her pity. Toughing this out was the only way he could keep up the image he was trying to hang on to. If he allowed his emotions to engulf him, he had no idea where it would all end up.

But it would be no place good.

"Do you want me to go up to help you?" Kenzie offered.

Was it his imagination, or had her voice softened a little? Keith stiffened, as if that could ward off any unwanted sentiment coming his way.

"The attic doesn't have enough room for two of us," Keith bit out. "Not with all this stuff crammed into it."

He didn't remember there being so many decorations. But then, he'd tried not to remember anything because initially, it had just been too painful for him. Amy's death had almost shattered him. She'd been the vital, happy one, the one who never became discouraged, no matter what.

After a while, not remembering was a better way to go for him. It was just easier to wipe his memory clean and pretend there hadn't been small, loving Christmases filled with laughter if not with presents.

"If you come down," Kenzie said, "then I can go up instead and you don't have to—"

He turned just enough to look down at her from his elevated position near the top of the ladder. "Do you *ever* stop talking?" he asked.

Kenzie treated it like a serious question, pretending she didn't hear the sorrow threatening to break through in his voice. "I do, on occasion."

"Can this be one of those occasions?" It wasn't really a question so much as a request.

Kenzie bit the inside of her bottom lip and really struggled not to say anything further. Not because she was insulted—she wasn't—but because in Keith's present state, although it went against everything she normally felt compelled to do, she had a feeling that silence would be easier for him to bear than bright, cheerful chatter.

He wasn't in a place right now where he would respond positively to banter.

So she stood at the bottom of the ladder, quietly waiting for Keith to hand one of the plastic containers of decorations down.

She'd almost given up hope that he actually would when Keith finally lowered the first box of silver-and-blue ornaments to her. He descended just enough rungs to cut the distance between them so that when she extended her arms up, she was able to take hold of the box.

Kenzie rose up on her toes as far as she could as she stretched her arms, angling so that he wouldn't have to bend down too far. The look Keith gave her silently told her she was trying too hard. Being Kenzie, she deliberately ignored the message. She was just happy that he'd come around enough to begin bringing down the decorations.

Every journey starts with the first step, she thought, heartened.

The prolonged process of retrieving the decorations and handing them down the ladder lasted close to an hour. And once all the boxes were finally down, Kenzie turned her attention to the tree stand.

"I'm going to get some food and water ready for the tree, and then I'll need help getting the tree into the stand," she told Keith.

He frowned. "Food and water? Room service for a Christmas tree?" he questioned, looking at her as if she'd lost her mind.

"The tree's a living thing," Kenzie reminded him. "Every living thing requires at least water. Most require water *and* food. Plant food," she explained, patting her skirt pocket. She took a packet out of it to show him. "When we bought the tree, the guy at the lot gave me this. He said it helps the tree last until after the holidays."

Keith shook his head, negating her plans. "It doesn't have to last until after the holidays. As far as I'm concerned, it doesn't have to last longer than a few days. After that, I'm out of here and the tree winds up on the garbage heap, waiting for collection."

She'd really been hoping that all this would have gotten him to change his mind, to stay awhile and at least begin to work through the anger and sadness she saw in his eyes. But he seemed determined to remain unhappy, to hang on to all those issues clearly haunting him.

"Then you are leaving right after the reception?" she asked quietly.

He did his best remain removed from her tone and not allow it to get to him. He deliberately blocked out the sadness he heard. "I'd be leaving right after the funeral if someone hadn't insisted on holding a reception right afterward."

She let that comment pass. There was no point in going into it now. Instead, she approached the situation logically. "It'll be late then. Why not fly out in the morning, when you're fresh?"

The first thing that came to him was to say that he wanted to leave Bedford behind him as soon as possible, but she had been very cheerful and upbeat about all this extra work and without complaint—never mind that he hadn't asked for it. He owed Kenzie, even if he didn't say so.

Keith supposed a few more hours here wouldn't make that much difference. "Maybe I will," he conceded.

Kenzie had already cleared away all the boxes he had handed down to her, taking them into the family room. When Keith came down the ladder with the last load, she took that box from him and quickly brought it into the house to join the others. By the time he had the ladder folding into itself and then neatly retracting into the ceiling, she was digging the tree stand out of the corner.

"About that help I asked for," she began tactfully, holding the stand aloft.

Keith's response was a sigh, but he didn't turn her down or even offer any excuses.

Following her into the house, he looked down at the offending blue spruce. "Might as well get this over with," he muttered, resigned. "Where do you want it?" he asked her.

Kenzie looked around the family room slowly, as if she had a vision.

"Where did you used to put the tree?" she asked.

Keith shrugged dismissively. "I don't know," he responded irritably, then shrugged again. "Anywhere."

She placed the stand down by the window, then looked over toward him. "Here?" It was a question, not a suggestion.

What did it matter? He didn't want it here to begin with. "Good a place as any," he responded.

"You really don't remember?" Kenzie asked incredulously.

Yes, he remembered. "It was the middle of the room," Keith bit out, glaring at her. "Happy now?"

Kenzie didn't answer that one way or the other. What she did say was "Thank you," followed by what he could only describe as a sweet, completely guileless smile.

The polite answer made him ashamed of his testiness and the temper he'd allowed to flare. But the woman was trying too hard to recreate something dead and not about to be resurrected.

Still, Keith told himself, he didn't have to be so curt. Apparently Kenzie couldn't help being a pain in the neck.

He blew out a breath, then murmured, "I didn't mean to bite your head off like that. Sorry."

Kenzie moved her head from side to side as if she were actually testing her neck to make sure it was all right. "Still attached," she announced with a wide grin that reached her eyes. "No harm done." With that, she moved the stand into the middle of the room. "Just help me get the tree into the stand and then I won't bother you anymore."

Keith laughed shortly. "Yeah, right. Like I believe that," he said, resurrecting his facade.

Even so, he picked the tree up from the floor and carried it, still bound, over to the stand.

He moved so quickly, he caught her off guard. Kenzie hurried over to him as he carried the tree. "Wait, let me help with that."

He refrained from saying that she'd only get in his way if she tried to carry the tree with him. "You just hold the stand still," Keith told her. "I'll handle the tree."

Kenzie could tell by his voice that he was straining. It made her feel guilty in addition to useless. "The tree's heavy," she insisted.

She knew that despite the fact that when they had carried it into the house together, she had brought up the top while he had picked up the bottom part before she could say anything. The angle he employed while carrying it assured him that the brunt of the weight was on his end. Even so, she could tell that the tree was more than a little on the heavy side.

"Nothing gets past you, does it?" Keith commented sarcastically, holding the tree still.

Kenzie had dropped to her knees and was moving as quickly as she could, tightening the stand's screws into place. The tricky part was making sure that all three screws were equally tightened, keeping the tree carefully balanced between them. She knew this couldn't be easy for him, keeping the spruce perfectly upright the way he was. "I should have called my brothers to come help."

"And I should have called the airlines and booked an earlier flight, but none of that's happening, so let's just work with what we've got, okay?" he told her, trying not to raise his voice. "Have you finished adjusting the screws yet?"

Kenzie shuffled around the perimeter. "Almost," she answered.

It felt as if she was vainly turning the screws, getting nowhere. And then, after what felt like an eternity, she couldn't move any of the three screws even half a turn further.

"Okay, test it," she told him, snaking her way back out from under the tree.

Rocking back on her heels, Kenzie took in a deep breath. Her first unobstructed one in a while, or so it felt.

Remaining somewhat skeptical, Keith slowly tested the tree's stability by partially releasing one of his hands from around its trunk.

The second he felt the tree beginning to list, he quickly closed his hand around the trunk again, holding it tightly. He'd never let go with his other hand.

"Not good enough," he told her.

Kenzie blew out a breath that sounded suspiciously more like a deep sigh.

"You liked saying that, didn't you?" It wasn't an accusation but an observation.

Keith inclined his head as if conceding the point. "It had its appeal."

Keith was fighting her every step of the way—but he was also ultimately going along with it, she noted happily. And that was the bottom line.

Inside all that bravado and aloof rhetoric he so liberally dispensed, there was a man who still cared. A man who did his best to appear distant and removed, but who was really the opposite upon closer examination.

And *that* was the man whom she wanted to reach, the one she wanted to extend her hand to and hold on tightly to so that he knew he wasn't alone.

Because she was there for him. And intended to be for as long as he needed her.

"Done yet?" Keith demanded as she once again moved

around the tree, reworking the three screws, trying to get a more equitable distribution of the tree's weight.

She didn't answer him immediately. Not until she'd tightened the last screw and satisfied herself that there was no way the base could possibly still wiggle.

"Done!" Kenzie finally declared in much the same voice that competing cowboys in a rodeo used when they'd secured the steer they had roped and brought down.

She crawled out from underneath the tree for a second time, her face somewhat flushed. Keith caught himself staring at the way the color infused her cheeks.

The next second, he roused himself and let go of the tree.

For a one long moment, the tree appeared to be almost perfect. The next, it began to list again, this time ever so slightly to one side.

Keith sighed. Then he looked at her face and knew exactly what she was thinking.

"It doesn't have to be perfect," he told her. "After all, it's just a tree."

Kenzie fisted her hands on her hips and gave him a look that he dreaded getting from teachers back in school.

"A *Christmas* tree," she corrected him, implying that made all the difference in the world. "And yes, it does. You give up too easy, O'Connell. Hold the tree," she ordered.

With that, Kenzie got back down on her hands and knees for the third time, crawled under the tree on her stomach and went back to work.

The woman, Keith thought as he held the tree as still as he could, was stubbornness personified.

He didn't realize, at least not immediately, that he was smiling as he thought it.

Chapter Twelve

"Okay, you proved your point," Keith conceded in grudging admiration.

It had taken Kenzie another fifteen minutes of adjusting and readjusting, but the Christmas tree they had brought into his house, looming at approximately seven and a half feet without taking the stand into account, was finally perfectly straight.

"You did it. The tree's straight. Your job is done," he pronounced.

"The tree's straight," Kenzie agreed, dusting herself off. "But the job's far from done yet." When she saw Keith arch a quizzical brow in her direction, she explained, "The decorations you brought down are still in their boxes. Job's not done until they're on the tree."

Keith shook his head as he blew out an impatient breath. "You're relentless, aren't you?"

Her smile rose into her eyes, highlighting her amusement at his assessment.

"I take vitamins," she quipped. "Don't worry," she was quick to assure him. "I'm not going to rope you into helping me. You can go do whatever it is you were planning on doing."

The fact was, he had no plans, other than to knock back a stiff drink or two to help relax him enough so that, with luck, he could fall asleep. The funeral was tomorrow, and although he told himself that he wasn't viewing the event emotionally, he was utterly wired about having to be there tomorrow.

He felt like a spring that would release at any second with just the slightest touch. That wasn't a good state to be in, he silently lectured himself.

She was brushing off the last of tiny, fuzzy lint that was clinging to the front of her light blue sweater. For just a fleeting moment, he envisioned his own fingers brushing it away.

Keith forced himself to focus on the moment instead. "Why are you doing this?" he asked her suddenly.

She never missed a beat as she answered, "Because a Christmas tree needs Christmas decorations. Otherwise, it's just a tree in the house that's lost its way."

Keith laughed under his breath as he shook his head. "Do you think these things up, or do they just come to you?"

She opened the first box and took out five decorations, depicting a family of colorfully dressed mice that appeared to have stepped right out of a children's cartoon. "How cute," she murmured under her breath.

Attaching a hook to each, she hung one decoration from each finger on her left hand, then turned toward the tree.

"If you're going to talk, grab a decoration," she told him. "I thought you weren't going to rope me into helping you," he reminded her even as he picked a gleaming mul-tiplaned silver decoration out of the box closest to him. The decoration cast a shower of rainbows as the light hit it. For just a moment, it threatened to stir an old memory, but he suppressed it.

"I don't see any rope," she replied, pretending to scan the immediate area before she turned an innocent face up to him. "Do you?"

"I stand corrected," he conceded wryly. He watched as she distributed the decorations in her hand, hanging them on different branches. "So why are you doing this? The truth," he specified.

Kenzie spared him one glance over her shoulder be-fore taking out another five decorations and repeating her procedure.

"Other than the fact that I love Christmas trees?" she asked.

He was trying to get to the unvarnished truth, con-vinced that people didn't go out of their way for other people without an ulterior motive. "Other than that," he prodded.

Hanging the last decorations, she went back for re-placements. She didn't have to think about her answer. It was something that had always guided her.

"Because it's a nice touch. Because it pulls a thread of continuity through what's happening. People leave us," she added in a more quiet voice, as if she would ever get used to the reality of that fact.

"You mean they die," he clarified.

She didn't like that word, never had. "They leave us," she continued doggedly. "But the traditions they leave behind continue, just like life."

"That's a lovely philosophy," he told her flippantly. She was on shaky ground in his opinion. She couldn't back that up with any amount of certainty. "How do you know my mother didn't stop celebrating Christmas right after Amy died?" he asked.

Kenzie paused, her hand hovering over the next box of decorations. There was a quiet certainty in her voice when she answered him. "She would have celebrated twice as hard, for Amy as well as for herself."

Kenzie was right—and he'd never understood why his mother had been so adamant about going all out that way. The holiday had lost all its meaning for him. Because Amy had always somehow been at the center of the celebration. She'd been the one who bridged any flares of temper that erupted between his mother and him.

Keith hung the decoration and then, for a moment, he contemplated just walking out of the room and leaving her to decorate the tree by herself.

But all this talk about the holiday had him thinking of Amy. With an inward sigh, he picked up another decoration, knowing Amy would have wanted him to.

"How did you know?" he asked in a low voice after a beat.

"I didn't, not definitively," she qualified. "It's just a feeling. I'd do the same thing myself in her place." She could see that Keith still didn't understand. "Celebrating that way helped your mother keep Amy's memory alive, made her feel that Amy was still there with her," she explained. "With both of you."

Stepping back to view their progress so far, Kenzie realized her oversight.

"Help me with the ladder," she told him, heading into the garage. "We forgot to put the star on the top."

Keith gave the tree a quick once-over. "Instead of dragging in the ladder, why don't you just leave the star off?" he suggested. "Looks fine without one."

Kenzie frowned. "It looks naked without a star," she insisted. The next moment, she reversed her position. After all, he'd gone along with the rest of it. Maybe he'd respond better if she cut him a break. "Okay, the star doesn't have to go on. But I still need to decorate the upper part of the tree." With that, she went into the garage.

Keith followed right behind her.

"That's too heavy," he told her, taking possession of the ladder.

"I'm stronger than I look," Kenzie protested, although she did like the fact that he was bringing the ladder into the house.

"You're also more annoying than you look," he countered as he brought the ladder into the family room. He set it up beside the tree.

Kenzie made no response to his comment. Instead, she took out another five decorations. By the time he turned around to face her, she had made her way up the ladder and was one step from the top.

Biting off a curse, Keith quickly circled around the ladder to get to her side of it. One hand braced against the top of the ladder, Kenzie was stretching to hang the decorations as high as she could place them.

Keith grabbed hold of the ladder on either side to steady it. "Are you trying to break your fool neck?" he accused her.

"Not particularly," she answered as if he'd asked a legitimate question. Her hold on the ladder's top rung tightened as she felt it sway ever so slightly beneath her. "But I just might if you grab the ladder like that again."

Choice words rose to his lips, but Keith managed to refrain from saying them. Instead, he told her, "Why don't you come down and I'll do that?"

As if he really wanted to, she thought, feeling there

was only so far she could push him before he just walked out. "No, that's okay. I—"

"I said come down." This time it wasn't a suggestion but an order, uttered through clenched teeth as he glared up at her.

She debated arguing with him, then decided having Keith insist like that was a good thing. It meant that he was involved in the process, at least for the moment.

"Coming down," she announced agreeably, making her way down the ladder.

The moment she had both feet back on the floor, Keith moved her out of the way and took Kenzie's place on the ladder.

In general, he wasn't as quick as she was when it came to hanging up decorations, or as limber when it came to running up and down the ladder, so the job wound up taking longer. But eventually, the upper half of the tree was finished.

As was, he noted, the bottom half of the tree. Kenzie had quietly emulated his progress by hanging up decorations on the bottom half of the tree, covering an equal amount of ground in about half the time. The entire tree was finished.

"Not bad," he grudgingly murmured.

"Not bad?" Kenzie echoed incredulously. "Why, it's beautiful!" she declared with feeling.

Keith merely shrugged, determined to sound far less enthusiastic, even though the truth was he'd enjoyed doing this with her. But if Kenzie caught a hint of that, he was certain that he would not hear the end of it, not until his plane finally took off.

"At least it's done," he said carelessly. "I'm beat. Unless you've got some magical trip to Neverland up your sleeve, I'm turning in." He looked her way, waiting for some last-minute pitch.

"There's been enough magic for one day," she told him. Maybe he was just exhausted and imagining things, but he could have sworn he saw her eyes gleaming. The next minute, she managed to catch him off guard again. "I'll be here in the morning," Kenzie told him as she gathered together her things.

He tried to make sense of what she'd just said. "I'm going to the funeral," he reminded her.

Kenzie slipped her purse onto her shoulder. "I know. I'm going, too."

He stared at Kenzie. He hadn't come right out and extended an invitation to her, so he had just assumed she wasn't attending. Was she doing it out of some misguided sense of obligation—or worse, out of pity?

He felt his back going up.

"You don't have to," he told Kenzie stiffly.

"I know that," she answered. Flashing a smile at him, she declared, "The tree looks great. See you tomorrow at eight."

With that, Kenzie went out the door, pulling it shut behind her.

Shaking his head, Keith flipped the front door's lock into place. Then, feeling close to exhausted, he went up to his old bedroom. He'd changed out of his clothes and had climbed into bed before he realized that he'd forgotten to have those two shots of scotch he'd initially wanted to help him unwind.

It was the last thing he thought of before he fell asleep.

It seemed as if he had just closed his eyes before he was opening them again. But night had come and gone, and now the blush of daylight was just beginning to make its way into his room.

With daylight came the ambivalent feelings he was too groggy to bury effectively yet. They loomed over him like monsters that had slipped out of his childhood closet.

Part of him wanted to skip the funeral entirely. His mother hadn't been there for him the past ten years of his life, he thought angrily. Why should he be there for her when she was being buried?

But if he didn't attend the funeral, he had a very strong feeling that Kenzie would come and find him. He wouldn't put it past her to drag him to the service, literally. He no longer felt he could place any limits on what the woman was capable of, or her tenacity, for that matter.

So with the greatest reluctance, Keith forced himself out of bed, showered, shaved and made himself presentable.

He stared at the man in the mirror, who was staring back at him with eyes that appeared hollow. He was as braced as he figured he could be to face this ordeal.

He might have been braced, but he discovered that he wasn't all that ready for it. When the doorbell rang a few minutes later, he all but jumped out of his skin as the sound echoed around him.

Keith came hurrying down the stairs. He reached the front door just as he heard the doorbell ring for a third time.

"Ghosts don't ring doorbells," she said.

It was the first thing Kenzie saw when the door opened, how very pale he looked. She took a quick guess as to the reason for his lack of color. The smile on her lips was neither teasing nor amused. It was understanding.

"I know that," he said curtly, congratulating himself that he hadn't actually snapped at her.

Kenzie appeared to take no offense at his tone. "Just something I thought I'd pass on," she told him glibly. And then she grew more serious as she looked him over again. "Are you going to be all right?"

The concern in her voice, which he equated to pity, helped lift him out of the emotional hole he'd suddenly fallen into.

"I'll be fine," he all but bit out.

Kenzie quickly assessed the situation. It sounded to her as if he wouldn't allow himself to give in to any emotional triggers. Apparently he would be a brick wall.

But even brick walls cracked if enough pressure was applied.

"Of course you will," Kenzie agreed, her voice chipper.

"That means you don't have to come," he told her pointedly, repeating what he'd said to her last night.

"I know I don't have to," she continued in the same agreeable tone, except that this time, she was more forceful. "But I *want* to." There was quiet resolution in her voice.

He inclined his head, knowing there was no arguing with her. If he was being honest with himself, he was grateful for her unspoken support.

"As long as it's your choice," he told her. "I'm not about to turn you away." The warm feeling he was experiencing told him just how grateful he was that she had elected to stick it out, no matter what he'd said to try to make her leave.

However, he wasn't about to admit his gratitude to Kenzie. If she knew how he felt, that might jeopardize things between them, throw them off balance. He didn't want to risk it.

The church was already close to packed when they arrived. Finding a parking space proved to be a challenge, and he had to circle the parking lot on both sides of the church before he found a spot.

Finding a pew would have been equally as difficult except that the first one had been reserved for the deceased's family. He was the only mourner who could lay claim to that. His father hadn't been in the picture for a very long time, and his mother had no siblings. With Amy gone, he was the only family member left.

In a move that was completely unplanned, he led Kenzie behind him as he slid into the pew.

Just before he took his seat, Keith was surprised to see that members of her family—the same people he had met for the first time only two days ago—were in the church, as well, clustered together in the next few pews. That meant they had been sitting there for a while now.

Lowering his head, he whispered to Kenzie, "Why is your family here?"

Kenzie looked over her shoulder and smiled at her mother before answering. "They're here in order to show support."

"But they didn't know my mother." At least, as far as he knew, none of them did.

The next moment, Kenzie confirmed his assumption. "No, but they know you."

It still didn't make any sense to him. "Does that mean that you strong-armed them into attending the funeral?" He wouldn't have put it past her.

But Kenzie shook her head. "No. I didn't have to. I'm the youngest. I learned from them, not the other way around. This is what my family's like. They didn't come here for me. They came here because of you. I think, given your situation, my mother's adopted you. She wants you to know that you're not alone."

Keith had no idea what to say to that, so he remained silent.

He maintained the same silence throughout the service, struggling hard against the unexpected waves of emotion that inexplicably beat against the beaches of his soul, wearing him down.

As the service was winding down, just when Keith thought his ordeal was finally coming to a close, the priest performing the service looked out on the rows of people he had been addressing.

"And now," the priest said, his deep, gentle voice going out to the very last pew, "if anyone here would like to add his or her own words to this service, please feel free to come up and say something about Mrs. O'Connell. Remember, it doesn't have to be polished. It just has to be from the heart. I'm sure that Dorothy would be very pleased."

A reluctance to be the first to speak kept people in their seats initially.

The priest looked around at the upturned faces, appearing to be searching for not just someone, but someone in particular.

And then his gaze honed in on Keith.

"Mr. O'Connell?" he called out, his tone meant to coax Dorothy's son out of his seat.

Keith began to move his head from side to side, wanting more than anything to be excused. If all else failed, he was going to point to his throat and just shake his head, begging off by means of a lie.

But Kenzie whispered into his ear, "Just say something about how you'll miss her sunny disposition and be done with it. If you don't, you'll always feel like there was some unfinished business left in the wake of her demise."

He kept his voice down, insisting, "I can't go up there and lie, gushing about how I'm going to miss the sound of her voice."

"Then don't lie," she countered. "Just pick your truths.

You have to do this. You've come this far," she reminded him. "You can't just fold at the eleventh hour."

What he wanted to do was tell her that yes, he could. But he knew she was right. If he didn't do this, everyone would know there had been ill feelings between his mother and him. There were, but it was no one's business but his.

So, although it went against everything he thought was right, Keith slowly rose to his feet and began to walk up to the pulpit.

Chapter Thirteen

Keith curled his fingers around either side of the pulpit, gripping it. He still wasn't sure how he had managed to make his way from the pew to the place vacated by the man who had been his mother's priest for the last thirty-one years. He couldn't remember putting one foot in front of the other.

His mouth felt like cotton and his mind was as close to empty as it had ever been.

What the hell was he doing up here?

He should never have gotten up, never allowed Kenzie to urge him on with that look of hers.

Now he was trapped up here.

His eyes shifted to the first pew. To Kenzie. She was smiling at him, her eyes urging him on.

Encouraging him.

And suddenly, just like that, his mind came alive.

"Looking around this church, I can see that my mother had a lot of friends. A lot of people are going to miss her now that she's gone. Since people are all different in the way they react to things, everyone will undoubtedly miss something else about my mother."

He could almost hear Kenzie cheering him on, like a mother watching her child take his first wobbly steps. He should have been resentful, he told himself.

For some odd reason, he wasn't.

"Me, I'll miss the mother I once knew. The one who stayed up late, putting the finishing touches on two dinosaur costumes so that my sister, Amy, and I wouldn't miss out on going trick-or-treating the next day. She stayed up late sewing, even though she had put in a full day's work and had to go in early the next morning to her second job. She worked two jobs because that's what it took to feed and clothe us."

He paused for a moment, reining in emotions that threatened to break free. It took him a couple more minutes before he could continue.

"I'll miss the mother who worked hard to help me memorize words for my spelling test so I could finally ace my retest instead of flunking it the way I'd been doing— spelling was never my strong suit," he added in an aside that had some in the church laughing in commiseration. "When I complained that I was too dumb to remember how to spell the words, she got angry with me and insisted that I wasn't. She got angry because I had run myself down and she didn't believe in doing that. Positive reinforcement was her thing."

He paused as his throat tightened. "I'll miss the mother who wouldn't quit, who refused to give up, even when things seemed hopeless." He took a breath before pushing on. "She lost her way after Amy died. I wish I could have helped her find it again, the way she used to help me find mine. I'll…" He pressed his lips together, feeling naked and exposed. "I'll miss my mother," he concluded in a quiet voice, and then stepped down.

He didn't remember taking his seat again, didn't remember actually even sitting down, either. And he was only vaguely aware that someone took his hand, threaded her fingers through his and lightly squeezed, conveying so many unspoken sentiments of comfort with that simple gesture.

Slowly, by degrees, as another voice began to speak from the pulpit about his mother, he became aware of Kenzie. Aware that it was her hand that had taken his, aware that she had been the one to squeeze it. Her eyes when they met his were filled not with pity but with sympathy.

Sympathy and tears.

"You did good," she whispered to him.

He couldn't answer her. He was afraid that his voice would break if he did. It bothered him that he could feel this way even after he had built up this tall wall around himself. The wall that was supposed to keep his feelings about his mother at bay and contained at all times.

He'd been keeping the wall in place for so long, he'd been certain that he had no feelings left, not for his mother, not for anyone. And yet there they were. Feelings. Feelings just waiting to ambush him. To prick him and make him bleed.

"I shouldn't have come," he told Kenzie when he could finally trust his voice not to break. The service had ended, and a church full of people had dutifully filed out and into their separate vehicles. They were all headed for the same place.

The cemetery.

The drive was a very short one, practically over before it began.

Kenzie remained steadfast. "You would have never forgiven yourself if you hadn't," she told him as they climbed out of the somber black sedan.

They fell into step, joining the flow of people heading toward the area of All Saints Cemetery that had just been prepared for the latest burial ceremony. It was to be his mother's final resting place.

Or at least where his mother's casket was going into the ground, he thought cynically. The dead didn't rest. They didn't do anything anymore.

"Not exactly thrilled with myself right now," he finally responded. He'd paused for so long, she thought he either hadn't heard her or, more likely, had chosen to ignore her.

"You can get through this," she told him with the conviction of someone who had utter faith in what she was saying. She was doing her best to convey that to him. "Just keep putting one foot in front of the other the way you've been doing."

What he wanted to do was put one foot in front of the other in the opposite direction and get as far away from the service—and her—as he could. For entirely different reasons. But he knew he couldn't, not without calling a great deal of attention to himself, which was the *last* thing he wanted to do.

So he made his way with the others to his mother's gravesite, acutely aware that Kenzie was right at his side every step of the way. Kenzie and that family of hers who seemed to insist on being there as a complete set—just the way they had been at the church.

He wanted to send her away, to send her whole family away. Yet in a strange way he couldn't begin to explain, he was grateful for their presence.

He sensed that they just wanted to be supportive for no other reason than, as Kenzie had said, he needed them to be.

He had to admit they were exceptional people. Just like she was.

Keith squared his shoulders and stood at the gravesite as the priest spoke words about his mother and her life that he barely heard. After a few minutes, it all became one continuous buzzing.

And then the casket was lowered and people were dropping roses onto it.

Where had all those roses come from? he wondered absently. This was winter, the third week in December. Weren't flowers meant for the spring?

He looked at Kenzie, and he had his answer. As with everything else, she must have taken care of this detail for him. She'd had the roses brought to the gravesite and distributed among the mourners.

She was always one step ahead. Certainly one step ahead of him.

"It's over," Kenzie whispered to him as the gathering at the gravesite began to break up. Taking his hand, she lightly tugged on it, indicating the direction he needed to take.

Because he suddenly felt drained, he let her lead, quietly following her out of the cemetery to the vehicle that stood waiting for them.

"You're doing very well," Kenzie said, her voice breaking into the endless silence riding with them in the vehicle.

"Don't patronize me," he told her tersely. Keith knew he had to come off like an angry, wounded bear. It was either that or break down. This was turning out to be a lot harder on him than he had anticipated.

"I'm not." The answer was neither defensive nor cloying. It was a simple matter-of-fact statement. "But you do still have an attitude problem," she pointed out. "People are just trying to be sympathetic, nothing more. Take it at face value and be gracious."

He swallowed the first words that rose to his lips. No matter what he felt, she didn't deserve to be shouted at. He let out a deep breath. It didn't help. His nerves felt frayed.

"Do I really have to go to the reception?" He knew the answer to that, but there was a part of him that was still hoping for a reprieve.

Kenzie merely looked at him. "It's being held at the house."

"That still doesn't answer my question," he told her, knowing he was being irrational, but still unable to refrain.

"Okay, then I'll answer it," she told him gamely as the driver entered Keith's development. "Yes, you need to go to the reception."

"Why? I said my piece at the funeral service. I attended the burial at the cemetery. The reception is just people milling around, talking over food."

"Well, you can talk, and you do eat. Shouldn't be a problem," she told him practically. And then she squeezed his hand. There was that silent encouragement again, he couldn't help thinking. But he didn't pull his hand away. "Just one more hurdle and then you can go back to being Mr. Congeniality and winning everyone over with your happy patter."

"Sarcasm?" He raised his eyebrow as if taking offense. "I just came back from the cemetery."

"That's why I toned it down," she told him, a wide, guileless smile on her lips.

He had no idea why he found that heartening—but he did.

The next few hours were a blur of people shaking his hand, offering words of condolence and relating stories he told himself he had no interest in hearing. Stories that convinced him in the last years of her life, his mother had cared for other people—any people—more than she had for him.

The sting of the angry words that marked their last encounter kept coming back to him over the course of the afternoon and evening, leaving a bitter taste in his mouth and an ache in his chest.

Just when he didn't think he could take much more, to his surprise the woman that Kenzie had hired to do the catering for the reception—a Mrs. Manetti, he thought she'd told him—came to his rescue by quietly telling the people that the reception would be closing down shortly.

After that, guests began taking their leave, pausing to say a few final words to him before going out the door.

And then, finally, the last of the guests were gone.

"That woman certainly knows how to clear a room," he commented to Kenzie, savoring the relief he was feeling.

Kenzie smiled as she nodded, watching the caterer preside over the room's cleanup. "Mrs. Manetti is good at reading people."

"I don't follow," he told Kenzie.

"I think she realized that you were reaching the end of your rope, and she could tell there was just so much more you could put up with. She probably said what she did so you could have some peace and quiet, let everything that transpired today settle and gel." She looked at him for a long, scrutinizing moment, then observed, "Apparently she was right. I think you're just about smiled out."

Well, she certainly had that right, Keith thought. The muscles of his face felt as if they were in danger of cramping up if he had to spend another five minutes smiling at well-intentioned strangers telling him what they deemed to be amusing stories about his mother.

Kenzie patted his face. "A really hot shower might help relax that."

"Yeah," he murmured, looking around the living room. It had emptied even faster than he had anticipated.

And as for Mrs. Manetti's crew, they were exceptionally efficient. The trays of food and beverages, both hard and soft, had been whisked away, and the extraneous plates and glasses that had littered the family room and living room were gone as if they had never existed.

Everything had been washed and put away in what amounted to a blink of an eye.

"It seems almost a little empty in comparison to earlier," Keith couldn't help commenting.

"It seems a *lot* empty," Kenzie corrected him with a laugh.

The next moment, she realized that just might be the trouble. As much as Keith had seemed as if he wanted to be alone, now she was hearing something else in his voice. There was almost a loneliness that she hadn't picked up on earlier.

"Listen, I don't really have anywhere to be—just some last minute presents waiting to be wrapped, but nothing that can't wait," she told him. "I can stay here for a while, keep you company."

Keith frowned slightly. He still didn't want any pity from her no matter how good she'd been about everything. "I don't need a babysitter."

"And I don't recall offering to be one," she told him matter-of-factly. "I do, however, remember offering to spend a little time with my friend." The television monitor, tucked within an entertainment unit over in the corner, caught her eye. "Maybe watch an old movie over some popcorn."

"What old movie?" he asked.

Her shoulders rose and fell gamely. She was secretly congratulating herself on getting him to open to the proposition. "You pick."

It didn't matter to him—with one exception. "I don't want to watch some sentimental tear-jerker."

"That's good, because neither do I." She didn't want him watching something weepy. He needed an upbeat movie, preferably a good comedy. "We can stream a movie—or simpler still, just channel surf."

She had a feeling it really wasn't about what was on the screen for him. As long as there was something flickering across it, making sufficient background noise, that just might be enough. She was hoping they'd wind up talking through it. He needed to talk.

"Why are you doing all this?" he asked out of the blue as she turned on the monitor. "Why are you handling everything for me, going these extra miles, being my buffer, my go-between?"

"That's simple enough to answer," she deadpanned. "I have this Girl Scout merit badge that I'm trying to earn." Kenzie struggled to keep a hint of a smile from curving the corners of her mouth.

"Seriously," Keith insisted.

She raised her eyebrows in feigned surprise. "You mean I'm *not* earning a Girl Scout merit badge for this? Bummer."

"Kenzie, why are you doing this?" he repeated, enunciated each word slowly and firmly.

She stopped teasing. "Because you're my friend. Because you're hurting. Because as a kid, I used to bring home stray puppies and feed them." She shrugged, as if she had no real say in the direction her behavior took. "It's a tough habit to break."

"So is making up stories and spitting out wisecracks," he observed wryly.

"No argument," Kenzie acknowledged. "But I don't know anyone like that." Sitting down on the sofa, she looked around the immediate area. "Where's your remote hiding?"

Keith nodded toward the other side of the coffee table. They both reached for it at the same time. And wound up grabbing opposite ends of the remote simultaneously.

Keith automatically pulled the remote—and because of that, her—to him before Kenzie could think to let it go. Unprepared for the sudden move, Kenzie lost her balance and wound up bumping up against his chest.

It was hard to say which of them was more startled by the very abrupt, sudden contact.

Surprise gave way to something far more basic.

Before he could stop himself, Keith cupped her face with his hands. The next moment, he brought his mouth down to hers.

Moved, emotional against his will, Keith kissed her to express his gratitude, to in effect say things that he couldn't find the right words to articulate.

He kissed her because it was the fastest and the simplest way to express himself and to make her realize that he was very aware just how much she had put herself out for him.

He meant to kiss her and just leave it at that.

But the kiss didn't wind up ending anything. Instead, it began something. By its very nature, it wound up opening up a whole volume of feelings he hadn't even been vaguely aware were there.

One kiss grew into another.

And another.

Each kiss was feeding upon the last and gaining in depth and breadth until they threatened to engulf not just him, but Kenzie, as well.

This was, a voice in his head whispered, the point of no return. This was where he stopped, took a breath and stepped back.

Move!

But none of that was happening.

The kiss was multiplying, mushrooming, demanding more and more from him. It was creating hopes and expectations that he was so very tempted to grasp hold of—and hold on to for dear life.

In her conscious mind, Kenzie knew this wasn't really Keith. It wasn't the man she had come to know or even the teenager she'd had such a huge crush on all those years ago.

Grief was making Keith act in a way he wouldn't if his soul hadn't fallen into some deep, dark abyss of hopelessness from which there was no return.

But there was *always* a way to return, Kenzie's mind argued. She had to let him know that so he wouldn't somehow wind up doing something he was going to regret deeply the moment he was thinking clearly again.

Any second now, she was going to pull her head back and make the wrong comment. The last thing she wanted was something to leave him feeling worse than before.

But how could this wondrous thing she was feeling be bad? something inside her argued.

Right now, it felt as if she was on fire. And the fire was good.

Better than good.

This was exactly what she'd always felt it would be like, kissing Keith.

Heaven in bright, neon lights.

Chapter Fourteen

There was liquid heat going through her veins. The word *more* echoed over and over in her head, obliterating any lingering thoughts of resistance.

Kenzie gave up even the slightest ghost of a protest, letting it disintegrate into nothingness. Melting as quickly as she was in the flame of his kiss.

Finally!

Her heart hammered wildly, joyfully embracing the feeling. After all this time, she was finally going to discover what it was like to make love with the man she'd once been so completely convinced was her soul mate.

The man she realized she'd always been in love with.

Keith had gone on to college, then left Bedford and Southern California altogether in the year after Amy had died, and she'd made her peace with that. Life for her had continued. She'd even tried her hand at a couple of semiserious relationships, but nothing ever took. There had never been anyone to fill her thoughts and dreams the way that Keith once had, never anyone whom she'd even come close to regarding as her soul mate.

No one she really wanted to spend the rest of her life with. That was because the position had always remained filled. Keith was the only man who qualified for that title—soul mate—then and now.

The very first time his lips had touched hers, she knew with certainty there was no point in really fighting her reaction to him, in pretending it was wrong, or happening for the wrong reasons.

No matter what tomorrow brought—and she was a big girl now—she didn't expect Keith to have some sort of a life-changing epiphany when dawn came. Didn't expect him to sweep her off her feet, declare he'd been blind up to this moment and he wanted to uproot his life, move back here and spend the rest of his days loving her just the way he was tonight.

Granted, it would have been wonderful…

But she was well aware that this wasn't some splashy 1940s big studio movie. This was life and infinitely more real than any so-called reality show. She knew not to expect anything more than what was happening at this very moment.

And what was happening this very moment was beyond words.

Beyond wonderful.

Everywhere Keith kissed her, everywhere he touched her, she felt the area quickening and coming vibrantly alive. She felt absolutely radiant with such a spectrum of feelings, of reactions, that it would have exhausted her to try to describe exactly what it was that she was experiencing, even to herself.

So she didn't even try.

She instead savored the overwhelming sensations. She

gave herself permission to squeeze every last drop out of what was happening, to soar beyond the highest pinnacle as sensation built on sensation within her body.

The second her skin ignited in response to Keith's hands, Kenzie eagerly tore away the physical barriers that existed between them. Starting with Keith's shirt, she worked her way down to the very last shred of clothing he had on.

It occurred to her only belatedly that she was pulling his clothing away from his body at the very same time that he was undressing hers.

And then there were no barriers, physical or otherwise.

Their bodies came together as if their very souls were magnetized, compelled to pull each other in.

She was his for the taking.

Keith had no idea what came over him. This had never happened to him before, not anywhere to this degree. Even when he was an adolescent doing his best to navigate through a sea of raging hormones, he had never felt like this, never experienced this all-encompassing need to make love the way he did right at this moment with Kenzie.

He told himself it was the grief fogging up his thinking, throwing him off balance. But he knew it was more than that. He wasn't just stumbling about, blindly feeling his way around. He wasn't blind. He could see with complete clarity.

And what he saw was Kenzie.

Nothing else but Kenzie.

She was his focus, his beacon, his guiding light—and she was drawing him in. Bringing him in to what could very well be his destiny.

It was completely irrational, but he felt as if he couldn't

continue existing in any manner, shape or form if he couldn't have Kenzie, if he couldn't make love with her tonight.

Now.

Struggling not to behave like some sort of deranged madman or rutting animal, Keith struggled to exercise supreme control over himself and move with patient restraint, not devour but savor the taste of her mouth, the feel of her body as his hands glided over her silken skin.

He had no idea what tomorrow would bring, and he was torn between the plans he'd set in stone—leaving here and never looking back—and the very new, formless, undefined feelings he was experiencing right at this moment.

Feelings, he realized, that had begun to take root from the very moment she had walked into his life again.

There was no denying, even as he continued making love to every inch of her body, that he was the very epitome of confusion and indecision. He, who had always tread so confidently, so clear-eyed through every step of his life, found himself stumbling now.

He couldn't think beyond the moment, certainly not about anything that lay on the horizon. All he could think about was now—that he had to have her now—because there could very well be no later.

Like a man who sensed he was dying at dawn, he made love with Kenzie as if he'd never get another opportunity to do so. Perhaps never even see her again after tonight.

Desperation created a passion of unimaginable proportions.

He made love with her as if he was on fire, made love to each and every part of her before he finally succumbed and, unable to hold himself back for even another tenth of a second—made love to *all* of her.

* * *

Her heart was pounding so hard, she was having trouble catching her breath. He was making her absolutely, deliciously crazy.

She arched her body toward each wonderful, cascading sensation as it first exploded within her, then fanned out into a countless myriad of lights.

She had no idea it was possible or how he managed to do it, but Keith was creating climax after climax within her. He brought her up and over so many times that she was convinced, as she finally lay there all but panting from sheer, thrilling exhaustion, that she had died and hadn't become completely aware of it.

The ecstasy she was experiencing launched her into a semiconscious, euphoric state.

Kenzie clung to it as if it were her life preserver.

While she didn't want to relinquish her hold on what was tantalizingly echoing through her body, she didn't think she could take more pleasure.

She almost giggled then because it was obvious, from the urgent way Keith was kissing her, that she would have to readjust her perceived and preconceived notions about her own limits.

Her capacity for pleasure was just going to have to increase—and *fast*.

Because he was ramping up the parameters.

With her last ounce of strength, Kenzie raised herself up on her elbows and captured his lips first, beginning a new and final round to the lovemaking that had begun so suddenly a luscious eternity ago.

Her taking the initiative almost made him crazy, instantly increasing the desire he felt, spiking it in his veins even as it all but brought him to his knees.

He deepened the kiss between them, then went on to

spread kisses along her body as she twisted and turned beneath his mouth. Every single part of her eagerly sought to be touched by his lips, anointed by his tongue. Each contact had her racing heart singing.

She wanted him.

Wanted him down to her very core, and she didn't know how much longer she could hold out. Her body was all but literally crying out for his.

"Make love with me now," Kenzie said hoarsely. It was half a command, half a plea.

There was no way he could resist even a second longer.

Her entreaty broke the very last band of control he had left.

Keith threaded his fingers through hers, felt her body arching up to press against his. She urged him on to the final union.

Even if his very life had depended on it, he couldn't have held back for a heartbeat longer. His body positioned over hers, Keith drove himself into her with as much power as he had left in his diminished arsenal.

The moment they were joined, a growing rhythm overtook them, dictating their final moments.

The tempo increased, urging them on faster and faster until they were all but racing toward the all-encompassing explosion, the culmination of everything that had come before.

And when they reached the top of the summit, tightly holding on to one another, the explosion shook their bodies, then rained down an exhilarating tranquility on them that was equal parts joy, euphoria and then delicious exhaustion.

After the ecstasy retreated into a warm feeling of wellbeing, Keith held her to him in a way he had never held anything before. Gently, tenderly, but with an underlying urgency, because he feared that the second he let go of her, everything—she, the feeling, *everything*—would just vanish as if it had never really existed.

So he held her until they both finally drifted off to sleep, each willing dawn to remain a thousand miles away.

But dawn came, the way it always had, the way it always would. It came and nudged aside the darkness, bringing with it the morning light.

Keith opened his eyes, more than a little surprised to find himself still here, in the family room of the house he had grown up in.

His mother's house.

The realization drove the last remnants of sleep away from him as if sleep had been a figment of his imagination,

He almost sat up then. Except that he couldn't. His mouth curved.

There was a woman with her head on his chest, and he couldn't sit up without disturbing her. If he disturbed her, it would probably wake her up.

So he lay there, his arms now lightly instead of tightly folded around her.

Feeling her breathe soothed him. He needed soothing right about now. A great deal had happened last night. He had a lot to think about. But he didn't want to think about anything.

He wanted the world to go away and this moment to be frozen in time so that nothing changed and this brand-new, wondrous feeling he was trying so desperately to hang on to would remain forever—or at the very least, last a little while longer.

That was all he wanted, just a little while longer—since eternity was apparently out of the question and off the table.

God, he was rambling on even in his own head.

At least he hadn't opened his mouth to let any of this out. He sought some sort of rational order he could easily slip everything that had happened into.

Good luck with that, he mocked himself.

Kenzie was stirring.

He froze.

Her hair was tickling his face. What could he say to her? *Should* he say anything to her, or just pretend to be asleep?

He opted for door number two—but it was too late. She'd picked up her head and was looking straight at him, so there was no use in pretending he was asleep.

Resigned, he murmured, "'Morning."

"Yes," Kenzie agreed, stretching like a cat against him and sending his temperature—not to mention his heart—soaring. "It is that." Her mouth curved, amused. Kenzie looked into his eyes, her smile growing wider. "You're still here. Is that a good sign?"

Evasiveness had become a habit. He sank into it naturally. "You were asleep on my chest. I couldn't leave."

"Ah, so it's just a sign, not a good one. You're here because you're too much of a gentleman to push me aside in order to make your getaway." She pretended to mull it over, then nodded. "Not as romantic as I would have hoped, but I'll take it."

"Um, Kenzie—" His voice faltered slightly. He had no idea what to say next, or at least how to phrase what he wanted to say next. Making love with her had entirely taken away his edge.

"Relax," Kenzie laughed, lovingly touching his cheek. "I'm just kidding. There's no reason for you to turn so pale."

"I didn't turn pale," he protested.

Kenzie rolled her eyes. "Oh, puh-lease. In comparison, you'd make a ghost look like he had a suntan." She laughed and the sound was oddly comforting. Even though he thought it was at his expense. "It's okay, Keith. Breathe." She touched his cheek again, as if that would somehow help calm him down. "We made love and it was beyond wonderful—at least for me. But I'm not expecting to hear our banns being announced at mass, and I'm not about to drag you off to look at wedding rings," she assured him, her eyes dancing with humor.

"We made love last night, but today is a new day, with new problems, new hurdles to leap over. If I'm not mistaken, it's the first day the house is going to be open to the public in hopes of enchanting them. So unless you're game to bring a whole new meaning to the term 'unwrapped presents under the Christmas tree,' I suggest we get up from under the tree, get dressed and clean the family room."

He blinked, trying to absorb her words. The woman talked faster than anyone he had ever known, and that included lawyers. "Then last night didn't mean anything to you?"

How could he possibly say that? she couldn't help wondering.

Maybe it was breaking some kind of unspoken law about admitting far too much, but she told him, "It meant *everything* to me. But it wasn't a proposal and I'm not about to demand one. So, like I said, let's get cracking and whip this house back into shape."

Gratitude overwhelmed him. Before he could think to stop himself, he went with instinct. Keith spun her around to face him and kissed her.

Kissed her long and hard with mounting feeling.

When she finally got herself to pull back, Kenzie drew

in a deep, deep breath and shook her head. The man definitely didn't understand the concept of a temporary retreat for the sake of getting things that needed doing done.

"You do that again and I'm not going to be responsible for what happens next. There's just so much self-control a woman should be expected to exercise, especially when confronted with a lover who's so incredibly hot," she told him with a wink.

And with that, Kenzie quickly put distance between them before all her good intentions went flying out the window and she threw herself into his arms.

Chapter Fifteen

"The tree is a very nice touch," Maizie said with warm approval later that morning. The words were addressed to Keith. True to her word, the lively agent had arrived early to make sure there were no last-minute hiccups she needed to smooth out before the open house got underway at one. "Glad to see you decided to take my advice. It really creates a family-friendly atmosphere."

Keith never believed in taking credit that didn't belong to him. Working in a law firm had taught him that doing so could bite him later. Besides, he wanted Kenzie to have her due.

"Actually, it was Kenzie who insisted on it," he said, nodding in Kenzie's direction.

Maizie looked toward the younger woman. If anything, the agent's smile just grew deeper.

"Well, she was right. This really makes it feel less like just another house on the market and more like a home. Unless they're looking strictly for investment purposes, prospective buyers react very positively to that sort of thing. They like knowing the house they're considering buying lends itself well to a family scenario." Maizie made her way from the family room to the kitchen. "Have you been staying here?" she asked him.

His first impulse was to deny it. But something told him the savvy little woman would somehow know he was lying. So he told her the truth.

"I wasn't going to, but—"

Keith abruptly stopped himself from explaining any further. There was no need for any confessions. This woman was his agent, and while she was an exceptionally nice, warm, intelligent woman, she was definitely not his priest.

Less than a month ago, he wouldn't have felt the need to say anything at all. Just what was going on with him? Keith silently demanded.

"Yes, I am," he finally admitted. "Why?"

"No reason," Maizie told him with a careless shrug that could have been interpreted in so many ways. "It's just that the house appears to be exceptionally neat." She turned a warm smile on him. "Someone raised you well."

He bit his tongue, swallowing the first answer that rose to his lips. The answer rejecting the idea that he'd been raised well at all. But if he were being totally honest, he would admit that he *had* been raised well. It was only in the aftermath of those years that everything fell to pieces.

"Yes, well, I thought the house wouldn't exactly show very well and attract buyers if it was a mess."

Maizie inclined her head, her eyes shining with humor. "Very true."

Finished looking around, Maizie set down the flyers she'd had run off on the coffee table in plain view of the entrance. The handouts enumerated the home's best features as well as its upgrades.

She turned to Keith. "Well, I hope you have somewhere to go today between one and five." Then, in case the reason for that was eluding him—this was, as far as she knew, his first time as a seller—Maizie told him, "It's customary not to have the home owner around during an open house. Makes it less awkward for everyone."

He hadn't actually thought about that since, initially, he hadn't planned even to be in town at this point. "Um, sure, I..."

"I'm taking him to my store so he can see where some of his family's items will be going until someone snaps them up and gives them a good home," Kenzie informed the agent cheerfully.

Maizie looked from Kenzie to her client. "Judging from his bewildered expression, I think you forgot to tell him about that, dear."

That was because she'd just thought of it, Kenzie silently answered. Ever the subtle saleswoman, she proceeded to sell Keith on the idea.

"It'll be interesting," she assured him. "And maybe you'll see something there you might want to buy to give someone as a Christmas present."

"Why would I want to do that?"

His answer made it sound as if...

"Wait, you don't give Christmas presents?" Kenzie stared at him, stunned. "To anyone?" she asked incredulously. "Not even to those senior law partners you work for?"

He looked at her with surprise. "That would just be a form of bribery. They wouldn't stand for it."

Kenzie blew out a breath. She had no idea that the situation was this bad. Keith's soul really needed rescuing.

Apparently of like mind with Kenzie, the look on Maizie's face was nothing if not sympathetic.

"I'd say you had your work cut out for you, dear," the older woman said before she left the room, saying she was retrieving her business cards from the trunk of her car.

Kenzie, meanwhile, was still frozen in place. "You were kidding, weren't you? About not giving any Christmas presents?" There was more than a hint of a hopeful note in her voice.

Keith shrugged off her question, telling himself that her obvious disappointment shouldn't have bothered him. *Why* was it bothering him? he silently demanded.

"Don't have anyone to give them to."

It was, in a nutshell, his go-to excuse for not participating in the holidays. With Amy gone and his mother heretofore inaccessible, Christmas and the trappings that went with it ceased to have any meaning to him.

This, Kenzie decided, would require drastic measures. And then a possible solution occurred to her.

"I have a better place to take you than my shop," she announced suddenly. "Just give me a few minutes to make a call."

It was getting so that he could almost read her mind. At least he could this time around. "I don't know what you think you need to do for me, but I assure you I do not need any—"

"Yeah, you do," she said, cutting him off. "Don't worry," she added, "It'll be painless."

And then she stopped talking because whoever she had just dialed on her cell phone had obviously picked up. Rather than continue her dialogue with Keith, Kenzie held up her finger in a silent instruction to stop his words midflow.

Kenzie turned away so he wouldn't overhear her. The

move was done out of habit, but he had to admit that his curiosity had been piqued—and his impatience was fueled. He didn't need whatever holiday sleight-of-hand Kenzie thought she was going to perform.

With that in mind, since she wasn't facing him, he decided he'd leave the house while she was talking. Slipping out the front door—the agent had already gone back inside and was doing something in one of the rooms—Keith came within a foot of making good his getaway.

Kenzie caught up to him just as he was about to get into his car. He'd opened the door and was going to slide in behind the steering wheel when he felt her hand on his shoulder.

"You're coming with me," she announced as if she didn't realize she had foiled his getaway.

He turned around to face her, impatience swaddling each word. "Kenzie, I don't need a babysitter."

"Good," she countered, "because no one's offering to babysit you." The significance of the words he'd chosen suddenly hit her. "If anything, you will be the one doing the sitting."

She'd totally lost him with that. "Come again?"

But Kenzie didn't go into any more detailed explanations. All she said was a very pregnant, "You'll see."

Keith could only think of one logical scenario as she commandeered the keys from him and told him to get into the passenger's seat. "Are you kidnapping me to a motel room?" The situation as he painted it was not without its rather large merits.

Starting the car, she pulled out of the driveway. "Well, you're half right."

"Which half?"

Kenzie spared him a glance as she took a right turn at the next through street. "I'm kidnapping you."

"Not to a motel room?" To anyone listening, it sounded as if Keith was kidding. He wasn't, at least not entirely.

Kenzie pretended to roll the thought over in her mind. "Maybe later. As a reward," she added.

"For me?" he questioned.

Even with her facing forward, he could see how deep her smile went. "For both of us."

Keith laughed, shaking his head. The woman was nothing if not unique. "Now you really have me curious."

"Good," she declared. To his frustration and surprise, she made no effort to explain anything further.

Keith tried another approach to unravel what she was up to. "Can I ask who you called?"

Kenzie inclined her head in a careless fashion. "You can ask."

It didn't take a philosopher to understand what she was saying. "But you won't tell me."

"I won't tell you," she confirmed, adding, "I figure it's more interesting for you if I just keep you guessing."

That sounded too much like a game, and he needed to let her know something right off the top. "Look, I'm not into playing games."

"Too bad." She sounded as if she genuinely meant that. "It actually might come in handy. Maybe it'll come back to you after a while."

"What the hell are you talking about?" Keith demanded, feeling as if he'd somehow gotten all tangled up and was sinking.

"Christmas, Keith. I'm talking about Christmas."

She wasn't going to tell him anything, he concluded. Since he was here, Keith decided that he might as well just let this all play itself out. Maybe there would finally be answers when she got to wherever it was she was going.

Sliding back in his seat, Keith pushed it into a resting position. "If you say so."

Kenzie laughed then and reached over to pat his arm, keeping her eyes on the road. "Not too far now," she promised.

As far as he was concerned, it had already gone way too far.

"We're here," she announced a little more than ten minutes later.

"Here?" Keith repeated, looking around. "Exactly where's 'here'?" he asked.

As far as he could make out, she had just turned onto a gravel-strewn parking lot. After driving only a few feet more, she came to a stop in front of a long, single-story building that was badly in need of paint not to mention some very crucially missing stucco work.

There was a sign across the front of the building, but the sun was in his eyes, so he couldn't make it out.

But Kenzie wasn't listening to him as she got out of the car. Instead, she seemed to be looking around for something.

Or someone, as it turned out.

The second she spotted who she was looking for, she broke into a wreath of smiles. A moment later, Kenzie's mystery person had joined them.

"You made it," Kenzie cried in relief.

Almost reluctantly, Keith got out of the car to see who she was talking to.

The next second, his mouth dropped open.

"Mrs. Bradshaw, I didn't expect to see you here," he said to the slender woman in gray slacks, a pink sweater and a matching hoodie.

"I have a habit of popping up in odd places," Kenzie's mother conceded. "Hello, dear." Andrea paused to greet him with a quick kiss against his cheek, treating him as if he were her son instead of just her daughter's...what? Her daughter's what? Keith silently demanded of himself.

He really hadn't figured out what to call their relationship—or if it actually *was* a relationship.

Turning toward her daughter, Andrea went on to tell her, "I brought everything, just the way you asked me to."

"Everything?" Keith echoed.

He was beginning to feel like a parrot, repeating words that became no clearer to him the second time around.

Taking pity on him, Kenzie turned toward him and said, "She means toys."

"Toys?" He was no more enlightened now than he had been a moment ago.

Kenzie pressed her lips together to keep from laughing at him. "All right, you'll have to learn how to speak in full sentences if you're going to help me."

"Help you with what?" Keith demanded. He was down that rabbit hole again, he thought irritably. And she wasn't helping. He was beginning to think she was enjoying his confusion.

"Better," Kenzie said, nodding her approval. "But still needs a little work."

In mounting desperation, he turned toward her mother. "What is she talking about?"

"I'm never quite sure, Keith," Andrea admitted, commiserating with him. "But I've learned that if you hang in there long enough, it eventually all makes sense after a bit."

"No big mystery," Kenzie told him, sounding, to his way of thinking, just a little too innocent as she added, "I'm playing Santa Claus, and you're my helper."

Keith realized her mother was in on this little scenario, as well, when Andrea said to her, "Really, dear, I don't

MARIE FERRARELLA   181

want to be stereotypical about this, but since Santa was a man, don't you think Keith should play Santa Claus and *you* should be *his* helper?"

Kenzie pretended that lightning had suddenly struck, clearing everything up.

"You know, that might make more sense, after all. You can be Santa Claus," she told him. And just to make it official, she produced a Santa suit, complete with a red cap from a bag that her mother handed her. She slipped the hat snugly on Keith's head. "There, it's official. I hereby dub you Santa Claus for a day! Now let's go get you into this getup so you can start making some very deserving little kids happy."

After five minutes and one detour into the kitchen so he could put on the suit, Keith stood frowning at the traditional costume that hung around his body. He'd been forced to put it on over his own clothes in an attempt to deal with its size, but it was still dangerously baggy and threatening to fall off at any moment.

"I really don't think I can do this," he told Kenzie as she fussed around him, using safety pins to decrease the size where she could.

"It would have been even looser on me," she told him, adding, "We have to work with what we have."

"No, we don't. *I* don't," he corrected her.

Kenzie stopped what she was doing, one last safety pin still in her hand. She didn't look at him with exasperation or annoyance. Instead, she searched her mind for a way to approach him logically instead of using emotions to win him over.

"Have you ever pleaded one of your cases before a judge?" she asked him quietly.

Was she kidding? He wasn't a law clerk. He was an accredited *lawyer*. "Yes, of course I have."

Nodding, Kenzie continued. "Was he a friendly judge?"

Subsequent judges had melded together, but not his first one. That man's dour face was still as vividly clear in his mind as if the trial had taken place yesterday. "Not particularly," he answered gruffly.

"Then I guess, since you didn't think it was a slam-dunk, you gave up." She said it as if it was a foregone conclusion.

"No, of course not."

"But you didn't win."

He saw where Kenzie was going with this. "Yes, I won."

Kenzie smiled, her argument made. "Then you can do this," she assured Keith with total confidence. "These kids are more than willing to meet you halfway. Having Santa Claus find them brings hope into their young lives. And the gifts in here," she told him, patting the side of the large sagging red sack, made out of the same material that his suit was, "will sell themselves. All you have to do is say 'Ho-ho-ho' and the toys in the bag will do the rest of your talking for you." She put on the finishing touch: pulling a white beard out of the same bag that had held his costume. After helping him put it on, she looked at him and grinned. "Hottest looking Santa I've ever seen, bar none. Ready?"

Keith was still not completely convinced he could pull this off. "No, I don't think I'm—"

He didn't get a chance to finish because she suddenly sang out, "Showtime!" grabbed hold of his hand and pulled him from the safety of the kitchen into the pure nerve-racking atmosphere of the homeless shelter's common room, where the parents and children spent time getting to know one another and hopefully made connections that would last them a lifetime. Or, at the very least, help get their minds off their situations for a little while.

"I sure hope you know what I'm doing," Keith said, eyeing the group of children he saw at the far end of the room.

"Absolutely. Bringing hope," she told him, looking pointedly at him.

He wasn't ready for this. Wasn't ready to interact with small, thin faces, all eagerly hoping that Santa had remembered them.

But ready or not, here they came, he thought as a group of children suddenly and enthusiastically surrounded him.

"What's in your bag, Mr. Santa?" one little blonde girl, who couldn't have been any older than six, asked as she tugged on Keith's sleeve.

For a split second, she reminded him of Amy when she had been that small. The same hair color, the same delicate bone structure.

And suddenly, it wasn't so hard playing Santa Claus any more. "Why don't we open it and see?" Keith answered, adding, "Who knows? There might even be something here for you."

"Really?" the little girl asked, her bright blue eyes growing to the size of the proverbial saucers as she turned them to the large bag Keith had managed to bring into the room.

"Really," Keith replied.

He pulled back the straining sides of the red bag and took out the first wrapped package. He pretended to examine it, shaking it slightly. And then he saw the lettering, ever so faint, across the front.

The word was Girl, telling him the gift was a safe one to give to a little girl. He couldn't help thinking the girl's whole future and how she approached it might very well be formed here, in this room, because Santa Claus had had time to fly his reindeer over to her part of the city and bring her a gift.

It was, Keith discovered, a very heady feeling.

And Kenzie had given it to him.

Chapter Sixteen

"Keep going, Santa," Kenzie urged him, whispering into his ear. The little girl squealed when she discovered a soft, furry yellow bear wearing a red T-shirt beneath the silver-and-green Christmas wrapping paper that she had sent flying in ripped pieces. "It looks like you're on a roll."

"I don't look anything like Santa Claus," he protested. Even with him sitting down, the jacket was pooling around him like a red lake.

"Granted, you're not exactly rotund, but you've got the suit. More importantly, you came in carrying a bag stuffed with toys, so you'll more than do," Kenzie told him. She could see that he needed just a little more convincing. "Try to think of yourself as the poor man's Santa Claus. Or, in this case, the poor child's Santa Claus."

Keith spared her another look as he surrendered. He couldn't very well find it in his heart to argue with that. Not when he was looking down at so many eager little faces.

Besides, he had to admit that seeing the girl smile and hearing her squeal of joy did feel good.

"Okay," he said in the deepest voice he could summon, waving the next child to come closer. "Let's see what's in this bag for you."

He didn't have to say it twice.

"I think you've found his element, Kenzie," her mother said to her as they both observed Keith in this new role. He would hand out a gift only after spending a couple of minutes talking to each new child. Andrea glanced at her before continuing. "He was always polite and well mannered, but this is definitely the happiest I've seen him."

Normally optimistic, exuberant and the first to lead the parade, this one time Kenzie was treading lightly, leery of assuming too much. "Someone once told me something about counting chickens," Kenzie replied, looking pointedly at her mother.

"Perhaps," Andrea conceded. She smiled at her daughter. "But after all, my love, it is Christmas, the season of miracles, and the kids seem more than willing to believe that your friend is Santa Claus."

"Santa Claus after a major crash diet," Kenzie pointed out, nodding at the way Keith's costume hung on his body.

Andrea laughed softly, shaking her head. "What happened to my dreamer?"

"It's uncharted territory, Mom. She decided to tread cautiously," Kenzie answered.

There was deep affection in Andrea's eyes as she looked at her youngest daughter. "So it's like that, is it?"

Kenzie could feel herself retreating, as if saying anything at all would jeopardize this happiness. Until now, she'd never been superstitious, but until now, she'd never felt like this before.

"No, I just—"

Something suddenly popped into Andrea's head. "Wait, isn't he the boy you had that huge crush on?" The moment she said it, it began making a great deal more sense.

Alarmed, Kenzie instantly pulled her mother aside. She was afraid that the next thing out of her mother's mouth would embarrass her beyond any hope of recovery.

"That was then," Kenzie insisted in a very firm, hoarse whisper.

In response, her mother smiled. "I see."

Oh, God, she should have flatly denied it instead. She hated lying, but there were consequences to this getting out. Her mother meant well, but Kenzie had a sinking feeling it would be only a matter of time—short time— before her mother spoke to Keith about "great loves that were meant to be" or something equally as embarrassing.

"Mother—" There was a desperate warning note in Kenzie's voice.

Andrea held her hands up as if that helped establish her innocence. "I didn't say a word, dear," she said. "Well, I have to be getting back. I just came with the toys the way you asked me to. But there's lots to do at home. Don't forget to come tomorrow," she reminded Kenzie as she began to leave. "Bring your friend."

The last sentence floated back to Kenzie in her mother's wake.

"How did you happen to find this place?"

Keith asked her the question when they were back in the shelter's overcrowded main office. The first thing he'd stripped off was the beard, which had been driving him crazy for the past three hours. He ran his hands over his face, trying not to give in to the overwhelming desire to scratch it and keep scratching.

The jacket and oversize pants were next. The last gift

had been given out, and after spending another hour in the children's midst, the children and Santa had parted company. He was tired, but there was an odd sort of contentment weaving its way through him that he had to admit he was enjoying.

Still, he was more than ready to go home.

Home.

It felt rather odd, after all this time had passed, to suddenly be applying that word to the house on Normandie Circle. He hadn't thought of it in that sense since he'd left. And yet, somewhere in the back of his mind, he supposed it had always been that. Possibly years from now it would still unofficially wear that label for him even if he never uttered the word again. The house on Normandie had been and would always be home.

Some of that, he knew, had to do with Kenzie. Maybe even a lot of it.

"I didn't exactly find this place," Kenzie was saying, answering his question. "Mrs. Manetti told me about it. She and her crew prepare food and bring it here every other week. Otherwise the shelter serves foods that are donated by discount stores. In her opinion, just because people have temporarily fallen on hard times doesn't mean they should only have three-day-old bread, powdered foods and fruits that were going to be thrown out."

"Mrs. Manetti," he repeated, the name nudging at a memory he couldn't quite get hold of. "Isn't that the woman who—"

"Catered your mother's funeral reception," Kenzie finished his sentence for him. "Yes, she is. She has a very big heart. When I once mentioned that observation to her, she just shrugged it off, saying it's her way of giving back to the community for her own good fortune."

Well, that explained the food he saw being served, but

not everything. "And the toys I was giving out today? Where did they come from?"

Kenzie's smile grew wider. "My mother and sisters have toy drives in their communities."

"Just your mother and sisters?" he questioned, sensing that there was some information missing. There were a lot of toys in that bag. "You don't have any part in it?"

Kenzie never felt comfortable talking about herself when it came to charitable deeds, but he'd asked her a direct question, so she was forced to give him an answer. "I might."

Folding the suit and placing it into the bag that Kenzie had brought it in, he laughed, shaking his head. They walked out of the shelter and got into her car. "I feel like I've just wandered into some old-fashioned feel-good movie."

"No, that'll come tomorrow," she told him glibly, driving away from the shelter.

Caught off guard, Keith looked at her, confused. "Tomorrow? What's tomorrow?"

She did her best to keep a straight face as she asked, "You mean besides being Christmas Eve?"

Keith suppressed a sigh. "Yes, besides being Christmas Eve."

"My mother invited you to the family Christmas party." When he made no response, she added, "I'll be there, too, seeing as how I'm part of the family and all."

"And I'll be on a plane for San Francisco," he told her.

She'd given herself a pep talk centered around the fact that what had happened last night would not change anything—but she hadn't expected it not to change anything so soon. She realized that he was leaving, but she wasn't ready to see him go so quickly.

"Really?" She packed a great deal of feeling into the

single word. "You don't want to be flying on Christmas Eve."

"Why not?" he challenged her. Then he reminded her, "A room full of kids thinks I'm Santa Claus. Santa Claus flies every Christmas Eve."

"Santa Claus doesn't fly," she contradicted him. "The reindeer do. If the reindeer were sitting on a plane, letting some pilot fly them—and you—it might not be all that safe on Christmas Eve. Even the reindeer know the pilot might have been celebrating just a little too much."

They were here, back at the house, she realized. The distance had managed just to disappear. She supposed the thought of his leaving so abruptly had caused her not to notice.

Kenzie pulled up in front of his house.

"You're reaching," he told her as they got out of her car.

The open house sign Mrs. Sommers had placed beside the for sale sign was gone. That meant the house was his again, at least for the night. He tried not to notice the sense of relief that came with the realization. He refused to explore what it might actually mean to him.

"I know, but you're tall. I have to reach," she quipped.

He laughed and shook his head again. "Kenzie, you're one of a kind."

"Considering the business I'm in, I'll take that as a compliment," she told him.

Keith began to go up the front walk. Kenzie, he discovered, was right behind him.

"You're coming in?" he asked, not entirely surprised at how good that thought made him feel.

"Well, I have to see what we'll be putting out for the sale tomorrow." She'd already told him that her aim tomorrow would be to appeal to shoppers who had put off finding the right gift until the last minute. "Besides," she continued as she followed him inside, "it would be kind of difficult for me to make dinner if I'm not in the house."

This was the first he was hearing about it. "You're making dinner?"

Kenzie nodded. "Unless you're rather have takeout, of course."

He had takeout all the time when he worked. He didn't believe in brown-bagging it, and evenings usually found him still at his desk, so ordering takeout seemed like the only logical way to go. But he didn't look forward to it anymore.

"No, I'm fine with you making dinner," he assured her quickly, not wanting her to change her mind. "I don't get much of a chance to eat a home-cooked meal."

Kenzie flashed a smile. She'd been pretty sure she wasn't going to need to twist his arm.

"Home cooked meal it is," she declared.

And then, maybe dessert, she added silently, knowing better than to count on it. This was all very undefined territory she was treading.

And maybe she was giving herself too much credit, but she had a strong hunch that he felt the exact same way about what was going on here. The man exuded sex appeal, but she suspected he was completely oblivious to that.

Ninety minutes later, after having seconds and then thirds, Keith realized he was dangerously close to needing to unbuckle his belt, or at least move it by a notch. He was stuffed—but happily so. The meal she had prepared for them—Sicilian chicken—had been so good, he couldn't stop himself from taking "just a little bit more" until "more" had added up to almost three full servings.

"Where did you learn to cook like that?" he asked

her, sitting back in his chair. He didn't want to leave the table just yet.

"Watching my mom," Kenzie replied. "And Mrs. Manetti's given me tips now and then. This was her recipe," she told him.

"How do you know her?" She had managed to arouse his curiosity on so many levels, and since he was asking questions, he figured he might as well throw that one into the mix.

"She and my mom are friends. They have been for a very long time."

As she talked, she began to gather the plates together, consolidating what had been left on the serving platters onto one.

"I think they were each other's bridesmaids. I know my mom was there for her when Mrs. Manetti lost her husband. And Mrs. Manetti returned the favor when my dad died." And then she smiled, remembering. "Mrs. Manetti was the one who encouraged my mother to start her own business, said that was the best way for her to get out into the world again and get on with the business of living. Mrs. Manetti told my mother that starting her own catering company was what really helped her function again."

"They both sound like extraordinary women," he told her. Accompanying the words was a pang he was quick to bury.

He had a strong feeling that if he didn't get up and start moving, he was going to wind up falling asleep right where he sat. Keith rose from the table and picked up his plate, taking it to the sink.

Kenzie was on her feet as well, carrying the platter to the counter. She covered it and placed it in the refrigerator.

"Most moms usually are," she told him, commenting on his observation.

She went back for the other plates, putting those in the sink on top of his plate.

Keith turned away from her. "Yes, well, we might have a difference of opinion on that," he said. There was a faint touch of bitterness in his voice.

What could have gone down between his mother and Keith to have made him so angry, even now, after her death? she wondered. Her sympathy went out to both.

"Some just don't have as easy a time of it as others," she told him.

Kenzie was really afraid this was going to eat straight into his gut. Putting her hands on his shoulders, she turned Keith around to face her. "It's Christmas, Keith. Don't you think it's time you forgave her?"

He was *not* about to get into this with her. He didn't want to spoil the evening—or the upbeat feeling that today and playing Santa Claus for the children had created.

"I don't want to talk about that now," he told her firmly.

Kenzie prided herself on knowing when to back off. "Fair enough. What do you want to talk about?"

That was the moment when he gave in to impulse, which he wasn't accustomed to doing. But then, none of what had been happening these last few days could be categorized as normal for him.

"We'll think of something," he told Kenzie just before he pulled her close and kissed her the way he had been aching to do all day long.

It didn't end there, as they both knew it wouldn't. Instead, one kiss blossomed into two, then three, then four, each kiss lasting longer, going deeper than the one before it.

Passions and desires instantly reheated in their blood, laying open the path that they had accidentally discovered last night. Except this time, there was no resistance, no hesitancy. Instead, there was the immediate joy of encountering the new and yet familiar feelings and reactions to the wondrous brand-new world that was waiting for them just a whisper of a shadow away.

A world neither one of them even tried to resist this time.

Resistance was futile, Kenzie caught herself thinking, remembering a clichéd line from a classic sci-fi series. Keith was making her close to crazy as he caused desire and gratification to leap almost simultaneously through her body.

She returned the favor as best she could, all too aware of the ironic fact that each moment she spent with him was one less moment she had left to spend with him. Unless something drastic happened to change his mind, he would be leaving her very soon.

He'd changed his mind about leaving tomorrow. He was going with her to the party at her mother's.

But what of the day after tomorrow? a small voice in her head—or was that her heart?—whispered.

And as they came together, creating that wondrous, temporary paradise for each other that she craved, she was left to wonder if she could stand watching him actually leave her.

She knew the answer to that even if she didn't want to admit it to herself.

Spent, exhausted, she lay beside Keith, missing him already.

"Wow," he murmured a moment later, too tired to pretend to be unaffected. "A few more times like that and I very well might not be able to move again." He felt her mouth curving in a smile against his chest as he held her. "What?" he asked, curious what had made her smile like that.

Curious, he realized, about everything having to do with her. Dangerous thoughts for a man who was leaving the day after tomorrow, he silently warned. Not just leaving, but for all intents and purpose, never returning to the region again.

"You just gave me an idea," she told him, her eyes dancing as she raised herself up on her elbow, her hair brushing tantalizingly along his skin.

He wasn't even sure just what he'd said, much less what it might have suggested to her. "What kind of an idea?" he asked.

"I plan to love you into a stupor." *So you can't leave.* "I don't want to waste my breath talking." She curled her body along his like a seductive snake.

"What do you want to waste it on?" he heard himself asking.

She was smiling into his eyes just before she answered him—kind of.

"Guess."

And then she didn't give him a chance to say anything further. He couldn't if he'd wanted to. Her mouth was sealed to his, creating blissful havoc.

Chapter Seventeen

It felt strange waking up beside her. Strange how very right it felt, even though he'd never allowed his barriers to be lowered to this extent, never spent the night with any woman he had made love with. Spending the night whispered of the beginnings of a commitment. And a commitment was something he had never wanted, never allowed himself to want.

And yet, here he was, of his own free will, finding a certain sort of comfort in the simple act of listening to her breathe.

Well, don't get used to it. You're leaving tomorrow, remember? If you don't, if you keep finding excuses to hang around, you're going to regret it. You know that you will.

His arm tightened around Kenzie, as if that could somehow hold reality—his reality—at bay a little while longer.

At least just for today.

He felt Kenzie stirring beside him. The next moment, her eyes opened and she smiled at him. "Hi."

Everything inside him smiled back at her.

"Hi yourself." He did his best not to sound distracted or give her any indication of the war that was currently being waged within him. "I didn't wake you, did I?" he asked, his arm automatically tightening around her when he thought about leaving Kenzie.

"I don't know," Kenzie admitted sleepily. "Did you shake me?"

"No." Technically, he hadn't, he told himself, knowing he was falling back on semantics.

"Then I guess you didn't wake me." Kenzie stretched, stifling a yawn, unaware of how sensual she looked or how something as simple as her stretching like that was arousing him. "Want breakfast?"

"Eventually," he told her, drawing her back into his arms.

And just like that, Kenzie was wide awake. "Oh. Dessert first," she said with approval, her eyes shining. "Good. I like dessert."

"You talk too much, Kenzie," he told her, beginning to kiss the sides of her neck and causing those delicious sensations to start leaping through her.

"So I've been told," Kenzie murmured just before he brought his mouth to hers and she couldn't say another word—and didn't want to.

"I was beginning to think you two weren't coming," Andrea said, opening the door to admit her daughter and Keith.

She hugged each warmly, starting with Keith, before either of them even had a chance to cross the threshold into the house.

Kenzie exchanged glances with Keith, her mouth curving as she thought of what had delayed them. "Wrapping presents took longer than we anticipated," she explained.

"*Wrapping* presents," Andrea repeated.

The expression on her mother's face told Kenzie that she wasn't fooled for a minute—and she couldn't have been more pleased about it.

Don't get used to it, Mom. He's leaving on a jet plane come tomorrow—or the day after, but he is leaving, just like the song says, she thought sadly.

Kenzie wasn't altogether sure if the silent caution echoing in her head was meant for her mother or for her.

Even standing here amid the warmth of family, with Keith right next to her, she could feel the ache beginning.

God, but she didn't want him to go.

"Well," Andrea was saying, hooking one arm through each of theirs, "as long as you're both finally here, that's all that counts." She beamed at each in turn, then announced, "It's official. We can start the Christmas party now."

"Your mother's kidding, right?" Keith said to her the moment Andrea moved on. "She really didn't mean she was holding up the party until we got here—did she?" he asked skeptically.

She would have loved to have reassured him—or, even simpler, pretended not to know the answer to his question. But if their time together was limited, she wouldn't mar it by lying, even though the answer would probably make him uneasy.

"My mother is a very happy, upbeat person, but certain things she doesn't kid about. Christmas parties aren't complete until everyone in the family attends. She's been like that ever since I can remember."

That might have been true, but in his opinion, Kenzie

seemed to be overlooking one very salient point. "I'm not family."

She shrugged as if the matter was out of her hands. "Apparently, you are—for tonight."

Maybe he shouldn't have come, after all, Keith thought. He was only getting further entrenched in a situation he had no business being in. He shouldn't allow her family to see him in a light that wasn't anywhere near accurate— no matter how seductive that light might temporarily be to him.

The next moment, however, as he was swept up in the festivities, the thought, born of self-preservation, vanished.

"Your mother shouldn't have bought me presents," he protested late that night when he and Kenzie had returned to his house.

"Don't worry about it," Kenzie assured him. "My mother loves buying presents. It makes her happy." She slipped off her coat and let it drape over the back of the sofa. She laced her hands through his as she looked up into his face, desperately trying not to think beyond the moment. "Consider it helping her find a reason to satisfy her shopping craving."

He shook his head as he marveled, "You know, the way you can twist things around until they fit the occasion, you would make quite a lawyer."

Kenzie demurred having the label applied to her. "Uh-uh, not my style. People don't like lawyers." She managed to get the line out while keeping a straight face.

He ran the back of his hand along her cheek. "Until they need one."

Kenzie could already feel herself melting. "Good point. And I suddenly find myself in desperate need of one."

Dropping his hands, she draped her arms around the back of his neck. She leaned into him just enough to have all the vital parts of their bodies touch. She could feel the sparks being set off already.

"And why would you be in desperate need of a lawyer?" he teased.

"Because we're standing under mistletoe." Kenzie grinned as she pointed over his head. "And I have this overwhelming, uncontrollable urge to kiss a lawyer."

Curious, he looked up. Kenzie was right. There *was* mistletoe hanging from the light fixture, and it was directly over their heads. He was certain the mistletoe hadn't been there when'd they left for her mother's party.

Or had it?

"Who put that there?" he asked her.

Her shoulders rose and fell in complete innocence. "Elves?" she guessed. "Enough with the small talk," Kenzie told him. "Like I said, I have this sudden need to fulfill a fantasy and kiss a lawyer."

Tomorrow he just might be on that flight back to the rest of his life. But he was still here tonight, and it was up to him to make the very most of every second he had. So he shoved the oppressive weight of his thoughts aside and did his best to grab a festive attitude.

"At your service, ma'am," he told her, closing his arms around Kenzie.

Her eyes shone as she replied, "I certainly hope so." And then she put him to the test.

It wasn't supposed to be this hard, Keith told himself early the next morning—Christmas morning. He should have been gone several days ago, not lingering like this, looking for yet another excuse to stay a day longer.

He had a life waiting for him in San Francisco, he silently insisted. A career to get back to. Here he was just floating around in limbo.

The bulk of his mother's possessions had already been sold and picked up, thanks to Kenzie's unique ability to sell ice to polar bears. What was left he'd decided to donate to the shelter where Kenzie volunteered rather than have her try to sell it on consignment at her shop.

He hadn't been sure how she would react to that when he proposed it on the way home last night. The straight donation meant she wouldn't be getting a percentage of the sale. But Kenzie, being Kenzie, had been happy about his decision.

"It's the right thing to do," she'd told him. "Trust me, it'll mean a lot more to someone at the shelter than it would to some shopper who'll most likely leave what she bought in her garage or the back of her closet once the novelty wears off."

The house, on the other hand, didn't seem to be generating enough interest, which in turn meant it wasn't about to sell soon. But then, given the season and what Mrs. Sommers had told him, Keith had to admit he wasn't really surprised. Since he didn't need the money, there was no urgency to sell the house.

There was also no need for him to hang around.

No real need except that he wanted to.

Which was why he needed to leave. Needed to leave *now*, before Kenzie looked at him and said something that would make him weaken. That would make him stay.

So while Kenzie ran an errand—dropping off Christmas gifts at the homes of the two assistants who worked for her—Keith packed his suitcase.

He'd almost given in to the temptation to leave before she returned—it would mean having to spend an extra hour at the airport, but then at least the break would be a clean one.

At the last moment, he decided to tell her goodbye in person. She deserved that.

Anything else would have been cowardly. Maybe it was vanity on his part, but he didn't want Kenzie to remember him that way—being too cowardly to face her. So he stayed, giving her an hour, waiting for the sound of her turning the doorknob and returning.

Waiting was agony.

And then he heard her opening the door.

The moment she walked in, Kenzie understood.

She didn't even have to see the suitcase standing on the floor behind the coffee table to know that Keith was leaving. And it wasn't even the suit he had on that gave him away. The expression on his face did it, the somber look in his eyes.

Her heart drained, her head throbbing, she started talking without comprehending what would come out of her mouth.

"You're leaving early," she said.

"No," he contradicted her, the word feeling wooden in his mouth, "I'm leaving late. I should have left two days ago. But I bumped back the ticket."

She knew that already. She'd overheard him doing it and kept praying he'd do it again—or throw away the ticket altogether.

This was where she had an opportunity to save face, to say something blasé and glib. This was where she began to distance herself from him.

She couldn't do it. Couldn't be anything but honest with him. The other facade wouldn't have been her. "I was hoping you bumped it back until the day after New Year's."

Not that he hadn't been tempted, but it would have been even harder with that much more time going by. "I would still have to leave," he pointed out.

"Maybe," she conceded. "But it wouldn't be today," she told him quietly.

Logic. He had to hang onto logic. Emotions would be his downfall. "Kenzie, I don't live here anymore."

She pressed her lips together, obviously trying not to cry. "I know." The words came out in a whisper.

If he'd left already, he wouldn't have to be agonizing through this conversation now. He didn't want to see her hurting. "My law firm is in San Francisco."

"I know," Kenzie repeated almost stoically.

His cell phone rang just then, and he glanced down at his pocket as if the phone was intruding.

"Better get that," she told him stiffly. "Might be your firm wanting to know what's keeping you."

You. What's keeping me is you, Keith told her silently.

But he knew that was exactly why he had to leave today. Leave *now*. Because if he didn't, he might not go at all, and he had to. Otherwise he wouldn't be who he really was.

So he turned away to answer his cell, trying to regroup. He didn't want to make this any harder for either of them.

Moving aside, he took his phone out of his pocket and glanced at the caller ID. Kenzie was right. One of the firm's senior partners was having his secretary call him, no doubt to verify that he would be on the five o'clock flight out of John Wayne Airport.

"Hello," he snapped. "This is O'Connell." And then he listened to the woman on the other end for a minute. Her end of the conversation was very sparse. And predictable.

"I'll be on it," he told the woman, his throat feeling incredibly dry as he forced the words out. He ended the call and tucked the phone back into his pocket before turning around to face Kenzie again.

He was stalling because he didn't know what to say to her or how to say it. The idea of the getaway he'd turned his back on earlier began to feel like a missed opportunity.

That didn't change the fact that he still had to get through this. Taking a breath, he forced himself to speak.

"I guess this is it," he began.

"I guess so," she agreed stiffly, her dry tone matching his.

He had to be honest with her even though he wanted to say anything that would take that stricken but brave look off her face. "I won't tell you I'll be back, because I don't know if I will. Maybe I'll have to come back when Mrs. Sommers sells the house—"

"She can mail you the papers," Kenzie said, her tone implying that there was no reason for him to return—at least, not if that was his only reason for coming back.

"I guess she can," he agreed.

With nothing left to stop him, Keith picked up his suitcase. More than anything, he wanted to take her into his arms, to kiss her one last time—long and hard, because this kiss was going to have to last him. But if he stopped to kiss her like that, he was fairly certain that he wouldn't make it out the door.

So instead, his hand just tightened around his suitcase—he did it to keep from grabbing her. "Goodbye, Kenzie. Thanks for everything."

She could feel the tears beginning to gather in her eyes. Damn it, Keith needed to leave before she broke down altogether. She didn't want him to see her crying. Didn't want him to think it was some cheap feminine ploy. Most of all, she didn't want to break down because if he saw her crying and still walked away, she knew she couldn't survive that sort of heartbreak.

So rather than make a comment, or give in to her natural instincts and throw her arms around him, or kiss him goodbye while saying something to him that she would regret, Kenzie just said goodbye and walked out the door ahead of him, her head held high.

She didn't pause to glance back, to see if he was watching her. She just looked straight ahead and walked as quickly as she could to her car. The second she got in, she closed the door.

Turning the key, she started the vehicle, telling herself over and over again not to cry until she had at least gotten out of his cul-de-sac.

She didn't quite make it.

The tears started coming before she had a chance to make the left turn onto the through street that ultimately led out of the development. Blinking madly didn't keep them at bay, didn't curb the flow.

A part of her had clung to the hope that he'd change his mind at the last minute.

But he hadn't.

Keith stood in his driveway, watching her drive away, struggling with the very strong desire to run after her and make her turn the car around and come back.

To what end? he asked himself. He had to leave. An extra hour or even an extra day wasn't going to change that. Being here in Bedford wasn't what his life was about anymore. He'd forged a new life for himself in San Francisco. It had taken him ten years to do it, but it was solid now and he had a commitment to the firm he worked for.

He couldn't just contemplate throwing all that away on a whim because he'd had an unexpectedly nice eight days here. People went away to exotic places on vacation, but they didn't suddenly uproot their entire lives and move there just because they had had a nice few days. That would have been completely crazy.

He knew better than that.

He knew exactly what he was leaving and what was waiting for him when the plane landed.

He knew.

Keith's hands tightened on the steering wheel as he pressed down harder on the accelerator. He told himself not to think because right now that would only serve to confuse matters.

Most of all, he told himself not to feel.

That used to be a lot easier to do when he had nothing to feel about, he thought.

Keith stepped on the gas harder, going faster. Trying to outrun his thoughts before they could catch up to him and make him turn around again.

Chapter Eighteen

Maizie hadn't intended to stop at the house on Normandie. She was just driving by to see if the flyers in the clear container beneath the for sale sign on the front lawn needed to be replenished. But when she saw Kenzie's car parked in the driveway, she pulled her own up to the curb just past the mailbox and got out.

The front door was locked, so she used her passkey, knocking as she slowly opened the door. She didn't want to walk in on something she shouldn't.

"Kenzie, are you in here?" she called out.

In response, a rather tired-looking Kenzie came out into the living room from the kitchen. "Right here, Mrs. Sommers."

There was a sadness about Kenzie that she immediately noticed. It went far beyond the smile the young woman was attempting to maintain. Maizie's first impulse was to ask her what was wrong, but she refrained. Kenzie would tell her if she wanted her to know.

Walking into the house, Maizie said, "I haven't seen Keith around for a few days now. Would you know where he is?"

She'd held two more open house events for this property. At the moment, all her other properties had gone into escrow or the owners had decided to hold off any further dealings until after the holidays, so she was concentrating the preponderance of her sale efforts on this house.

There'd been some foot traffic, but that had consisted mainly of people who were just curious, or were looking for new decorating ideas, or made a habit out of frequenting open houses, poking around the rooms to see how other people lived.

She hadn't seen Keith either of those days, but today, apparently Kenzie had come by to set up the last of the estate sales before having the rest of the furniture removed and given to charity. Quite honestly, Maizie had stopped when she saw her car because she was curious about how the two were getting along.

"He's home," Kenzie replied, doing her best to sound upbeat and friendly. She had a sinking feeling she was failing.

Maizie glanced over the younger woman's shoulder toward the rest of the house. Since Keith obviously wasn't here, she made the only logical assumption. "He's at your home?"

"No, his home," Kenzie replied stoically. "In San Francisco."

"Oh." Maizie searched her face, finding the answer before she asked. "When is he coming back?"

"I have no idea," Kenzie replied. She was doing her best not to let her voice crack, but it was getting harder and harder not to break down. "I don't think he's coming back."

"Oh, my dear, I am so sorry." Ever maternal, Maizie slipped her arm around the younger woman's shoulders. "How do you feel?" she asked, concerned since, after all, she had been the driving force behind bringing the two together.

Could she have been this wrong about them?

Kenzie wanted to say "Fine." She really did. In lieu of that, she would have said, "Okay." But the word that wound up coming out of her mouth was *"Lousy."*

"Oh, honey." Maizie's voice was filled with sympathy as she gave her another heartfelt squeeze. She did a quick review in her mind of all the instances she'd seen the two together. "Maybe he just needs a little time to wrap things up. I saw the way that man looked at you. A man doesn't look at a woman that way if he isn't really involved with her."

But Kenzie shook her head. No more delusions. She was determined to see clearly now, to see their relationship the way it was.

"I appreciate what you're trying to do, Mrs. Sommers. But I think you're wrong."

Stepping away from the older woman's comforting embrace, Kenzie snatched up her purse. The heck with the rest of the sale. She had to leave before she started crying. She absolutely refused to break down in front of anyone, even if that person was the most sympathetic person she had ever met besides her own mother.

She didn't want sympathy, Kenzie thought as she left the house. She wanted not to care. Most of all, she wanted not to ache so much.

Keith went into his firm's main office the morning after he arrived back. He went in early, stayed late and for the most part picked up his life just where he had left off.

Except that it didn't quite feel like his life. It felt more like a shell—a hollow, ill-fitting shell without depth, without dimensions.

Without substance.

He told himself that was because he'd had an unnatural break in his routine. Having his dormant emotions shaken up the way he had was a lot to deal with, and it would take a little time for things to get back to normal.

His normal.

Time. That was all he needed. Time.

Keith kept doggedly at it for two more days, trying to recapture the rhythm he felt he'd lost by going back to Bedford.

After the third day of almost nonstop work, he finally remembered to unpack. The suitcase had been standing by the front door all this time as if to remind him that he could just as easily take it to his car as up the stairs.

His car, he sternly told himself, was not an option. The only reason the suitcase would find its way to the car was if he were going to the airport—which he wasn't.

He took the suitcase upstairs.

Once there, he brought it to his bedroom and laid it on his bed. Snapping the locks open, he forced himself to concentrate on the mechanics of unpacking rather than allowing his mind to stray to a place more than four hundred miles away.

Being with Kenzie had been great, but it was over, he silently reminded himself. His time with her had just been a commercial in the program of his life, and he had to remember that.

Remember that he had worked—

Keith stopped dead, staring into his suitcase. Specifically, staring at what was right on top of his shirts.

Where had those come from?

He hadn't packed them, hadn't even *touched* them.

Letters covered the entire width and breadth of his suitcase. The moment he opened it, they began cascading out. They were the letters Kenzie had found, written by his mother. He picked one up.

The same letters he had told Kenzie to throw out.

"Kenzie, what are you trying to do to me? I said I didn't want to read them!" he shouted at the woman who was four hundred miles away.

Scooping up the letters into his arms, Keith threw them into the wastepaper basket in his bathroom.

As if in rebellion, the letters overwhelmed the container, and the basket just fell over on its side. The letters covered the basket rather than winding up inside it.

He cursed at the pile—and the woman who had snuck the letters into his suitcase—and stormed away.

When had she put those letters in there? Keith silently demanded, mystified. It had to have been just before he left the house. He'd had the suitcase open just prior to that, while he was packing, and his cell phone had rung. He'd turned away to talk. It must have happened then. If she'd snuck them into his suitcase sometime before, he would have seen the letters while he was packing.

The next question that occurred to him in giant neon letters was, *why* would she do this to him? Why would she actually pack up his old memories so that he'd be forced to confront them when he opened the suitcase?

Had she done it because he had chosen to leave her? Was forcing the letters to his attention her way of punishing him for going?

Despite what he would have labeled as evidence if this were a court of law, Keith couldn't bring himself to believe Kenzie would have done it for such a hurtful reason.

The Kenzie he knew didn't punish people, didn't seek revenge, no matter what.

The Kenzie you knew? How well does anyone know anyone? You were together a total of seven days. Not exactly a lifetime, is it—unless you're a fruit fly, he mocked himself.

Keith sat on the edge of his bed, staring angrily into his bathroom at the letters that were lying all over the wastebasket and the floor.

It was a dirty trick. Leaving Bedford—and Kenzie— was obviously the right thing to do.

This proved it.

She wasn't going to answer the knock on the door. She'd already begged off from attending the New Year's Eve party her brother was having, giving what she deemed was an Academy Award–worthy performance. She called in her regrets, sniffling and coughing as she pretended to be coming down with the flu.

She repeated her performance two more times—once for her pregnant sister, whom she had assured didn't want to be near someone coming down with the flu, and once for her mother, who had been alerted about her planned no-show by the others.

Her mother had been a harder sell. Andrea offered to forgo the party and ring in the new year with her and a hot bowl of homemade chicken soup. Since her mother made the world's best chicken soup, it had been a hard offer for her to refuse, given how she truly felt. The chicken soup would have been comforting.

But ultimately Kenzie managed to convince her mother that she was just too wiped out for any company. Besides, if her mother skipped the party "to hold my hot, sweaty hand, I'll never forgive myself." After a considerable amount of rhetoric had gone back and forth, Andrea relented and promised to have a good time for both of them.

"But I'll be by in the morning to check in on you," her mother added.

"Come at your own risk," Kenzie had told her, then sneezed. "I'll be here."

"Risk. Right." Andrea laughed. "Like I didn't nurse all five of you kids through coughs, colds, the flu and heaven only knows what all else. Get into bed, Kenzie, and get your rest. I'll see you tomorrow."

"Yes, Mom," Kenzie dutifully replied.

She hated lying like this, but she just couldn't take a room full of noisy family right now, all trying to cheer her up. Her sisters would probably offer to make a voodoo doll resembling Keith. She wasn't up to that, either.

She didn't want revenge. She just wanted him.

"And Happy New Year," her mother said before hanging up.

"Happy New Year," Kenzie echoed, disheartened. The last thing the new year would be was happy, Kenzie had thought as she put her cell phone away.

An hour later, she'd felt no different. But her mother obviously did, because that had to be her at the door, determined to feed her and try to raise her mood.

Kenzie was down to her last nerve, and she was in no mood to go on with her pretense.

So she decided to wait her mother out, ignoring the knocking that had only grown louder, in hopes that the woman would assume she was asleep, give up and go home. She had left only one fifteen-watt bulb on, so it certainly looked as if she'd gone to bed.

The fourth round of knocking told her that her mother wasn't giving up.

With a sigh, Kenzie got into character and shuffled to the door.

"There was no reason for you to come," Kenzie said in between coughs as she unlocked the door and opened it just a crack. She was still hoping to convince her mother to turn around and go home.

"We've got a slight difference of opinion on that," Keith told her just before he opened the door farther and walked in.

Stunned, Kenzie had let go of the door and stepped back, staring at Keith and wondering if she'd fallen asleep on the sofa and this was just a dream she was having.

"That was a lousy thing to do," Keith told her as he turned to face her.

Her mind scrambled.

The letters. He was talking about the letters.

"I'm sorry," she said, "but I thought you'd wind up regretting not reading them."

"Them?" he repeated as he looked at Kenzie, confused.

"The letters. That's what you're talking about, isn't it?"

He laughed shortly, his irritation coming through. "No."

"Then I don't understand," she admitted. She was too tired to try to talk her way out of anything. Two hours of crying had taken a huge toll on her brain capacity. "What's this lousy thing I did?"

"Like you don't know," he accused her. "You let me leave. You let me go four hundred miles away from you to find out that I didn't *want* to be four hundred miles away from you."

Kenzie stared at him, trying to make sense out of what he was saying and get it to jibe with the look she saw on his face.

"Are you happy or angry that you're here?" she asked.

"Can't you tell? I'm happy," he all but shouted at her.

At that moment, the solid wall of tension growing inside her began to disintegrate. "Could have fooled me," she told him.

"Why not?" he countered. "I tried to fool me. I tried to fool myself into believing I didn't want to be here. That being with you for seven days was enough and I didn't need any more. Well, I do," he told her firmly. "I need more. Lots more."

That persistent kernel of hope she had never been entirely successful at dissolving just popped inside her chest, spreading out to fill every single nook and cranny within her.

This time her smile was genuine. "How much more?" she asked.

"Does the word *forever* mean anything to you?" Keith asked.

Her smile went from ear to ear. Further, if possible. "Yeah. Heaven."

"Funny, me, too," Keith responded, drawing her into his arms.

God, it felt wonderful being held in his arms like this. It was where she knew she belonged. "What did you do with the letters?"

Keith looked into her eyes. He loved her. How could he have missed that? Or ever thought he could walk away from it when people spent their whole lives looking for what had just dropped into his lap? Was he crazy?

No, definitely not crazy—because this time, he was staying.

"What most people do with letters," he told her. "I read them. And I wish she'd sent them. If she went through the trouble of writing them, why wouldn't she have sent them?"

"Maybe she was afraid you wouldn't read them," Kenzie told him.

He really couldn't argue with that. Because even now, he'd almost thrown them out. "Yeah, maybe," he agreed. "I love you, Kenzie."

Her heart swelled almost to bursting. "I love you back." And then, because she was desperately trying not to dissolve in happy tears, she pretended to be playful as she asked, "So, now what?"

"You mean after I make love with you?"

Her smile could have lit up a corner of the entire city. "Yes."

He shrugged nonchalantly. "I do it again."

"And then?"

He grew serious. "I don't know. But we'll figure it out. As long as I have you, the details don't really matter."

What he was saying suddenly hit her. She looked at him, stunned. "You're leaving your firm?"

He nodded. "I already did."

She couldn't let him do that for her. He wouldn't be happy doing nothing. He was a man who needed goals to work toward. "Keith, you can't do that. You won't last a day not working."

"Who says I won't be working?" he asked. Before she could say anything, he continued. "One of the things my mother and I fought about before I left home was that I wanted to go into corporate law and my mother wanted me to go into some form of legal aid. She wanted me to help people who couldn't afford to hire a lawyer to represent them. I balked at that, saying that wasn't a way to earn a living. But now, looking back, I think maybe she had the right idea, after all. Besides, I've already earned a lot of money. How much more money does a person need?"

A minute ago, she hadn't thought it was possible to love him more than she did—but she was wrong. "Your mother would have been very proud of you."

He brushed his lips against Kenzie's, then paused for one last moment. This needed to be said. "Thank you for not throwing the letters out the way I told you to."

She'd known from the moment she found them that getting him to read the letters was the right thing to do. But packing them in his suitcase had been her last ditch play—her Hail Mary—to get him to reconsider and come back.

If her attempt had wound up failing, she would have known Keith wasn't the man she thought he was, after all.

But he was.

Kenzie laughed, weaving her arms around his neck. "Anytime you want someone not to do what you tell her to, I'm your woman."

I'm your woman.

He liked the sound of that.

"I'm going to hold you to that last part," Keith said just before he stopped all dialogue between them for a very long time.

Epilogue

Maizie Sommers was beaming as she slipped into the fourth pew from the front and took her place beside her two best friends.

She knew she looked like the proverbial cat who swallowed the canary, but she strongly felt she had good reason.

"I told you I was never wrong," she said in a low, very satisfied whisper.

Theresa turned to glance at her. "What are you talking about?"

"And whom are you talking to?" Cecilia asked, leaning forward to peer around Theresa and look at Maizie.

Maizie realized she sounded as if she were talking to herself. Thinking quickly, she rectified that.

"To both of you, of course, and I'm talking about Kenzie. About the last conversation we had just before New Year's Eve. She told me Keith had gone back to San Francisco the day after Christmas and she didn't think he was coming back. I told her I thought he was, and that was when Kenzie told me she thought I was wrong."

"And you said you never were," Theresa guessed. She and Cecilia exchanged glances. That was Maizie all right, confident—and with good reason, really, she thought proudly.

But Cecilia couldn't resist the opportunity to tease her. "What's the view like from Mount Olympus?" she asked.

The strains of the wedding march were just beginning, and the crowd rose to their feet to await the bride's appearance.

"The view is just fantastic," Maizie assured her friends just as the double doors at the rear of the church opened.

As the music swelled, Kenzie appeared on the arm of her oldest brother.

Maizie looked from the bride to the altar, where Keith stood beside Kenzie's other brother. The groom seemed completely mesmerized as he watched his bride coming toward him.

Mesmerized and incredibly happy.

If ever two people looked to be in love, it was these two, Maizie thought, the latest couple she and her friends had successfully matched.

"Absolutely fantastic," Maizie affirmed.

It was hard to tell who looked happiest, Theresa thought, taking in the scene: the bride, the groom—or Maizie.

The logical answer, Theresa decided, was all three.

* * * * *

MILLS & BOON®

Christmas Collection!

Unwind with a festive romance this Christmas
with our breathtakingly passionate heroes.
Order all books today and receive a free gift!

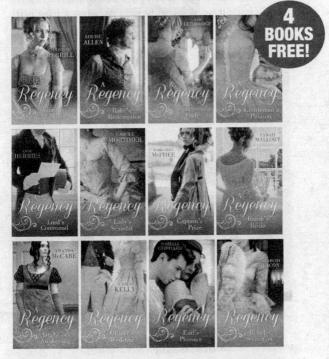
5_ST19

MILLS & BOON®

Cherish™

EXPERIENCE THE ULTIMATE RUSH OF FALLING IN LOVE

A sneak peek at next month's titles…

In stores from 20th November 2015:

In stores from 4th December 2015:

Available at WHSmith, Tesco, Asda, Eason, Amazon and Apple

Just can't wait?
Buy our books online a month before they hit the shops!
visit www.millsandboon.co.uk

These books are also available in eBook format!